SUPERSTAR

OTHER NOVELS BY J. SANTIAGO

Lex and Lu

Bliss

SUPERSTAR DUET
Five-Star
Superstar

SUPERSTAR

J. SANTIAGO

Visit my website at https://jsantiagoauthor.com
Cover designer: Elizabeth Mackey,
www.elizabethmackeygraphics.com
Editor and Interior Designer: Jovana Shirley, Unforeseen Editing,
www.unforeseenediting.com

This book is a work of fiction. Names, characters, places, and
incidents either are products of the author's imagination or are
used fictitiously. Any resemblance to actual persons, living or dead,
events, or locales is entirely coincidental.

Print ISBN: 978-0-9969558-5-0

To MMM
Team Tank!

To My Crew—
Gwen, Brandi, Patti, Jen, and Ronnique.

To Tauara, Xander, Nico, and Lucas.

ONE

FEBRUARY

Amber Johnson had traded her jeans and T-shirts for slacks and blouses three years ago when she first entered the Ayers Brown Field House as the Director of Operations for Coach Mickey Whitehurst.

As she crossed the parking lot in the few minutes before dawn, she reveled in the sense of anticipation coiling low in the pit of her stomach. Signing Day—the make-or-break culmination of years' worth of recruiting and plotting spread out over the course of a day.

She placed her thumb on the keypad, waiting for the sound of the releasing lock, before she pulled open the door to her office building. She rented a small house, miles from the hubbub of campus, an escape when she needed it. While the cozy bungalow offered comfort and solitude, she often found herself feeling more at home while wandering the halls of Ayers.

Amber made her way through the empty corridor, relishing the quiet, knowing it wouldn't last too much longer. Soon, the building would be a beehive of activity with coaches holed up in the war room, waiting for the National Letters of Intent to come through via fax and email; reporters clamoring for Whitey to share his thoughts about his recruiting class; compliance people milling about to verify future Mustangs; general hangers-on hoping to get an inside track on the Signing Day shenanigans. And she would be right in the middle of the action.

Dumping her bag on the chair in front of her desk, Amber ventured to the staff kitchen. Following Whitey's first national championship, his whole office space had been redesigned. The field house hardly resembled the place Amber remembered from her father's time on the staff. The kitchen alone boasted granite countertops, a dual stainless steel refrigerator that belonged in a five-star restaurant rather than a college football administrative building, and a complicated espresso machine that took up a large portion of the counter—an homage to Whitey's addiction to coffee drinks. She hadn't even liked coffee when she came to work here. Now, she couldn't begin her day without the strong brew. After starting the first pot, she scurried back to her office to gather her supplies for the day.

While Whitey stuck to legal pads and Sharpies, Amber had made use of her budget to get herself and her staff tablets. She did everything electronically, which drove her boss crazy. Although he teased her mercilessly about her technology obsession, she could access stats for him quicker than anyone else. She'd tried to convert him on numerous occasions, but he refused to give in. It was one of their many differences.

After she grabbed her coffee, she headed to the war room. Aside from her office, Amber spent the majority of her time in the communal room shared by all the coaches. Just like the kitchen, it represented the success of the Whitey Era. Last year, they'd replaced their magnetic dry-erase board with a remote-access screen. Amber could pull everything up on her tablet and project it onto the massive white surface. Whitey had joked about it looking like a New York Stock Exchange board, but Amber had countered with a response about how it should, as they were merely trading a different type of commodity. Her retort had garnered chuckles throughout the room, but no one had bothered to correct her. They knew she was right.

With her hands full, she transferred her paraphernalia to one hand and turned the knob. Whitey's presence didn't necessarily surprise her, but it did disappoint her.

"Good morning," she said as she sat on his right side, a metaphor for her position on his staff.

He glanced at his watch, taunting her, before he responded, "Good morning."

She didn't even try to fight the grin on her face. She nodded at the paper cup she still held in her hand. "Just the way you like it."

Whitey laughed then.

"Thanks for the coffee."

She inclined her head.

Reaching down, she unzipped her backpack and pulled out her tablet. Everything was up and running before Whitey took his second sip. He winced a little, and Amber wondered if it was because of the scalding coffee or the illumination of the screen in the otherwise lowly lit room.

She studied the recruiting board with the same level of knowledge and insight possessed by the other nine coaches on Whitey's staff. She was familiar with the strengths and weaknesses on their current team, the missing pieces they'd need to add to stay on top, and the X factor of each of the players.

"Any thoughts?"

She didn't have to be facing him to know he smiled.

"How many do you want?" he quipped.

The hinge on his chair squeaked right before she heard the familiar clunk of his heels hitting the table. Whitey's favorite pose had him shifted back, away from the table, with the soles of his shoes facing out.

"The important ones."

Amber had in her mind what was required to secure a top-five class. Whitey's public philosophy tended to veer toward filling his openings rather than having the press give his class a high rank. She argued that the perception was too important to the kids they were recruiting to not be worried about it. She also knew how competitive Whitey was, and while he liked to espouse his opinion on letting the press say what they wanted, his nature told her that he liked to be number one. She played an internal game, pitting her instincts against Whitey's knowledge. Lately, she'd found she was winning.

"Hmm...Deandre Pitts and Michael Walsh."

Bummer. "Really?" She heard the surprise in her voice and knew Whitey could identify it, too.

He chuckled.

At the sound, she turned to face him, her eyes narrowed. "You're messing with me? At five o'clock in the morning? After I brought you coffee?"

"Anytime is a good time."

"Seriously?" she mumbled.

His answer was another low laugh. "Dentarious Mitchell."

Amber nodded. *Exactly.*

"He's the one this year. We're deep at corner, but he's the unofficial leader. If we get him at noon, the rest will follow."

"Rest," she scoffed. "We have seventeen solid commitments. Nine of those kids will sign the papers at their first opportunity. I bet we'll have each NLI before Coach Hill walks in the door." She cut her eyes to him, and they shared a grin. Coach Hill was notoriously late. "The other eight of those commitments will get here soon after."

"That's true."

Something about the slow, drawn-out way he'd commented made her uneasy.

"So, who are you worried about?"

The door swung open behind them, diverting her attention. The coaching staff began to appear, and the noise level in the room increased dramatically as they all arrived and spoke at once. The anticipation she'd experienced earlier returned as people began to take their seats and provide their last-minute commentary on the recruiting class.

Lamarcus Steele and Nicky Stone sat across from her, like usual, as it afforded them the opportunity to share snarky looks. Steele winked at her, and Nicky delivered his trademark nod.

"Were you getting the worst Signing Day ever story from Whitey?" Coach Davenport inquired.

Amber turned in his direction. "No. No stories this morning. Just predictions."

"Ah. This is normally the time he likes to take us back a couple of years before he delivers his patented speech. 'It ain't over till the fat lady sings,'" Davenport said.

Snickers sounded from around the table.

"Well, it ain't," Whitey reiterated, as if they had forgotten one of his truisms.

"We know," chorused throughout the room, making Amber smirk.

But the good-natured teasing propelled Whitey right up onto his soapbox.

"Let's not forget that our livelihoods rest on the shoulders of seventeen- to twenty-two-year-old kids who are more interested in posting their every thought than actually taking the time to come up with one." His feet hit the floor, and he rolled forward to the table, signaling his business stance. "We might all think we know what's going to go down today, but these kids think pretty highly of themselves. I wouldn't put it past any of them to try to be today's big story with a surprise announcement."

Almost against her will, Amber's muscles tensed up, a sense of useless defensiveness making her cringe. She hoped Whitey wouldn't go there, wouldn't mention *his* name. Even though she attempted to keep her gaze from meeting Steele's across the table, there was little she could do when their eyes met. She read the sympathy there and responded with blank defiance, an attempt to appear unaffected.

"We don't need a Tank Howard moment," Whitey said, "so let's not take anything for granted today."

Ah, fuck. He had to go there.

Amber leaned back in her chair, the excitement for the dealings dissipating. Whitey continued to enlighten the room with his many signing-day lessons, but the mention of Tank's name was all it took for her to remember the last time she'd seen him at her father, Mike Franco's, wedding.

Even with a warning, Amber had been shocked when Tank Howard walked into the church. She hadn't seen Tank in over a year, but every emotion he'd ever invoked rushed through her, turning her inside out. It had been easy to elude him during the ceremony and for the beginning of the reception while all the traditional dances were happening and dinner was being served.

She avoided him, but there was no way to keep her from finding him in the crowd. Her first glimpse stole her breath—literally. She blamed it on her No Tank mantra. Following the NFL draft, she'd refused to watch a game, Google him, or moon over the *Sports Illustrated* cover featuring him after his NFL debut. So, this first time, it made her remember his beauty. On her second look, she noted the differences time had made in turning a man-child into a man. She wouldn't have believed his face could look more chiseled, but the leftover blurred edges from his childhood had given way to the finer angles of an adult. He'd also gained the mass she'd expected. Her third and final pass had her focusing on his date rather than him. The fact that he'd brought a woman to her father's wedding supplied her with a reason to own up to being pathetic and to start drinking heavily.

As she stood up to make her way to the restroom, she noted the unsteadiness of her walk. The leftover limp from her accident, coupled with a lot of beer, made her weave through the tables like a Weeble. The jingle running through her head brought a drunken smile to her face until she opened the door and came face-to-face with Tank's date. A flash of recognition in the beauty's eyes angered Amber.

"Hey." Without waiting for a response or inviting one, Amber hurried to the stall.

She took her time, hoping the girl would leave. When she heard the door to the restroom open, she hastily flushed the toilet and moved to the mirror, which had, only moments before, reflected the image of the beautiful woman with Tank. Amber studied her made-up face, her scar reflecting starkly in the fluorescent lighting. It hadn't occurred to her that she hardly considered it anymore. It was who she was, much like her deep brown eyes and ebony hair. She'd stopped being self-conscious about it long ago, mostly because of Tank Howard.

Rolling her eyes at her own sentimental foolishness, she fled from the restroom.

And stepped directly into the arms of Tank.

"Hey, Johnson, stop daydreaming," Whitey said at the exact moment Steele kicked her under the table.

Snapping back to the present, she caught Steele's knowing look before she turned her attention back to the proceedings around her.

She grabbed the remote from the center of the table and turned up the volume on ESPNU's Signing Day coverage, just in time for the retelling of the Tank Howard story. It was brief coverage now, merely a footnote in college football history. Most of the kids signing today had been ten or eleven when it happened. But, because of Tank's notoriety, it still got a mention. For a player who had received the Rookie of the Year award his first year and had made every pro bowl since entering the NFL, his story was still relevant. She turned away from the screen, tuning out the drama.

She should have prepared herself better. She had known to take precautions, build up tolerances. But she hoped that, one day, none of this would mean anything to her, that Tank Howard would only be an annotation in Amber Johnson's history.

Unconsciously, she raised her fingers to stroke the lines of her scar, the shriveled skin on her jaw and neck. The area was anesthetized.

If only her heart were numb to Tank.

TWO

Tank Howard struggled to open his eyes, even as the sun streamed through the plantation shutter slats he'd forgotten to shut the night before. Rolling onto his back, he tugged on the pillow next to him in an attempt to cover his face. When the pillow refused to budge, he glanced over to see the waves of hair draped across the expanse of the object he'd been seeking. He stifled a groan. Some sound must have escaped because Madison's brown eyes snapped open, meeting his.

"Forgot I was here, huh?" she teased with a knowing smile.

Her chipper morning persona was one of the many reasons he didn't often wake up next to her.

"Maybe," he conceded.

"I must have had more to drink than I thought."

"I figured when you Ubered here."

But he didn't need her explanation.

As the haze of sleep burned off, the events of the night before came back to him with a startling clarity. The huskiness of his voice and his sleep-crusted eyes were as much of a bitter reminder as the pounding of his head and the woman sprawled next to him.

He refrained from flinching when Madison's hand landed on his chest, and she slid closer to him. The tips of her nails raked lightly across his pecs as she nestled into the nook created by his wide-flung arm. Stopping on the outskirts of his nipple, the pad of her finger teased the center of the flat disk until it puckered for her. Tank felt himself stir, and while the thought of sinking between her legs was pleasant, his heavy head indicated it would be a bad idea.

He brought his hand up and gently patted her on the shoulder before he rolled away. Dropping a kiss on her head to soothe his rejection, he walked naked to his bathroom.

Madison was familiar with his rhythms. More like friends with benefits than any other moniker, they typically had an easy relationship.

He turned on the shower and stood beneath the punishing stream, eager to wash away the remnants of his descent into the bottom of a tequila bottle. Feeling a little more like himself, Tank left the shower and returned to his room to dress. Pulling on his boxer briefs, a faded pair of jeans, and a worn blue T-shirt, he sat on the side of the bed, better equipped to have a conversation.

Madison hadn't moved much since he left her. She smiled up at him with her guileless chocolate eyes. "Drowning your sorrows last night?"

He managed a smile. "Yes."

"It's been ten days. I thought you would have gotten over losing by this time."

"You would think that, right?" He was perfectly happy with allowing her to believe his binge drinking last night had been about his loss in the AFC Championship Game. It got him off the hook.

"So, is it really true?"

"I'm assuming I told you about Tilly last night?"

"You did." Her face lit up with her excitement over the news he'd shared with her. She clapped her hands with obvious glee. "I absolutely love weddings."

"This, I know," he agreed, smiling indulgently.

Madison Shepard was quite possibly one of the most cunning sideline reporters in the business. After facing her in the trenches, one would never know how much of a lighthearted, whimsical personality she had. Tank would relentlessly tease her about the crazy duality of her personality, but he'd find himself oddly proud of her when he watched her in action.

"How did you end up so drunk?"

"Girls' night. What can I say?" She shrugged before breaking out into a peal of giggles.

"I don't think I want any details."

She reached up, patted his cheek, and winked at him. "It's probably better that way." She moved to sit, clutching the sheet to her chest. "So, are there any plans for the engagement?"

Tank felt squirrelly all of a sudden. "Yeah," he answered, hoping to keep the anxious anticipation out of his voice. "Next Friday night."

"That's quick."

"Yeah, it's just a party. Nothing crazy. You know, Keira is pretty low-key."

"Don't tell me they're doing something at the Bear's Den?" she asked, incredulity in her voice.

Tank managed to laugh. "Not the Bear's Den—although I am sure that was her first thought. But I offered up my house, so we're going to do something here."

"I wanna help. I've got a great caterer who can do amazing things on short notice. We can stock the bar and do some small favors. I can make it seem like it's been planned for months."

Tank hesitated. He'd already known it would come to this. If he had written a script on how this conversation was going to go, he'd have nailed it. There was really no way to get out of having her act as the hostess for this party. "Thanks. But don't you have an assignment next weekend?"

"I can move some stuff around."

"Okay." It was easier to agree. Although it might complicate things, he wasn't sure he could face this part of his past without her unwavering support.

"What does the guest list look like?"

"Exactly what you think it looks like."

She smirked, and he knew she was remembering the last time he'd had to attend an event of this nature. He'd blocked the memory for the better part of the last two years. He didn't appreciate the knowing look in her eye. Things had been different between them then, so she'd handled her discovery in stride. He vaguely wondered what she'd think about a similar situation now. The knowing gleam she sent his way annoyed him.

Tank stood up, not really caring about her feelings in the moment. "I'm going to make some coffee."

He left his second-story bedroom, walking into the hallway.

When he'd signed his contract three years ago, he'd made two purchases—a modest town house and an outrageous car. He'd fallen in love with the new complex being built in the Oakhurst part of Decatur. The three-story homes were modern, sleek, and roomy enough for his needs. On his agent's advice, he'd bought two of the units and merged them. His top floor was split in half—part open deck, part playroom with a pool table, dartboard, and a TV large enough to take up one whole wall. The roll-up doors he'd installed gave it a loft-like feel. He loved the place. Though he'd bought it as a slightly anonymous owner, even his growing fame and recognition hadn't changed the way his neighbors viewed him. The close-knit community treated him like the guy they'd met when he moved in.

As he turned on the coffeemaker, he found himself speculating on what *she* would think of the place. The errant thought aggravated him. Suddenly impatient, he yanked open the cabinet above his head, grabbed a mug, pulled the pot from beneath the steady stream of steaming coffee, and filled the cup directly from the drip.

He trudged up the two flights of stairs to his third-floor loft. Throwing himself on the couch, he flipped on the TV and stared at it sightlessly.

Over the last week, he'd found himself thinking about Amber Johnson a lot. He blamed it on the inadvertent viewing of Signing Day coverage, but in reality, the triggered thoughts were numerous and random. Like the way his head coach would look at him sometimes or when he saw supply closets or the green and silver colors of his alma mater. It really didn't take that much once he let himself think about her. Like a favorite, poignant scene in a book, his brain seemed to be earmarked on the moment at the wedding when she'd ended up slamming into his body as she exited the restroom.

He could conjure it at will, remembering the split second they had settled into the embrace, their bodies reacting for them before their hearts could protest.

Her hands spread out on his chest, her fingers gently caressing, testing reality. He moved closer to her, and his steadying hands on her hips flexed. He'd been covertly watching her all day. He knew her hair was longer, her confidence stronger. He could tell by the way she held herself that she'd gotten more comfortable with her scars, more at ease with herself.

"Hi," he murmured. Then, he wanted to kick himself for the lame opening.

She immediately stepped back. Looking above him, maybe for divine intervention, she reached up, gathered her hair, and pulled it over her right shoulder, covering her scar.

Tank looked away from the motion, hurt by her discomfort with him.

"Hey," she returned finally, her gaze meeting his. "How are you?"

"Good."

"Congratulations on the Rookie of the Year honors."

"Thanks."

The awkwardness of the stilted conversation threw him. They'd never been awkward, even when trading insults in the beginning.

"Well, it's, uh, good to see you, but I should get back. I'm sure I'm supposed to be doing something." She took another step backward, putting more distance between them.

He almost let her walk away, but as she turned, he reached out, grabbing her hand. The jolt of desire raced through both of them, a convergence of need. Amber inhaled sharply, and Tank noted the pulse point beating in her neck.

His fingers moved without his acknowledgment, clasping her around the nape of her neck, his thumb finding its spot on the scarred skin of her jaw. Her eyes glazed over, and she shook her head—to deny what was between them, he guessed.

"Don't walk away yet," he begged. He heard the desperation in his voice and wondered where in the hell it'd come from.

Tank had never had to beg for anything. But this damn girl seemed to be the one thing he wanted but couldn't have.

She tugged against the hand holding hers—maybe attempting to break their connection, but he couldn't be sure. And, because he didn't want to know, he moved closer to her.

"Not yet," he whispered in her ear as he ran his nose along the perfect line of her neck. When she didn't resist, he placed kisses down the column before dragging his nose against her scar. "I can't believe I forgot your scent," he whispered, his voice rough with longing.

She'd been passive until, suddenly, she wasn't. Her hands came up to coast over his closely sheared head. Her body followed as she gave in to the same urge that had driven him to grab her hand.

Suddenly flush, their bodies molded together, he finally moved his mouth to meet hers. He sank into the kiss, not allowing her any space or options for escape. His tongue pushed against her lips, begging for the second time tonight for her to allow him something she seemed determined to withhold. But, this time, she acquiesced quickly, capitulating absolutely. He couldn't hold on to a thought as he got lost in the depths of her mouth. He wanted to sink into her completely, to lose himself in her like he hadn't been able to do with any other woman since her.

He slowly ended the kiss. He rested his forehead on hers, working to catch his breath. She fidgeted before seeking space.

They both glanced about, aware of the empty hallway directly outside of the restroom where, at any moment, someone might see them. It didn't matter to him, but he could tell she was bothered by it. Before she had a chance to end what they'd both willingly started, he searched for somewhere private. He couldn't see anything directly around them, so he grabbed ahold of her hand and pulled her to the other end of the hall where he turned into the massive lobby. He looked for a door, someplace he could get her alone.

"That's what the descent into the bottom of that bottle was about?" Madison's voice pulled Tank from his reverie.

He refocused on the TV, hoping to appear enthralled by the edition of *SportsCenter* playing in front of him. Slowly, he took a sip of his coffee before he looked up at her. "What?" he questioned, feigning confusion, like he didn't have any idea what she was talking about. But he knew. God, he knew, and yes, he wanted to shout, *Yes, I drained a bottle of tequila so that I wouldn't have to think about Amber Johnson walking into my house.*

"Amber will be here, right?" Madison settled herself on the arm of the couch.

He shifted uncomfortably before finally looking at her. "Possibly. Tilly wasn't sure."

Madison's eyes narrowed. "You're full of shit. There's no way she'd miss Keira and Tilly's engagement party."

His shoulders lifted in an involuntary shrug, one born of staunch denial and fading indifference. "I'm sure she'll make it. Along with Steele and Iman. Franco and Molly. Keira's family. Twenty to twenty-five people, tops."

Madison looked away from him, toward the open loft. She lifted her finger, the manicured pink tip tapping against the glossy surface of her lip in a cadence of calculation. "You know what that means?" she asked, cutting her eyes back, a glint of mischief on her face.

He cocked his head, bracing himself. "Nah. What does it mean?"

"We'd better lock all the closet doors."

With a groan, his head fell back to the couch in defeat.

THREE

When Tank had purchased his house he'd viewed it as an investment property, one he'd unload when the time was right. The clean lines of the space, the nonintrusive neighbors, and his access to the city outweighed the lack of a yard. He'd worked with the architect to build exactly what he wanted, and since he'd moved in, it had become his haven.

In the last ten days though, as Madison had been preparing for Keira and Tilly's engagement party, his home had become a place he wanted to escape. When the day arrived, Tank realized it was more than the commotion in his house that had been making him antsy; it was the thought of Amber attending the party.

It had been almost exactly two years since they saw or talked to each other. He supposed the time in between had dulled their last interaction. And it had. He hadn't thought about her in a long time. But, with the impending encounter, he found himself thinking about her—often.

Their lives were totally intermeshed. Amber's father was his coach. Her best friend, Keira, was marrying one of his closest friends, Tilly. And his other close friend Steele worked with her. Tank had a suspicion that Amber and Steele were much closer than he'd let on.

Tank might have skipped out on a couple of invitations when the likelihood of seeing her was involved, but with their many connections, he was amazed they had been able to avoid each other for such a long time and that he'd skillfully dodged any conversations about her. He wouldn't be surprised if their friends had made a pact after Franco's wedding to not mention Amber to him. He didn't know if she had a boyfriend, how she was doing at her job, or if her injuries from the accident had stopped taking a toll on her.

Amber Johnson existed in the vacuum of his past.

And, now, he wanted to know about her.

Grabbing his iPad from the docking station in his office, he stepped out into the kitchen and sat at the counter. Protein shake in hand, he opened Facebook. He didn't have an account anymore because his team's publicity department handled his social media. In a moment he could only label as insanity, he typed her name into the Search bar. And he got thousands of results, but none of them were her.

Must still not like social media.

He grinned, liking that he still knew at least one thing about her. But it only made him curious about other things. It was an impossible situation. He knew the people closest to her, but he couldn't ask any of them one single thing about her. Not what car she drove or what her address was or if she had a boyfriend.

He rubbed his hand over his head, trying to erase his thoughts. Agitated, he stood. Checking the time, he jogged upstairs to change into workout clothes. Grabbing his phone, he texted Steele.

Tank: ETA?

Steele: 15 minutes.

Tank: Hope you're ready to hit the gym.

Knowing he wouldn't be sitting around for much longer helped him relax. He definitely wanted to be absent when Madison's posse arrived, and if that meant leaving Steele to fend for himself, Tank would.

In his first off-season a couple of years ago, Tank had started swimming. One of the athletic trainers had suggested it as a way to keep in shape and expand his cardiovascular capabilities. He tried it and loved it, partly because it challenged him. He'd never been a strong swimmer, so he took some lessons, learning the proper techniques.

No matter how much swimming he had done, it never came naturally to him. He had to work at it, talk himself through it. The monotony of his internal dialogue—*Stroke, stroke, breathe, stroke*—enabled him to escape from the constant barrage of thoughts in his head.

Had a bad game? An hour of swimming allowed him new perspective on what he'd done wrong.

Got a random phone call from his absentee father? *Breathe, stroke.* Richard Howard who?

Lost the AFC Championship Game in spectacular fashion?

Well, swimming hadn't quite eased the ego-bashing of that game.

But, as he lowered himself into the tepid water, he hoped to achieve a level of blissful thoughtlessness today to specifically drown out the thoughts of Amber. He didn't want to rehash their last encounter. His one stumble through the portal of the past had been enough for him.

Steele followed him into the pool, jumping in to douse himself rather than the slow dip Tank preferred. He watched as Steele began his laps before joining him.

Tank liked to think he was solely responsible for convincing Steele to include swimming in his rehab regime.

Tank had been watching the game when Steele suffered the break to his femur that would end his career. He often wondered what the families of the injured players went through when the sports channels made the call to continually show the plays over and over again.

Tank had seen Steele go down, and before they even went back for the replay, he knew it was bad; the unnatural angle of the hit, the gangly fall, the prolonged inertness as Steele lay on the ground. But, on the replay, Tank swallowed the bile that had collected in his throat. And, as they continued to show it, to analyze it, Tank sat in horrified silence, his thoughts racing, his heart pounding.

If he'd been able to, he'd have been on a plane. But he was in his rookie season, on a road trip, too far away to get to Steele and hold his hand and ease his worries. Instead, he called Franco, who had called the team doctors, who'd made sure Steele would have the best of everything. Because Steele had come from absolutely nothing, and there was no one who could be in his corner when the horror of his future crystallized.

When Tank was able, he showed up at the hospital with information and options. He talked Steele through his recovery, then his rehab, and then his choices for his future.

Some strange twist of fate had put Lamarcus Steele in the path of Amber Johnson. And, while Tank and Steele could and did talk about anything, share everything, she was never part of the discussion.

Stroke, stroke, breathe, stroke.

They swam for an hour. Then, after they rinsed off and changed, they did some light weights. By the time they were finished, they were pleasantly tired and very hungry.

Tank drove them back to his home and parked, suggesting they walk to the pizza joint around the corner from his house. After they placed their order, they sat back in a booth and talked.

"Where are you headed to first when you can get back on the road?" Tank inquired.

"New Jersey, believe it or not. There's this player in Elizabeth that our Director of Ops thinks could be a good fit." Steele delivered this with a straight face and a direct look.

"Really?" Tank said, crossing his arms over his chest. "Director of Ops."

Steele returned his stare, not batting an eye. "Yeah."

"You can say her name, you know."

Steele cocked his head to the side. "Whose name?" he deadpanned.

"You're fucking funny."

Chuckling, Steele leaned back against the seat. "I'm just messing with you. Amber is all over this kid. Thinks he can be a player!"

"What do you think?"

"I think I trust her instincts."

Tank wasn't surprised. Amber was a football savant. Her analysis was spot-on—and not for a woman, for anyone. If she thought someone had talent, he would trust her, too.

Tank played with the wrapper of the straw, winding it over his finger, only to unwind it and do it all over again. He felt Steele studying him and looked up. "I'd trust her, too. She knows football."

"She does."

Neither of them said anything for a moment, the first awkward pause in their friendship.

"We're pretty—" they spoke at the same time, "You guys are—"

"We're tight," Steele admitted.

"I know," Tank confirmed.

The waitress delivered their food, interrupting their conversation. Serving up the pizza, they inhaled the first piece before Steele picked up the conversation right where they'd left off.

"When she first showed up, I didn't really know what to make of her. She didn't seem like she was the same person you'd lost your head over."

"Interesting way to describe it," Tank muttered.

"You know what I mean. You were riding high that year, and then, suddenly, you were in love. And it seemed weird to have her around. Anyway, we didn't become friends until I started rehab. I liked to go early before the guys were there. I didn't want to be around them. She worked out at the same time. We started talking, sharing war stories, and became friends."

"She's still rehabbing?" Tank couldn't help but ask. It had been a long time since her accident.

"Nah. But she still works out. It keeps her leg from stiffening up."

"Of course."

"We never talk about you."

The way Steele had said it sounded defensive, and Tank looked up from the piece of pizza in his hands and across the table to Steele.

At six foot five, Steele had been an incredible target as a receiver. His arms were covered in tattoos that you really couldn't make out because of his skin. Tank often teased him about it. He'd had twists in his hair as a player but sheared them off when he became a graduate assistant. He'd claimed he needed legitimacy. Tank had teased him about that, too.

Now, as he stared at Steele, Tank wondered about Steele's real feelings for Amber. Tank got that they were friends, but he suddenly knew there was more to it than that. His mind jumped, conjuring a picture of an altar with Steele and Amber standing on either side and Tank an attentive best man. He shook his head, pushing the image aside.

"Bro, it's cool. We were together for a few weeks a long time ago. You don't have to explain yourself to me." Tank issued his statement with confidence.

Relieved, Steele said, "I know. I felt bad for never saying anything. But we started hangin' soon after the wedding, and with the scene there, I just thought it would be better if I kept it to myself."

Tank forced a laugh. "Yeah, that was not one of my finer moments."

Steele shrugged. "Hers either."

Tank stopped himself from demanding Steele clarify the comment. He trusted Steele. Enough said.

"So, how you feeling about seeing her tonight?"

Tank narrowed his eyes, caught off guard by the question. "How about, since you and she don't talk about me, you and I don't talk about her?"

Steele's quick smile flashed white on his face. "You telling me to mind my own business?" Then, he laughed.

"Nah. I'm saying, there's nothing to talk about."

"Uh-huh," Steele grunted, mocking Tank with his knowing smile. "Whatever you say, bro."

They finished eating, an uneasy silence between them.

"Let's get out of here." Tank dropped some cash in the folder with the bill and then led the way to the exit.

As they started their walk back to his house, he once again found himself thinking about the evening ahead and the reappearance of Amber in his life.

Aren't friends supposed to be split up in a divorce? How come all of my friends are her friends? And why am I suddenly so curious about her?

The euphoric numbness from the pool disappeared.

Once they returned to the house, they retreated to their rooms to shower again and get ready.

Tank couldn't predict what the night would bring other than a reunion he hadn't ever wished for. And, while he could lament about the reality of having to deal with her tonight, he needed to understand that it didn't have to be anything.

SUPERSTAR

It had taken him all day to get there—to the one truth that would sustain him through the night. She was history. And, once he caught up with her in the present, he could put her and the memories of her back in the past—where they belonged.

FOUR

Amber opened the trunk of the Audi Q7 her dad had purchased for her two years ago and grabbed her team-issued rolling suitcase and valet. She hurried to the front door of her father's house and didn't hesitate to sling it open, the reverberation of it hitting the wall, announcing her arrival.

Just as she'd envisioned, her two-year-old twin half-siblings came barreling down the hallway toward her. Dropping her stuff where she stood, she met them partway and scooped their wiggly little bodies up into her arms. They squealed their delight as she rained kisses all over their faces.

"Could they be any more excited to see you?" Her father, Mike Franco asked from his lean against the wall.

"Well, I am the fun big sister," she reminded him between Alexis's and Andy's laughter.

"I'm not completely sure, but I think they've been asking for you all day. I'm guessing 'Ber is you." He winked at her before waving her to follow him to the kitchen. "I thought Steele was driving over with you?"

She reluctantly released the twins, dropping a kiss on top of each of their heads. As soon as she set them down, Franco pulled her into a quick hug. The children giggled before toddling off to get into something while out of the watchful eye of their father.

"He drove separately. He'll meet us tonight at the party." She sat down at the kitchen bar and propped her head on her hands. "I think he's missing the object of his bromance."

"Ah, I guess this is the first time they've seen each other since their seasons ended."

"Yeah. Before Steele heads back out on the recruiting trail, he needs his boy time."

Amber's unlikely friendship with Lamarcus Steele tended to sustain her because the rest of her friends and family lived hours away.

When she'd arrived on campus three years ago, Steele had been a senior on the team. She'd only known him as a rumored best friend of Tank Howard and a name on the roster of student-athletes she was responsible for taking care of and monitoring. Then, during the third game of that season, Steele suffered a career-ending injury. There were stories of Tank visiting Steele in the hospital and having his team doctors confer with Steele's team doctors. No one ever substantiated the stories, and Amber never asked.

It was during their mutual rehab sessions with heat or stim when they began to become friends. At first, because Steele was still a student-athlete, it mostly consisted of lamenting over coming back from an injury—what hurt, what didn't. But, when he became a graduate assistant, chasing a new dream, the friendship between them blossomed. Even after spending incredible amounts of time together and discussing any number of topics, it took six months before either of them acknowledged their respective relationships with Tank Howard.

"I imagine, they both need it," Franco added quietly.

Amber shrugged with true indifference. Steele and Tank's friendship didn't bother her. It was a separate entity, much like the relationship between Franco and Tank. If she wanted to avoid the concentric circles of her life and his, she'd have to move to Alaska and cut everyone off. As it was, she had been able to avoid seeing him for the last two years.

Although she'd evaded discussing the engagement party with everyone—Franco, Molly, Steele, and even Keira—she could admit she was nervous. Considering what had happened the last time they were together, she had a right to feel anxious.

What she didn't need was the fiery expectancy that had accompanied her on her ride. She'd chalked it up to her anticipation of seeing the twins.

But, now, in her father's whitewashed kitchen with the afternoon sun streaming in, she could feel the latent enthusiasm sprouting, growing inside her. She wanted to blame it on her Keira and Tilly's engagement and being with her family—anything other than the man who was hosting the party.

But, in the aftermath of her horrible, disfiguring car accident, she'd learned to be honest—at least with herself. And she wanted to see Tank. She wanted to talk to him and laugh with him. She wanted to trade anecdotes.

The thought of catching up with him scared her far more than the desire to touch him.

"How are you feeling about tonight?" Franco asked without hedging.

Grinning, she looked up at him. "I'm excited to see everyone."

"Vague, as usual." Franco leaned back on the counter, settling in.

Amber took him in. "You look good. Those pesky circles under your eyes seem to have disappeared." She loved teasing him about his second go-around as a parent.

"Well, it took only about fifteen months for the As to actually sleep through the night. Those undisturbed hours of shut-eye have done wonders for both of us."

As if they'd suspected the conversation had veered in their direction, Alexis and Andy came running back into the kitchen. Franco grabbed Alexis while Amber jumped down from the stool to get Andy.

"Hey, sweetness," she murmured into the rolls on his neck.

He giggled.

"Well, that's good. How's Molly doing?" Amber asked Franco.

Franco shoved his free hand into his thick black hair—a sign Amber recognized as stress.

"I think she's discovering how difficult it is to have a high-powered career in college athletics while also being a parent. And I'm not much help most of the year."

A niggling sense of worry pricked at Amber. "Is everything okay?"

A nervous chuckle escaped Franco's mouth, ratcheting up her unease. Alexis dropped her head to Franco's shoulder, snuggling in.

He placed a tender kiss on her forehead before looking back up to Amber. "You used to do the same thing—settle in on my hip, silently begging to stay in my arms." He stroked his daughter's light-brown locks. "It feels like a lifetime ago when I was parenting you."

Amber rolled her eyes. "You still parent me. Jeez, wasn't it you who wanted Steele to drive with me because you didn't want your twenty-six-year-old daughter driving three hours by herself?" she teased.

"Maybe," he agreed.

Neither one of them acknowledged how long it had been since Amber went to her father, seeking affection. Five years after the accident, they still managed to avoid the subject.

Up until Amber's debacle with Rowdy Daniels, Franco and Amber had had a very close relationship, their mutual love of football being one of many things they shared. In addition to the terrible scarring on her face and neck, the accident that had killed Rowdy almost destroyed her relationship with her father.

"Seriously, I know you don't want to talk about this, but are you good with going to Tank's house tonight?"

"I promise you, I am as okay as I can be."

Just because Amber's and Tank's parting words to each other had been mean and angry, the two years since their harrowing interaction had been good to both of them, and they could be adults for the sake of their friends.

"What's the plan for tonight?"

Franco glanced up at the clock. "Molly should be home soon. Our babysitter will be here around six o'clock. We can leave here around seven."

"About that, I think I am going to drive separately."

Andy started to wiggle in her arms, so she put him down on the floor and watched with amusement as he walked over and tugged on his sister's leg.

"Down!" he ordered.

Both Alexis and Franco seemed reluctant to let go of each other, but even at two, Alexis was powerless to say no to her demanding twin. Franco bent down and kissed his son before releasing his daughter.

Then, he looked over at Amber. "Why do you want to go by yourself?"

She glanced around the kitchen, trying to remember where she left her bags. Recalling the scene at the front door, she walked back through the hallway where her stuff lay in a heap in the foyer. Picking up her suitcase, she set it upright before retrieving her garment bag and hanging it on the coat rack by the entrance. Locating her purse, she headed back to where Franco was waiting for her.

She dropped the purse on the counter and rifled through it until she found the envelope. She pulled it out and presented it to her dad. "Take your wife out to dinner, and we'll meet at the party."

He opened it up and glanced down at the gift card inside. "Ruth's Chris? I guess Whitey is paying you well," he teased.

"You know he is."

"I can afford to take my wife out to dinner." His declaration vibrated with annoyance.

"I know you can. But I figured you might not have thought to do it. So, that one's for tonight, and this one"—she handed him a second envelope—"is for tomorrow night when I babysit."

He rolled his eyes, and she had to bite her lip to keep from laughing.

"She probably won't want to be away from the twins both nights."

"Convince her," Amber challenged.

He studied her, and Amber grew uncomfortable under his steady gaze. She couldn't tell what he was thinking or even what he saw when he looked at her. She hoped he felt her strength and resilience. She valued his opinion.

Did he see her as she was now, five years removed from the horror of her life in Oxford? Did the scar still crush him? Did he watch her walk and feel sorry for her? She didn't think he did anymore, but she could never really be sure.

Although she resented his worry about tonight, she could understand it. The last time she'd seen Tank at Franco's wedding, Franco had had to hold her as she heaved through sobs in the antechamber reserved for the wedding party.

Congratulations on finally finding a woman you love. Excuse me while I have a breakdown about the guy I used to love.

She almost groaned at the memory. Maybe she owed Franco.

"I've tried to figure out what I'm going to feel when I see him, but I keep coming up empty. I really can't predict it. It's been so long, and we've both had more experiences apart than we ever had together. It's stupid really. I'm not the first girl who's had her heart broken." She laughed normally because it seemed funny to her all of a sudden. "We were together for a couple of months and have not been together for three years. He's in a relationship. We live in different cities. Doesn't it seem kind of ridiculous to even think I wouldn't be okay tonight?"

The door from the garage opened suddenly, and Molly hurried into the kitchen. She smiled wide when she saw Amber and then hurried forward to drop her keys, purse, and messenger bag on the counter. She pulled Amber into a warm hug. "I hadn't heard from either of you, so I wasn't sure if you'd made it."

Amber and Molly stepped back from their embrace.

"You look great. Are you excited to see Keira?" Molly asked.

Amber laughed at the rapid-fire speech. "Did having kids make you talk faster?"

They spoke on the phone all the time and instant-messaged while at work. Since they both worked in college athletics, they had plenty to talk about, and Amber often relied on Molly for answering compliance questions.

Molly laughed at her question. "Maybe. Although I think I am so happy to go out tonight that my brain is working at warp speed."

Amber laughed with her. "Yes, I am excited to see Keira, and you are going out the next two nights, so don't fret."

Molly looked confused but quickly shook it off and made her way over to Franco. "Hey, babe," she murmured as she sank into her husband's space.

His arms immediately surrounded her, and they seemed to lose themselves in the hug. Both of their eyes closed as they took comfort in the embrace. Franco dropped his head and gave her an open-mouthed kiss that would have been hot if it hadn't been Amber's father displaying his passion for his wife.

Any concern Amber experienced talking to her father earlier dissipated instantly while she stood on the outskirts of their kiss. Being with the two of them, in their orbit, always left Amber a bit raw. She basked in their happiness, their obvious love and comfort with one another. Inevitably though, when she left them, the vacancies in her life would become gaping holes of regret and longing.

Now, with them immersed in a hug, silently communicating in a way Amber envied, she could only think of the last words Tank had tossed at her when she walked away from him at the wedding.

"I'm truly sorry," he said, the truth of his statement reflected in his eyes. "I mean, I hate what I did, but I'm more sorry about what's happened to you because of it. I thought you were hard when I first met you, but now, you just seem bitter and a little bit pathetic."

Her eyes widened, and the blow from his words hit her, making her flinch.

"I hope, for your sake, that you find a way to get over it." He looked her up and down, disgust replacing his apologetic gaze. "If what happened between us today is any indication of who you are now, you'll always be alone."

Then, he turned from her, walking back to the beautiful black woman waiting for him down the hall.

Amber flipped her hair, wrapping it around the right side of her neck, shaking off the haze of the memory. Like her protective cloak around the vulnerable skin, she longed to shield her heart from the confusing glimmers of hope and anticipation of seeing Tank.

FIVE

Keira had declared the engagement party attire casual, which Amber knew was for her benefit. But, over the last three years, after playing adult dress-up, she'd developed some fashion sense and her own style. Seared into her memory was the image of the last woman she'd seen with Tank, and tonight called for her A game. Her white shirt, stretch jeans, and mid-calf boots were accentuated with a brown leather blazer, thick belt, a stack of gold and copper bangles, and a thin infinity scarf. A knight with battle armor, she moved, unfettered by self-consciousness about the web of scarring on her face and neck.

Double-checking the address, she walked slowly toward the door while studying the surrounding area. Ranch-style houses from the sixties, which should have made the units appear out of place, flanked the modest but modern-looking town houses. The casual observer could note the change in the neighborhood. The hipster vibe reigned with the coffeehouse, swank but small restaurants, and requisite bars right around the corner. Amber immediately liked the area and wasn't the least bit surprised to find one of the NFL's leading men immersed in it.

Quintessential Tank. Threads of humility tangled up with all his ego.

Being here, seeing where he lived, loving where he lived, ramped up her anticipation. She stopped just short of knocking on the door, suddenly struck by the difference in her. She was about to enter Tank's house, and rather than the familiar rage and resentment, she felt giddy. She reached out and rang the doorbell. As she waited, she pretended like everything was under control and normal, but she was abruptly back at the wedding, her memories taking over.

The last time she'd seen Tank, the residue of anger had clung to her like oil on a mechanic's hands. Without any incentive to clean them, she let it settle and cake, thicken and stain. When he pulled her through the halls of The Fox Theatre at her father's wedding, she went willingly. The desire simmering between them was undeniable. But it wasn't overwhelming passion that fueled her acquiescence; it was blinding fury, simple rage. She hated him that night, and she wanted to fuck it out.

As he tried locked door after locked door, her frustration mounted.

"You're Tank Howard. One would guess you merely had to think, *Open sesame*, and the lock would just do your bidding."

Tank's answering chuckle should have made her smile. It didn't. It increased the agitated energy, making her caustic, so when the knob on one of the closets finally turned, it radiated through her. He gently pulled her inside, peering at her, his translucent green eyes searching hers for some connection before the darkness of the closet engulfed them. But she didn't need his soothing tonight.

She pushed forward, and her mouth landed on his before the door could shut. The wall behind him came quicker than she'd thought, and the momentum slammed her into his body. It was the perfect opening for what she wanted. Her hands were on his belt before her tongue entered his mouth. When his hands found her wrists, attempting to slow her, she pulled them free and went to work on the buttons of his shirt. He might have tried to neutralize the kiss, but she used his desire for her against him, working his body, his pleasure points, playing him like she was a maestro. She was a goddess, and she demanded his worship.

As if he suddenly understood where this was headed, his resistance stopped. His hands, instead of trying to slow her, reached down to her hips, and he gathered the material of her dress before hefting it, shoving it up around her waist. When he turned them so that her back was to the wall, she wanted to shout out in victory. When he didn't try to touch her or play with her, when he merely pushed her underwear to the side, a wicked smile curved her lips.

As she wrapped her legs around him, her mouth found his neck, his ear, and as he thrust up into her, she cried out, "Yes!"

His punishing rhythm was exactly what she craved, what she wanted, what she needed. Her hands were everywhere as he drilled into her. The sound of their bodies meeting slapped into the dark recesses of the closet, echoing in the tiny space, a consistent barrage of smacking skin and grunts. She tried to suppress the moans, but he moved his hand to rest lightly upon her throat, claiming her reactions.

Startled by the intimacy, she became more aggressive, mapping the increased mass of his body. The weight he'd had to gain rounded out the muscles he'd developed as a kid. His body at twenty-one had been stunning; his body at twenty-two was becoming a masterpiece. She had a fleeting notion of what he would be like in ten years, which she quickly squashed. There was no Tank in ten years. This was it. Her body tightened on the thought.

Tank paused, checking on her. "You okay?"

It hadn't dawned on her that Tank could read her. She didn't connect his knowledge of her, his care. But she fed on the hate sex. It filled her up, quenching the hunger pains she'd nurtured in the months apart.

She'd adjusted to the veil of darkness in the closet, enough to make out his luminescent stare. For the first time since he'd entered her, their eyes met. She imagined he could read the anger in hers because she could see the hurt and confusion in his. It should have penetrated her hardened heart, but it pissed her off instead.

Their gazes still locked, she lifted her hand from his shoulder and shoved two fingers into his mouth. He drew on them, and she felt herself clench around him. The lids of her eyes closed involuntarily, and when they reopened, his had darkened with desire. She pulled her hand away from his mouth and dropped her fingers between them to where they were joined. He groaned as she played with herself. He squeezed her ass, perhaps in warning, before he pounded into her again.

Her orgasm ripped through her. Dropping her head to his shoulder, she bit down, attempting to suppress the scream tearing out of her mouth. He grunted as both her body and teeth clamped around him. Continuing to thrust into her, he filled her up as he emptied.

The aftershocks of her climax died, she released the skin on his shoulder and muttered, "Fuck."

The awkwardness immediately descended. Unwrapping her legs, she dropped her normal left foot to the floor. His hands fell to her waist, anchoring her until she was steady.

Suddenly, the door in front of her opened, and she snapped back from the past.

"You need a special invitation to come in, Sunshine?"

It might have been the nickname, which she hadn't heard in years, or maybe it was just the heat of the memory she'd just conjured, but instead of the predicted anger, she looked up at Tank with a radiant smile.

"Hey."

"Are you coming in?" He tilted his head as he asked, and his dimples winked out at her. He stepped back and opened the door further, giving her space to get by him. Then, his gaze dipped down, and he reached forward. "Let me grab some of that."

The wine bottle she had tucked under her arm was suddenly confiscated. He placed it behind him on a table in the entranceway and then grabbed the bag containing the present for Tilly and Keira.

"Madison has some place for the gifts, but I'm not sure where, nor am I willing to mess with her master plan, so I'll leave this here," he explained as he dropped it next to the bottle of wine.

The casual mention of another woman should have gone unheeded, but she wanted to inhale sharply, her breath stolen. His back was still to her as he arranged her things. But, when he turned back to her, he didn't hesitate to step forward and pull her into a hug. It was quick but heartfelt, an embrace of friendship. She withheld another intake of breath, not wanting to get a close whiff of his scent.

"Good to see you," she said, meaning it.

"You, too." He opened his stance, and intending to move her, he placed his hand on the small of her back.

Without conscious thought, she stepped away. "Party this way?" she inquired, nodding her head toward the landing on the right.

He closed the door behind her and nodded. "Yep, right up those two flights of stairs."

"Trying to put me at a disadvantage, I see," she quipped with a smile.

He returned it. "There's an elevator," he offered.

"Of course there is." Again, she kept it light.

"Come on."

She followed him across the elevated entranceway, down two steps, and toward the back of the house. She quickly took in the sleek, contemporary lines of the decor, trying to keep her eyes off of her guide. Making their way through the kitchen, he turned down a hallway, presumably toward a garage. Two identical ornate doors were on the left. One had a doorknob.

"Garage," he explained. The other had a call button on the frame. "Elevator." He pressed the button, and it lit up.

"There you are," Madison exclaimed as the door to the elevator slid open.

Madison stepped forward and brushed a soft kiss on Tank's mouth. The touch, filled with familiarity and comfort, reminded Amber of the way Franco and Molly interacted. Madison's hand stole down and interlaced with Tank's before she turned toward Amber.

"I'm Madison," she introduced, sticking out her free right hand so that Amber could do nothing but shake it. "You must be Amber."

"Hi," Amber returned, releasing her hand at the appropriate time.

"I remember you from the wedding." Madison winked at her with a shit-eating grin on her face.

Amber found she had no idea what to make of the beautiful woman in front of her. She wanted to hate her, of course, but there was something too mischievous in Madison's gaze for Amber to feel anything but mild amusement.

"Right," Amber drawled out. "But we weren't really introduced, so it's nice to finally meet you."

"I came down to grab another bottle of wine. Give me a second, and I'll ride up with you."

"I'll get it," Tank offered. "You go up."

Madison laughed. "You just don't want to use the elevator."

"Maybe." He leaned over and dropped a kiss on her head before he turned and walked down the hall, leaving Amber in Madison's hands.

"Shall we go?"

Amber followed her into the elevator.

"He hates this thing. I don't think he's ever actually been in it. I think Hawk, his agent," she explained, as if Amber didn't know who Julian Hawkins was, "convinced him to put it in when he was having the loft built. It's super convenient for parties though because the best room is at the top of the house. I'm pretty sure Tank sat with the architect on every detail. You'll love it."

"I'm sure."

As if on cue, the elevator door opened, and Amber found herself looking out over Tank's rooftop loft. She quickly inventoried the space with its high ceilings, roll-up garage doors, pool table, massive entertainment center, and sparse but comfortable furnishings. She agreed; she loved it. She loved who filled it more. Keira and Tilly, Iman, Lamarcus, Franco and Molly. There were others, people Keira had mentioned, whom Amber would meet, but all the people who mattered to her were in this room, and she couldn't contain her smile.

She rushed out of the elevator and into Keira's waiting arms. Their embrace was long, drawn out, and full of sighs and murmurs of congratulations.

"You okay?" Keira whispered as they drew apart.

Amber should have expected the concern. Ever since the accident and the events leading up to it, Keira had worried about Amber. It had changed the dynamic of their relationship from best friends to one of overprotective big sister and resentful little sister. When Keira had gotten serious with football player Tilly Lace, things had changed again. Keira's family had not been open to the interracial relationship, and Amber had helped to ease the way with her friend's family.

Amber glanced over Keira's shoulder to where her parents stood.

"I'm so glad your parents came," Amber said soft enough so only Keira could hear.

"Me, too." Keira continued to study her though, and Amber knew her ploy was obvious. "I know you don't want to talk about it, but this has to be a lot to take in. I'm just making sure you're okay."

Amber glanced around to see if their conversation could be overheard but everyone around them was engaged or deliberately ignoring the reunion. She looked back to Keira. The happy, content aura of her best friend was palpable, and she could feel nothing but joy at being here to celebrate with her.

She pulled Keira in for another quick hug. "I'm really good. More than okay. I met Madison, and she escorted me up here." This earned her a horrified chuckle from Keira. "Your parents are here to celebrate with you, and I have all my favorite people in one place. Now, let's go get a drink."

They made their way to the bar set up on the deck outside. The lights of Atlanta dappled the skyline view in front of them. As they lifted their drinks in a toast, Amber celebrated more than just Keira and Tilly's engagement. She was lifting her glass to finally achieving freedom from her anger with Tank Howard. She was truly over him. The *eventually* Franco had promised her three years ago had arrived.

SIX

Tank could work a room. From the moment he'd stepped onto the Kensington State University campus as the nation's number one recruit, he'd been called on to meet with boosters and alumni, even the university president. He read crowds like he did defenses, constantly looking for weakness, strengths, breaks in the line. Then, he managed them like he did his offense—with well-honed efficiency.

But tonight was different.

His house was full of the people who'd watched him take his first stumbling steps into adulthood. They knew his history and, unfortunately, his hubris. It made for an interesting cocktail of familiarity and discomfiture.

Madison stood near him, a poodle prissily marking her territory. He didn't have to look over at her to see her protective stance, her hackles elegantly disguised in her semiformal black dress.

Across the room from him, Amber leaned in toward Iman, giving his young friend her undivided attention. Tank remembered her interest. It was never false. She couldn't pretend if she were on a stage and the director called for it. Her dark brown eyes could flash with anger, swim with jealousy, shine with laughter. He wondered if her emotions had been more easily discernible on her face before the indelicate scarring had marred its perfection. Right now, he could tell from where he stood that she was confused by something Iman had told her. Her eyes briefly cut to him, and he saw a look of derision tossed in his direction. He almost chuckled, wondering what he'd done to raise her ire.

God, he loved that about her. He could always count on a reaction.

What is that physics rule? For every action, there is an equal and opposite reaction.

The horrible aftermath of their frantic fucking in the closet came back to him as he stepped away from Madison and made his way out onto the deck to grab a drink.

"Heineken," he requested from the bartender Madison had hired. He ran his hands along the tiled countertop as he waited impatiently.

He wasn't a huge drinker, but the architect had insisted a built-in bar would enhance the space on resale. He could admit when he was wrong—most of the time.

The beer slid slowly across the couple of inches of space, and Tank nodded his appreciation to the guy. He grabbed a cocktail napkin and wrapped it around the icy-cold bottle. The standing space heaters kept the air warm enough, but it was still February.

He trudged toward the railing, looking for some peace among the white noise of the music, conversations, and laughter.

His attention was captivated by the view of the city spread out before him. He could see the infinite lights of the office buildings and high rises of Atlanta, a dappled galaxy dropped into suburban sprawl. He'd bet, if he focused really hard, he could see the illuminated sign of The Fox Theatre. Again, the memory of his last encounter with Amber nagged at him. He just wanted to forget that night, not relive it like a bad play over and over, attempting to figure out how he could have done it differently. *Really, how else could he have reacted when she shut down on him, even as his release soaked her thighs?*

He dropped his head to the railing, transported back to that moment when everything had exploded between them.

Tank knew the moment Amber's legs stopped shaking and the security of the wall behind her breached her lust-sated brain because she pushed his hands off of her waist and glared at him.

"You didn't fucking use anything."

His eyes narrowed on her. "I don't remember you asking me to suit up."

The resentment poured out of him, and he knew she felt it. He never had sex without a condom. It was rule number one of his mother, Chantel Jones's, list of things he needed to know. The circumstances of his birth had led his mother to make sure he kept himself baby-mama free, so it was an automatic response.

Woman in the vicinity? Condom in hand.

But he hadn't even thought about it. And, right now, he didn't want to give her that. Because, if she knew she had nothing to worry about, the exposure would be too much. He couldn't take her rejection a third time.

She brought her hands up and pushed against his chest, demanding room. The temptation to crowd her, to intimidate her with his size, was almost too great to fight. So, when he took a step back, it was with reluctance.

"Oh, that's right. It's my fault. Because any shitty, stupid thing you do comes down to me making you do it."

He scrubbed his hands over his face. "Christ!"

He took a deep breath, trying to rein in his fury, his emotions but she made him fucking crazy.

"You're on the pill, right?"

She broke eye contact and looked up at the ceiling.

Dread pooled in his belly.

"Of course," she said. "Amber to Tank's rescue." She looked back at him. "Pregnancy isn't what I'm worried about. It's more your whoring ways."

Bitch.

He wanted to scream the truth at her. Wanted to watch her inhale his confession and react to it. But he didn't want to be vulnerable to her anymore. The moment he let it out that he hadn't been with anyone since her, the balance of power would be firmly in her hands. If she wanted him in any other way than for what they'd just done, he'd probably risk it. But he knew better.

Glaring at her, he took an additional step back, letting the darkness seep between them. "I'll send you my blood test results."

"Make sure they're recent." The blackness of the closet couldn't hide her sneer.

His hands fisted and clenched against his thighs as anger vibrated through him. *This girl!*

She made him crazy.

And sad.

He studied her. The light aqua of her dress was barely discernable in the absence of light. He could draw the curves of her body, and he struggled with stick figures. He knew the lines, had them embedded on his psyche. He rubbed his fingers against his thumb, knowing exactly how the scars on her face and neck bumped and rolled under his touch.

Her rage, the most prominent emotion present, penetrated his hope. He'd buried it over the last year. He'd achieved so much in his rookie season. But he'd failed to overcome the regrets of his relationship with Amber. He'd hoped the year apart would dull her sense of betrayal, but he could admit now that not only had she not forgiven him, but she'd also harbored and fed her disappointment until he could no longer climb the heavily fortified walls of her heart.

The realization pissed him off. He turned away from her, grasping for the knob. Yanking the door open, he stormed out into the hall, his head downcast. He heard Amber fumble behind him, but he couldn't deal with her at the moment, so he kept moving.

"Tank?"

The sound of Madison's voice had his head jerking up. She stood a few feet in front of him, obviously confused by finding him tearing out of a closet. He didn't bother to try and mask any emotions. He imagined she saw his anger, his hurt, and his guilt prominently displayed.

Shaking his head, he moved toward her. "Sorry."

She shook her head, neither annoyed nor bewildered. He watched as she looked past him—to Amber, he assumed. Her eyes widened slightly, so the first emotion he could make out was surprise. He ignored it.

When he went to reach for her elbow to guide her away from his blunder, Amber spoke, "You'll let me know."

The hardness of the tone pushed him over the edge. He squeezed Madison's elbow before he turned away from her and stomped back to Amber.

The smack of a hand on his back made his head snap to the right, the memory folding in on itself and disappearing back into his mind.

Tilly stood there with a silly smile on his face. "My future mother-in-law wants a tour. You up to it, or are you okay with me leading a nosy woman through your house?"

Tank laughed. He was about to offer to lead the tour, but movement at the bar drew his attention. Amber leaned against it. No one else was on the deck, and he didn't want to lose the opportunity to have a conversation with her. He quickly scanned the scene inside, noting Madison was talking to Keira's mom.

"Have at it, man."

He ignored the knowing look in Tilly's eyes and turned back to the view, hoping she would come to him.

Tilly snickered behind his back and said in a low tone for only Tank to hear, "I got you, bro."

Tank didn't answer. None was needed.

Tank had met Tilly on his recruiting visit to Kensington, and they played together for three years. Tilly was a good college player and probably could have landed on a practice squad in the NFL, but he didn't want to wallow in obscurity when he had other options. Tank figured, in the next couple of years, Tilly would be managing the money of a lot of the league's players. The only reason he didn't work for Tank was because Tilly refused to take his business. Tilly said he valued Tank's friendship more than he wanted to be his business manager.

After witnessing the demise of Tank's college career and his early draft declaration, Tilly stayed with him every step of the way. He certainly didn't agree with Tank's choice, but he didn't judge him either.

Tank took a sip of his beer and waited. He could hear the din of her conversation with the bartender, the cadence of her voice sounding softly behind him. When it stopped, he knew she had seen him. Some vibe in the air shifted, and the muscles in his back tensed. He tried to maintain his casual stance, his view cast out toward the city, the beer hanging loosely between his clasped hands, so when she stepped to him, she'd believe he was surprised to be alone with her.

She approached the railing, and even if he hadn't known she was out here, his body would have responded.

When will that go away?

"Hey."

He stood up, turned to her, and leaned his hip against the railing, his view shifting from the lights of the city to the depths of her chocolate-colored eyes. The top of Amber's head came up higher than he'd expected. He hadn't noticed it earlier, but now, he could see she was taller. He looked down at her feet.

"Heels?" he questioned, the side of his mouth lifting into a half-smile.

She grinned. "Yes," she said, playfully raising her eyebrows. "It took me some time, but I can finally wear them." She shrugged. "In the whole scheme of things, it's not a big deal, but..." She paused. "God, I feel like such a girl saying this, but it's really exciting to be able to wear them."

"That's awesome." He left it at that.

She didn't want his praise, and although he knew what it meant for her, he could sense her reluctance to acknowledge his understanding of the feat.

She relaxed against the railing, her drink held in her hand. Then, she turned. "Wow," she murmured. She cast a quick glance at him before looking away again. "Amazing view."

"Right? I spend a lot of time out here."

"I can see why."

They stayed where they were with Amber taking in the city and Tank taking in Amber.

She finally spoke again, "This place suits you."

Her statement surprised him. "Yeah?"

"I love the neighborhood."

"Me, too."

The conversation was stilted, and Tank longed for their long-ago easy camaraderie, but he didn't know how to go back there, and he wasn't sure he'd cross the bridge if it somehow appeared before him.

"Madison tripped me up a little at our introduction."

Her frank declaration prompted a chuckle from him. "Yeah, like you, she doesn't do subtle well."

"Not that I didn't deserve it. That was a pretty shitty situation."

Tank couldn't help it when he stepped closer to her. He placed his hand on her shoulder, squeezing quickly before releasing it. Shaking his head, he decided an explanation was long overdue. "Madison and I weren't together at the wedding."

Her brow furrowed with confusion. "You weren't?"

"Nah. We were just friends. She thought it was funny, and I promise, she wasn't mad."

He didn't tell Amber about the conclusions he'd drawn after their frantic fucking in the closet.

So much had happened to him in the dark, dank, confined space. The feelings he harbored for her, the hope that she'd forgiven him—it was all a festering wound that she lanced when she pushed him out of and away from her. When he removed his hands from her waist, he detached himself from their past. The transformation, over a year coming, took merely a moment when he washed the scent of her from his hands in the restroom. And then he moved on to Madison.

"Hmm. Funny." Amber looked lost for a moment.

Tank regretted calling it funny. It was anything but.

"But you're together now." She bit her lip like she wished she could have somehow stopped the words or pulled them back.

Tank shrugged involuntarily. "We are."

He could tell her the true nature of their relationship, which was more symbiotic than loving, but he needed the distance his association with Madison provided. He needed the barrier because, when Amber peered up at him with those soulful eyes, he wanted things he knew he couldn't have.

He said nothing, and when the touring participants began to fill up the empty spaces of his rooftop deck, he found himself walking away from her yet again.

SEVEN

Relief raced through Amber, the tension in her muscles relaxing, as she left Tank's town house, following the parade of partygoers to one of the micropubs down the street. The short jaunt through the neighborhood reinforced her first impressions. She longed to stroll during daylight hours, so she could peruse the little shops and feel the intimate vibe. As she walked along, her hand curved around Steele's forearm, and she tried not to look around for Tank.

When he'd left her on the rooftop, she figured it was a good thing. The start-and-stop quality of their conversation depressed her as much as the knowledge of his relationship with Madison.

She was relieved that Madison and Tank hadn't been together at Franco's wedding. The disastrous encounter didn't beg for a cheating scandal. Amber remembered the look on Madison's face during her and Tank's graceless exit from the closet. While it hadn't been contemptuous, it hadn't necessarily been friendly. Amber's sobbing bout included a modicum of guilt for being the girl Tank had cheated with instead of the girl he cheated on. His declaration on the deck made her feel a little less horrible about their actions.

"Has it been as bad as you imagined?" Steele asked.

"No, it's been pretty easy."

"Good." They continued their walking, comfortable with the small stretches of silence. "Do you think you are finally over him?"

His question halted her in her tracks. He kept his pace, and her hand stayed glued to his arm, even as he pulled away from her. He stopped abruptly and turned back to her, the distance between them and the rest of the group growing.

Steele was so tall that she normally needed to keep extra space between them to save her neck. But, now, he stood a little out of her reach, and she peered across the night to him. His eyes matched his skin, so the only color was the white around his black pupils and the flash of teeth in his mouth. In his stare, she glimpsed a flash of something she'd never seen before—or maybe she had chosen to ignore it or maybe she was imagining it.

She shook her head, clearing it. "Yeah."

"Yeah, you're over him?"

When she nodded, he looked away from her. She felt some change between them, and when his eyes came back to hers, she knew.

"How do you know you're over him?"

Shrugging, she answered him as honestly as she could, "I'm not angry anymore. I can look at him and talk to him and not feel that tremendous hurt. For so long, anytime I thought about him, I could feel the heat of my anger pumping through my body—like the night I'd walked in on him with his dick in some girl's mouth. It was no different. It didn't go away. But, tonight, I didn't feel any of that."

Steele took a small step toward her. For a man with a size fourteen shoe, the slight shuffle moved him infinitely closer. Warily watching him, she braced for his next action. She didn't know what to feel. Of course she'd thought about the possibility of something more with Steele, but she always held back, not wanting to come between him and Tank. As she stood on the precipice, straddling the line between friendship and more than friendship, she didn't know if she wanted to jump.

His go-go-gadget arm lifted from his side, and she waited as his hand engulfed her neck. His thumb touched her cheek, and his fingers curled around her nape. Leaning forward, he captured her lips in a tender kiss, an exchange of air. He hovered there, waiting for her. Indecision stayed her. Curiosity mobilized her. Closing the distance, she pressed her lips against his—once, lightly—before her tongue swiped the seam of his lips, asking for entrance. His mouth opened, and she got her first taste of him. They explored each other with sweeping strokes.

The hand on her neck tightened in her hair, and his other hand landed on her hip, pulling her closer. The angle changed with his proximity, and her head dropped back. Warmth seeped into her belly as Lamarcus deepened the kiss.

His lips mastered the feel of hers, and when he broke the kiss, he dropped small kisses across her mouth and along her jaw. His thumb stroked her cheek as he took a step away from her. Her eyes blinked open, and she found Steele studying her. The flicker of uncertainty in his stare made her nervous. They didn't speak.

And, in the absence of conversation, thoughts began to whirl through her brain. The kiss had been good. She imagined that sex with Lamarcus would be better—better than any sex she'd had in the last two years. They were best friends; they shared secrets. He was a good man, one who wouldn't solve his problems with stupid, hurtful decisions.

Lamarcus's traced along her chin once more before he pulled her forward into his chest, his hands resettling, intertwining behind her back. She relaxed into the embrace and looped her arms around him. Her heels gave her an added touch of height, but even with them, his size dwarfed her. Dropping her head onto his chest, she sighed. She loved him, but she wasn't sure she could love him in any other way than she did now.

"That was interesting," Steele ventured.

Amber couldn't help her giggle. "It was."

"I always wondered, you know?"

She nodded against his chest.

"Maybe I should have done that when we first started hanging out," he said.

"Maybe."

"It kind of felt like kissing my sister."

She could feel his smile in the words.

"Okay. I'm not sure that was the best analogy, but we can go with that."

Steele must have been concerned about her reaction because he pulled back from her and set her away from him, keeping his hands on her shoulders. "It was weird for you, too, right?"

His horror of her feeling something different than him was pretty humorous, and she contemplated punking him. But she didn't need to mess with their friendship any more than the kiss might have.

She smiled reassuringly. "Yeah, it was weird for me, too."

"It wasn't bad," he clarified. "You can kiss."

Laughing, she said, "Thanks, dude. You're making me feel awesome."

He chuckled and then squeezed her shoulders. "I expected something different." The simple statement lingered in the air between them. "All this time we've been hanging out...I mean, you're the perfect woman. You can talk football better than most men. You understand my injury and what it meant for me when my life plan got ripped away. You get me, and I thought we'd just fit." He looked away from her, as if he were embarrassed by the confession.

Amber reached up and cupped his jaw. "Steele, I get it. And I'm not offended. That kiss was a long time coming. And, believe me when I say, it seemed like the a great situation. I swear, everyone has been waiting for it." She grinned up at him. "But there's something to be said for chemistry." Winking, she dropped her hand and pulled out of his grip. "Let's go get a drink."

Steele turned and offered his arm. She placed her hand back into the familiar spot, and the two of them continued their trek to the bar. The quiet between them was comfortable, the kiss seemingly forgotten.

The uneven cadence of her walk compared to Steele's was a broken metronome in the white noise of the street, and Amber found herself thinking about the slightly awkward few minutes when they'd both realized it wasn't going to happen between them. Disappointment flooded her. They were a good fit for each other, and she hated the lack of a spark.

She'd known, as soon as he'd run his hand on the left side of her face rather than the right, he couldn't be for her. How it had come to one simple motion was something a highly paid psychologist would have to untangle. Since Tank, no one had touched the marred part of her face. She didn't know if it was repulsion because of the angry appearance, if it was fear of hurting her, or maybe it was just plain denial, but no one was brave enough to confront the ugliness of her past that illuminated her face like a beacon on a foggy night. Without even thinking about it, she reached up and ran her hand over the twisted terrain, the cold touch a welcome respite to the deadened skin running from her lip along her jawline and down the length of her neck.

The road bent to the right, opening up into a concentration of retail, with the lights from the halogen signs lighting up the street. Their destination was across the road, a couple of doors down from where they stood. Stopping for traffic, they waited on the side of the street.

Amber scanned the area, looking for people, but it seemed everyone had already made it into the bar. She could hear the whispers of music from the outside deck in the back and the chatter of voices. She had a moment and a question.

She squeezed Steele's arm, and he turned toward her.

"Since we've survived the weirdness of that kiss, I need to ask you a question."

Steele's brow furrowed. He nodded instead of answering, so she gathered the tattered shreds of her dignity.

Taking a deep breath, she spit it out, "You didn't touch my scar."

His eyes widened in surprise, but she refused to stop the train of thought.

"No one has. I've been with my fair share of men in the last couple of years. No one touches it. It's like they are afraid it's contagious. I'd thought you'd be different. But you weren't."

She glanced away from him, the guilt in his eyes too much for her to take while she bared her deepest fears. Her face heated with embarrassment. They'd shared a lot of things—work woes, rehab stories, childhood memories. But, at the moment of her confession, she realized they'd never gone this deep. And she suddenly wanted to take it back. Her curiosity could be satisfied another way, with someone she didn't care about, whose answer probably wouldn't matter to her all that much.

As she struggled with her discomfiture, another horrible thought dawned on her, and she almost flinched with the knowledge. Tank was the only person in her life who had seen her scars and accepted them and what they were. Then, he'd gotten past them. But he really never let her forget they were there. It was why he had been so special to her. While everyone else wanted to pretend like they didn't exist, Tank Howard had claimed them and her.

Fuck. No wonder I can't let him go.

She thought she had. When Lamarcus had asked her before they kissed, she'd been confident in her answer. But, now, she was unsure. She wasn't over him. She was just over the anger. Tears welled in her eyes, and she was grateful she wasn't facing Steele. Biting her lip to contain an embarrassing, sobering sob, she worked to get her emotions under control.

Then, Steele's paw of a hand landed on the ravaged skin, and he turned her back to him. His fingers trailed over every inch of her lips and jaw and down her neck. He could basically palm the whole area in one touch. She closed her eyes, the intensity of the moment stark.

"I don't know," he said quietly. The roughened pads of his fingers stayed against her trampled neck. "I guess I thought it would hurt or you would hate it. You never talk about it, so I just started to ignore it. I'm sorry."

"It's okay," she said on a sigh.

He dropped his head to hers, landing a quick kiss on her forehead.

"You guys coming in or what?"

Amber's eyes snapped open as both she and Steele jumped away from each other. Steele turned, his back now facing Amber. She wanted to stay behind him, hiding from Tank, but she took a step to the side, so they appeared as a united front.

Tank stood in front of them, his hands shoved into the pockets of his dress pants. She'd seen him dressed up a couple of times—most notably on the night he'd won the Heisman when he was decked out in a suit. Tonight, he wore charcoal-colored trousers and a white dress shirt. It was tailored to fit his shoulders to perfection, a fit you could only get customized. The white of his shirt against his cocoa-colored skin seemed to enhance his green eyes. Those eyes on a white guy would be nice, but with his mixed blood, they peered out with an eerie brilliance that could only be deemed as beautiful. With her seconds-old realizations bouncing around in her brain, it was hard to look him in the eye.

No one spoke, and in the ensuing silence, Amber wasn't quite sure whose court the conversational ball had been lobbed to. She looked between Steele and Tank, who seemed to be engaged in some silent communication. She started to fidget, shifting her weight from left to right.

"So, shall we go?" Tank asked, holding his hands out to indicate which way they should walk.

"Yeah," Amber responded, thankful for the direction.

The three of them crossed the street together and then made their way into the bar.

"Drink?" Tank asked.

Amber couldn't help her glance over at Steele. He appeared to be shell-shocked, a bit guilty if she could trust her read. He refused to look at her, instead peering around the bar—taking it in or hiding, she didn't know. When she pulled her eyes away from her friend, she found herself caught in Tank's snare.

He nodded his head toward Steele. "He ordering for you?"

She sensed some sarcasm but couldn't be sure. "Nah. I'll have a beer."

"There are about a hundred selections. Can you be more specific?"

She shook her head, feeling out of place and nervous. Then, Tank picked up a menu from a nearby table and shoved it at her. She took it from him and focused on the choices in front of her.

"A hefeweizen," she said, passing the menu to Steele.

He shook his head. "They have anything stronger?" he asked Tank.

Tank chuckled, but the smile seemed false even though she was no longer an expert on him. Maybe she was merely projecting. But as Tank and Steele walked to the bar, she was uneasy.

Why did Tank have to walk up at exactly that moment?

Because I have the luck of the damned.

EIGHT

Tank hadn't been prepared for the jealous rage that made the muscles in his shoulders bunch and his fists clench. Visions of pummeling his best friend flashed through his mind, the sick fantasy unfurling a malicious smile. The ire tangoed in his bloodstream, looping and dipping, all fire and passion. The heavy wooden barstools appeared to be able to cause a vicious commotion, and he dragged his fingers across the wooden slat, subconsciously weighing the sturdy chairs.

Walking through the bar with a quiet Steele following him, he worked to talk himself down. As they waited for the bartender to acknowledge them, Steele placed both hands on the bar and dropped his head between his shoulders, casting out the vibe of a remorseful puppy. Tank kept his head forward, his eyes fixed on the mirror in front of him. The reflection included a downtrodden Steele, a confused Amber, and an oblivious Madison, all collected in one scene, a snapshot of his suddenly complicated life.

"Hey, man," Shane, the neighborhood bartender, said as he stuck out his hand to greet Tank. "What can I get you?"

Tank clasped his hand before nodding to Steele. "Preference?"

"Tequila," he grunted.

"Patrón," Tank clarified. Then, he nodded to Shane and added, "Two," before turning and leaning his left hip on the bar. He briefly studied Steele.

"We good?"

Tank didn't quite know how to respond to the question. He was the furthest thing from good, but he had no right to the anger he stubbornly nursed. He'd watched them kiss and then talk. The intimacy of the interaction between the two of them shredded him. Then, the guilt hit. Steele's history read like *The Blind Side* without an adoptive family and a happy ending. He deserved something good.

But could he stand it if Steele's good happened to include Amber?

"Yeah, we're good," he answered, hoping like hell that Steele didn't note the grinding of his teeth as he forced the words out of his mouth.

The bartender plunked the two shots and a saltshaker in front of them before he set a small white plate filled with limes down on the bar. Tank smirked at the dude, wondering if it was wishful thinking on Shane's part or if he wasn't very good at hiding his state of mind. Tank reached for the shot at the same time as Steele. They clinked glasses, and with a nod to each other, they slammed the liquor. Tank's throat almost seized up as the taste of the tequila triggered his gag reflex, a leftover reaction from his binge drinking a couple of weeks ago.

Carefully placing the glass on the counter, Tank waved Shane over. "Another round and a hefeweizen," he requested, suddenly remembering Amber's order. He dug his wallet out of his pocket and tossed his credit card on the bar. "Start a tab," he instructed before turning his back to the bar and surveying the scene.

He found Amber without even knowing he was looking. She was tucked into a corner with Iman in what looked like their second serious discussion of the night. Curious, he grabbed the beer Shane had delivered and left Steele.

He walked directly to Amber and Iman. Reaching between them, he thrust the beer into her hand.

"I was just wondering what a girl had to do around here to get a drink," she teased, her eyes twinkling, as she winked at Tank.

"Yeah, sorry about that. I might have been sidetracked."

"Tequila will do that to you."

Tank regarded Iman and Amber. "You two look way too serious for a celebration."

Iman shrugged and glanced away with a roll of his eyes. Tank shifted his gaze to Amber, the question apparent.

She shrugged, too. "We're agreeing to disagree on his choice of an agent."

"Like I had a choice," Iman mumbled.

Tank shook his head. "Been there, done that," he directed to Amber.

Her eyebrows rose, her interested piqued. "You two have had this conversation?" she asked Tank.

"Numerous times. He's damn stubborn."

Iman finished his drink and walked away, his annoyance a second skin.

Tank turned his attention to her. "He doesn't like to listen."

"You tried to talk to him about it?"

"I sent Hawk to meet with him. But Iman had it in his head that Hawk was spread too thin with too many guys already. I'm not sure who's been advising him, but he didn't want to hear anything I had to say. Tilly tried to talk to him, too."

"That makes me feel better."

Her comment irked him. "Why?"

She looked away from him, clearly uncomfortable with answering him. She raised the glass to her mouth and took a sip. A slight ring of foam formed on her top lip, her tongue sneaking out to lick it. Tank felt a trickle of desire low in his belly, and he almost groaned. His interest focused on her mouth as he imagined tracing it with his tongue, relearning her flavor. When she turned back to him, he'd forgotten all about being annoyed.

"I thought you left him hanging." She didn't flinch from her delivery. Rather, she leveled him with an unapologetic glint.

He didn't know whether to be offended or pissed, but she effectively doused the flickers of desire that had been threatening to engulf him.

He smiled ruefully. "Seriously, Sunshine?" The deliberate use of her nickname earned him a narrowing of her eyes. "You have that little faith in me?" His question hung between them, the meaning so much larger than Iman Perry.

"When it comes to your friends, I have a lot of faith in you."

Her answer brought them back to Iman, and Tank took a moment to formulate his response.

People were all around them, their friends, but he grabbed her elbow and stepped in closer. "Iman got himself into some trouble. Nothing crazy, but when that happened, his confidence in his ability to get drafted dropped. And I think he got some shitty advice. When I found out who he'd signed with, I was pissed, but it was too late."

"Do you think he has a chance?"

"Do you?"

"Yes. Obviously not in an early round, but he could go somewhere."

"Without going to the Combine, it will be harder for him, especially because Kensington State isn't going to draw anyone for a pro day. I think he can do it, but it's going to be a lot of work, and I don't know if he's committed to it."

"That's all true. But he is really talented, and someone will be willing to take a chance on him."

He smiled at her assessment, surprised at her optimism. "I hope so." He took a step away from her, returning them to a respectable distance. "You like what you're doing?"

Conversation was easier than it had been at his house. Maybe the neutral territory helped. But they were talking, and she was smiling at him. He wasn't ready to forgo his opportunity to catch up with her. As a discussion topic, jobs were easy.

"I do," she answered. "It's different every day, and I get to be around football, so what's not to like?"

"There's something not to like about every job."

She cocked her head to the side, studying him. "There are things about your job you don't like?"

"Of course."

"Like?"

"Losing."

"Ha. That's an occupational hazard. Your job is almost always going to end on a loss."

"Yes"—he grinned—"except when we win the Super Bowl."

"Hasn't happened yet," she teased.

His hearty laugh filled the space between them, and she met his eyes with a big grin of her own. He acknowledged the irony of laughing with her about him losing. He hadn't been able to think about their last game of the season without gut-wrenching frustration, and suddenly, she'd made a joke about it, and he was laughing.

"So, what don't you like about it?" he prompted.

Amber didn't answer for a moment, seeming to think about what she wanted to say.

"Come on. Don't think about it so hard. First thought."

Resigned, she answered, "The first thing that came to mind was ego."

Again, he found himself laughing. "Managing egos is definitely not your forte."

"Hey," she grumbled, slapping lightly on his arm, attempting to pull off being angry. "I manage them just fine. I don't necessarily enjoy doing it."

"You're so good at it though."

He couldn't hide the playful note in his voice, and she giggled. The sound was so foreign, it made him mute. He hadn't heard her laugh like that since the night of his last college football game. The first time he'd heard it, the rustiness reminded him of an unoiled hinge. But then it began to come easier and flowed more naturally from her. Hearing it now, without the crustiness of disuse, made him want to laugh harder.

"You ready to get out of here?"

Tank turned to see Steele standing behind him. Hiding his irritation, he moved back, letting Steele into the small circle of two. Glancing back at Amber, he noted she and Steele were engaged in some silent communication. Their connection made him crazy.

"Now?"

Steele shifted uncomfortably, and Tank wondered what the hell was going on with his friend.

"Yeah, now. Franco and Molly are heading out, and it would be easier to leave with them."

Amber appeared confused, but she nodded. "Okay, let me run to the restroom." She set her empty glass on the table a few feet behind them before she turned to Tank. "It was good talking to you."

She stepped to him and leaned in, pressing a quick kiss on his cheek. It was over before he could react or even say good-bye. She disappeared into the hallway where the restrooms were located. Both he and Steele watched her depart.

Then, Steele turned back to him and glared. "What the hell are you doing?" he whispered furiously.

Tank resisted the urge to roll his eyes. "Being friendly."

"Well, friendly for you and Amber isn't really a thing, is it?"

"Jealous?"

Steele chuckled sarcastically. "I don't have anything to be jealous of."

His statement reminded Tank of what he'd happened onto earlier in the night, and just like that, the stupid envy and helpless anger descended on him again. He refused to let Steele see his reaction or pick up on the seething beast trying to roar its head. The kiss had bothered him, but seeing Steele's hand lingering on what he considered to be his spot on Amber's body had killed him.

Did Steele know how the touch of a hand soothed what she'd described as the burn under her skin? God, did Steele know what it did to her if he dragged his tongue along the webbing under her jawbone?

Surely, he did, and it made Tank fucking crazy to realize someone else could have such intimate knowledge of her.

But what did he think she'd been doing for the past three years?

Tank knew her well enough to know that she hadn't been celibate.

He wanted to scrape his hand over his head, but Steele knew his frustration tells, and he absolutely refused to put his feelings on display for his friend.

When had he ever made an effort to pretend for Steele?

He couldn't wait for this fiasco of a night to be over. Then, he'd just have to make it through the wedding and probably some baptisms.

Could he lose Tilly as a best friend between now and these certain life milestones he'd be forced to attend with Amber?

"Hey, babe," Madison said, slipping her fingers around his arm. "Hey, Steele," she greeted. Tank might have grunted a greeting to her, but she continued on, as if she hadn't expected either of them to answer, "Looks like people are heading out. You two ready to go?"

"Yeah," Tank said.

"I'm going to head home with Amber," Steele responded.

Is that a knife twisting in my back?

Madison got wide-eyed. "Ooh! I've been hoping you would finally make your move," she cooed.

Tank felt every muscle, tendon, and ligament in his body tighten and snap.

Steele chuckled and sheepishly looked away, as if he were a seventh grader who'd just had his crush outed.

"I've got to close my tab. Be back in a few." Tank bent down and brushed a kiss across Madison's mouth.

He made his way to the bar and paid his tab. As he turned around to move back toward the door, he saw Amber and Steele leaving together with her clutching his arm. Right as they crossed the threshold, she turned, catching Tank's glare. She gifted him with a hesitant smile and a fluttery wave before she exited. Steele didn't look back.

Tank didn't remember much of the walk home. The two shots of tequila had hardly been enough to get him drunk. He was inebriated on a cocktail of jealousy, anger, and betrayal.

Feeling reckless and slightly desperate, he pinned Madison against the door the moment they entered his house. In a graceless, emotionless manner, he wrapped her legs around his waist. He was thankful for the dress she wore. Fumbling through their clothes was easy. But nothing else about their encounter was. Her mouth tasted wrong, the cloying scent of her perfume jumbled his thoughts, and the smooth surface of her manicured fingernails as they dug into the flesh on his back annoyed him. Lost in the regrets of the past, he moved in and out of her with a scary emotional distance. When her body tightened around his, her climax making her shudder, he held her close, all the while struggling against the desire to get away from her. Inelegantly, he pulled out of her and unwrapped her legs from around his waist. He waited until she was steady, and then he released her. He zipped up his pants, his unresolved erection making the task difficult.

"Were you fucking me or fucking her out of your system?" she asked stoically.

He had an answer for her, but it wasn't one either of them wanted to hear.

NINE

MARCH

Amber glanced at the corner of her computer screen and noted the time. She had about ten minutes before she would have to head out to the first spring practice of the year. Whitey didn't require her presence on the sideline, but when her schedule permitted, she tended to spend at least an hour on the practice field, watching.

Today, the weather had dawned crisp and clear without the threat of the soupy humidity ever present on the field in the fall. She'd take a March afternoon over an August afternoon anytime. Plus, she was eager to see the future of their team. They'd lost some key positions on both sides of the ball, but they had a number of players who'd red-shirted the year before. They were hungry to make an impression before the new signing class entered the fray in the fall.

While this was considered the off-season because they didn't have a game every weekend, it was really a misnomer. College athletics didn't really have an off-season. There were times when they didn't have to be at the stadium for fifteen-hour Saturdays, but it didn't mean they weren't busy.

Camps and recruiting ruled Amber's downtime. Almost immediately following the spring game, the recruiting calendar would open up to allow for contacts and evaluations. Her coaches would be off in literally ten different directions, cultivating the youngsters eager to be a part of the next great recruiting class. As they came in off the road, they'd gear up for the eight camp sessions they had scheduled for the summer.

And the student-athletes didn't go home anymore. Summers were spent taking classes, lifting weights, and playing seven on seven.

Midway through June, their incoming class would arrive. There'd be paperwork and physicals and monitoring to manage. Just as their freshmen were getting acclimated to life on campus, it would be August, and two-a-day practice sessions would start.

So, her hashtag for the last three years had been #thereisnooffseason.

Thankfully.

Because Atlanta had fucked with her head.

She'd been a little worried about the engagement party; of course she had. As far as a party, it had gone off without a hitch, and Amber had a good time. Being with all those people again, at one time, was refreshing and fun. Spending time with the As and Franco and Molly was restorative. Helping Keira find the perfect wedding dress was a memory Amber would cherish for the rest of her life. Giving Iman a hard time about his choices and making sure he had things to think about tapped into some part of her she hadn't known existed. She liked trying to help him find his way even if she was a little too late. Overall, her time in Atlanta was awesome. Even seeing Tank.

But, since she'd gotten home, her head resembled a minefield. Trigger points surrounded her that, weeks before, had been innocuous events and items. Like Jamal Jeffries who had merely walked into her office to ask about his scholarship check, wearing Tank's number. Or reviewing some footage on a young quarterback who feinted sideways, a step vaguely resembling a trademark Tank Howard evasion. Last Tuesday, she'd turned on the TV in her office to find it on the NFL Network, replaying some footage of the AFC Championship Game. Helplessly drawn in, she watched Tank, resplendent even during an ass-kicking. He was suddenly everywhere, and she didn't even have the shield of her anger to provide protection.

She stopped briefly at the desk of her administrative assistant. Lauren faced outward, so her back was to the door of Amber's office. She was more gatekeeper than anything.

"I'm about to head out to practice. Anything I need to handle before I go?" Amber asked.

Lauren looked over at Amber from her computer. She picked up an envelope on her desk and handed it to Amber. "This came from Miss Eva. She said they're the dates Whitey wanted to run by you for the speaker."

Amber grabbed it and nodded. "I really wish he would learn to email," she said, shaking her head.

Lauren laughed. Whitey's technology aversion was something of a standing joke among the staff. "He would save some trees."

"Truth." Amber unwrapped the string on the campus mail and pulled the paper out. She handed the envelope back to Lauren and looked over the dates. Turning the paper so that Lauren could see, they both chuckled at Whitey's scrawl. "Seriously, a whole piece of paper to write down two dates. He could have texted me." Amber dropped it on the desk and leaned over to better see the computer. "Can you pull up my calendar?"

Lauren quickly clicked through a couple of screens and brought up the requested information.

After a quick scan, Amber nodded. "Okay. Go ahead and add this to the players' calendars, and set up text reminders for their phones for twenty-four hours and another for one hour and fifteen minutes in advance."

"Got it."

Amber grabbed the paper, crumbled it up, and shot it into Lauren's trash can, holding her pose. It dropped in, and Amber threw her hands up, walking backward, as she made the goal sign. "All right. I'm on the field if you need me."

"Do you know what this is about?" Lauren asked, tossing her head in the direction of Amber's makeshift basketball hoop.

"I don't. Some speaker. Whitey was kind of vague."

"Okay. I'll just put *Speaker* on the calendar."

"Perfect." Amber turned and walked through the outer door of their office space.

The Football Operations area was separate from the offices, which was why Amber spent a lot of her time in the meeting room, directly in the hub of their world. They'd obviously redesigned the building before she arrived. She would have directed them to do it differently. All the coaches' offices had a wall of windows, so their view opened up to the practice fields. The regulation-size turf surface boasted state-of-the-art video technology, so the coaches could record practice and analyze plays. At the far end was an indoor facility for stormy weather. It made scheduling practices predictable and her job easier. But it didn't stop her from marveling at the money invested in their program.

She took the elevator down to the ground floor that housed the locker and training rooms. Everything around here was locked down. The outside doors and players' locker room required thumbprints for access. To enter Whitey's office suite, the iris of your eye had to be authenticated. They didn't use codes because those could be given out, like secrets on the black market.

Amber placed her thumb on the reader and entered the hallway leading directly to the field. She blinked against the blast of sun as the door opened. Hastily sliding her sunglasses into place, she made her way to the field.

Even with unlimited access and being around the sport all the time, there was something about that first whiff of the air around practice. She couldn't claim turf had a smell—if it did, it probably held the sweat of all the previous players—but some scent always permeated the space around her when she was on a football field. She was sure it was more about the collective hopes and dreams of the players and coaches, but whatever it was, she craved it.

Most people, when asked to conjure their safe place, would come up with beaches or blankets, people they loved, or places they wanted to go. The gridiron was her safe place. Maybe it was the memory of her time as a kid, standing with her father, completely confident of her place in the world. When she'd come here three years ago, she'd needed it without knowing why.

Amber meandered around the field, watching the drills, taking note of what she saw.

When the coaches met later in the day to recap, she liked to have her own impressions. She wouldn't share them because it wasn't her place. But, in her head, she'd compare what they said to what she'd observed. And she would keep track.

She found herself watching the receivers who were working with one of the promising quarterbacks and Steele. She enjoyed his coaching style. His explanations to his players were spot-on. He encouraged them while correcting them, and he understood how to capitalize on their strengths. She didn't know if he would ever master the political piece of being a head coach, but he had the player-development part of it down to a science. He glanced up and inadvertently met her gaze. He offered a tentative smile and then turned his attention back to his players.

Since Atlanta, their relationship had suffered. Steele had vacationed from there, and when he'd returned last week, their interactions had been strained. He'd say she was acting like a girl and imagining it, but she knew she wasn't. They still hung out, but the ease of their friendship seemed to be stuck on the corner of Peachtree Street and Oakhurst, jammed up in the traffic of a kiss and a stroke. She didn't regret either action, but she definitely regretted the lack of chemistry.

Nicky came up and tapped her on the shoulder, ducking to the left when she looked right.

"You are such a child." She laughed when she got him to stop messing with her.

"You love that about me," he responded.

"I do."

She absolutely did love her some Nicky Stone. He was a good ole Southern boy from Mississippi who loved to hunt and fish. The gentle giant had been a bone-crushing linebacker, which always struck Amber as odd because of his easygoing nature. He'd been working for Whitey for two years when Amber joined the staff. They'd become fast friends as the youngest members of Whitey's elite group, and then they had adopted Steele when he joined the ranks.

"Where's the boss?"

Amber looked around, confused. "He's not here?"

"Nope. During our meeting, he told us he'd be late, but I thought he'd be here by now."

Amber lifted her phone and tapped on it, searching for a text or an email from Whitey's administrative assistant, Miss Eva. She didn't find anything but a missed call from Franco, which she ignored.

"Did he say why he was going to be late?"

Whitey didn't clear his schedule with her, but he normally kept her in the loop.

Nicky shrugged and then began to back away from her, on his way to his guys. "He was meeting some VIP and wanted to show him around. Gotta go. Catch up later?"

"Yeah. Day one tradition," she responded as he bounced away from her, as eager to be back on the field as she was.

Amber took one more look around, searching for Whitey. She glanced back at her phone, noting the time. She wanted to stay and watch, but she also wanted to know what Whitey was up to. Turning, she made her way back toward the locker room entrance, acknowledging the trainers and other random staff with nods as she passed.

She pulled open the heavy door and stepped into the hallway. She quickly ditched her sunglasses, sliding them up onto her head, pulling her hair back with it. She didn't often do this because it left her scar exposed, and while she was fairly comfortable with it, she didn't like to draw attention to it. But the hallway was dim and deserted. The door at the other end opened, and Amber recognized Whitey's voice before her eyes fully adjusted to the interior light.

"What is so important that you are late to practice?" she chided.

Whitey laughed before stepping back and holding the door for someone. "I told you she keeps me on my toes," he joked.

Amber hadn't realized someone was with Whitey, and immediately, she regretted calling him out. She was always brutally honest with him but was also respectful enough to know when to give him shit and when to hold back. Typically, in front of other people, mum was the word. Her cheeks colored with embarrassment.

She closed the distance between them. "I apologize," she started, offering her hand in greeting.

"No worries."

The familiar voice washed over her, and her eyes snapped up to meet his.

Tank fucking Howard.

She looked between Tank and Whitey, clearly shocked to see the two of them palling around together. A litany of sentences was poised on the tip of her tongue—questions, accusations—but she remained mute, merely staring at Tank.

"Tank Howard, this is Amber Johnson, my Director of Operations. Anything you need, she's your girl."

The smile widened on Tank's face, making his stupid dimples pop. "Perfect," Tank murmured, his gaze locked on her.

"I've got to get to practice, but we'll talk tomorrow. Remember, anything you need, total access. Amber will handle everything."

She watched helplessly as Whitey flew out of the corridor, the clank of the door handle releasing snapping her from her stupor.

"What are you doing here?" she managed to say.

Tank smirked. "I know people."

TEN

Amber and Tank remained in the corridor, appraising each other. Tank continued to smile cheekily at her—a big, fat, happy Cheshire Cat grin. Amber's stomach rolled with both awareness and anticipation.

And his response? *"I know people."*

She'd thrown the same expression at him when they first met, using her anonymity to her advantage.

She couldn't help but smile back at him when the three words penetrated the haze of surprise.

"Ah, you remember," he stated.

She fought against the heady giddiness of the shared memory. "I do."

"Good."

She couldn't help her reaction to him. He was dressed casually in jeans, a T-shirt, and sneakers. He had graced a number of magazine covers with his football regalia, but looking at him now, there was no doubt he could do justice as a model.

She glanced away to get a handle on her thoughts. "Uh, so Whitey mentioned full access. What do you need from me?"

"That's a loaded question," he said, chuckling softly.

She took a step back, searching for more distance between them. She needed some space. Clearing her throat, she tried again. "What exactly are you doing here?"

"Training. Off-season training."

"Why?" she blurted.

He rubbed his hand over his head. Amber had seen him do that hundreds of times when he got nervous or anxious or if he didn't know quite what to say.

He's nervous. "I mean, why would you come here to train?"

"Change of scenery."

"Whatever," she said, suddenly impatient with him. "So, you need access to the weight room and training room?"

"Whitey said he could get me a locker, too."

"Of course."

"And the practice field."

Her eyes widened at the access he was being granted. "Okay. Let's head upstairs and see what we can do."

She led the way to her office. They didn't speak as they entered the elevator or when they exited. As he followed her, he remained silent. Most people asked questions or commented about the facility. Tank said nothing, for which she was grateful because her mind was whirling in too many directions for her to hold on to any one coherent thought other than the question flashing like a grand marquee in her brain.

What the hell is he doing here?

Opening the door to her office, Amber led Tank through the reception area. When Lauren looked up at them, her eyes widened in disbelief.

"Lauren," Amber said, stopping in front of her desk, "this is Tank Howard. He needs to get set up with access around the building. Are you available to take him around?"

Amber needed a moment, or ten, without his presence. Lauren looked at Amber with a smile one might expect a lottery winner to wear.

"Oh, of course," she stuttered before standing up and coming around the desk. She held her hand out, and Tank took it. "Pleasure to meet you," she cooed.

Amber had to fight to keep from calling her assistant out on her fangirling. They had Hall of Famers in here all the time. During football season, it was like a parade of the famous, but Tank Howard had managed to throw Lauren off her game.

"Nice to meet you," Tank responded. If being pawned off surprised him, he didn't show it.

"Uh, right this way," Lauren said.

Amber refused to watch them as they strode through the outer doors, instead turning and beating a quick path to the sanctuary of her office. She sat down heavily and stared at the blank screen of the computer in front of her.

What is happening here?

She toyed with the pen on her desk, twirling it around in an endless circle, her focus on the aimless spinning.

Unthinkingly, she turned on the TV. An image of Madison Shepard dominated the picture. Her hair was perfectly coifed, and her eyes shimmered with glib mischief. The volume muted, Amber could only stare at the woman involved with Tank. That she was so beautiful hurt a bit. That she seemed to be fun and cool hurt more. That she'd thrown a kick-ass engagement party for Amber's best friend...well, that dug the hurt a little deeper. She wanted to turn the TV off, but she continued to study the woman on the screen. Amber had never really envied anyone for anything. She always accepted what she had and who she was and embraced it. But faced with the seeming perfection of Madison Shepard, Amber found that she could indeed want what someone else had. Acknowledging that pissed her off, so she punched the off button with a little too much emphasis.

She had plenty to keep her occupied, a hefty to-do list waiting for her on her computer. Tapping the mouse, she brought it to life and attempted to busy herself with work instead of pointless imaginings of Tank. She opened her summer camp folder and started going through the minute-by-minute schedules, looking for possible unintended breaks or hard-to-meet timelines. For fifteen minutes, she pretended to be concentrating before she gave up and closed the file. She reached for her cell phone and pulled up the contact before she could think better of it.

Tilly answered on the first ring. "Hey. You okay?"

That he opened with this might have been a red flag, but since she rarely called him, she didn't even flinch.

"Yes, everything's good. How are you?"

"Fine," he said after a slight pause, telling her he was confused by the phone call without having to say a word. There was dead air before he asked, "What's going on?"

"Uh, Tank Howard showed up here today."

Silence.

"I'm sorry. What?" Tilly finally responded.

"So, you didn't know?"

Another pause. "No."

A sigh escaped her.

"I'm assuming you talked to him?"

"Of course. I mean, Whitey ordered me to get him full access to the facility. So, yes, we talked."

"What?"

"Apparently, he's going to be training here."

Then, Tilly began to chuckle.

"This is so not funny."

"Oh, yes, it is," he managed to say between laughs.

"No, it's really not. What is he doing here?"

Tilly finally controlled his laughter. He took a deep breath. "I have no idea. He didn't say a word to me. Did you ask his partner in crime?"

Amber couldn't help but roll her eyes. Tilly and Tank were best friends, but Tank was also really close to Steele. For whatever reason, Tilly and Steele didn't mix. Both of them acted like little girls who were sharing a best friend. Normally, she loved to tease them about their stupid little rivalry, but she wasn't in a joking mood.

"No. He's at practice."

"Well, I bet he knows what's going on."

"You're ridiculous," she muttered.

"If he didn't talk to me about it, I'm pretty sure he talked to Steele."

"Yeah, probably," she responded. Right now, talking to Steele about Tank was about as appealing as talking to Tank.

"You all right?"

"Yeah, all good."

It was late.

Nicky and Amber sat at a high table in the corner of their favorite sports bar. Steele had neglected to join them. His absence didn't faze Nicky in the least, but Amber was starting to think Steele was deliberately avoiding her. And more and more, she was regretting the kiss they'd shared. Their curiosity wasn't worth the price of their friendship.

"So, wait, why did he say he couldn't make it?" she asked again.

Nicky barely glanced from the wall of TVs to answer her, "He must have partied too hard on his vacation because he's got his head stuck where the sun don't shine." Nicky's little Southern witticisms barely registered anymore. He pulled his attention away from the basketball game they were watching. "So, who you got this year?"

"You seriously think I'm giving you any of my secrets?"

"Your streak is ending." He threw his hands in the air, a victory sign. "This year, I will be the king."

"Such a sore loser." She laughed. "If we could actually bet money on March Madness, I'd be rich."

Nicky snorted. "Two years in a row, and you're too big for your britches."

Amber shook her head, laughing at him.

"Still got room for me?"

Amber and Nicky shifted to look behind them, surprised to see Steele standing there.

"Absolutely. Grab a chair." Nicky nodded in the direction of a table to the right of him where there seemed to be an extra.

Steele went to the table as Nicky and Amber exchanged confused glances.

He returned with the stool in tow and swung it around before sitting. "What are we drinking?"

"Stella," Nicky informed him.

He raised his hand with three fingers aloft and pointed to the half-full beer bottles on the table. Their regular waitress nodded to him from the bar.

Then, leaning forward, he dropped his elbows to the table. "Sorry I'm late."

"Thought you weren't coming," Amber commented without judgment.

"I had something I couldn't get out of."

Three weeks ago, Steele would have told them everything. Nicky must have noted the lack of details, too, because he bumped his knee against Amber's under the table.

"It's cool," Nicky responded. "I haven't even been able to catch up with you today. How cool is it that Tank Howard is going to be here for the next couple of weeks?"

Amber's eyes widened at his proclamation.

Steele looked away before answering, "Pretty awesome."

"How come you didn't tell me, man? Was it on the down-low?"

The waitress placed the beers in front of them. "You done with this?" she asked Amber as she eyed the almost empty bottle.

"Yeah," Steele answered. "She doesn't drink the ass-warm part."

Amber smiled weakly before nodding her head. The girl cleared their empties and turned back toward the crowded room, leaving them.

"So?" Nicky prompted.

"Yeah…" Steele took a long sip of his beer. Then, placing it in front of himself, he looked directly at Amber when he responded with, "I didn't know he was coming."

"What?" Amber demanded, unable to keep the surprise out of her voice.

"Seriously. He left me a message saying he wanted to talk to me when I was on vacation, but I didn't have a chance to get back to him."

Amber wanted to call bullshit, but there was something going on with Steele that he wasn't ready to talk about, and she understood what that felt like. She got his motivation for his silence and could deal with his lack of sharing.

Tank Howard though? She didn't understand him at all. *What was he up to?*

Lauren had taken him to do all the necessary tasks that afternoon. Amber deliberately left her office to take care of some paperwork with Compliance so that she wouldn't be around when he returned. Tank was never one to ask for permission or to explain his actions. She blamed his unilateral approach to life on the constant deference he'd grown up with—the catering of his teachers, coaches, and administrators since he was deemed a five-star athlete. In college, he'd discussed things with Franco before and she knew he was a little bit afraid of his mother, which tended to make her laugh when she thought about it. Maybe, knowing all of that, she shouldn't have been surprised that neither Tilly nor Steele had been consulted or even notified.

The three of them hung out for a while longer before they paid their tab and headed out. They came across Nicky's car first.

"I've got her," Steele assured Nicky as he got into his car.

Amber and Steele maneuvered through the lot.

She clicked the locks but didn't make a move to open the door. Instead, she leaned back on her car and looked up at Steele. "We okay?"

"Yeah," he said on an annoyed sigh.

Her lips tightened in frustration. "What's up with you?" When he looked away from her, her vexation increased. "God! I wish we'd never kissed!"

She pushed off her door and turned away from him. Before she could pull the handle to open the door, his long fingers curled around her arm, and he whipped her around. Her startled gaze met his angry glare. He moved into her, his hand leaving her arm and meeting his other to frame her face. He dropped his head so that his lips were hovering above hers.

"Do you really wish that?" he asked.

Their dark eyes locked on each other, and she tried to garner clues as to what he was feeling. But she couldn't get a handle on what she was feeling. Part of her responded to the look in his eye, his hand on her scar, his full lips a mere centimeter away. She licked her lips, perhaps in invitation. Steele's eyes widened. He pressed his mouth against hers. A fleeting touch was all he gave her. Her belly tightened, but even then, she couldn't discern if it was nerves or desire. When she didn't move, he released her, stepped back, and looked away. He shook his head a little, dispelling something.

"He's here for you," Steele said matter-of-factly.

Amber's brow furrowed. "What are you talking about?"

Their eyes clashed—his flashing with some unknown emotion, hers heavy with confusion.

"Tank. There's one reason for him to be here." He shrugged his shoulders. "He came for you."

ELEVEN

Tank fished his workout gear out of his suitcase and shoved it in his duffel bag along with his shoes, a towel, his travel dopp kit, and slides. He double-checked to make sure he had everything he needed. Then, he zipped it up and dropped it near the front door before heading to the kitchen.

Hawk secured the place, sight unseen. The two-bedroom bungalow fit Tank's needs perfectly. It was situated in a sprawling family neighborhood that was far enough away from campus for Tank to appreciate the quiet. The best part was the lap pool and Jacuzzi the owners had recently installed. Although Hawk had thought Tank was crazy when he shared his plan, he'd done everything to make sure Tank would have what he needed. He'd even rented him a modest Range Rover, so Tank could leave his conspicuous Maserati sitting in his Atlanta garage. Tank would have appreciated its speed and handling on the drive here, but he'd made what he thought was a mature decision to leave his prized possession back home.

Tank grabbed the Bullet from the cabinet and began mixing a healthy smoothie. He was anxious to get to campus this morning, and he didn't want to waste time with making a big breakfast. He smiled as he thought of Amber's reaction to seeing him yesterday. If he could, he'd do it all over again just to enjoy the play of emotions across her face. The surprise, he'd expected. He'd planned exactly what he was going to say to the inevitable question of what he was doing there, and he hadn't been disappointed when she responded. He hadn't even had to prompt the memory. It was waiting for him to tease it, and her unpredicted smile was worth every second of his plotting.

He hadn't gotten to spend any time with her yesterday, but he learned a great deal about her, and his respect for her amplified exponentially.

Coach "Whitey" Whitehurst was one of the most respected coaches in college football. His reputation for being an offensive genius was rivaled only by stories of his hard-ass nature. It wasn't uncommon for people, both inside and outside of his circle, to refer to him as an asshole. Yet, here Amber stood, Whitey's right-hand person.

Tank hadn't even provoked the man yesterday. He never asked a single question about Amber or mentioned her name. Whitey had no idea of the connection between the two. But it didn't stop Whitey from bragging about her or from pointing out her responsibilities as they toured the building. Tank had absolutely no right, but he was proud as hell.

He poured his drink into a to-go cup, supplied by Hawk, and headed out the door.

He popped the trunk on the SUV and shoved his workout gear into the back. As he was about to close it, he remembered he'd put his phone in the front pocket, so he wouldn't forget it. He reached back into the bag to grab it, almost afraid to power it up. He'd turned it off the moment he left Amber to go on his tour with Lauren. He knew what would follow and figured he deserved a twenty-four-hour hiatus on all phone calls. His phone buzzed, an indication of the stored messages and waiting texts.

Sliding into the front seat of the car, he put the key in the ignition and turned it on. Then, with the car idling, he picked up the phone, keyed in his passcode, and perused the missed calls, voice mail notifications, and texts with a combination of amusement and dread.

Surprisingly, there weren't many calls—really only two that he thought might be related to his presence here. He didn't even listen to the messages. He merely hit the callback cue for Tilly. It barely began to ring when Tilly answered.

"What the hell are you doing?" he demanded before he broke into laughter.

Tank smiled, pleased with Tilly's response. "Training."

"Sure you are," Tilly ribbed. "Dude, this is so much bigger than me asking Keira to marry me, and you didn't even have the decency to give me a heads-up."

Chuckling, Tank waited, sure there was more. With the Bluetooth engaged, he put the SUV in reverse and headed out of the neighborhood.

"I had to hear about it from Amber."

Tank slammed the brakes a little too hard at the Stop sign and sputtered, "Amber called you, not Keira?"

"Yep. Wanted to know what you were doing. It was actually pretty awesome to not have an answer for her. The only shitty part was that I didn't have an answer for her best friend."

"Oh, you mean, the woman you're marrying?" Tank laughed. He continued through the intersection and made his way out onto the main road.

"Exactly." Their laughter died down, but Tank could still hear the smile in Tilly's voice when he asked, "Seriously though, what are you doing?"

Tank took a deep breath. "I just need to know, bro."

Tilly sighed. "Now?"

Now?

It was an appropriate question and one Tank had a ready answer for. Not just now. He'd always wanted her. The night she'd discovered him with another girl and run out of his apartment, it'd taken every bit of strength he had to remain sitting on that couch and not run after her. When she'd shoved him out of the hotel room in New York, he'd wanted to rip the door off and carry her out, caveman-style. At the wedding, he'd wanted to keep her wrapped around him while he was buried deep. But her anger provided a visible force field that no amount of firepower could breach because she hadn't forgiven him.

"Always, man."

Tank arrived at the Ayers Brown Field House about ten minutes later. He sat, staring at the building, contemplating his day. It was early, so parking was easy. He saw Amber's car sitting in the same spot as yesterday, the closest one to the front door.

First one in, last one out, he thought.

Glancing around, he noted Steele's car. Tank still hadn't talked to him. If there was one thing that bothered him about showing up here, it was that he hadn't warned Steele. He'd wondered, when he powered up his phone, if there would be a message from his friend. Surely, he and Amber had talked about it. If Tilly had been her first call, Steele would have been her second. But Steele hadn't called him. In fact, he hadn't spoken to his friend since the engagement party. Radio silence.

Shrugging with the uncertainty of his decision Tank turned off the car and went to search for Steele.

The building was impressive. He'd been here seven years earlier on his official visit. But a lot had happened since then, including a couple of national championships and an influx of funds. He took the elevator to the coaches' offices, making sure to stay away from the Operations side of the hallway. He slipped in the front office, heading in the direction he remembered from his tour yesterday.

Steele's door was slightly ajar, and Tank pushed it open, leaning against the jamb. Steele sat back in his office chair situated behind his desk, his feet on the bookcase on the left side. He must be enjoying the view out of the wall of windows.

Tank took his time, looking around Steele's office. The walls were painted in their school colors of red and black. There, on the right wall, the one opposite his desk, was a wall wrap of past players on the field with an image of Steele making a one-handed catch in the end zone. Tank smiled at Steele's incredible talent that was immortalized on the walls of his office.

"Nice picture," Tank commented.

Steele's chair swiveled quickly, bringing him around to face Tank. "Hey, man," he responded, getting up and coming around his desk to greet Tank. "Heard you were here," he said, grasping Tank's hand and pulling him in for the one-armed man hug. "Thanks for the heads-up." He punctuated this with a slap to Tank's head.

"Bro, I tried to call you. Twice. Return your damn calls."

"Sorry, man. Vacation. I was off the grid for two weeks."

"So, that's why you didn't roll out the welcome mat for me?"

Steele grinned. "You know it." He walked back around to sit behind his desk. "So, you're training here?"

"I figured you could be my training partner." Tank sat in the chair in front of the desk, reclined with his legs stretched out and crossed at the ankle.

Steele dropped his elbows on his desk, seeming to consider Tank's request. "Well," he drawled, "you can join us. We already went today though. Five in the morning."

Tank shrugged his shoulders. "Not a problem. Can you catch some balls?"

For a brief moment, a light shone in Steele's dark eyes before it quickly faded. "Yeah, man."

"I've gotta work out, but I wanna throw the ball around."

Tank had his schedule figured out. With the help of some of his team trainers and some input from Franco, he knew what he wanted the off-season to look like. It would be fun to be able to train with Steele. They'd never gotten the opportunity to play together, and it was one of the regrets he harbored in his mind over his choice of schools.

"We can definitely do that." Steele laid-back stance a reflection of Tank's. "How long are you here for?"

"Maybe a month. We'll see how things go."

Steele looked away from him, contemplative. Tank hadn't let himself feel guilt for showing up on Steele's doorstep, virtually unannounced. But, sitting in his friend's office, the slow, slick slide of it settled between his shoulder blades, making itself known. Steele had no idea Tank had seen him kiss Amber. He couldn't know what had been set in motion by Tank's voyeurism. For the briefest of seconds, he'd thought that perhaps he should back off and let Steele have his shot. But it was fleeting. If seeing them kiss could get him to leave Atlanta, he was going to follow through even if it made him a bit of an asshole for not being honest with one of his best friends.

"You're not going to ask why?" Tank ventured, not able to withstand the silence any longer.

"Don't need to. I know exactly why you're here."

Tank's fingers clenched in reflex, gripping the armrests. He was suddenly nervous.

Steele shrugged. "You came for Amber, right?"

Tank chuckled because Steele looked so damn smug that it was funny. "I don't know that I'd put it quite like that. I'd like to spend some time with her. See where it goes."

"And, because you are who you are, you think you can just walk into her world, get all up in her professional life, and it's going to be okay?"

Tank's smile wanted to slip, but he fought to hold it in place. There was a dull ringing in his ears that sounded like a gauntlet had hit Steele's desk. Tank didn't want this to be some sort of competition between them.

So, he said what he should have said before he rearranged his life, "Are you interested in her? Do you want me to back off?" He had no idea what his reaction would be if Steele said yes and yes. He'd find some graceful way to exit, or maybe he'd take out his best friend. Either reaction seemed reasonable and acceptable.

But Steele just shook his head. "It ain't that, man. I just think it was a little over the top of you to show up here."

Tank looked away from Steele and pretended to consider it. Like he hadn't already thought through the pros and cons of showing up here. The thing was, with their schedules, time was a precious commodity. He had it right now, and he had to use it to his advantage. He couldn't be sure if it was just his nature to seize opportunities or if he'd nurtured that quality during his years on the field. He saw an opening, and he ran toward it. This was his opening with Amber. He was sure of it.

"Maybe," he conceded.

He might have said more, but they were interrupted.

"Steele, meeting," Amber said from outside before she turned the corner and stopped abruptly. Her eyes widened briefly before she managed to control the expression on her face. "Hey." She nodded to Tank before looking at Steele. "We gotta go."

Steele glanced at the watch on his wrist. "Coming." He stood hastily and grabbed the iPad from his desk. "Sorry, man. Gotta work."

Tank nodded.

Steele made his way around the desk, and Tank stood to follow them out. Amber led the way with Steele close behind her. Tank's destination was in the opposite direction. He fought to keep from turning his head to snatch one more glance of her. But he couldn't resist.

He looked back over his shoulder, taking in the view. He loved seeing her in her element, wielding power, controlling tempo. He came here, interested in the girl he'd known, the one he couldn't quite get out of his head. But he was completely enthralled with the woman she'd become in his absence.

TWELVE

Amber left the office when the sun was setting, coloring the sky with shades of purple, pink, and orange. Sunsets normally caused her to stop and appreciate. But, today, she hurried to her car, the beauty of the fading day around her hardly a blip on the radar of her racing mind. She yanked the door open and shoved her three bags into the passenger seat. Then, she climbed in and leaned back against the driver seat, releasing a shuddering breath. She shut the door and pressed the ignition button, dropping the fob into the center console already littered with an empty bottle of water, this morning's coffee indulgence, and three gum wrappers she had yet to clean out. Shaking her head, she sighed again, this time at the debris spread over her usually pristine car.

Her life had gotten infinitely more complicated in the last week, and she found herself scattered and jumpy.

She blamed Tank.

Not because they'd had a conversation or because he'd approached her or interfered in her life in any way. He'd been in town for a week and she'd barely seen him.

And that's the problem, she reluctantly admitted to herself. *Damn Steele for his hasty declaration about Tank, and damn Tank for his inaction.* She huffed out a breath powerful enough to blow her bangs away from her face.

When Steele had told her that Tank came for her, she'd met his statement with a morbid sense of anticipation, disbelief, and horror. Because she wasn't quite certain she could handle a direct confrontation with Tank—for so many reasons but mostly self-preservation. She'd prepared herself, even practiced what she would say to him, how she would deny him. In front of her bathroom mirror, she'd turned him down—gently, harshly, and somewhere in between.

With the distance of a week and too much time in between to think, she was no longer certain of what she would say if he decided to talk to her.

How did she go from dreading a conversation with him to hoping they'd at least run into each other?

Word on the street said he was around a lot. Yet she hadn't even seen him since she came upon him in Steele's office, an encounter that hardly counted because they didn't talk to each other. She was an allied army with intelligence pointing to a sneak attack. She strategized for a frontal onslaught, but now, she wondered if she should have prepared to be flanked. No matter the plan, she'd grown so restless and careless that she considered darting out into the open as bait.

Sick of the introspection, she turned on the radio. Needing some upbeat music, she pulled up her workout playlist and hit play. Ready to leave, she shifted into reverse. Glancing up from the rear camera display, she watched from her parking spot as the double doors to Ayers opened.

Tank appeared in the open space between them, his head down as he perused his phone. She observed him from her hidden vantage point, a guiltless voyeur. He wore gray sweats with the Atlanta emblem emblazoned high up on his thigh. His loose-fitting T-shirt billowed around him, except where it hugged his biceps, prominently flashing the taut muscles. His black socks and slides rounded out his post-workout clothes.

She remained poised over her steering wheel, her hand squeezing the gearshift, constricting in rhythm with the slightly faster pacing of her heart. His scent drifted around her, an imagining of her olfactory glands as they wept for a chance to experience his distinctive smell. Unconsciously, her left hand rose and rubbed her nose. She started to wonder how long she could continue to stare at him when his head snapped up, and his eyes found hers.

Ah, there you are.

Their connection was all clichés—electricity, heat, zing—a veritable writer's feast of words to describe their conductivity. Her fight-or-flight response kicked in, and she almost jammed her foot down on the pedal to reverse out of there as quickly as possible. Before she could make a move, her hand slammed the gear into park, and she almost laughed as her internal battle produced such automatic responses in her body while her head and heart duked it out.

A reluctant grin formed, and Tank must have seen it because his mouth responded in answer. He pocketed his phone and made his way over to her. In an effort to create some distance, she rolled down the passenger window, forcing a door, a seat, and a console in between them. He ducked down, dropped his elbows on the ledge, and then leaned forward. An infinitesimal part of her pictured the window rolling up, closing down the opportunity, but then he spoke, and her mind started conjuring all sorts of other endings.

"Hey, Sunshine."

Normally, his nickname grated and chafed against the nerve endings of her pride, but the murmur of it soothed everything out, and she smiled softly.

"Hey there, Superstar."

He grinned. Then, he dropped his head and shook it. "Always got a comeback." He chuckled.

She smiled cheekily, enjoying him. His green eyes twinkled in amusement, and she found she liked the expression on his face and her responsibility in getting him to light up like that.

"You just leaving now?"

She nodded.

"Did you get here at five again?"

She arched her brow in question. Then, she shrugged. "Yeah. Stalk much?" Even as the sarcastic retort left her mouth, warmth seeped through her at the thought of him knowing her schedule.

He merely smiled in acceptance, like he would have been disappointed with any other response. "I see your car when I get here in the morning." He didn't seem to expect a response, so she didn't offer anything up. "Have you eaten? Because I've been following my nutritionist's meal schedule for me to a tee, and my body wants to cheat."

Amber snorted. "Like that's a shocker."

He closed his eyes in dismay, realizing what he'd said, and regret settled into the lines of his shoulders. "Real smooth," he muttered before looking up at her again. "Shit," he sighed.

Amber rolled her eyes, feeling sorry for him for some stupid reason.

"I thought this place was famous for barbeque. Any chance I can get you to go to dinner with me?"

His gaze didn't waver as he looked over at her. The earlier amusement had faded, dulling the pretty green depths. She'd still never seen such beautiful eyes on anyone else. His black lashes stuck out long and straight, framing the translucence. Watching him, she fell right into them, caught in their focus. If he'd vacillated she could probably figure out a way to say no. But his draw was too much, and she found herself nodding.

"Get in. I'll drive."

She saw the surprise but pretended not to, glancing down to grab each of her bags and transferring them to the backseat. Tank opened the back door and placed his duffel bag down before getting in.

"Nice ride," he commented.

She nodded as she put the car into reverse and backed out of the parking lot. "Yeah, it was all Franco. He insisted, and I resisted for a while, but then I figured, why not?" She dished out a smug smile before she whipped the car out of the parking lot and flew down the road. Maybe she wanted to impress him a bit with her mad driving skills, but mostly, she needed some control between them, and if she could only capture it as she drove, it would have to be enough.

"This place suits you."

"You got that from being here for one week?"

He nodded and shrugged. "Yeah, I did."

She wondered if he would elaborate, but when he seemed content to let the silence hang between them, she cranked her playlist and drove. His confidence in her place filled her in some way. It was the dangerous thing about Tank Howard.

Even three years ago, when they'd briefly been together, he'd shored her up, given her strength, and made her want things she hadn't known she'd want again. She remembered how long it had been since she really laughed, how old and decrepit hers had sounded. By the time they were over, she took it back. All those pesky little pieces of herself she'd tried to get rid of after the accident, she Humpty-Dumptied them so that she was whole. There was some saying about being able to take something away, causing the smallest ripple—like an Olympic diver making the tiniest splash. Walking away from him was like that. He'd given her so much of herself back that when he crashed in such a spectacular fashion, she was able to move on and grow.

It didn't take them long to get to Piggy's, a complete dive of a building with the best barbeque she'd ever tasted. Tank didn't even bat an eyelash when she pulled into the sandy parking lot and turned off the car.

"I swear, the food is amazing," she qualified as she made her way out of the car.

He followed her through the heavy wooden door into the dimly lit bar. There were flashing neon beer signs and picnic tables for dining. Decorating the walls were pictures of past football greats. No one in this town even pretended to care about other sports, so all the pigskin paraphernalia was appropriate.

Amber took a table in the back corner. The waitress was quick to come and take their orders before heading off to stand at the bar, casting longing looks in Tank's direction.

"That happen a lot?" Amber couldn't help but ask.

"What?"

She scoffed. "The fangirl stuff."

He chuckled. "I guess. I don't really pay attention. The places I hang out at home, the people know me, so they don't make a big deal out of it. Every once in a while, if some of us go out together, we can attract a crowd, but for the most part, I hardly even notice."

"How's training?"

He placed his elbows on the table and clasped his hands, leaning forward, eating up some of the space between them. He smiled wide. "It's good. I like being in a different place. The change of scenery was a good idea." He paused as the waitress dropped their beers on the table. Then, he returned his gaze to her. "I feel more focused, ya know? And it's been great, having Steele to throw to."

Amber choked on the sip of beer she had just taken. "Steele's catching balls for you?" she asked, not even trying to disguise her surprise. "How's he doing? Is his leg holding up?"

Tank's brow furrowed. "He didn't tell you?"

She shook her head.

There was confusion on his face, but he shook it off. "He's doing awesome. I've had a blast, having his hands waiting for me down the field."

"Still your one regret?" The question flew out of her mouth, the filter gone. Another Tank Effect.

He looked away and shook his head before returning his gaze to her. "No. I have a much bigger regret." He let the statement sit between them, his eyes boring into hers. As quickly as the seriousness had descended though, he flashed a smile and said, "But, yes, I regret never having the chance to play with Steele."

Their food arrived, and they moved on to small conversations, nothing more personal than their current favorite players and their preseason predictions. As they finished up, they got into a heated battle about who would win each of the divisions and who would make it to the Super Bowl.

Tank grabbed a napkin. "You got a pen in your purse?" he asked.

She narrowed her eyes at him. "Yeah. Why?"

"You're talking a lot of smack right now about my team. I'm calling your bluff."

She smiled and then shrugged before digging a pen out of her purse.

"Go ahead," he said, "and write your division champs and Super Bowl winner on one side. I'll write mine on the other. And we'll see who wins."

"What does the winner get?" She could feel him drawing her in like a Venus flytrap, and she didn't even care. She enjoyed him, his company, his wit, his intelligence.

His eyes twinkled. "Winner's choice."

Amber grabbed the pen and wrote down her selections. Then, she passed it to him, facedown. "No looking," she declared.

Laughing, he slid the napkin toward him, the side with the writing down. Picking up the pen, he scribbled his picks. Then, he looked up. "Do we get to compare now?"

"Absolutely not. After the Super Bowl."

He smirked. "I'll probably be at Disney World."

She laughed loudly. "Such a cocky bastard."

He winked at her, and she laughed harder.

"Okay, so who gets to keep it?"

"I do." She pulled it back from him and grabbed her wallet. Folding it up, she slid it into one of the compartments. Picking up her phone, she pulled up her calendar and looked to the next year. When she scrolled through, she clicked on Monday, February 6, and typed in, *Super Bowl Predictions Unveiled*. Then, she pulled up Invitees and glanced up at him. "What's your email?"

As she waited for him to respond, she briefly considered the easy camaraderie between them. He should come with a damn warning—*highly likable, unbelievably beautiful, shockingly down-to-earth*. She found herself wondering how three years as one of the NFL's most recognizable players hadn't changed him much, hadn't changed their dynamic much.

They continued to stare at each other until he recited his email. She clicked Send. His phone dinged, and he slid it out of his pocket. He glanced down at the alert and snickered.

Looking up at her, he said, "It's a date."

THIRTEEN

Tank knew exactly what he was doing when he entered the training table—the dining hall reserved for the players—and handed his debit card to the gatekeeper. There'd been no training table at Kensington State, so this was a new experience he enjoyed. He imagined, if he had to formulate a list of things he would have liked as a college student-athlete, access to good food would have been one of them. He looked around and deliberately picked a table somewhat out of the way. He tried hard not to draw attention to himself. This was an experiment in switching tactics. He'd done the avoidance thing with Amber, and he could appreciate its effectiveness. But, after their night at the barbeque joint, he wasn't okay with staying away from her.

There was a moment, a split second really, when the men on the field part, much like the Red Sea, with an opening only wide enough for a sure-footed athlete to tiptoe through before dodging the tackles on his way to a touchdown. Tank considered his dinner with Amber one of those moments because, much like those first tentative steps in the direction of a hole, once he'd made the move, she opened up in front of him.

Their impromptu dinner a couple of nights ago had strengthened Tank's resolve. He hadn't meant to waver, but once he settled into her place a couple of weeks ago and spent time with Steele, he questioned his decision to barge into her world. *Among other things, how would they make a relationship work with their jobs?* He couldn't be away from Atlanta long, and she wouldn't be able to leave either. The logistics seemed impossible. They didn't own their weekends. Tank had pictured her with him in Atlanta. But, now, he knew she belonged here. She was amazing at her job, and when he'd told her she fit here, he'd meant it. So, why bother to go down a road neither of them would be able to follow? He'd almost conceded. Then, he'd stepped outside one evening, and she'd been there, studying him.

He'd enjoyed glimpses of her since, and it wasn't enough. If anything, their dinner had made it all that more important. They were so beyond the physical connection she'd always been okay with exploring. On some fundamental, basic level, he needed her— not just in his bed, but also in his life.

He walked leisurely through the cafeteria, checking his choices. He hadn't been exaggerating when he told Amber he stuck to his nutritionist's plans. Here, it was easy to meet her exact standards. Every dish had the nutritional content broken down.

He couldn't resist slipping his phone out of his pocket and snapping a quick picture to send to his dietician, especially after his cheat session the other night. While he had it out, he glanced at the time, knowing Amber would be there soon. So, maybe he had been stalking her a little—just enough to know what time she arrived in the morning, what days she worked out, when she ate lunch, and when she left. He'd come by the information rather haphazardly because, much to his disbelief, she was a creature of habit.

He grabbed what he wanted and then made his way to his table. He just sat when she walked in, and she instantly zeroed in on him. The only indication of her reaction was an almost imperceptible widening of her eyes that most people would have missed. She nodded to him before taking a tray and getting food. It was like she knew exactly what was on the menu because she didn't stop to read the placards, nor did she look around. Like everything, she had a purpose. He noticed a slight tightening of her hands on her tray when she went to get a drink, and he smiled, knowing she was figuring out what to do. He hoped she wanted to see him as badly as he wanted to see her.

Amber pushed her cup against the drink lever, and he could discern the internal battle as she gnawed on the corner of her lip, a spot he liked to think of as his. Placing her glass down on the tray, she turned abruptly and made her way to him. He didn't even try to look away. What would be the point of that? He was beyond trying to pretend with her.

"Hey," she said as she took the seat across from him. "How are you?"

Tank leaned back in his chair, basking in his view. Her dark hair fell straight, past her shoulders, and she let it hang, covering her scars. He had to stop himself from reaching across the expanse of the table to cup her jaw.

"Hey. All's good."

She messed with her tray, taking all the plates off before moving it to the side. When she was done, she looked over at him. "How's the food?"

He looked down at his untouched lunch and then chuckled. "I'll let you know."

Her gaze followed, and she colored slightly. Then, she shrugged. "But you've eaten here before, right?"

"I have, and it is good. I like that I don't have to think about what I'll be putting in my body. I'm a big fan."

"Ah, still feeling guilty about cheating the other night?"

She winked at him, lessening the blow, and he grinned.

"Worthy cause." He pulled his gaze away from her, forcing himself to concentrate on the food in front of him.

They ate in silence, both watching the TVs strategically placed around the room. He wasn't uncomfortable, but he couldn't come up with a suitable topic of conversation.

"So, you're our mystery speaker tonight, huh?" she asked.

He'd wondered when the topic would come up. "I am." He didn't elaborate.

Smiling, she said, "That's all I get?"

"What more do you want?" he quipped. *Whatever you want, you can have.*

She picked up her drink and took a long sip on her straw. Tank's stomach bottomed out as he watched her wrap her lips around it, release it, and then lick her lips with a swipe of her tongue. His gaze dropped, and stupid followed. If he had to speak in that moment, he was sure only gibberish would come out of his mouth.

"Okay, mystery man, what's the big deal?"

His eyes snapped back to hers, and he shook his head, trying to dislodge the fantasy of her mouth on his. "No mystery." He looked down at the remaining food on his tray and then pushed it away, no longer hungry. "You've seen the documentary *Broke*?"

"Unfortunately."

He nodded. "Yeah, it's pretty depressing."

"Ridiculous."

He lifted his brow, surprised at the vehemence of the word as it left her mouth. "Money management—that's the topic."

She paused to consider him, and he could tell by the derisive look on her face that she had an opinion on the subject.

"Don't take this the wrong way, but what do you know about money management? Actually, let me rephrase. What do you have to know about money management? Don't you have someone who does that for you?"

He fought the smile that threatened. He had known she wouldn't make this easy, and she didn't disappoint. He didn't mind talking about this, and her attitude was unsurprising. There was no way in hell he'd be telling her the topic of his next speaking engagement.

"Yes, I pay someone to manage my money. And I have Tilly always whispering in my ear about making sure I stay on top of it, telling me I need to be as fluent about my portfolio as I am about the plays we run."

"He's such a know-it-all," she teased.

He snickered. "Yes, he is."

"Okay, so you know how much money you have. What can you possibly tell these kids?"

Her skepticism amused him.

"It started in college."

"What do you mean?"

"I always had a plan for my scholarship checks. I mean, I paid my rent and bought food. But I also paid myself a little from every check." He leaned forward, placing his elbows on the table. "I can't even remember who told me to do that, but I stashed a little bit of every check—for emergencies or stuff. I was always on Iman to do the same, but he had his little obsession with tats and shoes."

She laughed. "Little?"

"Exactly. Look, no kid comes to college, knowing what to do with their money. For a lot of them, it's the first time they've ever had any money, let alone their own money. You throw the Pell Grant in there and then this miscellaneous expense stuff? That's a lot of money to be responsible for."

"How do you know about the miscellaneous expense?"

He hated the answer he had to give her. "Hawk keeps me informed."

She rolled her eyes. "Of course he does."

"I only know the basics, that kids get it on top of their scholarship check to cover other expenses like travel." He waved his hand, trying to encompass all the little things. "I'm not an expert. I don't want to be. But, if one kid will listen and try to be responsible for the money coming into and out of his hands, then that's good enough for me. I just want them to be aware. Because, once they leave here, it's not Monopoly money anymore."

"Monopoly money?"

"It just seems like it when you're in college. You're not thinking about what's next, right? Tuition is paid automatically. We used to get money for our room and board. Even if you blew money on something you shouldn't have, you wouldn't starve because you were going to get food. Monopoly money. No one is tracking it; no one is asking you what you are doing with it."

"That's an interesting perspective."

"It is what it is."

"What was the biggest surprise for you when you got out?"

"With money?"

"Yeah."

Tank didn't have a ready answer. He should have, but it took him a moment to come up with one. "Taxes."

"Like you actually do your own taxes."

He laughed. "Absolutely not. But we have to pay taxes in every state we play in. Say I work for four hours a year in Green Bay; then, I have to pay Wisconsin taxes. There's not even a chance I could do my own taxes."

He expected a laugh or a smile out of her, but her attention was diverted to the TV behind him. He glanced up, seeing a mirror view of what she saw, and he felt the ease between them evaporate.

Madison's image dominated the screen. She was standing outside of a stadium, reporting on her take on the upcoming draft. They both continued to watch. Whatever she was saying swallowed up the din of the conversations going on around them. His gaze dipped from the TV back to Amber, and he watched her watch Madison. He'd have given anything to know what she was thinking. Her jaw tightened so subtly, he would have missed it if he hadn't been studying her so intently.

"It's over," he murmured. It slipped out, a confession not required and said so softly that he questioned whether it'd actually come out of his mouth.

When her eyes dropped back to his, he knew he had. Her lips parted, like she was going to say something. Then, she shook her head and returned her gaze to the TV. When Madison flipped it back to the studio, Amber began to bus her spot, placing her plate and utensils back on the tray with deliberation. He didn't want to have this conversation here—really, he didn't want to have it at all—but he had to say something.

She was about to stand when he reached out and placed his hand on top of hers.

She glanced up at him with some unnamed emotion swimming in her eyes. He thought she was going to pull her hand away, but she stilled instead and waited for him, granting permission for him to speak.

Suddenly nervous and mentally kicking himself for his lack of preparedness, he blurted the first thing that came to his mind, "It's done. I wouldn't have come here if Madison and I were still together."

He silently pleaded with her to understand. She nodded, a movement so slight that he wondered if he'd imagined it.

"This is going to sound bad, but you have to trust me on this." He knew he was taking a chance, using that word, but he didn't know any word comparable. "Madison and I, we've always been more friends than anything else."

She scoffed, pulling her hand from his.

He snapped his hand back from the table and held both of them up in surrender. "Friends with benefits, absolutely. But that's all it's ever been. For both of us."

"You don't owe me any explanations, Tank," she said as she stood. "I gotta get back to work." She picked up her tray, dished out a strained smile, and headed toward the conveyer belt where the dirty dishes belonged.

He tracked her the whole way as she smiled at some of the players and nodded to some of the staff. He watched her as she placed her tray down and spoke briefly to the guys in the kitchen. Even as she walked out the door, his hungry gaze stayed trained on her.

Fuck. Today wasn't supposed to end like this.

SUPERSTAR

In the battle for her heart, the score was even.
Tank—1, Amber—1.

FOURTEEN

Amber grabbed the steaks from the fridge and arranged them on a platter to haul out to the grill. She'd marinated them this morning, knowing the guys would be over for the Sweet Sixteen games. Their printed-out brackets dangled from the magnet on her refrigerator with hers on top. She was up on both Steele and Nicky and feeling pretty confident that her winning streak would remain unbroken.

The noise from the TV and the preparation for dinner kept her hands and mind occupied. She pulled out vegetables and cheese and went about fixing up a plate. Amber enjoyed entertaining and cooking. Inherited from her Italian grandmother, she loved when her house was full of people, and she was feeding them.

Three years ago, she'd craved only solitude. Now, solitude was her worst enemy because time alone to think meant unwanted thoughts about Tank Howard.

Like the fiasco of lunch. When she'd scurried from the dining hall earlier in the day, she'd gone directly to her office where she quickly barricaded herself behind her closed door. As she leaned against it, she struggled to catch her breath. There'd been a moment when she forgot about the sordid past she shared with Tank. She looked at him and saw only possibility. Then, Madison Shepard's beautiful face filled the screen behind Tank. It was like an artist's odd rendering of everything she wished for overshadowed by a harsh reality. He sat in front of her in all his casual beauty, but the specter of Madison was larger than life.

Amber sighed and continued chopping broccoli and carrots, the sharp blade of the knife against the raw vegetables therapeutic. When the front door opened, she continued her work.

"Honey, I'm home," Nicky joked. "And I brought company."

Amber didn't even lift her head. She kept chopping and waited for Nicky's entrance.

"Just fire up the grill," Amber said. When his greeting registered, she quickly looked up, suddenly nervous about whom Nicky brought to her house.

"Y'all know each other, right?" Nicky said as he turned the corner and headed to the fridge, depositing a six-pack of beer before picking up the steaks from the counter. "Oh, good. You made extra. I thought I'd have to share mine. And you know I don't like to share my meat." He laughed at his stupid comment.

But Amber was too busy studying Tank to do much more than roll her eyes.

"I hope you don't mind me crashing the party," Tank said.

The knife was paused midair as Amber gathered herself. The consummate hostess, she never turned away anyone—from Nicky's obnoxious cousins to occasional women he'd show up with. So, she plastered a smile on her face when Tank stopped to look at her, waiting for her approval.

"No, no problem at all."

Nicky smiled wide. "I figured you'd love to pick his brain. You appreciate good football more than anyone I know. So, for bringin' a soon-to-be legend to your house, I'm thinkin' I get the biggest, primest steak tonight."

Amber found herself on the verge of laughter as Nicky flashed a proud grin in her direction. She looked at Tank, who seemed to be enjoying himself—whether at her expense or Nicky's, she couldn't be sure.

"Steele's not here yet?" Nicky turned and moved toward the sliding door off the kitchen without waiting for the obvious answer. "I'll get the grill started. Almost game time." With a lazy pull on the door, he scooted sideways through the opening and disappeared onto the deck.

Tank fidgeted and ran his hand over his head, the familiar gesture causing Amber to stare fixedly at him. His eyes darted all around. She knew the look on his face. It was a mirror of her own from her venture into his house four weeks ago. Curiosity. Interest.

He wanted to study everything about her house. He didn't have to say it because she recognized the look in his eyes.

His gaze settled on her. They stood, transfixed.

He moved toward her, and her hand clenched in anticipation on the knife. She felt the edge of the wooden handle, the raised rivet biting into her finger. He slowly kept coming. When he was inches from her, on the side of her body, he raised his hand, and his finger swept up the side of her neck, tracing along her scar. He dropped his hand and took a slight step away. She struggled to keep her reaction masked, but every particle in her body heaved a silent, breathy sigh.

"I'll go if you want me to," he said low. "I drove myself, so I can leave if you say the word." He drew a shuddering breath that reverberated within her. "But please let me stay."

It would be so much easier for her if she forced him to go. She knew he'd make it easy on her, providing an excuse to Nicky, exonerating her.

An image of Madison flashed in front of her, the carrots and broccoli disappearing in favor of Tank's beautiful friend with benefits. She forced herself to make a final cut, the snap of the crisp vegetable like a shot in the room.

The front door opened, and Tank took another step away from her. The space between them was greater, but the heat of his body near her warmed her right side. Steele stepped into the kitchen before Amber could grant or deny Tank's request. He faltered at the threshold, like he'd hit some invisible force field.

Amber made herself look directly at Steele before she abandoned her chore and stepped to the fridge. "Need a beer?" she asked the room at large.

"Hey," Steele said. "Yeah, to the beer."

Amber handed one to Steele, but Tank declined with a shake of his head when she moved to give him one. She kept it for herself, knowing she was going to need it.

Steele popped the cap, pulled open the hidden garbage can, and dropped it in before he turned to Tank. "What are you doing here?"

Amber noted the antagonism in Steele's voice, and she looked at Tank, confused.

"Nicky invited me," Tank said confidently, no trace of the pleading man from moments before.

"Figures," Steele returned with a roll of his eyes. Then, he turned to Amber. "You okay with him being here?"

His attitude pissed her off. She didn't appreciate Steele being rude to a guest in her house. She narrowed her eyes, aware they saw her bristling at the question.

"Yep," she said shortly. She picked up the appetizers she'd been working on and shoved them at Steele. "Why don't you both go keep Nicky company while I finish up in here?"

Dismissed, they turned toward the deck door and trudged out, their normally easy camaraderie noticeably absent. With them gone, she finished with dinner, mulling over Tank's presence and Steele's attitude.

After the less than ideal beginning, Amber expected the tension-filled evening to drag out. But, once they ate and parked themselves in front of her TV, they settled into the familiar atmosphere of trash-talking and critiquing.

"How can they call that blocking? His feet were planted. It's clearly an offensive foul," Amber lamented when her team's foul count put the other team in the bonus.

"He was still moving. His right foot wasn't set. You'll see on the replay," Tank explained.

"Whatever. Offensive foul," she repeated.

Tank chuckled, and she couldn't resist looking his way.

Amber thought she was familiar with Tank's arsenal of expressions, but when he glanced over at her while they waited for the replay, some previously unknown sentiment was there. She couldn't name what she saw, but the rawness of the unguarded moment—something like longing and tenderness—took her by surprise. It was a look she feared because a vulnerable Tank was one she didn't think she could resist.

He noticed her looking at him and glanced back toward the TV. The moment was gone when the slow-motion foul flashed on the screen, and then their eyes met again. This time, he smirked at her—enjoying being right about his assessment, she guessed.

Shrugging like she didn't care that he was right, she stood. "Anyone want another beer?"

Nicky and Steele nodded in answer, unaware of the moment between her and Tank.

She needed a reprieve from him. Walking into the kitchen and placing her hands on the counter, she inhaled a Tank-free breath. She cleaned up the remnants of her cooking. Normally she insisted on the boys' help, but the mindless tasks of loading the dishwasher and wiping the counters helped to clear her head.

The dynamics in the next room were troubling. Aside from the situation with Tank, she worried about Steele. His antagonism with Tank earlier had been odd. But, now, it almost seemed as if she'd imagined it because he and Tank had been fine once they started eating dinner. She'd never hung out with the both of them, so she wasn't sure of the interaction between them. Tank hadn't even seemed bothered by Steele's posturing when he first arrived, so maybe he was used to it. She couldn't be sure, and she had no desire to broach the subject with either one of them. She finished up and grabbed the promised beers. Taking a deep breath, she made her way back into the fray.

"Dude, you're tappin' that?" Nicky asked as he glanced at the TV and smacked Tank on the arm.

Amber stood, motionless, waiting for Tank's answer.

"Nah, man," Tank answered.

He was in the exact spot as when Amber had walked out earlier. His big body took up a section of the couch with his legs spread and his elbows resting on his knees. He looked relaxed, but Amber could see the tightening of his jaw.

"Whatever," Steele scoffed.

Amber took a step back, not wanting to interrupt their conversation.

Tank turned his head toward Steele. Even from her vantage point, Amber could tell that Tank was pissed.

"Lamarcus, you might want to keep your mouth shut since you have no idea what you're talking about."

"Who says I don't know what I'm talking about?" Steele stared at Tank with some thinly veiled anger in his eyes.

Then, he glanced up as if he detected Amber standing there. Tank turned his head, following the direction of Steele's gaze. Both men studied her. She shrugged, hopefully showcasing her indifference to the whole conversation. Nicky looked up, too, and held out his hand for the beer.

"How'd you even meet Madison?" Nicky asked Tank, oblivious to all the tension in the room.

Steele scoffed. "I introduced them."

His answer stunned Amber. "You did?" Her question sounded loud in the room. Glancing back and forth between Tank and Steele, she waited for one of them to answer her.

"He did," Tank confirmed.

There was no inflection to his answer, and Amber had no idea what to make of it.

"Damn, Steele, you never told me you knew her."

"Barely," Tank said. "She came here to interview Steele after his injury."

Amber swiveled back and forth with the tennis volley of information being cast between them.

"Really?" she asked, incredulous.

Steele nodded. "Tank brought his doctor to check on me, and Madison was here for an interview about the kid whose career blew up so spectacularly on national television in front of millions of viewers. Real human-interest story," he finished sarcastically.

"Complete vulture," Tank agreed.

Then, they both laughed, the tension seeming to drain away.

"So, you've been dating her for that long?" Nicky continued.

Amber wanted to hit him with the bottle in her hand. She couldn't believe his cluelessness.

Tank shook his head. "We never really dated."

"But everyone thinks that," Nicky kept on. "So, wait, you don't date. But you mess around, right? Please tell me you mess around."

Amber watched in fascination as Tank squirmed in his seat. He cleared his throat and rubbed his hand over his head. She almost laughed at his discomfort. She looked to Steele to share in Tank's embarrassment, but Steele's face was a hardened mask of pure annoyance.

Tank stared Amber in the eye when he responded, "We did. For a while. But we don't anymore."

A big smile spread over Nicky's face. "Dude, I wish I could claim that."

Tank shook his head and then diverted his attention back to the game.

"I'm gonna head out," Steele said, standing.

"Yeah, I should probably go, too. Do you need any help with cleaning up?" Tank asked before he stood.

"Uh, no. I've got it."

Nicky looked around the room, seemingly confused by the turn of events. "All right, guess that's my cue."

Amber almost laughed at him. He'd gotten the cue to leave but obviously missed the one about the very uncomfortable topic of Madison Shepard.

They moved out in single-file order with Amber following, eager for some solitude to think about all the craziness she'd heard in the last few minutes. She said good-bye to them and closed the door. Leaning against it, she shut her eyes and played back all she'd learned in the last half hour.

Steele had been responsible for Tank and Madison knowing each other. Tank and Madison were over, but Steele hadn't necessarily bought Tank's declaration. And Steele had seemed awfully pissed about all the Tank and Madison talk. That made her wonder why Steele had tried to kiss her all of a sudden.

Did he really want her, or was he just trying to thwart Tank? Or was Steele trying to forget that he had a thing for Madison Shepard?

Because what Amber had seen on Steele's face looked a lot like jealousy.

FIFTEEN

APRIL

Amber wanted to stay away from the presentation but found she couldn't. She hadn't been invited or informed about the content of Tank's talk, and she found she couldn't control her interest in it or his ability to speak. She wanted to know what he was going to say and how the players were going to react.

The auditorium had a control room, much like you'd expect for a theater production, with windows looking out and more knobs and buttons than a recording studio. Amber quietly entered the room and was surprised to see Steele sitting in one of the rolling chairs, completely focused on the podium at the front of the room. She suspected he was curious, too. She sat without a word.

Tank stood in the center of the presentation area. Dressed in slacks and a button-down shirt, he exuded confidence. She'd missed the beginning, but he held their attention captive. From her vantage point, she could see that each player's eyes were glued to the front of the room. There was no playing with phones or lolling heads.

Point for Tank.

"I'm going to solely focus on men's violence against women, but don't think for one minute that it doesn't go both ways or that there aren't other forms of sexual assault that aren't just as important. But in here"—he waved his hand between himself and the players sitting around him—"it's about us football players and who we are when we step off the field." He paused and made eye contact with a number of the men in front of him.

"We play a violent sport. You're here because you hit hard"—he looked into the eyes of one of their defensive backs—"or you can take a hit"—eye contact with their quarterback—"or because, when you step onto the field, you become a beast. How many of you have ever watched *Looney Tunes*?" He acknowledged some of the hands around the room. He clicked the button on the remote in his hand, and the screen behind him illuminated. "Ralph E. Wolf and Sam Sheepdog. Take a look."

A clip of the cartoon played, and she immediately related to the characters clocking in for work and spending the day trying to outwit and best each other. She smiled. *Clever.*

A couple of laughs sounded from around the room.

When it ended, Tank began again, "I want you to remember this clip. We'll come back to it." He paused and moved closer to them. "How many of you have heard the phrase, *No means no*?"

Almost every hand in the place went up.

"How many of you believe it?"

Again, hands went up.

"Awesome. I'm going to run through some scenarios with you, and I want you to tell me if, in these instances, no means no." He walked closer to them, his face completely serious. "It's just us here. No coaches, no administrators. No judgment. This only works if you're honest with yourself."

Then, he walked them through easy scenarios, which they responded to. There were some arguments, some honest answers, and some not-so-honest answers. Amber watched from above, feeling slightly guilty for spying, but she couldn't make herself leave. It was too important. What he was talking about, the lessons he was imparting—she didn't want to miss it.

"All right, this one's hard. You're with a girl, both of you naked, in bed. Condom is on. You are seconds away from penetration. She says no."

"That's bullshit, man."

Tank smiled and shrugged in acknowledgment. "Okay. But what do you do?"

"If the fish is in the fryer, you can't take it out."

Tank nodded. "I get you. But she said no."

"How are you supposed to stop when you are that close? Some things ain't possible."

"That ever happened to you?"

Tank nodded. "Yes, it has."

"What'd you do?"

"I stopped."

"Bet your hand got a workout."

Tank smiled ruefully. "Maybe."

"Seriously, you stopped? What happened?"

"I told her she had to leave." His response got some chuckles.

"For real?"

Tank rubbed his hand over his head, and then his face got serious. "I was already in. So, when she said no, I thought I was hearing things. Like maybe my roommate had the TV on some crime show, and that measly *no* had come in through the thin walls. I remember my eyes opening real wide. I looked down at her.

"She was crying. 'No. I said, no.'

"So, I stopped, pulled out, and rolled over on the bed. I thought, *Shit, I hope she said that after I was in and not before.* I wasn't sure, so I asked her. She got hysterical and told me she was sorry but that she shouldn't be there with me. I'm not going to lie. I was kind of an asshole to her, but she left.

"And I was scared for a couple of days. I didn't know if she was going to go to the police or the university or a boyfriend or her parents. I consoled myself with knowing I'd responded the moment I heard her, but I gotta tell you, I was nervous that it was going to blow up in my face. Thankfully, I never saw her again."

His last statement garnered some snickers. But no one spoke.

Tank looked up to the ceiling, like he needed strength or something. Then, he looked back to his audience. "If you're ever tempted to hurt a woman, pretend it's someone you love. Your mother, sister, grandmother, aunt, former teacher. If you hate your mother because she walked out on you, think about any woman in your life who has treated you well. Think about how you would feel if a man used his strength against a woman you cared about."

The room remained quiet.

Tank seemed to be gearing up for something big, and as Amber watched him, she silently offered him her fortitude.

"About a year after that incident, I was dating a girl. She'd had a boyfriend for a while, long before we met. Things started to go bad. She knew she had to get out, but he was a football player, and everyone on campus thought he was a good guy. But he was toying with her, making her doubt herself, alienating her from her friends and family. She'd had enough. One night, he wanted to have sex with her, and she told him no. She fought him, but let's face it, a hundred-twenty-pound woman is no match for anyone in this room. So, he took what he wanted because he figured it was his right. They were a couple; they'd had sex lots of times. But, this time, she didn't want it. Is that rape?"

A pin could have dropped in the room, and everyone would have heard it.

A flush of shame crept up Amber's body, and her sense of exposure amplified.

Why was he bringing that up? Why was he talking about her experience?

She held herself rigid. She was afraid, if she moved, then Steele would know how much this was affecting her, and she didn't want him to know about her past. She'd only ever told Tank about what had happened that night. A shiver ran up her spine, and her hands quaked, tremors making them unsteady. She sensed Steele turn and look at her, but she didn't have the guts to return his stare. She remained facing forward, hoping he wouldn't make a connection.

"It is rape. And, when she told me her story, two things happened to me. I was overwhelmed by the trust she had in me. For a woman to live through that and then relive it, sharing it with someone, takes a crazy amount of courage. More courage than it takes for us to walk onto a field, knowing we are going to get hit by big men."

There were some chuckles, and Tank smiled, flashing his dimples.

"According to the Rape, Abuse & Incest National Network, two of three sexual assaults are never reported. Think about that for a moment. And then think about someone you know surviving that and feeling safe enough to talk about it." He let that statement hover in the room.

"The other thing that happened when she told me was that I was so thankful I'd stopped when I heard that whispered *no*. I don't ever want anyone to feel powerless and violated." Tank turned and moved back a little, giving them some space from his formidable presence.

He paused, and Amber took comfort in the silence of the room. His deliberate break allowed her to collect herself, her thoughts, her memories, her fears.

"All right, why did I show you that cartoon?"

She'd forgotten about it. Apparently, everyone in the room had forgotten about it. The student-athletes looked around at each other.

"Crickets," he joked. "Need to watch it again?"

"Yeah."

Tank cued it up and replayed it.

When it ended, he stood in front of them and said one word, "Why?"

"What happens at the office stays at the office," someone yelled out.

Tank chuckled. "Close enough."

Jamal stood, and Amber felt her heart squeeze. She didn't play favorites, but if she did, he would reap the benefits.

"When we play football, we have to be aggressive. But we should leave it on the field. When we walk off the field or clock out, we need to leave the aggression and power behind us."

Tank nodded his approval. "Being a man is hard. Being a good man is harder. I'm asking you to be great men. To take the opportunity afforded to you because of your ability and to use it in a positive manner. People are watching, children are watching, your mama is watching. Make them proud."

It didn't call for applause, but how else could they respond to such a powerful presentation? So they clapped. They'd been moved, and she could feel it, even in the protected box far away from the action.

When the assembly broke up, it did so slowly. The student-athletes trickled out with some staying behind to talk to Tank. Amber and Steele remained above, still caught in the trap of his words.

Suddenly, in the dark, Steele grabbed her hand and squeezed. "I'm sorry," he said.

She shrugged, unwilling to speak, afraid of the fragile hold she had on her emotions. What she was feeling wasn't fair, and she knew it. The tentacles of betrayal snaked out from her heart, crushing the life out of the fragile trust building between her and Tank.

"I never knew what made him want to do these speeches. I should have guessed."

Amber's head whipped around in his direction. "Speeches?" she croaked, her voice rough with feeling.

Steele tightened his grasp on her hand again, probably all too aware of the state of her feelings. "Yeah. He does a couple of them a year at different schools."

"What?" She didn't try to hide the surprise in her response.

Relief and confusion coursed through her, a churning rapid of emotions bubbling over. Knowing this was something he did consistently somehow made it better, which didn't necessarily make any sense to her. But knowing he hadn't regurgitated her story here for some selfish end steadied her somewhat.

She had so many questions for Tank. Yesterday, she hadn't thought there was any reason to ask questions whose answers she wasn't sure she could handle. But, today, right now, curiosity burned through her, leaving behind a wasteland of unknowns she could no longer live with.

"He's been doing this since he started in the league," Steele explained.

"You've seen it?"

"Nah. First time. And I'm not sure I need a repeat," he joked.

"No," she responded, unknowingly shaking her head. "Once is enough."

"He wouldn't have wanted you to see this."

"No. I'm sure he wouldn't have."

SIXTEEN

Tank always took his time exiting after this presentation. Someone always wanted to talk, sometimes argue and sometimes explain. He'd learned early on to take his time with packing up to give these young men an opportunity to get something off their chests if they needed to. He'd become Pandora with a side of priest as he lifted the top on a shitstorm of an issue and then hung around for the splatter. He wasn't good at doling out advice, but he'd found he was good at listening, and often, that was what was needed.

Tonight, he hung around for longer than he'd anticipated, mostly because he'd gotten into a discussion with Jamal Jeffries.

By the time Tank made his way toward the exit doors, it was well past ten o'clock.

Checking his phone on his way out of Ayers had become something of a habit. He noted a message from his mother and Tilly—two phone calls he needed to return. There was a missed call from Madison, but she hadn't left a message, so he figured it was nothing important.

He pulled his keys from his pants pocket and clicked the unlock button. As he went to throw his bag in the car, he saw Amber's car sitting in its usual spot. A prickle of unease crept up his spine. He didn't consider himself an intuitive guy, especially when it came to Amber Johnson, but seeing her car here so late concerned him.

Over the last few weeks, he'd learned her routines, and he was surprised by the predictability of her schedule. Shutting the car door, he turned back toward the building. If she was still here, something was up. It could have been work, but for some reason, he doubted that. He hoped like hell she hadn't seen his presentation or heard about the content. He didn't think her knowledge of it would bode well for him.

He checked her office, and when the Operations unit was shut up tight, he made his way toward the meeting room. He knew she spent a lot of time there during the day and figured, if it was work-related, a good chance existed that he'd find her there. When he found it empty, he sat down in one of the chairs and pulled out his phone. Some sixth sense told him not to text Steele, so the inquiry went to Nicky.

> *Tank: If Amber's at work but not in her office or the conference room, where would she be?*
>
> *Nicky: Is this a trick question? LOL.*
>
> *Tank: No. Really.*
>
> *Nicky: Film room. Second floor.*

Nicky's response had been instantaneous; he didn't even have to think about it.

So, Tank took the stairs down to the second floor and picked his way through the halls, looking for the film room. After a series of locked doors, he finally tugged on a knob that turned. He stepped into a room dimly lit with small overhead lights. The telltale glow of a couple of computer screens illuminated Amber.

Purple Beats was wrapped around the back of her head, and glasses he didn't know she needed sat low on the bridge of her nose. Her bangs were pushed to the side, the rest of her hair pulled back into a low ponytail, leaving the scar on display. The now natural set of her face left her mouth pulled on the right in a slight frown. Absorbed in whatever she was doing, she didn't even look up at him as he leaned against the door, studying her. Her eyes flicked back and forth on the screen. She looked like she'd worked a seventeen-hour day, and Tank was fairly certain he'd never seen her look more beautiful.

What is it about this girl?

He didn't want to startle her, but he found he wanted her undivided attention focused on him. He could almost hear her response to his thought. She'd laugh and tell him that his ego demanded everyone's attention. But he knew, the only attention he craved like an addict was hers.

Unable to take the obscurity any longer, he shoved away from the wall and stepped forward so that he stood in the slice of open space between the computer screens. The shadow he cast forced her to look up.

The shock he'd expected to see on her face was absent, replaced with an unfamiliar glint he couldn't name.

She sat back in her chair and pulled the headphones from her ears, dropping them around her neck. "Hey."

Tank nodded and looked down to the screens in front of her. "What are you still doing here?"

"Scouting," she said.

Then, she glanced away from him. He couldn't get a read on her expression, but he detected something like embarrassment.

"That part of your job?" Tank continued to loom over her.

Smiling, she shook her head. "No, it's not. Just something I like to do."

Tank was sure his confusion was evident. He wanted to push her to continue, but he waited for her to decide what she was willing to share. He couldn't contain his nosiness, so he tried to steal a look at what she was watching. A play was frozen, paused in the middle of unfolding. He took in the scene, noting a hole in the defensive line. It was small enough to discourage most offensive players but big enough to tiptoe through to split the defense. He didn't know how the play would unfold, but he knew what he would do if he were on the field.

"How does it play out?" he inquired.

She scooted the chair forward, pulled the mouse toward her, and hit play. Tank watched as the quarterback eyed the hole but didn't react, instead stepping left and absorbing a hit from the guard on that side who'd filled the gap.

"Should have stepped into the space," Tank commented without taking his eyes from the screen.

"Exactly. He has a big body, is really quick, and has a great arm. But he has no vision, no creativity. That drops him from a four- to a three-star. You could argue coaching or confidence. But you see him watch that hole open up, and he just can't envision himself stepping into it. You could teach him to read the defenses better, but you can't teach heart."

Tank turned his head slightly, just in time to see her shrug with indifference.

"It's too bad because his physique is incredible."

Her analysis was spot-on.

In his final season at Kensington, after he'd found out who she was and they were able to talk football, she'd astonished him with her take on his play. Things she said to him after games would come up with the coaching staff the following week during film review. She had an uncanny ability to break down plays on both sides of the ball. They were undefeated that season, so her postgame review of his play never bothered him—tweaks, small misses—because when you were winning, nothing really bothered you. He wasn't quite sure how he'd react to her picking apart his play during the AFC Championship Game. He imagined his ego would take a beating as any memory of that game still made him cringe.

Tired of looming over the table, Tank walked around and pulled up another rolling chair. "What else you got?" he asked.

She turned her head toward him, but once again, Tank couldn't figure out what she was thinking. They stared at each other for a minute before she made some room for his chair and pulled up the next video.

Tank and Amber scouted fifteen players, ranging from age fourteen to seventeen. Mostly, they agreed on the ratings with a couple of exceptions. Tank found her to be a much more critical evaluator of talent. Where he would have awarded four stars, she would point out what was missing and try to talk him into agreeing on three. She won most of their arguments—not because he'd let her, but because she'd made valid points that he couldn't always counter.

Amber was about to pull up another video but stopped to adjust her glasses and rub her eyes.

"Tired?" Tank asked.

He could stay up all night just to spend this time with her, but she looked wrecked.

Perched now on the edge of her chair, she stretched her arms over her head, unconsciously thrusting her chest out. Tank fought to maintain his appreciative sigh at the sight, but their close proximity had long since been messing with his brain and his ability to keep his hands to himself. His hands itched to touch her, and his mouth watered every time the space between them decreased as they moved in to study a play. His want for her was limitless, and in that second, with her innocent yet provocative stretch, he thought he was going to lose the tentative hold on his libido. He pushed his chair slightly back, so her outthrust breasts weren't in his direct line of sight.

"I'm a little tired." She dropped her arms and looked over at him. She must have noticed the leer on his face because she smirked.

He answered with a shake of his head, a denial of what she knew she had seen. She chuckled softly, and he couldn't help but give in to the grin tugging at his lips.

She rolled her chair away from him.

Cocking his head to the side, he said, "That inch of space isn't going to help."

Her laughter split the air and the tension in the room.

That! That sound.

"I love your laugh," he admitted, no longer able to deny himself. He reached forward and ran his finger along the edge of her jaw. "God, I love that sound."

But the touch of his finger had strangled the sound in her throat, and she merely looked at him, her eyes awash with a million questions.

"Why?" she asked.

He wanted to feign ignorance and explain how her laughter was like the first sound of Christmas to a kid. But he knew she wasn't asking about that. His hand dropped back to his thigh, and he took a second to collect his scattered thoughts. He didn't want to get this wrong. It was too important. He glanced away, knowing his answer was going to be inadequate, and he wasn't ready to disappoint her again.

"Are you mad at me for using your story?" he asked, swinging his gaze back to her, showcasing his greatest worry.

Slowly, she shook her head. "I don't think so," she started before glancing up at the ceiling. "I was stunned. You were stunning, mesmerizing." She dropped her arms to her knees. "I was so proud of you because what you'd said was so important. I'm not sure I can even get words around it, ya know?" Her pause was about composure. "But, when you went there, my first thought was that you were an asshole. I couldn't believe you'd used my story to further your cause—which I am not even sure I know what that is. But then Steele told me you'd been doing this for a while, and then I didn't really care that you'd used my story. It was a confusing hour." She sat back. "Tell me why, Tank."

"I hated that story." He rubbed his hand over his head, frustrated with his inarticulate response. He liked having her close, so he copied her earlier position, elbows on his knees, a seesaw of positions between them. "I hated it. I wished all sorts of bad shit on a guy who was already dead and also on Southern cops in small football towns.

"But, later, with some distance, I got that it was a bigger issue than me just being pissed that someone I cared about had been hurt. It could and did happen to people, and I had a forum to talk about it." A sheepish grin appeared on his face. "Hawk is all about public image and insisted I have some cause I could get behind. It was easy from there. I watched some presentations by TeamUP and talked to some of their trainers. I went to a private train-the-trainer session. Then, one of their people helped me craft my presentation. And I didn't intend to include your story or in any way violate your trust." He grabbed her hand. "You know that, right?"

She didn't pull away from him, which he considered a minor victory. But it took her a second to answer him with a nod.

"It came out during my practice session, and the guy working with me really liked that I could give them a starting point to connect with such a violent act. So, it stayed."

"Okay."

He squeezed her hand. "Since few people knew about our shared past, I knew I could keep it safe. Ya feel me?"

"So, Franco's never seen it? Because he would connect the dots. He would know."

Ah, I should have thought of that.

Tank shook his head. "He's never seen it. We don't advertise it. But I'm committed to it now. Especially now. But, if you want me to take it out, I will. Just say the word."

"No. Keep it." She conceded like it was no big deal, but it was a gift, and he knew it.

"Thank you."

She was inches away from him, and he didn't want her to wonder anymore.

"You said something else earlier about not knowing why I was here. I want to clarify."

She radiated skepticism, but he pushed forward. He released her hand, grabbing the arms of her chair. The wheels conceded to his gentle pull, rolling her closer until their knees touched. He lifted his hand and laid it on her jaw, the scarred tissue so familiar. Her eyes closed, a deep sigh escaped her parted lips, and the pulse point on her neck jumped. Tank reveled in her response, still there for him. He dropped a quick, lightweight kiss on her mouth before he pulled away. Her lids fluttered open, and she stared up at him.

"I'm here for you."

Then, he kissed her.

SEVENTEEN

It was a perfect first kiss.

Even though it probably numbered in the hundreds between them. A first because—the man in front of her, the one with his hands strategically placed on her right jaw and her left hip—this man was different than the man-child he'd been. Every dip of his tongue, nip on her lip, exploration of the cavern of her mouth was a first. A perfect first kiss.

A diving-board kiss that made her want to plunge into the warm, languid pool of Tank Howard. She wanted to swim to the bottom and touch the deepest part of him. She wanted to wade through the rhythm of the blood pumping through his body. She wanted to splash and dip, to stroke and breathe, to hold her breath and sink until she had to surface to inhale his air.

She was going to fucking drown.

Tank ended the kiss and dropped his forehead to hers while she struggled to get control of herself.

"Come home with me," he whispered, "or let me come home with you."

He dropped his mouth to hers again and nibbled on her bottom lip before dragging tiny kisses across the shredded skin on her jaw and neck. Her heart rate kicked up, and every part of her body clenched in response.

Needing sanity, she pushed off the ground with her feet and sent the chair rolling back, leaving Tank's mouth hanging open and her heated skin cool. With a little bit of space between them, she was able to regulate her ragged breathing, but she had to shake her head to try to regain her composure.

When she was sure she could handle it, she looked at Tank. His green eyes were heavy with desire and want. But he didn't push. She knew he could move in for the kill, convince her with his body to continue their night, but he waited patiently for her to make a decision. His patience was one of those subtle differences separating the man from the boy. Tank of three years ago would have pushed once, thrown his hands in the air, and walked away, expecting her to follow. The impulse seemed to be gone or leashed because he didn't press, didn't seem to expect her acquiescence. Instead, he watched her, probably looking for signs of her thought process. He would be disappointed. Her brain had atrophied. Thoughts lay trampled, her fears scattered. She was a desolate wasteland of nothingness. She couldn't gather a litany of objections even though she knew there were many and they would eventually make themselves known.

But, right at this moment, she wanted him.

Amber stood up and held her hand out to him. His fingers intertwined with hers as he followed. It was one beautifully choreographed moment. They didn't speak, but so many things passed between them. He gently squeezed her fingers with his, acknowledging what was there and what was sure to follow. He brought her hand up and pressed her palm against his open mouth. Her eyes closed involuntarily.

She let go of his hand and turned to the equipment in front of her. She closed out of the windows, saved her spreadsheet to her shared drive, and shut down the computer. The break from the moment helped her gather her senses.

This foray with Tank didn't have to mean anything or everything. It could just be a giving-in, a concession to the wonder. *What would it be like with a clean slate?*

She'd played their last two moments together numerous times over the last few years. In the hotel room, on the night he'd won the Heisman, he'd brought his hope, and she'd brought her good-bye. And, at the wedding, she'd carried all her hurt and anger. And maybe some hate.

So, she couldn't even begin to guess what it would be like to just offer him her desire.

When everything was closed out and she had no excuse to delay, she turned back to him. He immediately reached for her hand again, maybe wanting to remind her of the connection between them, maybe just needing to touch her.

He let her lead them from the room, through the halls, and down the stairs to the atrium. As she stepped outside, she realized she didn't have her stuff.

"Shit," she exclaimed as the door closed behind them. "I have to go get my things."

"Okay. Do you want me to wait here or come with you?"

"Can you get me back here at four thirty?"

He chuckled. "What time would I have to get up if you went back upstairs?"

"Five," she responded cheekily.

He tugged on her hand, walking her to his car. "Figured."

He unlocked the car and walked her around to the passenger side to open her door. He waited for her to get in, and then he pulled on the seat belt, leaning over her and locking it in place. He overwhelmed her with his size and his proximity.

She quirked an eyebrow at him, trying to take some control. "Really?"

He turned his head, and at the same time, each of his hands wrapped around one of her wrists. His body moved minutely. He merely stared at her, but a myriad of emotions swirled around him. Where her page was blank, his was covered with scribbles and doodles, none of which she could decipher.

"Really." He smirked, covering his emotions with a familiar face.

She shrugged, the movement reminding her that he still held her wrists. He dropped a quick, chaste kiss on her mouth before he removed himself and closed the door.

He walked behind the Range Rover, and Amber watched him in the rearview mirror as he stopped and ran his hand over his head. For the first time, Amber thought he might be more nervous than her. The notion filled her with an uneasy sense of power. Then, he moved, and it was gone.

Tank yanked on the door and slid gracefully into the seat. He turned on the car, leaned his arms on the steering wheel, and turned to face her.

Snickering, he said, "My place or yours?"

She couldn't help her answering laugh. "Yours," she said without hesitation. No need to have lingering memories of Tank Howard in her bed.

He reversed out of the parking lot and began the drive.

Amber looked at the time on the dash. "I didn't realize it was so late," she remarked.

Tank took his eyes off the road for a split second to look at her. "Four thirty's going to come quick."

"I hope not."

He shook his head but couldn't hide his grin. "Gutter."

"I am always surprised at how late it is when I watch film."

Tank nodded. "Tell me about that."

"What do you want to know?"

"You said it's not part of your responsibilities. But that spreadsheet of yours is pretty impressive. What do you love about it?"

His question caught her off guard. Of course he would phrase it like that. He had spent an hour with her and knew she loved it.

"That's an interesting way to ask."

"What you love about it?" He glanced at her, and when she nodded, he shrugged. "You do love it, right?"

"I do."

"Why?"

She never talked about it with anyone. Steele and Nicky knew she looked at film, but they had no idea how much time she spent analyzing players. There was something about being able to spot talent and determine if it would become something or go to waste.

She'd been doing it since she realized she had access to all of this film. For three years, she'd looked at thousands of players. She'd rated them and then followed their careers, tracking their successes and failures. She didn't listen to the expert opinions on them. Instead, she'd created her own evaluation. It took a lot to earn five stars from her.

"I just love that part of it. The scouting more than the recruiting. You can tell so much from watching film over a couple of years."

"Do you share your opinions?"

"No."

"I find that hard to believe," he quipped.

She rolled her eyes. "It's not really about that. I mean, I love pitting my knowledge against Whitey's, but he doesn't know I'm doing it."

"I don't know about that."

"What do you mean?"

"I've spent some time with him over the last couple of weeks. I don't think your extracurricular activities are much of a secret."

"He knows I watch the film, but he doesn't know the extent. And I don't ever offer up any contradictions."

"But he asks you, doesn't he?"

She thought about it for a moment and found herself smiling. "He does."

Things got quiet between them, the low hum of the music the only sound in the car. Amber thought about what he'd said and revealed. As wrapped up in himself as Tank could be, he happened to be pretty damn observant. She'd forgotten that about him, probably because it was one of his more endearing qualities—his ability to notice the people around him.

They quickly arrived at his house, and Amber's previously lost inhibitions returned. As Tank pulled the Range Rover into the garage of the bungalow, the regrets and prohibitions rose from their lust-induced death. She didn't even have to name it because she knew exactly what thought beast was waiting to roar in its all-mighty voice.

The thing about Tank was just that—Tank. He made her feel everything. Fear, hope, completeness, loneliness, jealousy, pride. He came with all these feeling triggers. She'd existed the last three years in relative happiness, perhaps born from a desire to be numb. But she was content with her life, her job, her choices. She was even content with the choice she was about to make.

Tank found his way to her door, opening it before she even realized he'd stepped out of the car. She unbuckled her seat belt and stood, trapped between the V of the door and Tank. He smiled down at her and linked their hands before he turned and led her into the house. She didn't bother to look around. This wasn't his place. There was no need to study the furnishings. There were no Tank secrets on display in this temporary house. So, she followed him as he beat a determined path to the bedroom.

She was ready for him, more ready than she'd ever been, and in the moment, there was clarity.

Closure.

For a split second.

Tank stopped at the foot of the California-king bed and maneuvered her around, so they faced each other. He looked like he was about to say something. But she was already there and didn't need any crazy assurances, so she grabbed the bottom of her shirt and pulled it up over her head, foregoing the buttons. She stood in her bra and skirt in front of him. His eyes dropped down, and she watched as he took a very slow inventory. She reached behind her back and slid the zipper down, letting her skirt fall to her feet.

Tank groaned.

She smiled in victory.

But, when she stepped toward him, he shuffled back, keeping a buffer between them.

Her hands landed on her hips with annoyance, and her smile slipped away.

"Really?" she sputtered, her voice startlingly husky.

He had the audacity to laugh while his hands made a sign of surrender. He kept the distance between them but reached up to cup her jaw. One swipe of his thumb against her scar, and her body temperature rose while white-hot heat collected in her belly.

"I just need to be clear about what this is."

She was trying really hard to concentrate on his words, but the gentle sweeping of his fingers on her neck and mouth made it difficult. "Sex, right? I get it."

He snickered. "Yes, definitely sex. But..."

He stumbled on his words, and she didn't know how to get them to move forward. She stood in front of him, practically naked, his want for her a thriving presence in the room.

"But?"

He took a deep breath. His hand lingered on her scar, and his eyes locked on hers. "But so much more."

Those four words made her stop and wish for her clothes. This time, she took a step back, and Tank's hand dropped to his side.

"Let's not get ahead of ourselves," she murmured.

Tank looked like he was going to argue with her as his eyes narrowed, and he took what she could only term a calming breath. Then, he grabbed her hips in his hands and yanked her forward, his body absorbing her momentum and melding perfectly with hers.

Her hands meandered up his chest before meeting in a clasp behind his neck.

She'd meant it. She didn't want to build this up between them, to think they were on the cusp of some brilliant love story. She wanted him. He wanted her. End. Stop.

But, as his hands encircled her waist and her nails lightly traced the almost shaved part of his head, their bodies merged together in a perfect line. Heat infused every part of her as her blood got hot. Her skin fired, and the space between her legs turned liquid.

They didn't kiss. Rather, their mouths exchanged quickening breaths, like they needed each other's air to live. The pounding of her heart reverberated in time with the pounding of his, her right breast almost vibrating with the rhythm of it. In all the rage of their desire, the overwhelming emotion she could name infused her with panic. Because, even though they were in the midst of a sexual inferno, she felt an all-consuming sense of serenity.

EIGHTEEN

Tank had made pressure his bitch on more than one occasion. He never hesitated or questioned his decisions. In a game, quick thinking and taking action were imperatives.

But, suddenly, he hesitated.

He'd pictured a conversation, a plan between them, a sort of outline of expectations before anything happened. Maybe that was optimistic or even naive.

When had any part of their relationship gone as planned?

On the threshold of being with Amber again, Tank wondered if he should have wined and dined her more, courted her.

As her nails lightly scraped against the back of his neck and her body moved against his, he lost all sense of his plan.

"God, I've missed you," he murmured, his mouth incapable of keeping the thought locked down.

Amber chuckled against him, her smile a fraction from his mouth. He couldn't stop himself from swooping down and capturing it with a gentle nip on her bottom lip.

She pulled away from him. With an smirk, she said, "Show me how much you've missed me."

Tank laughed and then stepped into the gap. He bent down and picked her up in a fireman's carry. He walked to the bed with her giggling body writhing on his shoulder. Then, he dipped and deposited her onto the bed. He leaned over her, his arms on either side of her hips, and he grinned down at her startled expression.

Amber reached out, wrapped her arms around his neck, and pulled him down. Their upturned mouths met in a chaste kiss.

One, two, three small pecks, lips against lips, before Tank's mouth opened, and he licked along the seam of hers. She opened on a small gasp, and Tank pressed forward, his mouth the frontal assault. His hands twitched on the sides of her, eager to claim, but he held back, wanting to enjoy being lost in her.

Their kiss in the film room had been mind-blowing. Kissing was one of those things he hadn't done a lot of in the past couple of years. It had been too intimate for what he had in mind. Even with Madison, soul-sucking kisses hadn't been on the menu. But, with Amber, he could happily be lost in her mouth for days. And, while his body begged for more, he continued to explore her mouth.

He could tell the second Amber began to get impatient because the grip on his neck tightened as she tried to pull his body down on top of hers. When he resisted, her leg came up around his waist, and she tried to leverage her slight weight against his. He couldn't help the laughter that rumbled through his chest. She turned her head away from him, the only way to break his hold on her mouth. Her eyes flew open and met his. He knew the lust-filled, blown pupil look of her gaze mirrored his. They were both far gone.

"More," she demanded.

He dropped a kiss on her nose. "I know. A lot more."

"No. Now!"

He smiled but conceded by dropping his body on top of hers, aligning them for optimum contact, his groin cradled in the pocket between her thighs. Even with his clothes still on, he could feel the heat of her. The intimate meeting of his cock with her wet heat pulled a hungry groan from both of them.

"Fuck," he sighed.

She arched up and tightened the grip of her arms and legs, gluing their bodies together.

"So good," she murmured.

It was so good. So good that he needed a moment to revel in it. Having her in his arms, in his rented house, was like some far-reaching goal fulfillment. He knew this was what he wanted, but being on the verge of sinking back into her body made him soar. It was like winning the Heisman, being number one in the draft, earning the Rookie of the Year award rolled into one.

So, while she writhed and bucked against him, silently pining for orgasmic bliss, Tank exulted in the second—before it was suddenly too much and his body demanded more. He slid his hand under her, unhooking her bra with deftness. He leaned to the side, resting on his left elbow, before slipping his finger in the center of the material and pulling it down to reveal her perfect breasts. He dipped his head and dropped a kiss on each nipple, eliciting a moan from her.

"Seriously, enough with the fucking seduction, Tank," she said breathlessly.

He looked up at her lust-filled eyes and laughed. "Always so impatient. And that mouth of yours. Always so damn dirty."

She rolled her eyes and then reached over to start unbuttoning his shirt. "You have way too many clothes on. Naked. Now."

He let her work on his shirt while he undid the belt, button, and zipper of his pants. He shucked them off with a shove of his hands and a hook with his foot. Then, he knelt and peeled off his shirt.

"Better?" He threw his hands out, showcasing his almost-naked form.

"Almost," Amber commented as she eyed his boxer briefs.

She rolled over and got to her knees, kneeling directly in front of him. Her fingers hooked his underwear on each side, and she slid them down to pool at his bent knees. He mimicked her movements and divested her of her panties, so they were naked, facing each other on their knees.

He leaned over to the nightstand, opened the drawer, and pulled out a condom. Ripping it open, he sheathed himself. He moved slowly, savoring the moment, the anticipation of having a naked Amber looking at him with want, need.

He'd wanted to take this slow, draw it out, but now, with her hungry eyes focused on his body, he found that he couldn't wait. The mattress depressed as he inched toward her, pitching her just slightly forward. Tank's hands snaked out, his fingers eagerly gripping her waist. His thumbs caressed the taut skin of her stomach for a millisecond before his grasp tightened, and he lifted her. She knew instinctually what he wanted, and she responded by wrapping her arms around his neck and her legs around his waist.

In one perfect movement, he thrust upward as he pulled her down onto him. The sounds of their mutual delight rang out in the room, a guttural cacophony of satisfied moans.

Neither of them moved. They froze, eyes closed, relishing the feel of each other. Amber's hair teased his fingertips, and he could tell without seeing her that her head dropped back. His eyes sprang open, and he dove for her neck, her jaw, the most perfect part of her. His tongue started at the bottom of the spider web, tracing the intricate lattice up her throat, until he came to the deep gouge at her jawline, fanning from her now-imperfect lips.

Amber's breathing tripled, her heart thumping so that Tank could feel her pulse thundering at her neck. He toyed with her scar, loving the feel of it under his mouth. He knew it was her most pronounced erogenous zone, and he loved to drive her crazy. And he was because her hips started moving,

"That's it, Sunshine," he cooed near her mouth, the words amping her up even more.

"Let me move," she pleaded as her nails dug into the back of his neck.

He couldn't restrain the chuckle that escaped him as he moved her once up and then back down. "Go ahead, Sunny. Mark me again. I love it."

When she didn't flinch at his use of her nickname, he knew she was too far gone, and her response to him snapped the last of his restraint. He dropped one of his hands from her to the bed, and as gently as he could, he laid them down. He started to slowly pump into her, cherishing the feel of her.

"More," she demanded.

"That's it. Tell me how you want it."

"Just…more."

He unwrapped her leg from his back and moved it up so that her knee kissed her shoulder. He shifted, thrusting up, bumping against her clit with the force of the movement. She sputtered, some nonsensical words leaving her mouth, as her hand moved down to the top of his ass, and she directed his actions. His pace increased, his attempt at controlling them gone.

He couldn't get enough of her. He wanted to consume her, have her consume him. He could feel his orgasm brewing. He let go of her leg and moved his hand between them, wanting her to get there with him.

"So close," she gasped.

"I know," he stated with confidence as he could feel her muscles starting to tighten on him, to clamp down and pulse.

He dropped his head and lightly bit her scar as he worked her clit. Then, she was coming, hard and fast, gasping.

Tank looked up at her. He didn't think she would do it, but she opened her eyes and stared directly at him, the ecstasy blazing. And that was all it took for him to let go.

Tank shifted and dropped to the bed beside her. He caught his breath and then rolled out of bed to deal with the condom. He strolled back in the room, crawled next to her, and pulled her up against him. He anticipated her fighting him, wanting the space between them. But she settled against him and dropped her hand to his chest. It moved in a lazy rhythm up and down, tracing random lines and shapes.

"You ever call me Sunny again, and I'm going to hurt you," she said before pinching his chest and following it with a kiss.

Tank responded with a laugh. "That's what you've got for me?"

"You know I hate that. I can barely stand Sunshine."

He kissed the top of her head. "You love to pretend you hate it, but deep down, you love it."

"You keep telling yourself that."

He chuckled.

She picked her head up and looked at him, shifting so that she was almost leaning over him. "That was…" She looked away. "What can I say that won't make your ego blow up like a frickin' balloon?"

Tank laughed. "Nothing." He held her gaze. "Your response told me everything." The moment became heated, and his body immediately responded. Then, he shrugged. "But I can help you with some adjectives. Incredible." He slightly lifted his head and lightly kissed her, basically touching his lips to hers. "Earth-shattering."

She smiled at him then, and he knew she was feeling it, too. He kissed her jaw, and her eyelids drooped.

"Amazing."

"You and your damn ego. You don't even need anyone to feed it. You can manage it all by yourself."

"Truth," he said, smiling at her.

She dropped back down onto his chest, and the length of the sudden silence made him nervous.

He ran his hand up her side, tracing the line of her arm, until his hand interlocked with hers on his chest. "What are you thinking?"

When she squirmed against him, he braced himself. In the past, for Amber, thinking was on par with bumping up against his ego. It never led to anything good.

"It doesn't really matter, but what's up with you and Madison?"

The question shouldn't have surprised him; in fact, he wanted to have this conversation with her. "What do you want to know?" He needed to let her lead this because, if he did, he'd probably gloss over details she wanted.

"How…well, when did it start? You said you weren't together at the wedding."

"We weren't." He continued to hold her hand.

She blew out a frustrated breath. "Just give me a timeline."

He snickered, his chest vibrating with it. She squeezed his hand, demanding something.

"After the wedding, I, uh…binged for a while. I definitely didn't want a relationship, and Madison and I crossed paths a couple of times, but we just hung out. We got to be friends though. I got a little bored with the hit-and-run one-night stands. We just kind of agreed to get together when she was in town."

"After the wedding, you binged? What'd you do before that?"

Tank tried to withhold the tensing of his body. "Um, yeah…not a lot."

Amber sat up, pulling the sheet to cover her breasts. Looking down at him, she asked, "Are you going to explain that?"

He cleared his throat. "From the time I left you in that hotel room until the wedding, I wasn't with anyone."

Amber's eyes got wide. She blinked, like a newborn baby trying to adjust to a reality outside its mother womb. Tank tried to hold her gaze, but heat moved up his neck, and he knew Amber could see the embarrassed blush staining his skin. He shouldn't be embarrassed, but he knew she'd want to know why, and that was a truth he wasn't sure she wanted to hear right now.

"Why?" She reached out and ran her hand across his cheek. Then, she smiled mischievously. "Yeah, that boyish blush isn't going to get you out of explaining."

He laughed. Then, he reached out and pulled her down on top of him. She threw her leg over his hip, so she was straddling him, the sheet forgotten. She looked down on him like a queen surveying her domain. She tilted her head and cocked her eyebrow. Her hands slid up his chest, lingering on his cheeks, before she dropped down and kissed him hard, demanding his response.

"Why?" she whispered against his mouth.

Perhaps it was the kiss or the demanding tone of her voice, or maybe it was her naked body rubbing against his.

"I kept thinking you'd come back to me."

NINETEEN

Amber cued up the film and leaned back in her chair. She had a rare couple of free hours in the middle of the week, and she found herself in the film room, watching the AFC Championship Game.

When Tank had left the hotel room three years ago, she'd promised herself she'd stay away from all things Tank. It was a hefty promise. *How could she love football and not watch one of the best players in the game, who happened to be on her favorite team and was coached by her father?* For that first season, Franco called her and expected some feedback. It took him the entire five months to realize that she refused to watch his games. He'd never brought it up directly, but he'd stopped asking.

The game she was watching bothered Tank. She knew he wasn't over the routing he'd experienced. For a player who hadn't had to deal with loss often, it was a devastating blow. Amber wanted to know what had happened.

They'd briefly touched on it the night before. They'd touched on a lot of things. She didn't get one second of sleep, partly because she didn't want to miss out on one moment with him. The conversation was almost as good as the sex. She only paused once the whole night. When he told her he'd thought she was going to come back, she almost got up and left. In that second, she knew vulnerable Tank was a lethal injection to her heart. He was everything she wanted and nothing she needed. Being with him was Russian roulette. She could protect herself, but eventually, the chamber in the gun would be filled with a bullet. The trick would be to get out before she got shot.

She'd waited until she knew Tank and Steele were working out before she snuck away to her sanctuary of the film room. And she watched and took note. She saw his mistakes and assessed the damage. She broke it all down. As she sat back with all her conclusions, the door opened.

Looking up from the computer screens in front of her, she was only mildly surprised to find a freshly showered Tank smiling at her from the door.

"Hey."

"Hey yourself. Good workout?"

He nodded. "Surprisingly, yes. Maybe setting my expectations low helped make it feel like a good workout."

Dropping her elbows onto the table in front of her, she smiled at him mischievously. "Why the low expectations?"

His dimples peeked out as he returned her smile. "Sleep and energy deprivation."

"Ah. Well, maybe you should plan better."

"Oh, I think my planning was spot-on." He walked to the table and peered over the monitors, looking straight at her. "Scouting?"

"Sort of," she answered vaguely.

His eyes narrowed. "Sort of?"

She shrugged.

Then, he leaned over and dropped a kiss on her forehead. The gesture spoke of familiarity and sweetness. "I have a question for you."

"Shoot."

"I have to go back to Atlanta this weekend."

"Is that a question?"

He grinned. "I was wondering if you want to come with me."

She tipped back in the chair. "Well, we're a week and a half away from the spring game. We'll definitely have practice on Saturday."

"I thought about that. I can wait, and we can go Saturday afternoon."

She considered it. She could see Franco, Molly, and the kids if she went. She didn't often take the time to head there when she had an opportunity. She missed them, and she wanted to spend time with them. She tried not to think about what Franco would say when she showed up with Tank. Although she knew her father pretty well, it was one reaction she didn't think she could script.

"More incentive?" he asked. "I talked to Tilly. They are having some people over Saturday night. We can surprise them. And, if you want to see Franco, I can take you there while I go meet with Hawk."

She almost laughed at all the carrots he was dangling. She wanted to go, no matter what, but it was good to have a couple of excuses and not just the desire to hang out with him as the only reason.

"I'd love to see the As. Let me talk to Franco and see if they'll be around."

"Great."

"So, did you tell Tilly about last night?" She hoped he hadn't, but she couldn't be sure. Even now, it felt odd that their respective best friends were getting married to each other. "Because I haven't even told Keira yet."

He laughed. "Actually, I didn't. I knew I needed to go back, so I talked to him at the beginning of the week. I'm sure Keira would love to see you. And it would get Tilly off the hook with wedding stuff if her maid of honor was around."

She chuckled. "He'd better get used to this. Keira has been planning her wedding since she was five. It's going to be a long year."

"He already said they should just elope."

They laughed some more.

Then, Tank came around the side of the table and took a seat. "So, are we scouting?" he asked as he looked at the monitors. He did a double take when he noticed the uniforms, the game, the play frozen in front of him. He rubbed his hand over his head. Turning to her, he asked, "Why are you watching this?" A trace of accusation and embarrassment colored his tone.

"I was curious." She almost reached out to touch, reassurance for both of them maybe, but she stayed her hand.

"You were curious about the worst game of my career?" The question flew out of his mouth, the accusation heavier this time.

Easy.

She wasn't sure how to play this.

Tank had always taken her analysis well. He'd never gotten defensive if she lobbed some constructive criticism his way. But he also hadn't gotten stomped and humiliated in a game that millions of people were watching. Even worse, she knew he was going to hate what she had to say because the loss of the game had nothing to do with the Xs and Os; it had everything to do with his leadership.

His eyes flickered back and forth between the screens and her. Frozen in front of him was one hell of an ugly sack, a picture of his body pinned under the left tackle. Something in his eyes flashed when he studied the scene, like he remembered the crunch of the helmet on his shoulder pad. Maybe his body remembered the impact of the hit that had driven his right shoulder into the unforgiving ground. Possibly, he could recall the smell of the field as his facemask sprayed a healthy dose of grass and dirt up into his nose. It could have been anything, but she guessed he remembered it all.

"You could at least acknowledge it was the worst game." He was pissed.

Part of her wanted to laugh at the return of man-child Tank, who basically wept when his precious ego was bruised.

"Well," Amber began, "based on the score, I would guess it was. But, because I haven't seen you play since college, I don't know."

His jaw dropped, incredulity a mask on his face. "You haven't seen any of my professional games?"

"No."

His eyes literally bugged out of his head. She had this image of him having to force his eyes back into his sockets, and she worked hard to smother her smile and laughter.

"Why not?"

She waved him off, not deigning to answer his question.

He shifted in the chair, obviously uncomfortable. Then, he nodded. "So, what'd you think?"

She bit her top lip, fighting another smile. She couldn't help it; she found him so cute when he was in a huff. It inserted some humanity into the perfect specimen of Tank Howard, and it made her like him even more. His arrogance was insidious, but his vulnerability was endearing.

"I think it's hard to throw and run an offense when you're clenching," she said her piece, putting it out there in the film-room universe. Then, she waited for the explosion.

Tank's eyes blinked, like residue was in the way of him seeing clearly. "Did you..." he sputtered. He looked around and then back at her. "Did you just say it's hard to throw when I'm clenching?"

Amber smirked. "Yep."

Tank leaned back in the chair and cackled. His laughter filled the space, permeating the air, and he looked at her with a big, dopey smile on his face. She returned it.

"That's your expert analysis?" he said, the smile lingering.

"Yeah, dude. You lost that game because of nerves."

"Clenching?"

"Right, clenching."

He reached up and rubbed his index finger and thumb across his chin. He pinned her with his gaze, which had somehow darkened with lust. "What can *you* do when you're clenching?"

Amber's whole body infused with heat, her nipples tightening, and she thought she could come just by the look on his face. She swallowed audibly. "This isn't about me."

But he was definitely making it about her.

He inched his chair forward, the little plastic wheels rolling unhurriedly on the industrial carpet. Amber inched hers back, wanting but not wanting what his heated stare was promising.

"There's a wall behind you," he said softly.

She should have looked but found she couldn't tear her eyes away from his. Her chair halted, the caster refusing to budge, and Tank's body and chair came closer and closer until their knees knocked lightly together. His hand snaked between her legs and moved at a snail's pace up her inner thigh.

"Are you clenching?" he whispered, leaning forward so that his head was near her ear. He nipped the lobe, lightly pulling on it with his teeth.

She tried belatedly to clamp her thighs together, but he clutched at one of her knees and held it apart from the other.

"You are," he declared. "I can feel it, and I'm inches away from verifying it."

Forget clenching; she was about to combust. He moved his hand between her legs, shoved her panties aside, and swiped one finger into her wet heat.

"So hot," he whispered. Then, he dropped his mouth to her jaw and sucked on her scar. "Clench, baby," he said.

And, just like that, she was coming, thrusting against his hand and tightly gripping the arms of her chair as she rode it out. When her breathing regulated, she felt his smile against her jaw, and she couldn't help it when she smiled, too.

He kissed her hard but quick and then rested his forehead against hers. "That was so hot," he murmured.

She didn't even have a response to that, so she shoved his body away from hers, needing some room to collect herself. She couldn't quite believe what had just happened. One minute, he was angry, and the next, he was laughing. Then, he was making her come. Talk about a mood swing.

She reached for the table and pulled the chair forward, back into the position where she'd started. She clicked through and shut down the video. When she felt like she had some modicum of control over herself, she looked back over at Tank.

"Is that how you deal with criticism?" she quipped.

He laughed. "Uh, not usually. Franco doesn't do it for me."

Her nose scrunched up. "Ew."

His smile lingered as he looked at her. She reveled in it. When it was genuine, he glowed.

Then, he got serious, and he turned his attention to the blackened screens. "You're the first person to tell me that. I mean, Franco and I haven't really talked about it, but our offensive coordinator made me sit in a two-hour-long review of everything I had done wrong."

"Well, in all fairness to Skip, you did a lot wrong."

He nodded. "I did."

"You never looked comfortable out there. That's not the Tank Howard I'm used to seeing."

"How would you know? You said you hadn't seen me play." He turned toward her again, "How come you haven't watched?"

She took a deep breath, held the gun to her head, and pulled the trigger. "The easiest way to get over you was to block you out. I couldn't watch you play, watch your success, while wanting to move on."

He reached out to her, sliding his index finger against her jawline. "I get that."

Things were too serious all of a sudden. She longed for the crazy laughter or even the sexual tension from earlier. She could deal with that. But introspection and regrets? She wasn't ready for all that. She'd walked away from him for a damn good reason, and she wasn't going to question what she'd had to do to get through it.

She moved her face away from him and stood, breaking the moment. "So, Atlanta?" she said. "When do we leave?"

TWENTY

Amber rolled onto her back and lifted Alexis above her head, making *vroom, vroom* noises as her baby sister flung her arms out wide, pretending to be an airplane.

"Coming in for a rough landing," Amber warned as she let her arms fall a little to the side.

A full-belly shriek flew from Alexis's mouth. Amber slowly dropped her arms, letting Alexis lie softly on her, stomach to stomach. Her little body still shook with helpless giggles as Amber wrapped Alexis up in her arms. Amber had all of two full seconds of snuggling before Andy jumped next to her head, begging for his turn.

"Me, me, 'Ber. Me."

Amber released Alexis, who scrambled out of the way, giving her twin his turn.

"One more," Franco said.

Amber, Alexis, and Andy all turned to the doorway, looking over to their father, who was leaning against the jamb.

"Nap time," Franco stated.

"No sleepy," Andy protested, even as his little fist unconsciously reached up to rub his eye.

Amber stifled a giggle of her own. "Okay, Pops," she said before she grabbed Andy's sturdy body and boosted him up above her head.

"Plane, Daddy!" Andy yelled in between his laughter.

"I see," Franco agreed. "A jet, I think."

"Jet!" Andy yelled.

"Coming in for a landing," Amber said, intending to give her tired arms a rest.

But Franco swooped in and grabbed Andy right out of the air amid Amber's surprised laughter and Alexis's screams of protest. Franco turned toward his little girl and swung her up with his other arm.

Looking over his shoulder to Amber, he said, "I'll be back," before he left her sprawled in the middle of the playroom.

"I'll be here," she promised, grinning.

She didn't even bother to try to get up. She was exhausted from her fitful sleep the night before, their early morning departure to Atlanta, and then entertaining the twins for the last couple of hours. The sudden quiet of the room made her shift uncomfortably as the thoughts she'd tried to keep at bay were given rein in her crowded head.

After a spectacular practice yesterday, Whitey had given the team the weekend off. Amber almost called Tank and asked to leave for Atlanta a day early. But a day early was a night early, and she wasn't quite ready to spend another night with him. After the day in the film room, she'd found ways to keep her distance, the intensity of their exchange a little too much for her to handle. She'd rather hastily agreed to come here with him, but she needed to remind them both what this was—nothing more than having fun. She planned to manage her feelings for Tank, to truly just hang out with him.

Amber rubbed her hand over her eyes and then rolled over before getting to her feet. Wandering into the kitchen, she grabbed a bottle of water from the fridge. When she closed the door, she stood, studying the pictures and drawings adhered to the stainless steel with cute little ceramic football magnets. A Christmas picture of her and Andy snagged her attention. They were facing each other, and Andy had his hands on the sides of her face. They wore matching Santa hats and grins, adoring each other with their identical chocolate eyes. A shaft of love pierced through her. She thought about one of her conversations with Franco regarding Molly's difficulty in mixing her high-powered career with motherhood. For the first time in years, Amber wondered about what she wanted, how she wanted her life to look.

"I think that's one of my favorite pictures," Franco said as he made his way into the room. "Molly had one framed for me to put in my office." He walked to her and pulled her into a brief hug. Nudging her out of the way, he opened the door and pulled out a water bottle for himself. "I might like it as much as our headset picture." She smiled at him, easily recalling the picture of her and Franco in the press box during a football game, headsets in place, with identical expressions.

"I didn't see it until just now. It's really good."

"It is." He turned away from the picture. "The As are down. Wanna enjoy the weather on the deck?"

Amber didn't answer. She merely turned and walked toward the French doors. Pulling them open, she strolled onto the brick patio and sank into one of the plush chairs. She leaned back and dropped her head.

When she heard Franco sit, she rolled her head to the side and looked over at him. "These chairs are nicer than anything I have in my house."

Franco chuckled. "When I was your age, I was using milk crates as bookshelves. Pretty sure you're doing better than I was." He leaned back and dropped his feet onto the coffee table in front of him. "Is something wrong with your car?"

Amber took a deep breath. She had known this conversation was going to happen, but she'd hoped she could put if off for a little bit longer. She could hedge, but to merely prolong the inevitable didn't seem like such a good idea.

"No, I drove over with Tank." She kept her eyes on her father even though she was tempted to look away.

He blinked, but no other emotion showed on his face. "Tank Howard?"

Amber rolled her eyes, not even bothering to answer. Franco looked away from her, surveying the backyard, as if he needed some view that didn't include her. The silence stretched between them. She waited for him to respond or react, but nothing came. She wasn't sure what she had expected from him. Outrage, horror, anger? But as they continued to lounge in the crisp April air, Franco's lack of a reaction bothered her.

"Nothing?" she asked, unable to sit in silence any longer.

Franco laughed drily. "What do you want me to say? I haven't commented on your personal life in years. You want me to start now?"

Amber shuffled forward in her chair, dropping her elbows onto her knees and plopping her chin on her fists. She didn't say anything for a moment as she really thought about his response. He was right; she knew that. After their last, most memorable fight, Franco had been careful, allowing her to do whatever she wanted without offering any advice. Even at his wedding, when she'd sobbed in his arms, he hadn't said anything about her actions.

"Yes," she said into the void.

"Yes what?" Franco asked, studying her.

She looked directly at him. "I want you to give me your opinion."

Franco took a deep breath. "I thought Madison was a good fit for Tank."

She halted, a visual flinch at Franco's brutally honesty. She didn't know how to respond to Franco's statement, and he didn't even try to explain himself. His gaze never wavered from hers. She swallowed audibly, maybe trying to hold down the doubts bubbling like bile in her stomach. Attempting to hide her questions from her father, she looked away from him. Grabbing her water bottle, more for something to do than to quench a thirst, she tried to resume her relaxed, laid-back pose.

"Just be careful," Franco warned.

He might have been about to say more, but the door behind him opened, and Molly came out. She walked to Franco and dropped a kiss on top of his head before turning to Amber. Amber stood, and they embraced warmly.

"I'm so glad you are here. Were the twins excited?" Molly stepped back and studied Amber. "Did I interrupt something?" she asked.

Amber loved Molly for many reasons, but one of them was that Molly was always cognizant of Franco's relationship with his daughter.

Molly looked back and forth between them. "And did you get a new car?" she asked Amber.

Her last question made both Amber and Franco laugh.

"No, it's a friend's."

"Friend? Right," Franco interjected sarcastically.

"What am I missing?" Molly asked.

Franco stood. He wrapped his arms around Molly and kissed her right below her ear. Amber watched the two of them with a sense of envy she didn't normally acknowledge. Franco murmured something only Molly could hear. Molly smiled. They were sickeningly in love.

"I'm going to check on the twins. Do you want something to drink?" Franco asked.

Molly glanced at her watch and then looked at Franco. "I'll take a beer."

He laughed. "You got it," he said as he made his way inside.

Molly dropped into the chair vacated by Franco and looked up at Amber. "Why don't you tell me what I interrupted?"

Amber sat and plopped her feet onto the table. Besides Nicky and Steele, Amber was close to two other people—Keira and Molly. So, it didn't seem weird to want to spill her guts to her father's wife. She knew she'd have to have this same conversation later tonight with Keira, and she didn't necessarily mind a practice run. Plus, Molly had a modicum of distance, whereas Keira tended to take Tank's actions more personally.

Amber didn't even need to take a deep breath to tell Molly. "I came to Atlanta with Tank. I dropped him off at his house. That's his car outside."

"Oh," Molly said.

"Oh?"

"Oh."

"That's all you've got?"

Molly sat back. Then, she sat forward. "I'm not really sure what to say. What do you mean, you came here with Tank? Isn't Tank here?"

"He's been in Alabama, at State, for the last four weeks. Training."

"Training?"

"Training."

"Okay, if anyone were listening to this conversation, they would think we were crazy," Molly observed.

That made Amber laugh and relax.

"So, why don't you tell me what the hell is going on?"

"Tank showed up at State couple of weeks ago." Amber got the opening statement out, but she wasn't really sure where to go from there. She searched for some explanation that would make sense, but she wasn't sure she could explain Tank's motivations because she didn't understand them herself.

"Are you sleeping with him?" Molly asked, tact apparently not required.

Heat crept up Amber's neck.

Molly sighed. "No direct answer needed." She looked away. "What about Madison?"

"Fuck," Amber whispered. "Why is everyone so frickin' worried about her?"

Molly's gaze returned to Amber. "Don't be stupid. I'm not worried about Madison. I am absolutely concerned about you."

"You don't need to be concerned about me. I'm fine. Tank is in town now. I know he won't be much longer. When he leaves, he leaves. No harm, no foul." When she said the words, she believed them.

Molly studied her, skepticism clearly etched in the lines of her face and the wary gaze she cast. "Do you really believe that?"

Amber thought about Molly's question. She hadn't been introspective about her actions with Tank. She knew what this was between them—nothing more than she'd let it be. It was easy to follow her impulses with him. She wasn't going to let herself love him again. He'd broken her trust long ago, and the breach, an irreparable mistake, couldn't be forgotten. She was smarter this time. But she couldn't deny the frayed tether still inexplicably binding them together. She wanted to ride this wave with him right now, but she knew she would be able to get off when the time came.

"Yes," she finally answered.

Molly cocked her head to the side, her tell when she was going to deliver her verdict. In another incarnation, Amber clearly saw Molly as an impartial judge, doling out wisdom with the bang of a gavel.

"Did you think that at the wedding?" Molly asked, throwing Amber off-kilter.

Amber stuttered to come up with a response. *The wedding.* She'd had no thoughts at the wedding. She'd been driven by primal need. "It's different. I was raw then, and it was the first time we'd seen each other in a long time. I was drunk. There are a hundred ways this is different."

Molly lifted her brow and leveled Amber with a look that called bullshit. Amber had a brief thought that the As would struggle to get anything over on either one of their parents.

"Look," Molly began, "you're asking me to believe that you can be rational about your feelings for this man. But I saw you in the aftermath of him tearing through your life like a tornado. All the debris left in his wake wasn't pretty. For that matter, I don't blame him or you. It's the combination of the two of you. And I understand, Amber. Because it's the way I am about Franco. I couldn't be casual about being involved with him either. The difference is that I'm honest with myself about what I feel and how completely stupid he can make me. I'm not going to try and talk you out of whatever it is you think you're doing. I'm just saying, you need to be real about it."

"I am being real about this," Amber stated indignantly.

She was mad for no specific reason. Molly's assessment of Tank and her was no great surprise.

Molly shrugged. "Great. Then, it shouldn't bother you when I tell you that I agree with Franco."

Amber's brow furrowed. "About what?"

"I thought Madison was perfect for Tank."

TWENTY-ONE

Tank's meeting with Hawk finished early. He had time to kill, so he found himself at the pool, drowning his restlessness with slicing strokes through the water. Impatiently, he waited for the time to pass. He and Amber had gotten up really early, and he'd expected to be tired, but he was oddly wired, some nervous energy coursing through him. He hadn't heard from Amber since she dropped him off at his town house earlier. He knew she'd soak up the time with her family, but thoughts of her had plagued him all day, and her radio silence made him impatient and edgy.

Their tangled web of relationships could be a hindrance and a help. Today, he figured it was an obstacle. All the people who'd lived through the destruction of his relationship with Amber were going to see them together. They would have an opinion, and he knew they weren't favorable.

What went through Franco's head when Amber told him she came to Atlanta with Tank?

He thought maybe Tilly was pulling for them, but he couldn't be sure. Tank's choices those years ago had driven a wedge between him and Tilly, too.

Tank heaved himself out of the pool, uncertainty dripping off him like the chlorinated water. He stood and yanked open his bag. Grabbing his phone, he texted Amber. It was getting late, and they needed to get ready to head to Tilly's. He waited for the little bubbles to appear. At the lack of a response, he stuffed the phone in his bag and threw his sweats on top of his long Speedo tights. He left the pool and moved through the rec center, on his way to his car. His sudden anger had him pulling open the door and throwing his body into the seat. He would have loved to be on an open straightaway, so he could gun the engine and let the speed burn off the tension still coiled in his muscles.

It was a short drive to his home, and as he pulled into the garage, he breathed a sigh of relief. The Range Rover sat in the bay next to where he parked. He sat back in the driver's seat and tried to will the stress to leave his body. She was there. He was finally able to name the fear that had been bothering him all day. He was afraid she was going to find a way to get away from him when he needed time to try to convince her to take a chance on him again.

He exited the car, pulling his bag from the back. The wet tights clung to his legs, and his damp sweatpants hung heavily from his hips. His T-shirt was stained with darks spots where the water clung to his skin before seeping into the fabric. He shook his head at his ridiculously hasty departure from the pool. He could have at least dried off, but he'd let an unnatural panic rule his actions.

Opening the entryway door, he left his stuff in the mudroom before entering the kitchen. He glanced around, looking for telltale signs of Amber. The keys to the Range Rover sat haphazardly on the counter, the tag from the rental agency sticking straight up in the air. Amber's purse and cell phone littered the space, and the trickle of relief now gushed in earnest. He placed his hands on the counter and hung his head.

"Fuck," he whispered.

"You okay?" he heard Amber say before he looked up and met her stare.

She stood at the bottom of the stairs, clothed in one of his T-shirts. Her hair was wet, and her face was scrubbed free of makeup. She held on to the railing that curved elegantly up the staircase.

"Yeah, I'm good," he said, recovering.

Her eyes perused him. "Swimming?"

He nodded, not really trusting himself to speak. He wanted to ask her if they were okay, if she'd changed her mind. Since he'd picked her up early this morning, uncertainty had been there between them. He wanted to dispel the doubt and insecurity.

"Yeah. Burning off some energy."

A mischievous glint made her eyes sparkle as she let them roam over him again. Her blatant examination made his blood pulse.

"I could have helped with that," she quipped.

Her hand dropped from the railing, and she took a predatory step in his direction. He watched her stalk toward him, and his body responded the way it always did when he was around her. Something in the way she looked at him felt off, but he couldn't convince his body to deny what she obviously wanted.

When she reached him, she wrapped a hand around the nape of his neck and pulled his head down. She kissed him lightly on the corner of his mouth while her other hand landed on his tightly restrained erection. After one caress, both of her hands moved to the waistband of his sweats. She pushed them down, her fingertips pointed to his toes. As his pants dropped, her hands roamed back up his thighs, over the swimming suit now adhered to his body.

"These look"—she swiped his length, squeezing—"hot and...really uncomfortable."

Her assessment made them both laugh.

Amber slid her hands around his hips and under the waistband. As she worked her hands down over his ass, there was an audible sucking sound as the spandex released its grip. They snickered. One hand ventured around to the front and gently pulled the band over his distended length. Then, she pushed him back against the counter. She followed the Speedo down to the floor and sank to her knees in front of him.

His eyes closed involuntarily as she kissed his leaking tip. His hands gripped the counter as she swallowed him down. He was lost in the warm, wet depths of her mouth. She'd never sucked him off before. It was an errant thought in his mind that was rapidly becoming blank, like her mouth was an eraser wiping away all the crazy, disheartening thoughts he'd worriedly written earlier in the day.

He had things he wanted to discuss with her, but, like dust, they scattered. He had nothing but what she was doing to him, how good she was making him feel. His hips began to cant without any knowledge of him asking them to move. He was lost, drowning.

He opened his eyes, wanting to have this visual memory for easy retrieval. His eyes found hers as they stared up at him, almost like she'd willed him to look at her. Their gazes locked as they both remembered the only other blow job between them, the one Amber walked in on, the one responsible for the end of their relationship. They both flinched, blinking. He wanted to beg her to replace that memory with this one. He wanted to tell her how much he loved her. His mouth opened, but the only sound was a groan of completion as he came.

Tank showered and got ready while Amber dried her hair and dressed. They'd barely spoken since Tank helped her off her knees in the kitchen. Instead of easing him, their encounter at the counter in his kitchen had put him even further on edge.

He left his room and headed upstairs to the loft. Turning on the TV, he focused his attention on *SportsCenter*. He pulled up Uber on his phone and put in a request. He was going to need more than one drink tonight. He wanted to talk to Amber, but as the minutes dragged on and the time to leave drew near, he figured she was avoiding it.

"Hey," she said, her voice pulling him from his thoughts.

He turned toward where she stood, waiting for him. She looked like the girl he had fallen in love with and some person he'd never met before, all at the same time. Gone was that crazy platinum-blonde hair, replaced by her dark-as-night black tresses. It still hit her shoulders, but her bangs were longer now. Her eyes were lined with black, emphasizing the slightly almond shape she inherited from her father. She sported jeans, but she wore a flowery purple shirt that was ultra feminine with its sheer overlay. She had on purple flats, and her jewelry perfectly accessorized her outfit. It was Amber but not. Like version 2.0 or something.

"You look great," he said, standing from the couch and making his way to her. He leaned down, and his lips met hers in a whisper of a kiss. "You ready?"

She took an audible breath. "I think so." She was uneasy, and for the first time, she wasn't trying to hide it from him.

He stepped closer to her and reached down with both of his hands, lacing them together with hers. Tank let his head rest on the top of hers. "Why are you nervous?" he asked.

He didn't think she'd answer because information exchange didn't seem to be in their wheelhouse today. But she surprised him.

"The thought of being with you around anyone feels weird."

He knew she wasn't trying to be insensitive, but her words cut just the same.

Needing to lighten the mood, he clutched his chest. "You're killing me, Smalls," he cried dramatically.

"*The Sandlot*," she said, "I love that movie."

His ploy worked. Amber relaxed as she graced him with her first genuine smile of the day. She held out her hand to him and he took it.

"You're silly," she said as she turned to the stairs. But he tugged her toward the elevator.

The car was waiting outside. Tank locked the door and handed Amber his keys. She dropped them in her purse, like they'd been there before. He opened the door and waited for her to slide in across the seat. Then, he followed her in, swallowing the space in between them. He reached over and grabbed Amber's hand. The tension between them eased as they settled into the ten-minute drive to where Tilly lived in Virginia-Highland.

"You excited to see Keira?" Tank asked.

He kept her hand in his, rubbing his thumb across hers, the ebb and flow further lessening the strain between them. It wasn't until she raised her head to meet his eyes that he realized she'd been intently studying their hands.

"I am. But, to be honest, I'm not all that excited about getting sucked into wedding plans. She probably should have chosen a better maid of honor. Planning meals for over one hundred people on the road? I'm your girl. Oohing and aahing over satin dresses? Not so much."

Tank chuckled. "You know, she probably already knows that about you."

Amber smirked. "I know."

"Plus, Madison loves that shit. She'll take care of all the stuff you hate."

Amber's whole body tensed beside him, and her hand, still clasped in his, curled into an impenetrable fist, breaking their connection. Without any purchase, Tank pulled his hand away.

"I didn't know Madison was in the wedding."

"I got that," Tank answered ruefully.

Amber turned toward him. "Are they really that close?"

"Yeah, they're pretty close," Tank responded. "Didn't you know they were friends?" He should have feigned conversational interest rather than shocked disbelief, but the words were out of his mouth before he could even think about it.

Rather than the indignant response he expected, Amber just sighed and looked away from him.

"Apparently not," she answered softly.

Tank studied her as he lamented his colossal misstep. She wasn't ready for him. He hadn't done enough to build up what was between them. He'd let one night of great sex convince him that he'd won her over. But, from the moment this trip had started earlier in the day, he'd been second-guessing himself and his decision to bring her to Atlanta. He needed to move slower. Just because he knew she was it for him didn't mean she was ready to admit and accept that he was it for her.

When the car pulled up in front of Tilly's brick bungalow, Amber threw the door open and scrambled out. Her back was to him when he alighted from the car, and he stepped up behind her, sliding his hands around her waist, pulling her back against him. He breathed her in, and the sheer fulfillment he experienced with Amber in his arms overwhelmed him. His grip tightened on her, his fingers exerting the magnitude of his want. Amber melted against him and dropped her head onto his chest. She tipped her head back and pressed a light kiss on his jaw.

"Come on," he murmured. He nudged her forward, allowing his hands to fall away.

They maneuvered up the walkway and climbed the three steps onto the porch. Amber knocked on the door.

"Keira's pictures of the house didn't really do it justice," she commented while they waited.

"Tilly said the guy he bought the house from did a really good job on the renovation."

"He did. But I can see he left some of the original stuff." She waved at the front door, stepping to the side to do her best Vanna White impression. "This door is definitely original."

Tank shrugged. "I have no idea. I bought a brand-new house for a reason."

Amber held her hands up. "I get it. No HGTV for you."

Tank would have responded, but the door opened.

Tilly's massive frame filled the space, and he smiled wide when he saw Tank. "What's up, man?" he asked as his hand shot out, pulling Tank in for a hug.

Tank returned the hug and then stepped back, reaching a hand out for Amber.

"I've brought a surprise for Keira," Tank explained as he tugged her in front of him.

"Sunshine!" Tilly exclaimed. He reached down and lifted her into a hug.

The warmth of his welcome allowed Tank a modicum of relief. In the few seconds he watched Tilly hugging Amber, Tank realized how incredibly stressed he had been about bringing her here and the reception they would receive from Tilly and Keira. He reveled in the release. He looked up, wanting to communicate that to Tilly.

But Tilly's gaze reflected anything but welcome. It was more warning. A warning Tank didn't get a chance to digest.

"You didn't let me know you were really coming." Tilly explained.

"Yeah, sorry about that. I thought it'd be fun to surprise Keira after all."

Tilly shook his head. "Will be," he confirmed. Then he rubbed his chin, his eyes shifting away. "But there's a...surprise for you too."

The foyer opened to a dining room on the right and a living room on the left. Tilly directed Amber through the dining room but stayed Tank with a hand on his arm.

Tank narrowed his eyes, understanding dawning. "Madison's here?" he murmured.

Before Amber could get clear, before Tilly could answer, Madison waltzed through the living room, directly into Tank's arms.

TWENTY-TWO

Tilly hadn't uttered any derivative of the word *sun* in Amber's presence in the last couple of years. So, when he called her Sunshine, her heart melted. He could have contracted an airplane to write his approval of her showing up on his doorstep with Tank, and it wouldn't have resonated as loudly as his greeting. When Madison slung her arms around Tank, Tilly stepped to Amber, throwing his arm around her shoulder, steadying her against the sight of Madison in Tank's embrace. He didn't need to bother.

"Where's Keira?" Amber asked as she kept moving, leaving Tank standing in the foyer.

"Come on. I'll take you to her."

"Okay. But, later, you need to give me a tour. I am loving this house, and I've only seen the front stoop."

He grinned big, the slash of white against his dark skin lighting him up. And, as always, a happy Tilly made her happy. Although their relationship had had an inauspicious beginning, on one of the worst nights of her life, Tilly Lace stabilized her as the avalanche of Tank Howard tumbled down around her.

"I knew you would like it," Tilly said as he guided her through the foyer and dining room.

Her glances were cursory, but the workmanship of the house showed in every line of molding and detail of the coffered ceilings and the chair rail in the dining room. Someone else might have renovated the house, but the bold slashes of color were all Keira. As much as she liked Tank's home, she loved this one more.

Tilly pulled up abruptly in the kitchen, and Amber stopped to avoid walking into him. He turned to her and put his index finger against his lips, which were tilted up at the corners. She nodded her head.

"Keira?"

"T."

"I've got a surprise for you."

"We have guests," she stage-whispered.

Amber stifled a giggle as Tilly laughed.

"Not that kind of surprise," he responded loudly. "But maybe later," he said as softly as his baritone voice would allow.

Amber quaked with suppressed laughter as Tilly grabbed her hand and pulled her forward into the kitchen. Keira sprang up from the barstool at the imposing marble kitchen counter and ran forward, almost knocking Amber to the floor with her enthusiastic hug. Tilly must have anticipated the overly exuberant display because he braced Amber.

"Oh my God. I can't believe you're here," Keira gushed as she continued to rock Amber back and forth in her embrace. Then, she stopped suddenly. "Wait." She pulled back but kept her hands locked on Amber's biceps, as if she were afraid Amber would vanish if she didn't hold on. "Why are you here? How are you here?" Keira's brain must have made some sort of connection because, all of a sudden, her mouth paused, wide open, like a gaping fish. "Shit."

Amber was tempted to let her stew but found she couldn't do it. "I came with Tank."

Keira's eyes closed. "Shit."

"You already said that," Amber reminded her with a fond smile.

"So, you already know Madison is here?"

"Yep."

Keira gulped audibly. "You came with Tank."

"I did."

Keira laughed. "Let me introduce you around. Then, I am going to grab us a couple of beers, and you are going to tell me what the hell is going on."

Keira released the death grip on Amber and turned back to the kitchen where a couple of other women flanked the counter. For the first time, Amber took note of the amount of people in the house. She followed Keira over to the group. In the midst of the introductions, Amber noticed Tank remained sequestered somewhere with Madison. She didn't want it to bother her, but she couldn't pretend. She graced Keira's friends with her halfhearted attention, and when Keira grabbed two unopened beers and pulled her through the house, she trailed behind her like a mindless lamb.

"There's a koi pond in the back of the property," Keira said as they made their way outside. "It's really cool, but I already told Tilly that it's gotta go before we have kids."

"Always planning ahead," Amber remarked.

Keira led her to a pair of benches and made her sit across from her. "I need to be able to see your face as we have this conversation," she explained.

Amber rolled her eyes.

"That's exactly why I need to be facing you." They both snickered. "It's so good to see you."

"You have no idea," Amber returned, reaching forward to briefly touch Keira's hand. "I really needed to see you and Tilly."

Keira perched on the edge of the bench and leaned forward, so there was hardly any space between her and Amber. Her giddiness slipped away as she stared Amber down and pronounced, "Start talking."

Amber huffed out a startled laugh before she told Keira everything—from the moment Tank had shown up on campus to their arrival at Tilly's house. Keira listened intently. Aside from some facial expressions during the story, Keira let her talk. As she spoke, some truths nestled in the spaces between her head and her heart, providing some much-needed clarity.

"So, I have to know," she demanded earnestly to Keira, "what's your take on Madison and Tank?"

Every doubt and question from the day, from the last couple of weeks, coalesced into this one all-important truth.

Keira sat back on the bench then, and the intensity of the conversation shifted. No longer did the burden of the story rest on Amber's shoulders. Twilight had fallen around them, and the sounds of the city crept in. As she waited for Keira's response, Amber noticed the constant flow of the water circulating in the koi pond. Laughter from the deck snagged her attention as she recognized the deep chuckle of Tilly and the familiar laugh of Tank. She smiled involuntarily.

Keira mimicked Amber's posture, resting her elbows on her knees. "Tank and Madison are really good friends who have…well, had sex. They trust each other, which made their sexual relationship convenient and easy. I don't think, at any point, either of them saw any future in what they were doing. Having said that, I think everyone who's been around them for the last year probably thinks they are perfect for each other because they see them together, and they notice the ease. I don't operate like that. The whole friends-with-benefits concept has always seemed too cold and unemotional so it's been difficult for me to understand their relationship. But I'm close to both of them individually, and I can tell you, neither one of them is in love with the other. They love each other, much like you love Nicky." Keira let her words sink in. Then, she tapped Amber's knee. "I'm not sure exactly what you are asking me. If you want to know if you are going to have to deal with Madison while you are with Tank, I'd have to answer yes."

Amber felt the weight of Keira's stare and turned to look at her.

"Can you handle that?" Keira asked.

"I don't know."

"Can you handle all that comes with being associated with Tank Howard?"

Amber chuckled. "Who the fuck knows?"

"So, what are you doing?"

Amber broke their staring contest. *Well, isn't that the question of the day? What am I doing?*

She was exploring the differences between the Tank from then and the Tank now. She was reveling in the feel of Tank's hands on her body. She was asking herself questions about her future for the first time in years. Today, she'd been worrying, but before she'd made the journey to Atlanta, she'd been enjoying. The possibility of failure was so much greater than the possibility of success. Together, they were the perfect storm—a convergence of forces that was both beautiful and frightening. To take a chance on Tank could bring her startling happiness, but she appreciated the likelihood of utter desolation, too. She didn't have any newfound wisdom to direct her, but she wouldn't have come this weekend if she wasn't willing to take a chance. The realization hit her hard. And, while a part of her wanted to gasp in surprise, most of her wanted to enjoy the release of her relief.

The silence must have stretched too long for Keira because she nudged Amber again, repeating her question, as if Amber might not have heard her the first time, "So, what are you doing?"

Amber nudged her back. "Not fighting it."

Keira laughed. "Okay then."

Amber stood. "I've monopolized the hostess enough."

"Yeah," Keira concurred. "Plus, our beers were empty some time ago."

Amber bent down and snagged the forgotten bottles from beneath both benches. "So, how's the wedding planning going?"

"Uh, can we table that one?" Keira said.

Amber heard the disheartening tone of Keira's voice and reached out to grab her hand. "Parents giving you a hard time?"

"Seriously, Amber, I can't do this right now."

Amber squeezed her hand before releasing it. "Anything you need, okay? If there's a downtime in my job, this is probably it, so just ask."

Keira pulled up, taking a deep breath, before moving to rejoin the party. Amber stopped in front of her, but Keira looked up, away from Amber's prying gaze. Amber watched as her best friend gathered herself, quelling the watering of her eyes with a few more deep breaths. When Keira had herself under control, she hugged Amber. Then, she turned and continued up the slate steps to the patio.

Amber dumped the bottles in the recycling can before she surveyed the people outside. Tank and Tilly stood with a group of men. Solely based on their size, Amber assumed they played football. Tank's back was to her, so she took a moment to study the men he was with, but her perusal was cut short when Tank turned, opening up space for her in his circle. She warmed at the sight of him and the gesture.

She didn't hesitate as she walked forward and slid under his extended left arm. He switched his beer from his left hand to his right after giving her the spot on his left, so her right side was tucked safely into his chest, allowing her left side to be more prevalent. He curled his arm around her, pulling her in close, and dropped a kiss on her head.

She noticed so many things about him in that moment.

He didn't break in conversation or make a big deal about her being there, like he'd done it a thousand times before and this was no different. Even though it was. He'd just announced to his friends whom he was with, and he couldn't have been more obvious about it if he'd screamed it from the rafters. And, without any words, he let her know he would wait for her signal to introduce her.

So, when she tilted her head up to look at him and he met her gaze, all her little doubts and fears slid away, like water through her hands. She leaned up and pressed a kiss on the underside of his jaw.

He dipped his head, his mouth finding her ear. "Hi," he whispered. The caress of his breath across her ear caused a full-body shiver that she managed to suppress. "It's good to see you," he continued.

She wanted to argue that she hadn't been gone that long, but then it hit her. He hadn't seen her all day. She'd been hiding in the shadows of her doubt, lurking in the dark corners of her fear. And he knew, when she'd crawled into the space he provided her, that something had changed. She smiled against his chest, and she knew he could feel it because he squeezed her shoulder.

The conversation around them had ceased. Maybe it was the natural seven-minute lull, or maybe the guys around them wanted an introduction. Tank gave her another kiss on the head and then turned to his friends. Amber straightened from the hug and looked up.

"This is Amber Johnson," he began. "Amber, this is Remy Stevens"—he pointed with his beer bottle and index finger—"Nick Baskins, Lucas Smith, Karlos Smith—no relation to Lucas"—everyone chuckled, the clarification apparently well-worn—"and you know Tilly."

Amber stepped forward and shook their hands. There were no surprised glances or questioning brows raised, and Amber briefly wondered if they already knew about her.

"In the interest of full-disclosure," Tank continued, "you won't ever hear me refer to them by their real names again." Everyone in the circle laughed. "Nick started off as Mad Dog, but it's since morphed into Doggy. Lucas has always been Lucky. Karlos is just Los. And Remy is Deuce."

"It's nice to meet you," Amber said.

Once she had their names, everything clicked in her brain. She knew their positions and stats, their strengths and weaknesses on the field. Lucky and Los were Tank's favorite receivers, Doggy was his center, and Deuce was one of the corners.

"Do I dare ask about your nickname?"

Tank laughed. "You already know my nickname is Tank."

But she was watching his teammates laugh with him and knew they didn't call him that. Her eyes narrowed.

"You look really familiar," Lucky said. "Do I know you?"

Amber looked around at the guys in the circle as they all studied her. The mention of Tank's nickname was forgotten as they tried to figure out who she was. Amber glanced up at Tank, and he merely raised his brow, telling her the ball was in her court.

"I probably remind you of your coach. Mike Franco is my dad."

There was a moment of shocked silence before they all started talking and laughing at once. Tank resettled Amber under his arm, tucked up tight against him, and he breathed deep, the exhalation reverberating against Amber's side. She smiled. She didn't have to see his expression to know he was happy.

They stayed like that, out on the deck, always touching, as the night went on. People came and went. Tank introduced her to everyone. She basked in his attention, aware of him always. He found every way to touch her, and by the time they were ready to leave, she couldn't wait to get to his house to have him alone.

It wasn't until they were in the car on the way home that Amber realized she hadn't seen Madison the rest of the night. The party wasn't that big, so either Madison avoided her, or she left.

Amber was going to let it go but found she couldn't. "Did Madison leave?"

"She did," Tank replied.

"Because of me?"

Tank was quiet, probably debating on what to tell her. Then, he cupped her face in both of his hands and lightly kissed her. He was touching her and intently gazing at her. "No," he finally said. He kissed her again, a gentle touch of his lips to hers. "Because of *us.*"

TWENTY-THREE

The opened roll-up door on the loft allowed the cool night air to drift over their panting naked bodies, and the sound of the occasional car driving by mixed with their calming breaths. Tank's hand moved leisurely up and down Amber's back, his constant need to touch her at play. Amber nuzzled her head up under his chin, intermittently sprinkling kisses on his chest, neck, and jaw.

If he could freeze a moment, bottle a feeling, sell an emotion, it would be this aftermath of their amazing connection, which they'd illustrated with every touch, word, and sigh of the last hour. He was reluctant to move or talk, for fear of their moment ending. The difference between how he felt right now and how he'd felt after she went down on him in the kitchen were worlds away. And it bothered him. So, rather than bask in the ease of the moment, he took a deep breath and stepped into the abyss of conversation.

"What was that about? Earlier, in the kitchen?" he asked. His survey of her back and hip never faltered as the words fell from his mouth.

But Amber tensed nonetheless, her body stiffening and her breath caught between an inhalation and exhalation. "I didn't know a blow job needed an explanation," she answered flippantly.

He held back his desire to chuckle. *Oh, Sunshine.*

When he didn't answer, she muttered, "You didn't need explanations in the past."

A combination of fury and shame hit him like a battering ram. He flipped them, so he loomed above her. Grabbing her hands, he pinned them over her head. The look on her face assured him that she knew he was mad, but he wasn't sure she could understand the flare of embarrassment and sense of disgrace he lived with whenever he thought of that night.

He didn't say anything, trying to collect his thoughts and not put any more distance between them. So, he dropped his head and kissed her, gently at first. Her surprise at his mouth on hers was evident in the gasp he swallowed. She capitulated immediately and kissed him back, attempting to deepen the contact. But Tank pulled away and then released her wrists, threading their fingers together. His head dipped, and he ran his lips along her scar, worshipping the damaged part of her that he barely noticed anymore.

Tank lifted his head and rolled off of her, swinging his legs over the side of the couch. He bent over, propping himself up by placing his elbows on his knees. He turned his head, gazing out into the night sky that was visible through the open loft door.

"I'm sorry," Amber said in a voice that penetrated the tension between them.

"It's fine," Tank responded. He just needed a minute to think about what he wanted to say to her, so he stood up. Reaching for his discarded pants, he put them on. "Time-out," he grunted, his back still facing her. He withdrew and wandered out to the deck. His thoughts were a wicked brew cooking in a cauldron of the past.

In that hotel room on the night he'd won the Heisman, she'd warned him that she wouldn't be able to forget. And maybe she shouldn't. Maybe he shouldn't try to forget either. He'd been a child who made a stupid decision. He wanted to think he'd be smarter now. But, twice today, that moment had haunted both of them.

How exactly do we move on?

Amber's hand landed on his back, warm against his rapidly cooling skin. Her arms encircled his body, and she clasped her hands and squeezed, both of them settling into the contact. Her lips landed between his shoulder blades, and she sucked on his skin with an open-mouthed kiss.

"I'm sorry," she murmured again. "So sorry."

"You have nothing to be sorry about," he sighed.

"I do." She kissed him again "The kitchen—it was all about distance. I needed some distance." Her insistence on keeping her mouth adhered to his skin muffled her words.

He wanted to understand her and how her brain worked. He needed a compass, a road map, a fucking GPS. She pressed closer to him, and he suddenly got it because he needed distance now. Her proximity scrambled his brain. He removed her hands from his stomach and turned around wide, making her take a step back. His gray button-down shirt draped on her frame, leaving enough of her skin exposed to tempt a saint. He scuttled away, his hands in a surrender position, and took a seat on one of the barstools that was several feet away from her.

She watched his mad dash with a look of confusion.

Cocking her head, she studied him. She stepped forward and then thought better of it. She shuffled to the side and leaned against the back of the outdoor sofa.

"I was with Franco and Molly all day. Their reactions to me showing up in your car were different than I'd thought."

Tank smirked. "I'm sure Franco is cleaning his shotgun as we speak."

Amber smiled. "Nah. Their biggest concern..." She paused. "That's probably not the right word. But they thought that you and Madison were the real deal. And I guess it's just hard for everyone to think you could switch gears so quickly." She looked away from him, but he waited because he knew there was more. "And, while I didn't want that to bother me, it did."

Tank's eyes narrowed. "I'll come back to Madison, but why didn't you want it to bother you?"

"Because I'm not ready for this to be more than just sex between us."

"Ah," Tank sighed as he tried to fight the hurt he experienced at her words. "Well, that explains the kitchen blow job."

He shook his head. *Really, how could he be hurt by their earlier sexual encounter?* It had been hot as hell, and there weren't many better places to be than in her mouth.

"Jesus, you act like you didn't get anything out of it. If you were so offended, why didn't you stop me?"

Tank barked out a laugh. "Stop you from blowing me? Really? Have you seen you and what you can do with your mouth?"

Amber's laughter split the night air, and the tension between them faded away. Tank watched her laughing with a weird sense of pride for putting such a carefree smile on her face. He wanted to see her like that all the time. He captured it in his mind, this piece of Amber he knew she rarely showed the world, and here, she let him get glimpses.

"Come here," he said gruffly.

She smirked at him. "You sure you can handle being close to me?" she teased.

He tried to fight the smile pulling at the corners of his mouth. She could be so cute sometimes.

"Oh, yeah," he answered, looking her up and down, devouring her. "I can handle it, you, anytime."

Like a fish caught on a line, he reeled her in. She sauntered toward him, the playful smile still lighting her face. She stepped right between his legs, and his hands immediately sought her hips, but he didn't pull her closer.

He kept some distance between them, so he could see her face while he said what he should have said from the beginning, "I need for you to listen to me." He didn't proceed, instead waiting.

When she understood what he wanted, she nodded her head.

"There was no switching gears. From the outside, maybe I can understand what Franco's saying. But all anyone has seen between Madison and me is friendship." He held up his hand at her attempted protest. "Yes, we had a sexual relationship. But it was just easier than being involved with anyone else. Madison has known I've been in love with you since she saw us stumble out of that damn closet at the wedding. She didn't require anything more from me. And maybe that makes me an asshole for taking what was offered, but I can assure you that Madison knew exactly what we had. It's why she left tonight. She doesn't want to mess this up for me. She understands how much I want this"—he waved his hand back and forth between them—"you." He ran his fingers along her jaw and kissed her quick. He pulled back from the kiss before the temptation to lose himself in her became too much to fight.

"So, what happened earlier..." He paused. He got stuck here because he knew he was going to sound like a whiny little boy, but he didn't want to keep anything from her.

She gave him a saucy smile.

"You can do that anytime you want," he stated.

She gave him what he wanted when she laughed at his declaration.

Then, he sobered. "But not like that. Not chasing something cheap between us because this is all so much more than sex."

She looked away. He panicked, scrambling, like he would in the pocket on a missed block. But, when her brown eyes locked back on him, it wasn't distance he saw. Questions and fears lurked there, things he could understand and hope to assuage. Immediately, he thought of their shared memory of his betrayal, and he knew another moment of indecision. He pulled her close, and when she came easily, relief coursed through him. His hands moved from her hips and up her back, and he cradled the nape of her neck with both of them, his thumbs teasing the skin along her jaw.

As much as it pained him, he needed to take this slow, build her trust. It was the only way.

"More than anything, I want you to trust me. But I know trust takes time—under normal circumstances. So, let's just take this slow and see where it goes."

It was so hard to put the brakes on what he wanted with her. But pushing too hard was like trying to come back from an injury too fast. It'd only lead to more pain and more time recovering. He didn't want to be sidelined forever. And he was more than willing to do the work, to build up all the muscles around the injury, to nurture it.

"I can do that," she agreed with something like a rueful smile.

"And I need for you to level with me. If I'm moving too fast or pushing too hard, you have to tell me." He continued to caress her jaw, but he never pulled his eyes from hers.

"I can do that, too."

"But, most importantly, if you really feel the need to blow me, I'll take one for the team. I promise."

They both laughed.

Then, abruptly, Amber dropped her head onto his shoulder, like a tired toddler cuddling up for the night. He held her, one hand digging into her hair and the other on her lower back. Her exhaustion showed in the lines of her body and the slow tug of her weight on his. He scooped her up. Carrying her, he made his way inside and shut the loft door with the push of a button. He walked to the elevator and waited for the door to open.

"Would you mind coming to brunch with a friend of mine?" Tank asked as he walked into the elevator.

She barely lifted her head from his shoulder when she responded, "Not at all."

Tank dropped a kiss on her jaw as the elevator dropped to the second floor. He took her to his bedroom and set her down on the bed. He sat next to her, and they smiled at each other, some new understanding blossoming between them.

"You mind stopping at my grandmother's near Kensington on the way home tomorrow?" she asked. It came out confident, but her eyes spoke of her nervousness.

"Did you just invite me to Sunday dinner? With Franco? And the As?"

She smiled sleepily. "You remember Sunday dinner?"

He wanted to say that he remembered everything, but he was done pushing for the night. "Yeah, I remember something about it."

"So, yes?"

"Of course," he said.

He stood up, and Amber reached out, grabbing his hand, stopping him from moving away. He looked at her questioningly.

"I have to ask you something, and I want you to be honest with me."

He almost sighed his frustration but stopped himself. "I will always tell you the truth."

"Truth was never a problem with us," she said. Before he could respond, she asked, "What's your nickname?"

He smiled and hated that he'd promised to answer. "You're going to laugh."

She shrugged but smiled.

"Five."

Her eyes narrowed. "I don't get it. It's not your number, so what's that about?"

This time, he did sigh. "It's short for Five-Star General."

She managed to just hold back her laughter. "Because?"

"I'm always barking out orders on the field."

And, when she laughed, he didn't care that it was at his expense. He just started the countdown until he could make her do it again.

TWENTY-FOUR

Tank pulled the Range Rover into a spot right along Piedmont Avenue, about fifty steps from The Flying Biscuit Café—their brunch destination. Amber tried not to roll her eyes at his luck. When she teased him about it, he merely smirked. Tank exited the car and was opening her door by the time she reached down to get her purse. Linking hands, they darted across the street and made their way inside.

"So, who are we meeting?" Amber asked as they weaved through the crowd of patrons waiting for a seat.

Tank turned to her and grinned, his dimples winking at her. "The minion."

Amber cocked her head, studying him, attempting to figure out what he was talking about. He'd pulled on a flat-billed Atlanta Braves hat right before they left the house. With his gray hoodie, jeans, and Nikes, he looked like an overdeveloped kid. He was absolutely adorable, and Amber hated that he rocked every look—the superstar athlete, the dressed up mentor, the casual Sunday brunchgoer. *Did any role look bad on him?*

"Minion?"

"Remember the guy who worked out with me my last year? Who drove your car to my place? The guy who prompted you to school me on the people you called minions?"

Amber laughed. At the time, she'd been a little arrogant and maybe a little self-righteous when she spouted off about what she considered the minions who hung around college football programs. "Wow! Do you have to remember everything?" she asked flippantly.

"Trust me when I say, I tried really hard to forget. I just never really mastered it."

Their eyes locked while the conversations and chaos around them faded to the background. The exchange had been light, but suddenly, everything about it was deep.

"Can I help you?" the hostess asked, breaking the intensity of their stare.

Amber and Tank turned to her. The girl looked back and forth between them, obviously aware she was interrupting a moment. Amber observed as the girl's eyes widened with recognition when her gaze rested on Tank. But she didn't say anything to alert anyone around them.

"We're meeting someone," Tank answered. He glanced around the restaurant.

"There's a guy around the corner, waiting for his party. Do you want to take a look?"

Tank nodded and reached again for Amber's hand. "Thanks," he said as he pulled Amber past the stand.

They made their way through the restaurant. The place was packed with people, and they had to shimmy to fit through some of the tighter areas.

"That's him," Tank commented. He pulled Amber in front of him and guided her to the table.

Ryan stood, greeting Tank with both warmth and familiarity. They embraced with the one-armed man hug, giving Amber an opportunity to study Ryan. If Tank hadn't explained who he was, Amber never would have made the connection. She'd seen him from about fifty yards away once and through the window of Tank's car another time. A slightly built dude, his obvious confidence gave him an appearance of being bigger. He had dark hair and light-blue eyes that seemed razor sharp even though they hadn't focused on her. He seemed to take everything in at once. And, when his gaze shifted her way, she knew he recognized her.

"Ryan Shields, this is Amber Johnson."

"Nice to meet you," Amber said, reaching out a hand while she noted a look that resembled satisfaction on Ryan's face.

"Nice to see you again, Amber," he returned.

Then, he laughed and winked at Tank. Tank flashed an embarrassed smile at his friend and shook his head.

"Shut up," Tank said softly to Ryan as they all sat down.

The waitress was on them immediately, and Amber wondered if the hostess had spread the word about a celebrity in their midst. They ordered coffee, but Amber needed to peruse the menu. As she did that, Ryan and Tank caught up on each other's lives. She heard bits and pieces of the conversation, enough to know that they kept in pretty good contact with each other. She thought perhaps she was being vetted and wasn't sure how she felt about that. The waitress delivered their coffee and took their orders.

Tank pulled Amber into the conversation as soon as the girl stepped away from their table. "Ryan's a scout for Tennessee. I thought it'd be cool for the two of you to meet."

Amber couldn't figure out Tank's angle, but she could tell he was up to something. Amber turned her attention to Ryan as Tank explained her intricate scouting system for young players. Ryan managed to split his attention between Amber and Tank, listening to Tank pontificate about what she did and shrewdly observing Amber's reaction to everything Tank was saying. Amber fought hard to mask her wonder at Tank's explanations. She didn't realize how much he'd gleaned from sitting in the film room with her on those two occasions. And, while his detailed delineation was impressive, the pride she heard in his voice caught her completely off guard.

Their food was delivered, and still, they talked about players. Amber relaxed into the conversation, comfortable with the company and the topic. Ryan's insightful questions about the youngest kids she'd scouted proved to her that he knew what he was talking about. So, when Tank redirected the topic, she didn't notice. Instead, she found herself sharing her opinions about the upcoming draft with Ryan, something she wouldn't have normally done because she wasn't quite as secure in her evaluation of NFL talent. They easily agreed on the first-round draft picks, and it wasn't until their plates were being cleared that she understood what was happening.

"It's not the top guys that are hard to pick out, right? I mean, everyone gets to see them week in and week out. It's the diamonds in the rough that set you apart as a scout and organization," she theorized.

"That's true," Ryan agreed. "Finding the guy who no one is looking for is often what makes good teams great."

Amber nodded along with his statement.

"So, who are your diamonds this year?" he slipped in.

"That's easy. Michael Chambers, Austin Redding, and Harriman Perry."

"Really? Why?" Ryan prompted.

"Chambers is undersized, for sure. But he's quick and smart. Check his stats. The number of tackles he's accumulated cannot be a fluke." She'd been sitting back in the chair, but now, she moved forward, placed her elbows on the freshly cleared table, and earnestly leaned in. "Redding is just patient. Here's a kid who didn't get an opportunity to start for three long years. Comes in as a senior, is the team captain, and picks up some key interceptions. He's a tad slow, but sometimes, you can overlook that. And Iman, physically, he's a beast. He's grown since he got to college, so he's six-five with a shocking wingspan, and his hands…" She gave an appreciative sigh. "His hands are sticky. You put that ball in his vicinity, and he's coming down with it."

Ryan smiled wide. Then, he looked at Tank and winked. "Should have known Franco's daughter would know what she was talking about."

Amber deliberately rammed her shoulder into Tank's arm as they strolled away from The Flying Biscuit Café and into Piedmont Park.

"You think you're so smart," she remarked, withholding the smile she wanted to share with him.

Tank grinned. "Nah. I was supposed to hook up with Ryan anyway. Just saw an opportunity."

"I had no idea you were such a manipulator."

Tank gasped, as if in horror. Feigning hurt, he said, "Manipulator?"

Amber rolled her eyes. Tank threw his arm around her shoulder, pulled her closer to him, and dropped a kiss on the top of her head.

His shoulders moved up and down in a shrug she could feel. "Who knows if it will do any good? But Ryan knows a lot of people. Thought it might be worth a shot since Iman's agent sucks."

Amber couldn't help the warmth seeping through her. He could have sent her flowers every day for a year, and it wouldn't have affected her as much as him trying to help Iman. She was always impressed with the way Tank treated his friends. Even on his worst days and his best, riding high on being Tank Howard, he was always a bit of a sweetheart to his boys. It was both endearing and annoying, as trying to maintain any type of objectivity kept getting churned up in his wake.

"Where are Tilly and Keira meeting us?"

"Over by the baseball fields."

They ambled along, not in any hurry. It was a perfect April day with a crisp blue sky, a light breeze, and a slight chill in the air. The park was busy with Sunday activities. They skirted a game of Ultimate Frisbee, weaved around intimate family picnics, and laughed at a little boy trying hard to ride a bike.

"Keira all right?" Tank asked suddenly, breaking the comfortable silence.

Amber slowed her pace to a crawl and thought about his question. "I don't think so. I'm worried actually."

"Did she say something last night?"

"No, and that's the problem. When I asked how things were going with her parents, she basically avoided it. So, I left it alone."

"What's up with that?" he asked, the frustration evident in his voice.

They stopped walking, and Tank's arm dropped from around her shoulder. He grabbed her hand, seemingly needing to touch her.

Amber looked away from him. "I know, right? It's 2017, people! They are really against the whole relationship. You'd think, after three years of Keira and Tilly being together, that her parents would have accepted it and moved on." She squeezed Tank's hand before her gaze found his again. "It's crazy. Her parents are like my parents, and to find out that they are racist bigots is really difficult to take in. How do I still respect them and love them when one of their fundamental beliefs is so different than mine and so abhorrent?"

Tank's eyes flashed with anger, and the moment between them got really heavy.

"Dictionary?" she quipped in an attempt to lighten things up.

Tank laughed. Then, he bent down, dug his shoulder into her hip, and lifted her off the ground. He smacked her lightly on the ass as her head cascaded down his back, landing right next to his butt. "You're such a little shit," he teased.

Then, he took off at a fast clip, over the remaining real estate between where they'd stopped and where they were supposed to meet Keira and Tilly. Amber laughed the whole way. Tank stopped abruptly. She pushed up by setting her hands on his ass and lifting her body. But, apparently, Tank had no intention of putting her down because his hand clamped down on her thigh, holding her in place.

"Whatcha got there?" she heard Tilly say.

"A smart girl with a smart mouth," Tank responded.

Amber could hear the laughter in his voice, and while she wanted to be annoyed by his response and his refusal to let her go, she found herself grinning instead. Feeling a little mischievous, she let her hands slide down and around his muscular butt. Tank inhaled sharply, but it didn't stop her from then pulling up his shirt and jacket and nipping the spot right above where his jeans hung on him. She did it hard enough to make him react, but she got nothing. So, she gently bit him again and then soothed the spot with an open-mouthed kiss. Tank's hands landed on her hips, and he pulled her down from his shoulder. He turned her around in front of him and pulled her back against him, his fingers squeezing her hips.

"You are so going to pay for that later," he whispered in her ear before releasing her so that she could hug their friends.

She practically ran to Tilly and threw her arms around him. "Hey!" she said enthusiastically. When he released her, she looked around for Keira. "Where's my girl?"

Tilly's smile dropped from his face, and everything about him looked defeated. "Sunday. Church with her parents."

"Oh," she answered, but she couldn't mask the confusion in her voice. "What's going on, Tilly?"

He turned and made his way to a picnic table, sitting heavily. Tank and Amber followed, taking seats across from him.

"I wish I had an answer for you. Her parents are being crazy, and she's getting sucked into it because of the wedding." He paused, but Amber knew he had more to say. "Before we decided to get married, she was all, 'Fuck them and their small-minded bullshit.' But, as soon as I asked her to marry me, she's been giving into them on everything. We should have just eloped," he finished on a sigh. Amber was about to respond when Tilly started talking again, "You know she's the only white girl I've ever dated?"

Tank and Amber said, "Really?" at the same time.

Tank nudged her with his leg under the table, but she resisted looking at him.

"I was never interested in white girls. Then, I met her, and it just didn't matter, ya know? You just love who you love."

Amber's eyes welled with tears, but she fought valiantly to hold it back. So many things about his statement hit her that she didn't like. Tilly sounded hopeless and resigned, not at all his jovial self. And, right at this moment, she didn't want to acknowledge that the heart wanted what it wanted, regardless of the obstacles and regrets.

She thought about Keira last night, and once again, she knew she'd been a shitty friend. Keira had needed her last night, and she'd been all about herself. She glanced over at Tank, who was studying Tilly.

Amber looked down at her watch. "Hey, if I'm going to go see the As, I probably need to leave now."

Tank turned to her, completely confused by her on-the-fly help-Tilly plan. "Okay," he said, his eyes narrowing.

She gave him a quick wink before she explained to Tilly, "Since we won't be able to make it to Nona's tonight, I'm going to see Franco, Molly, and the As one more time before we head out. We figured you could get Tank to me later. Does that work for you?"

"What were you going to do if Keira came?" Tilly asked, totally onto her.

"Bring her with me," she said, her tone calling into question his sanity.

He smiled knowingly. "Right, Sunshine."

Tank stood, and Amber followed.

He fished his keys out of his pocket, and when he handed them to her, he leaned down and said, "I owe you one."

She smiled at him, gave him a quick kiss, and took off, leaving the best friends alone.

TWENTY-FIVE

The sound of Amber's phone alarm blaring was a sort of rude punctuation mark at the end of her weekend. Bleary-eyed, Amber swiped her finger across the face of her phone and rolled over, burying her head in her pillow.

She vaguely remembered slowly coming awake in the car last night when Tank pulled into her driveway. He'd helped her inside, given her a chaste kiss, and then left. Her disappointment caused by his absence stayed buried in her chest, a dull little cut reminding her of the fleeting nature of her time with Tank over the weekend.

But she could hide under her covers for only so long. With an inelegant grunt, she threw the covers off and huffed it to the shower, hoping a long, busy day could stay all the insecurities and questions, like a last meal before a lethal injection.

When she pulled into her spot in the parking lot of Ayers less than an hour later, Amber was pleasantly surprised to find she'd beaten Whitey to the office. As petty as it seemed, a little smile curved her mouth. She'd take a victory, no matter how small.

Finding her way to her office, she mentally reviewed the week. With the spring game and visits, both official and unofficial, the coaches' clinic, and the game-day management, it promised to be busy. The eventful week spread out in front of her, a tasty buffet of oblivion and denial. She could work Tank Howard out of her system. *Really, what the hell had she been thinking when she took a trip to Tank La-La Land this weekend?* She could not allow herself to fall for him again.

Sitting at her desk, she turned on her computer and began organizing her tasks for the day. She tried like hell to get lost in her list, but everything was prepped and ready. Her first year, she'd experimented; her second year, she'd perfected. Now, she merely played all the parts she knew by heart. Sighing, she dropped her head to her desk.

She heard the outer door of the suite open and sat up, rolling her chair closer to the computer, pretending to be engrossed in something on the screen. She heard Nicky before she saw him, and the relief for the distraction of her friend was immediate. He bounded into her office, like Tigger in a grown man's body.

"What's up, celebrity?" he said jovially, his voice loud in the silence around her.

She smiled before his greeting penetrated. Her brow furrowed. "Celebrity?" she questioned.

"Why didn't ya tell me you and my man Tank were a thing?" He dropped into the chair in front of her desk. There was no censure in his voice. Rather, he looked a little fascinated with the turn of events.

Amber shook her head at him, still confused. "What are you talking about?"

"If you are gonna date this dude, you have to set up some Google Alerts."

"Nicky," she teased, "please tell me you don't have Google Alerts for Tank Howard." Her tone was light, playful, but her stomach seized with nerves.

Nicky actually blushed while Amber tried not to sputter with laughter.

"Seriously?" she asked.

"Just Google him and look at the images," Nicky said.

"No," she said indignantly. Amber had spent the last three years of her life not cyberstalking Tank. She refused to start now.

"Fine," Nicky agreed before pulling out his phone.

Before she could stop him or shield her eyes, he stood and pushed the phone in her face. She had a crazy flashback of the last time someone had shoved a phone in her face and asked her to look at a picture. When Franco discovered the picture of Tank and Amber in an intimate embrace, her little world had been rocked. Shaking off the memory, she reluctantly glanced at the picture in front of her. It was like a celebrity-sighting picture in a popular magazine, the one where anyone with a phone had caught a celebrity doing everyday things, like grocery shopping—or in Tank's case, dodging across a street on the way to brunch. Even with his Braves hat firmly in place, you could see who he was. His hand was clasped in Amber's, and they were both smiling, probably laughing at her comment about parking. The people in the photo enthralled her. Even though they weren't looking at each other, the connection between them was as obvious as the identical smiles on their faces. Thankfully, the picture was on her left side, so you couldn't see her scars.

She dragged her eyes away from the photo and looked up at Nicky with a shrug. "We were grabbing brunch."

"Uh-huh. Did you see the caption?"

Rolling her eyes, she responded with a firm, "No."

"I'll read it to ya. *Did the Shepard*—that's with a capital S—*lose its sheep?*" Nicky wiggled his eyebrows up and down. "Get it? Shepard? Sheep?" Then, he laughed.

And Amber wanted to throw up. Gathering herself, she shrugged again, going for nonchalance. "That's the stupidest caption I've ever heard."

"Yep. So stupid, it's funny." Nicky leaned back in his seat. "So, wanna talk about it?"

"No, I don't." She glanced at her computer, clicking on her calendar. "And I have a meeting in ten that I need to get ready for."

The joking, carefree Nicky disappeared right before her eyes, and she was suddenly gazing into the very focused eyes of her friend. Here, with that look, she could see how intimidating he must be on the field.

"I'm not sure what's going on with you two, but just be careful."

Touched by his concern but unwilling to acknowledge a need for it, she grabbed her tablet from her desk and stood. "There's no reason for you to worry about me." She waited for him to stand, and they walked together out of the office suite. "You know me well enough to know, I can handle Tank Howard," she quipped.

Maybe it was the confidence with which she delivered the line or her unflappable attitude about the picture, but she knew she'd played it right when the shroud of serious Nicky lifted.

"You can handle anything, tough girl," he said, holding out his fist.

She bumped fists with him, their hands pulling back and spreading, a well-choreographed explosion of a handshake. With a mutual wink at each other, they made their way to the war room. As they walked, Amber's mood lightened. Her momentary shock and anger over the picture faded. She was in her safe place, and her worries over Tank could be buried under the person she was when she entered her domain. Most of the coaches were already seated, and she took her place at Whitey's right side. Across from her, Steele sat, engrossed in a discussion with Stone, the defensive coordinator.

"Let's get started," Whitey bellowed over the chatter in the room. "I hope everyone enjoyed their weekend off."

There were some murmurs around the table, quietly spoken platitudes of thanks for a surprise break.

Whitey waved them off. "I want to review some film first. While most of you were lazing around this weekend, one member of our staff was working overtime to get some hands-on training with one of football's greats."

As everyone looked to the screen, a chuckle rumbled from somewhere in the room. Amber turned to the sound, and when she looked back, the picture Nicky had shoved in her face flashed on the screen. It was followed by a series of pictures of Tank throwing her over his shoulder and sprinting through the park. The whole room erupted in laughter, and Amber's face flooded with heat. Someone banged on the table in hilarity, and Nicky literally fell out of his chair. She'd never been so mortified.

She spun in her chair to glare at Whitey, but he had his head thrown back, obviously proud of his introduction to today's prank. She gave up and shook her head, laughing in spite of her total embarrassment. She'd worked with most of the men in this room for the last three years, so she made sure to show no fear. There was no way she could let them think she couldn't handle their ribbing, or they'd amp it up, like sharks circling blood in the water.

Whitey rolled his chair back up to the table, signaling an end to the joking. Like middle school boys exclaiming over a fart, it took some time for all the snickers to die down.

"All right, let's get back on task," Whitey announced. "Amber, walk us through the week, please."

She made quick announcements having learned her coaches had short attention spans for administrative bullshit. She reminded them that everything was scheduled into their phones, as were automated prompts so that they'd know exactly where to be. Then, she turned the meeting back over to Whitey, and they began to actually review film.

Amber tried to stay in it, to listen to what was happening around her, but her head was all over the place. Nicky's unexpected concern this morning, Tank's abandonment the night before, Keira's issue with her parents. She couldn't focus on any one thing in particular as thoughts flitted circuitously.

Her phone vibrated with a text. Looking down, she saw it was from Tank. Unlocking her phone, she clicked on her Messages app.

Tank: Can I see you later?

She didn't respond.

The Sunshine in her wanted to tell him he could have stayed with her last night. He'd basically unloaded her from the car and split. She was really confused but tired, too, so she slipped into bed and tried to forget how disappointed she was that he hadn't wanted to stay with her.

She contemplated answering him with a text that said, *I have to wash my hair.*

While she was figuring out how to respond, her phone vibrated with a second text.

Tank: We need to talk.

Little tentacles of unease danced up her spine. They did need to talk. She'd been hoping they were going to talk last night because he'd given her a lot to think about over the weekend. But, with Tank, everything had to happen on his timeline. Like him showing up here in his off-season—when it was convenient for him.

For the last three years, everything Amber had done, every action and decision, she'd handled on her own—when the time was right for her. She knew there would come a time, if she wanted to have what Franco and Molly had, when she'd have to learn to compromise and think about the needs and wants of someone other than herself. And she could admit, even as her ire began to prickle at Tank's text, that she had enjoyed herself this weekend.

Her life and Tank's were seamlessly sewn together in so many ways. They shared friends and interests. *But, even if she could forgive him everything and truly trust him, how would their lives come together?* She had a life and job here; he had a life and job there. And, although they were similar, their jobs made their lives completely incompatible.

She lifted her head from her phone, unsure of her next step. Steele sat across from her, studying her. Their gazes met, and his narrowed. He looked at her with some odd combination of pity and anger. Her phone buzzed again. Pulling her eyes away from Steele, she looked down, wondering what Tank had texted this time.

But the text was from Steele.

Lamarcus: He's going to hurt you again.

She almost laughed, wondering how long a text took to be delivered when you were sitting five feet away from the sender. She didn't have any assurances for Steele, and she didn't need to give him any. So far, Tank hadn't hurt her, but in the last couple of weeks, Steele had with his attitude and complete withdrawal from their friendship. So, she answered him as honestly as she could.

Amber: Maybe.

As she sent her text, another came in.

Tank: Please.

She could deny an arrogant Tank. She could deny a bossy Tank. But a pleading Tank? Yeah, there was no way she could deny him.

Amber: Working late. My house at 9.

TWENTY-SIX

Tank folded the last of his clothes and tucked them into his overflowing suitcase. No matter where he traveled or for what purpose, his travel bag always seemed overwhelmed on the way home, like his clothes had overindulged during the trip and put on some weight. He closed it and then pulled the second zipper open, providing him the additional room he needed to shut it.

He did a final lap around the house, looking for any evidence he'd been there. There were no abandoned chargers or papers strewed about. The place looked unlived-in and clean. He'd come here, knowing he had a limited amount of time, but the end date had come sooner than he expected, giving credence to the old adage, *Time flies when you're having fun.*

He wasn't sure where he'd be spending the night tonight, but he hoped it wasn't in this rental property. Grabbing the suitcase, he hauled it outside and put it in the back of the Range Rover.

He checked the time on his phone as he got into the car and smiled when he remembered Amber's snarky instructions to meet her at nine o'clock. He could almost picture her exasperated face and hear her aggravated sigh when she'd finally responded. He was minimally shocked she hadn't hit him with some stupid excuse about washing her hair or cleaning her carpets to get out of seeing him. He would have deserved it.

If he'd had a plan in mind for yesterday, it had veered completely off script. They were supposed to have brunch and hang out with their best friends, and then he was supposed to meet the whole Franco crew. He was pretty excited about the prospect.

Amber leaving him in the park so that he could console Tilly both annoyed and touched him. And Tilly needed it. Just an afternoon of hanging out, shooting pool, and watching basketball did wonders. Tilly didn't say much, but Tank could tell that his friend was worried.

When he'd finally met up with Amber again, the ride back was quiet. She was exhausted from entertaining the twins, and she'd had a couple of beers with Franco and Molly. So, after driving about ten miles, her head lolled against the window, and she was out. They needed to talk, but he didn't mind the reprieve.

Leaving her by herself last night hadn't been planned either. But he knew they needed to discuss his impending departure and what that meant. Letting her sleep alone was the ultimate sacrifice though. He didn't know how many opportunities he was going to get to share her bed, and ducking one of them was like passing on a winning lottery ticket.

He contemplated the coming conversation on his drive to her house. Hawk had forwarded the pictures of Tank and Amber that had already made the rounds with the Atlanta media. Hawk wanted a statement, but Tank wasn't ready for that. He didn't want to do anything to jinx the fragile bond he'd built with Amber. Probably, if it wasn't for his association with Madison, this might have flown under the radar.

He'd missed a call from her earlier, but he didn't want to talk to Madison until he'd worked through everything with Amber. His greatest worry now was that he had to get back to Atlanta. He knew it was the wrong time to leave when he and Amber were just getting started, but he could play hooky for only so long before the demands of his job, endorsements, and promotions kicked in.

He arrived at Amber's at precisely nine o'clock. Her front porch light was on, as was the light in the kitchen. He left his suitcase because there was no way he was going to misstep with presumption. He ambled around the front of the car and up the walkway, and then he knocked on the door. He didn't have to wait long for her to open the door for him.

He didn't even pause. He pulled her into his arms. There was no hesitation as her arms wrapped around his neck, and she relaxed into the embrace. Tank ran his hands up and down her back, memorizing the feel of her in his arms, a sensation he could hopefully retrieve later when he was alone in Atlanta.

She raised her mouth while tugging on his neck. He bent, and she placed her mouth on the lobe of his ear, biting gently. He suppressed a full-body shudder, losing the battle to not react to her. If they had sex tonight, it had to happen after all the cards were on the table. She kissed the spot right below his ear, a particularly sensitive point on his body that she was all-too familiar with, and he forgot all about his noble ideas. He slid his hands down her back and over her butt, and then he gripped her thighs before lifting her. He moved forward a couple of steps until her back was against the wall.

"Hi," he finally said before he planted small kisses against her lips, over her left jaw, and then to her right side, tracing the deep groove from the corner of her mouth and along the webbing.

Her mouth dropped open, and she gulped for air, like a fish out of water. Every muscle in her body went lax against him, and every muscle in his body hardened.

Amber gasped something that he couldn't quite make out because he was lost in this vortex of air, a wind tunnel amplifying every rough inhalation she dragged through her lungs.

She stiffened and said loudly, "Baa!"

Movement between them ceased. He kept his mouth open against her jaw because he was afraid to look up at her and acknowledge that he got the joke.

"Baa!" she repeated but this time with the perfect delivery of a wayward sheep.

Tank burst out laughing, his body shaking with mirth. He couldn't even form words, but he could move, so he hefted her from her perch on the wall and walked them to the living room. Still laughing, he sat on the couch and situated her on his lap. Their eyes met, hers sparkling with mischief.

"Guess you saw the picture," he managed to say, even as the urge to giggle—yes, giggle—remained.

"Oh, I saw the *pictures*," she concurred, emphasizing the plural form of the word. "In fact, the whole staff got to see the pictures. Whitey got a kick out of telling them that one of his staff members had gone above and beyond over the weekend to get some hands-on training from a football great."

Tank couldn't control the guffaw that exploded out of his mouth.

"Silly me," she continued, "I was looking around the room, trying to figure out who got the drop on me with impressing Whitey." She rolled her eyes. "Because I'm super-fucking competitive like that," she drolly reminded him.

He tried to control his hilarity, but it took several minutes and a plethora of comments from Amber like, "Glad you find this so funny," and "Go ahead, bruh. Get it all out."

When he finally used up his monthly allotment of laughter, he got serious quickly. "I am really sorry. Honestly, I had no idea there was anyone around to even take note of us." He wanted to add that it was hard to notice anything when he was around her, but he imagined she'd think he was playing her. "That's one of the reasons I texted you earlier. I was hoping to give you a heads-up."

"For some strange reason, Nicky set up Google Alerts on you, and he showed me the picture of us on the street."

He didn't think she was trying to make him feel worse, but her explanation made him feel like a complete ass. He should have been better prepared and should have at least given some thought to exposing her to the media. He wasn't a huge story in Atlanta, but every once in a while, on a slow news day, he could be a story in the off-season. Some infinitesimal part of him wondered if Madison had set him up, but he couldn't get his head around her selling him out like that.

"I am so sorry."

She shrugged. "Now, we know."

"Baa?" he teased. "Really?"

She smirked and then laughed. "What do you want from me? I had all day to come up with something."

Fuck, she makes me happy.

He didn't even want to broach the next topic because he was enjoying her response to everything. He wouldn't have predicted her approach to this. He'd figured she'd be so pissed at him and skittish because of it. That she could joke about it and laugh off her embarrassment in front of the whole staff kind of amazed him. She was so much less guarded than she had been at twenty-three. He loved her confidence. He wondered about all the things she'd experienced in their time apart that helped her grow into this strong, independent woman he had sitting on his lap.

He couldn't stop himself from dropping a quick kiss on her mouth. He reluctantly pulled back and set her away from him. Her sitting on his lap was distracting, to say the least.

"What's up?" she asked, all business. The tone of her question bothered him.

"Hawk wants me to make a statement."

"About us?"

This time, he heard skepticism in her voice.

"At least about the end of my relationship with Madison."

"Huh."

He narrowed his eyes. "What does *huh* mean?"

Her gaze darted away from him. "Ya know, you had me convinced that your relationship with Madison was no big deal."

"It wasn't," he insisted, not at all happy with where she seemed to be going with this.

"Well, if it wasn't, why does it need to be addressed? Why am I feeling like a home wrecker?"

He managed to hold back the rolling of his eyes. "Madison left the party the other night for us. She's a good friend. But she's also been my date for the last year, so those people who follow the celebrity-gossip scene think we're together."

"Yeah, I get all of that." Amber waved her hand, like she was pushing his words out of her way. "What does Madison say?"

"I haven't talked to her about it."

Amber looked at him and raised her brow. "Really?" she virtually scoffed.

Tank shook his head. "Yeah, really. I wanted to talk to you first."

"Look, Tank, your world is not my world. So, whatever you feel like you need to do, do it. But I don't want to be outed—or whatever you call it. So, say we are old friends or something, but I want my name kept out of it, and I don't want anyone to think we are together."

He was tempted to argue, but right now, it wasn't a fight he thought he could win, and he had a bigger battle ahead of him. "Fine. I'll talk to Madison, and I'll keep you in the loop on whatever we come up with."

"Perfect," she said flippantly.

He reached over on the couch and plucked her off the cushion he'd set her on only moments ago. "Is your leg okay?" he asked as she straddled him.

She nodded before she put her arms on his shoulders and looked down at him, meeting his eyes for the first time since they'd started talking about the pictures.

He took a fortifying breath. "I have to go back to Atlanta tomorrow."

She leaned away from him, barely restraining a slight flinch. "Okay," she said.

He could feel her withdrawal from him, and just as she made to stand and move away from him, his hands clamped down on her hips, holding her in place. "Don't do that," he said softly.

"Do what?"

"Pull away from me."

They stared at each other. His hands flexed on her hips, and her body relaxed marginally. He couldn't quite figure out what to say, so he stayed like he was with her weight on him, her hands cupping his neck, her dark brown eyes boring into him.

"It's shitty timing," he explained, "but I want to do this with you, try to do this."

Amber's eyes got wide and then narrowed as his words suddenly made sense to her, and she didn't like the meaning. "Long distance?"

He smiled briefly. "It's only two hours away," he said, pointing out the obvious.

"Yes, two hours. But we both have erratic schedules and hardly any corresponding time off."

He had anticipated this response, so he'd done his research. "Actually, May is pretty light for both of us, so I think we would be able to see each other at will. I know camps pick up for you in June, so I can do the traveling until we have mini camp. Then, July is downtime for you. And I know you have a mandatory couple of weeks off during that time. You can come to me, and we'll make it work. Then, we just take it day by day from there."

He was proud of himself for anticipating her concerns and giving her a concrete plan. He waited for her reaction, but she looked catatonic.

"Say something," he murmured. "Anything."

"We can cut bait right now. No harm, no foul."

"Uh, anything but that."

She considered, studying him, trying to discern his secrets. He wished she'd had mind-reading capabilities, so she could tap into his brain and know how completely serious he was about her.

"Let's say," she started slowly, like she was thinking up the words as she went, "we do that, and we're successful with the long distance from now until our seasons start." She paused.

Tank waited, and when she didn't continue, he prompted her, "We will be."

"Right. So, we're in this relationship, and then we both work twenty-four/seven for five months—actually, six for me—right through Signing Day. What then? We try to continue a relationship when we have no possibility of seeing each other? Skype and FaceTime go only so far."

"There are days, bye weeks, which are not at the same time, but I can come here during mine, and you can come to me during yours because we play at home on your bye weekend."

"Are you hearing yourself?" she asked incredulously.

"You are the only one who needs to hear me."

"You're fucking crazy," she said, laughing.

"Yeah, well, I happen to be fucking crazy about you."

TWENTY-SEVEN

MAY

Amber allowed herself another glance at the top right corner of her computer screen where the minutes of the day were moving at a glacial pace. In the amount of time it had taken this day to pass, Amber figured a mountain could have risen from beneath the shifting plates of the Earth's surface. She knew her sense of anticipation was the cause, but it had been a really long month since Tank slipped out of her bed on the morning he had to return to Atlanta. Much like Amber had predicted, two aborted trips over the last four weeks had left Skype as their only visual communication. She'd long since wished for teleportation as a superpower.

April had been busy with the spring game and then planning for the contact and evaluation periods for her coaches. But, now, with everyone on the road, she was at loose ends because work was slow. And she missed Tank. Mostly though, she blamed it on being bored and not having any distractions to take her mind off of who was waiting for her in Atlanta.

Aside from talking every night, Tank had started trying to stump her with football trivia. He kept a running total of their game. She was currently winning—by a lot.

Sometime during the month, Tank had discovered that he didn't know general facts about her, so she started getting what he called Amber Fun Facts texts.

What's your favorite color?

What's number five on your top ten movie list?

If you could hang out with any famous person for a day, past or present, who would it be?

She'd answered.

Green.

Remember the Titans.

Vince Lombardi.

If he'd asked her what about him surprised her the most, she would have said, *Your ability to be freaking adorable.*

She'd thought the distance and time apart would prove to him, and to her, that they couldn't make this work. Instead, she found herself wondering if there was a career out there that would challenge her but let her be close to him. And that scared the shit out of her.

At four forty-five, she couldn't hold back any longer. She shut down her computer and began organizing her desk so that, when she came in on Monday morning, she'd be ready to go. She heard voices in the outer office but ignored them.

She picked up her phone and sent Tank a quick text that she was getting on the road and hoped to be there for a late dinner. Making her way out of the office, her mind on the two-hour drive and Tank at the end of it, she wasn't prepared when Lamarcus Steele filled her doorway. His hands were braced on the jamb across the top of the door. With the muscles of his arms taut, he was a framed picture of masculine grace.

"Going somewhere?" he asked, sarcasm threaded through his words.

"What are you doing here? Shouldn't you be in South Florida?" She hoped to appear unflappable, but she wasn't sure she pulled it off. Even though she missed their easy friendship and relaxed interactions, she was impatient with his antagonistic attitude.

"Finished early and caught an earlier flight."

"Oh." She shrugged. She would love to push him out of the way and continue out the door, but he didn't seem to be moving. "I'm on my way out."

His eyes surveyed her, moving slowly down and then up. "Thanks for the information. I probably couldn't have figured that out on my own."

"Ya know, Steele, I'm pretty much over your shit. If you need something work-related, let me know, and I'll take care of it. But, otherwise..." She let the statement drift between them.

Steele studied her with a good degree of petulance before some unknown emotion flashed quickly. "Look, I'd rather be anywhere else, but Nicky needed me to do something for him."

"Do you need something from me to do it?"

He shook his head, his eyes never leaving her. "It has to do with you, but it's not work-related."

Amber almost growled her annoyance, but instead, she turned around. She dropped her purse at the side of the desk and then leaned against the front of it. Steele, seeming reluctant, finally let his hands fall and walked into her office. He dropped into one of the two chairs. His long legs almost touched hers until he shifted them to the side and crossed his left leg over his right knee.

He shook his head, and Amber got the feeling that he wished he were anywhere but in her office.

"I don't want to do this," he stated, confirming her thoughts.

She rolled her eyes. "Just get it over with."

"You know Nicky's weird obsession with Tank?"

She actually smiled because she did know. "Yeah," she said, almost laughing, "Google Alerts."

"Yeah," Steele concurred before he rubbed his hand over his face. He shifted in his seat, dropping his leg and sitting up straight. "So, he saw something this morning and wanted you to see it."

Amber's stomach conducted a little tuck-and-roll exercise before settling. "Let's see it."

All bravado, she held her hand out for what she presumed would be his phone with some crazy picture on it. He pushed up with his feet and reached back to grab his phone from his pocket.

He made quick work of the passcode and of finding the picture. Then, he placed the phone in her hand.

She kept her eyes trained on him, prolonging the inevitable. Then, she looked down. Tank was sitting at a table in some funky little café that had tiny two-top tables and mismatched wrought iron chairs. The colors in the restaurant reminded her of a carnival, all bright and jovial, some fantastical eclectic place she could see herself falling in love with. She noted all of that—the interior design, the furniture, the cute bar in the background—before she saw what her friends wanted her to see. A suit-clad Tank Howard leaning across a table, smirking at Madison. His jacket was strewed casually behind him, and his tie was flipped around, like he wanted to avoid splatter. Madison was laughing at something.

And Amber was fine.

She shrugged and held the phone out to him. "So, he's having lunch with a friend. Big deal."

"Yeah, big deal. That was my response."

"Really?" she said skeptically. "Your response to this picture was, *No big deal?* You expect me to believe that?"

"You've got this all under control, right?" He quirked his brow at her.

"I do."

"Right. So, no big deal. You know, except for the hand-holding."

She wanted to ignore him. But, instead, she focused on the picture again. Just like before, she looked at everything but what she needed to see. Then, she zeroed in on the hand-holding. Under the table, Tank's hand was intertwined with Madison's, casually resting on her knee. It looked intimate. It looked like two lovers enjoying lunch. It looked like something far more serious than friends.

But whatever.

She shrugged with feigned indifference and dropped Steele's phone in his waiting hand.

"Thanks," she said shortly. "Is that all? Because I gotta get on the road."

Steele shook his head, like a disappointed parent who knew his child was making the wrong decision but was going to let her learn her lesson the hard way. "Un-fucking-believable. Seriously? You're still going to go see him this weekend?"

"That's not really any of your business."

"God, he has both of you fooled. I don't get it. Why are you setting yourself up to get hurt?"

"Again, that stopped being your business when you kicked me out of our friendship."

"I didn't kick you out. I just couldn't stand to watch you make the same mistake. And, this time, someone else is going to get hurt, too."

"They aren't together." Her voice rose, anger vibrating through her. It wasn't even the picture. It was Steele.

"They were together at the engagement party. I know they fucked when they got home."

"Why do you even know that?" she asked, cringing. "Aren't you guys a little too old to be sharing locker-room stories about your conquests?"

Steele shook his head. "For two smart women, you and Madison are fucking stupid."

"You seem awfully concerned about Madison. You barely even know her."

"Are you kidding me? Who do you think I've hung out with every time I've been with Tank over the last two years? If you want to pretend like you're not going to have to deal with them as a couple, you're delusional. She might be accepting of you two being together, but they are a package deal. There's no way Madison is out of Tank's life. Just like him to get to have his cake and eat her—I mean, it, too."

He smirked, like he'd made some funny joke. It was an action she'd seen him make thousands of times when they shared jokes and sarcastic retorts. It was a look she was so familiar with, like an old, comfortable blanket you could wrap up in every night.

Hurt sliced through her.

"You know," Amber said, cocking her head and studying him, "for claiming to be his best friend, you sure seem to resent the hell out of him."

It was a low blow but a perfect strike because Steele's whole demeanor changed. The accusation pissed him off, and she could see it.

"Yeah, well, he's living the life I was supposed to have," he sneered.

His reaction exploded between them like a bomb, shrapnel carving up their relationship, leaving bloody pieces of their friendship strewed about the room. When the dust and ash cleared and they were able to take stock of the atmosphere between them, neither one of them could make eye contact. The loathing and resentment of his statement shocked her. The loathing and resentment in his statement seemed to have set him free.

He hauled his massive frame out of the chair and turned, leaving her with all his doubts, presumptions, and truths. The cloak of reality sat heavily upon her.

TWENTY-EIGHT

Tank rubbed his sweaty palms down his jean-clad thighs as he waited impatiently in his kitchen, trying to figure out what to do with the flowers he'd bought. He pulled out a vase and then pushed it aside, so he could hand them to Amber when she walked in the door. But he looked like a pussy, standing in his kitchen, with a big bouquet of flowers, so he set them down again and wiped his hands on his pants.

Fuck! He couldn't believe how nervous he was.

He had the whole seduction plan worked out. His overwhelming need to provide Amber with a perfect weekend had driven him insane. Everything that would occur over the next forty-eight hours needed to be perfect. He knew he couldn't sustain the illusion, but this first time, like a used-car salesman, he wanted to sell her on a car in less than mint condition.

The pressure.

Amber was supposed to arrive at any moment.

When he'd left her in bed all those weeks ago, he'd essentially skipped out of her room because she was going to give their relationship a go. The hopefulness sustained him for the first two weeks they were apart. Then, their first rendezvous got canceled.

And he thought, *No big deal.*

But, when two weeks had slipped into three and then fallen into four, he'd begun to curse Skype. Skype, he decided, was a big fucking tease. He'd convinced himself that being able to see her daily would make the distance thing easier. But, really, it made it that much harder. Yeah, he saw her, looking her best and her worst, on good days and bad. But he couldn't do a damn thing about it. When she smiled at him, excited about something, he couldn't kiss her senseless and run his fingers along that perfectly imperfect jaw of hers. He could only meet her smile with one of his own. And, on the couple of days when she was in a crappy mood, instead of being able to help her forget, he got to sit on the other side of a computer screen and remind her how shitty this deal was. Staring at her across an Internet connection really fucking sucked. But he refused to tell her that. There was no way he was providing Sunshine with anything other than fairies and rainbows.

When he thought of the future, he only did it in vague outlines because, if he looked too hard or really thought about how this would work during the fall, he would lose some of his optimism. The off-season was peewee football. His body didn't hurt like he was a ninety-year-old man. His head didn't feel like exploding because of the inevitable mistakes he'd made. He wasn't exhausted. He didn't get on a plane biweekly, traveling to different cities. The ups and downs were little ripples on a lake rather than the ten-foot surf of a hurricane. If he were struggling now with the realities of their relationship, he'd drive himself crazy during the season.

So, he buried it with flowers, good wine, and amazing take-out food. And he continued to wipe his sweaty palms on his jeans because he couldn't let those fears surface, and he couldn't share them with Amber. He had to be cool and unflustered.

He surveyed the kitchen one more time. He frowned when he noted the time. Amber should have already arrived. He picked up his phone and called her. The direct path to voice mail concerned him, but without any means to get in touch with her, he tried to relax.

Resigned, he grabbed a beer from the fridge and headed up to his rooftop. From his perch up there, he could see the street in both directions. Rather than stand in the kitchen, worrying over how to give a girl flowers, he stood against the railing, looking out over the city. She still hadn't arrived by the time he finished his beer, and his concern amplified. He was reluctant to worry Franco or Keira, so he waited, really impatiently, getting more frantic as the time wore on.

When he saw Amber's Audi racing down the hill to the left of his town house, he turned abruptly and jumped on the elevator. He wanted to be waiting when she got here, so he could shake her or something like that.

Tank opened the garage door. The casual pose he struck belied the anger, annoyance, and relief he was fighting.

Amber pulled into the bay and shut off the car. Tank's ire built as he watched her blasé exit. His worry had morphed into some crazy ire he wasn't used to experiencing.

"Hey," she said as she shut the door.

He studied her from his post. She didn't seem particularly excited to see him. She ducked his gaze, finding all sorts of interesting things on the floor and in her car as she shuffled around to the tailgate and pulled it open. His vision of a movie scene where she hurdled into his arms as soon as she saw him disappeared like a rabbit in a magician's hat. Instead of excited, she looked defiant, like she had a reason to be mad.

"Thought you'd be here sooner," he said. He tried for detached and uninterested, merely an observant boyfriend.

She glanced at him through the back windowpane of her small SUV. "Sorry," she muttered, the word muffled in the space between them. "Something came up at work."

He waited until she had her bag and then felt like an ass for not helping her with it. Ambling toward her, he grabbed the straps from her dangling hand. He dropped the bag at their feet and reached up to cup her chin with both hands. He stared into the chocolate depths of her eyes. His thumbs stroked along the line of her jaw. Tank's hands curved around, trailing lazy touches against her nape before delving into her hair.

He tugged her head back before he dropped his mouth onto hers. He tested her response with a touch and a retreat. Her mouth followed his, and when they met the second time, he pressed a little harder. Her lips parted on a sigh, and her tongue tentatively licked against his mouth, begging for more. He didn't hesitate to open up for her. The kiss, a familiar dance, grew more urgent as their bodies craned to get closer. Increasingly desperate and needy, they clung to each other.

Tank's hands couldn't decide what they wanted to touch. They roamed with a mind of their own, untangling from her hair, following the line of her spine, caressing the curve of her ass. His hands were relentless creatures, ever so needy and greedy as hell.

His fingers were agents of touch, her delicate curves their prey. While his mouth plundered hers, his hands pillaged her body.

Regretfully, he pulled away from her mouth. They both gasped, like they'd just realized they needed air to breathe. Tank's hands never stopped perusing her body, but he took a moment to look her over, to lap up the sight of her.

"It's so good to feel you," he murmured, their eyes locked on each other.

She shuddered against him, his wayward fingers finding the outline of her breast and ghosting over it, even as he waited for her to say something. Her heavy-lidded eyes shut.

"You have no idea," she muttered.

He dropped his head and nuzzled his mouth up against the hinge of her jaw. "Oh, I have an idea." He continued to eat at the skin below her ear. "I have a number of ideas."

"Take me inside," she said.

He scooped her up and carried her into the house. He didn't stop to pick up the flowers he'd worried about all day. Instead, he sprinted up the stairs and burst into his bedroom. He gently placed her in the center of his bed.

Leaning over her, his hands fisted by her side. She stared up at him, desire infusing the air between them. Having her in his house, in his bed was everything he wanted and needed.

"I'm getting rid of these clothes," he said.

She nodded. "Yours, too."

He unbuttoned and unzipped her jeans with deftness. As he pulled them down her legs, his gaze gobbled her up, and he dropped tiny kisses on her navel, the top of her thigh, her knee, her ankle. She squirmed against him, eager for him. Her panties followed. Impatiently, she sat up and pulled her shirt over her head, whipping it across the bed so that it landed on the edge, dangling daintily.

Tank smiled wickedly, enjoying the mutual shedding of their clothes. They were naked in record time.

He looked her over, thirsty for the sight of her. "Ah, Sunny, you're killing me."

His fingers then followed his line of sight, touching all the places he'd visually caressed. Down from the top of her head, his two hands drifted lazily—framing her face, sweeping down her neck and across her collarbone, circling her belly button and finally coming to rest in between her thighs.

Staring into her fathomless brown eyes, he murmured, "So ready for me."

"Always."

He wanted to worship and savor her, to somehow communicate the longing

He smiled as he climbed up her body. But it was short-lived as he slid inside her. He could only drop his head into the crook of her neck and breathe deep. Amber's legs wrapped around him, and her hands clasped his back, pulling him closer. They moved together—slowly yet desperately, as he buried four weeks of pent-up lust and longing inside her perfect body.

He wanted to go deeper, slide so fully into her that she'd take him with her when she left. Even wrapped up in her, he couldn't get far enough in. He pulled out of her arms and untangled her legs from his waist. Going up onto his knees, he grabbed her hips and pulled her up to meet his thrust.

"Oh God!" she moaned.

He chased their release, pounding into her, taking in her flushed body, her half-slit eyes. He saw it all, and he wanted more. He wanted all of her. He couldn't hold on much longer. He wanted to run his tongue along her jaw, but he couldn't get to it from this position.

He gripped her waist again and drove in hard. Two thrusts were all it took for them to crash over the edge. Tank lowered her hips and then collapsed onto her. He stayed there, allowing them both to catch their breaths.

When his heart stopped attempting to beat out of his chest and the air in his lungs came out in a slow, even rhythm, he rolled, taking Amber with him. She immediately snuggled into her spot underneath his chin.

"Hi," he murmured, kissing her head and running his hands up and down her back.

"Hi yourself."

He could hear the smile in her voice.

"You were late," he remarked.

She tensed slightly. "Yeah, work."

He needed diplomacy for his next sentence. "Maybe you could let me know if you are going to be late. I was worried."

He waited for her to give him shit, but she merely sighed, "Yeah."

"Is everything okay?" he asked.

She didn't say anything for a bit. The sun had set while they made love, and the color of twilight filled his room. He got still in the silence, trying to figure out what the hesitation was about.

He shifted out from under her, maneuvering her so that he could look down on her and see her face. "Hey," he nudged, "you okay?"

Amber looked up at him, her eyes searching his for something. She reached up, her hand curving around the back of his neck, her blunt nails tracing some indefinable pattern. She drew his head down and lightly brushed her lips across his. "Now, everything is perfect."

TWENTY-NINE

Amber perched on the edge of the chair, her chin resting on her fist, as she studied Keira across the bistro table. Keira looked stressed and tired, the dark circles staining the skin below her eyes, a sign of strain. Worry had skirted Amber's consciousness since her last trip to Atlanta. But she needed to have this conversation face-to-face, so she'd waited, allowing Keira's vague answers and convenient missed calls to permeate their friendship over the last couple of weeks. But, now, she could ask the nagging questions that had been circulating in her head like gnats on a humid summer day.

The waitress dropped their plates in front of them, and Amber gave Keira time to pour ketchup onto her burger, arrange her fries just so, and daintily take her first bite of her lunch before she allowed herself to start the inquisition.

"You never told me why you ditched me the last time I was in town," Amber began.

She reached over and plucked a fry from Keira's plate. Keira smacked her hand and then reached for her lemonade. She took a sip, set the glass down, and began toying with her food.

"Yeah, I just decided to go to church with my parents. Kind of a last-minute thing." Keira seemed to be concentrating hard on rearranging her fries.

"Oh. Have you been doing that often in the last couple of years?"

Keira sighed. "You know I haven't." She spun her plate around, her preoccupation with her food continuing to keep her eyes cast down.

"Huh."

Keira finally looked up. "You are not subtle," she remarked drolly.

Amber shrugged. "I wasn't trying to be."

"Right."

"Do you want to talk about what's going on with your parents?"

Amber had always been the reluctant talker in their relationship. She got it—the need to hold some things close to the chest. But she also understood the value of being able to share the burden. It was a lesson she'd learned too late—too late to save herself a lot of misery. She didn't want Keira to experience that sense of regret and the persistent what-ifs that tended to knock around in your brain when you had misgivings about your actions.

Keira didn't answer her.

Amber was navigating unfamiliar ground. "I know I'm not one to talk," she ventured, "but I think I've learned the value of having someone listen when you can't quite figure things out for yourself."

"You're going to think I'm crazy. Or maybe a coward. I'm not sure which." Keira looked beyond her, as if her eyes connecting with Amber's would give something away.

"Try me," Amber suggested.

Keira took a deep breath. "I didn't think it would matter. Ya know, the last three years, I thought my parents had come around. I mean, I knew they weren't loving the idea of me and Tilly, but I thought they had come to at least understand that we meant something to each other. Ya know?"

Amber couldn't tell if it was a rhetorical question or if Keira was expecting a response, so she nodded her head and mumbled, "Uh-huh."

"I thought they knew it would happen. That Tilly and I would want to get married. But they were shocked. I wish I could explain the looks on their faces when we went to the house to tell them. It was like I'd told them I was a drug runner and had just been arrested and was going to jail for the rest of my life. Their faces...they just looked...horrified."

"I'm so sorry," Amber whispered. She already knew this part of the story, but she refused to interrupt.

"And their reaction appalled Tilly. He was so hurt because he'd thought they'd accepted him." Keira reached over and drained her drink. "Anyway, since then, things have been pretty awful. They don't want Tilly paying for the wedding. They insist on paying for it, but they only want to pay for it if we do it their way. Part of me wants to elope. Part of me wants to just give in. Part of me wants to call the whole thing off."

Amber's eyes got wide, and she tried to hide her dismay by grabbing her own drink.

"This is where I get crazy. Are we always going to have to deal with this kind of narrow-minded bullshit? Yes, he's black, and I'm white. What the fuck does it matter?" Her voice got higher, and she waved her hand around like she was batting away flies. "Except, all of a sudden, it does matter. I look for people's reactions to us. I anticipate snide looks and ignorance. I feel defiant all the time. And I think, *What about our kids? What will they have to experience? Who is going to judge them because they are interracial?* It's been driving me insane. I just..." She looked away, out the front window of the restaurant. "I just don't know if I can live like this." Turning back to Amber, she said, "I think I might call off the wedding."

Keira could have run a knife through Amber's heart, and Amber wouldn't have been as shocked as she was at Keira's pronouncement.

She slowly shook her head, as if she could scatter Keira's words and make the idea disperse. "You can't mean that," she blurted.

Keira smiled sadly. "I can't do this to Tilly. I can't walk around, second-guessing us because of what other people think. But that's what I do now. It's not fair to him and—shit!" Tears flooded her eyes and spilled over, cascading down her cheeks.

Amber pulled her napkin out of her lap and held it out to Keira. Keira snatched it away and wiped it over her nose and under her eyes, pressing hard to stanch the flow. Amber sat uncomfortably in her chair while Keira worked to get her emotions under control.

Amber had wanted to talk to Keira, but she didn't want to know this. She didn't want to have to think of Tilly and how heartbroken he would be if she left him. Keira was right about one thing. Amber did think she was a coward.

"Have you talked to Tilly about this?" Amber inquired.

Keira shook her head.

"Don't you think you owe him that?"

Keira shrugged. Then, her indifference seemed to hit her, and she quickly said, "Yeah, of course."

"Ya know, Tank unilaterally decided the end of our relationship."

Keira looked indignant. "This is hardly the same. I'm not going to go out and cheat on Tilly."

"No, you're not. You're just going to rip his heart out because you are dealing with being a minority all of a sudden."

Keira's mouth slackened.

"So, people look at you because you're different. So the fuck what? You've blended in your whole life. You grew up in a town that was basically settled by your ancestors, and everyone around you looked the same. Think about how Tilly has felt every time he walks into your house. But you know what? He's stayed, and he loves you even though your parents are complete assholes. And, now, you're thinking about walking away from him because people might judge you for being with a black man? Seriously?"

"That's not what I said, Amber!" Keira whispered furiously.

Amber knew Keira was seething.

"No, it's not what you said. But isn't that what you meant? You've just decided to walk away from him without even telling him how you are feeling and what you are suddenly experiencing." Amber took a deep breath. "I'm not a minority, and I can't even imagine what it feels like to always be one of just a few. But I know what it's like to be judged because of how you look. And it takes a thick skin. It's okay if you don't have one yet. But you'd better fucking grow one. Because you owe that to the man you fell in love with."

"Says the girl who is the master of denial."

Amber cocked a brow. "This powwow isn't about me."

"Well, maybe it should be."

"You're deferring a lot. What are you really scared of?"

Keira didn't speak for a long time, and Amber was content to allow her to come to terms with the real issue.

Keira ran her hands through her hair in frustration and helplessness. "I'm afraid that our marriage can't survive without the support of my family."

"I get that. So would Tilly." Amber leaned back in her chair. "I am absolutely the last person qualified to give you advice. But I just think you are underestimating your fiancé and yourself. I get that you're scared and torn. But none of this mattered before you got engaged. So, I think you need to figure out why it's such an issue now." She glanced down at her phone. "And I hate to get the last word in"—she smiled, trying to take some of the bite out of their interaction—"but I've gotta go. I'm supposed to meet Tank at Franco's in twenty minutes."

Keira's eyebrows shot up, and for the first time since their lunch began, she looked like herself. "Well, that ought to be fun."

"I know, right?"

"How's it going?"

Amber didn't even try to fight the involuntary curve of her lips at the thought of Tank. She shrugged though, reluctant to show her excitement. "It's good. But that doesn't necessarily mean I'm looking forward to hanging out with the whole family today."

"So, why are you?" Keira looked too giddy, enjoying turning the tables and asking some hard questions of her own.

Amber pondered her answer. "Well, as much as I would like to spend the whole entire weekend in Tank's bed, it seems safer to be around other people."

"Hmm, that's an interesting take."

"Yeah, well, full doses of Tank Howard can be deadly."

"How's that?"

"It's easy to get caught up in the fantasy of him. The reality is pretty harsh, so I've found myself limiting our one-on-one interactions. Lunch with you, dinner with Franco and the kids. Perspective."

"Or you know, seeing if he fits into your life."

"There's no fitting in. My life isn't here. And his has to be."

"Talk about denial."

Amber laughed. "No denial. I am being straight-up honest with myself about this whole thing."

"Okay," Keira said simply. There were other words, but she held them back, and Amber was grateful.

She didn't want to talk to Keira about all the doubts Steele had managed to stir up yesterday. Keira wasn't exactly a Lamarcus Steele fan—mostly because of Tilly. Suddenly, Tilly's weird distrust of Steele seemed to make some sense to Amber, and she didn't like the feeling. She wanted to think the guy she'd been so close with over the last couple of years was just in a weird place and that Tilly was merely insecure over his place in Tank's pecking order of friends. But that assessment didn't sit well with her either.

"Seriously, I have to get on the road," Amber said before she dropped money on the table and turned toward the door. But the devil inside her reared its head, and she found herself moving back to where Keira remained. "Hey, have you seen Madison?"

A self-satisfied smirk settled on Keira's face. Then, she shook her head. "She's been out of pocket. She's been working on some report."

"Oh. Okay. I'll talk to you tomorrow." She started for the exit again.

"Tilly and I are busy tomorrow, so don't call, asking us to meet you for brunch or dinner or anything. And I think all of Tank's boys are otherwise engaged, too."

There was a mischievous twinkle in her friend's eye, and even though Amber was the reason for it, she was thankful to see it.

"You're an evil bitch," Amber said with a wide smile. "Love you anyway."

THIRTY

The drive to Franco and Molly's house seemed both infinite and brief. As much as Amber wanted to deny the little pockets of excitement at the thought of seeing Tank, it was hard to do in the confines of her head. Sometimes, you just had to go with it because the constant battle to remain disengaged was exhausting.

Her meeting with Steele yesterday had been disheartening for a number of reasons. Either one of her closest friends was lying to her and manipulating her or Tank was being less than honest about his interactions with Madison. Not much chance of a win in that scenario.

Keira's information about Madison had made Amber feel better. But was she secure enough to be okay with Madison as a permanent fixture in Tank's life? She wasn't so sure.

On her drive to Atlanta yesterday, she'd made the decision to trust Tank—for the time being. That was why she didn't say anything to him about her confrontation with Steele. It appeared to be a good decision. And, based on the night they'd had, it was the right decision. The dinner he'd ordered, the goddamn flowers. He was a walking orgasm. His nervous retelling about his utter cluelessness about what to do with the flowers had her gasping with hilarity. A nervous Tank Howard was like a billboard of a hot fireman with a helpless puppy. Panty-melting, panty-dropping, panty-combusting. And he was rewarded well for his cold take-out dinner and the forgotten, wilted flowers.

But, with all of that, she was relieved that she'd planned ahead and arranged a lunch with Keira and a dinner at her dad's. She and

Tank needed perspective—or at least, she did. A whole weekend with Tank had to come with an escape clause. *How else could she be expected to maintain any distance when he was being sweet and sexy as hell?*

When she finally pulled into Franco's driveway, she was excited about all the people waiting for her—the As, Molly, Franco, and Tank.

Is there such thing as a quintuplet crown?

She jumped out of the car and practically ran to the door. She didn't bother knocking. She entered an eerily quiet house. Glancing at her watch, she knew the twins had already napped, and she found herself bummed at the lack of activity. She'd been bracing herself for the tackle she usually got when she walked in the door. She made her way down the hall, toward the kitchen. Peeking around the corner, she was surprised to find Molly standing at the counter, chopping vegetables.

"Seriously?" she asked.

Molly turned her head. "Oh, were you expecting a welcoming committee?" She grinned at Amber and then placed the knife and the carrot she'd been dicing onto the counter.

Molly came over and greeted her with a warm hug. Amber found herself leaning into it, accepting all the warmth and love Molly always gave to her so freely.

When she stepped away from the embrace, she looked around the kitchen, her curiosity getting the best of her. "Where are the As?"

"Oh, sweetie, your baby siblings got a better offer."

Amber tried not to let her disappointment show. "They're not here?"

"They're here."

Amber frowned.

Molly nodded to the patio. "Take a look."

Her face scrunched up with confusion, but she made her way over to the French doors. She attempted a fleeting glance, but when she took in the sight in front of her, she couldn't look away. Tank, Franco, Alexis, and Andy were playing football—Tank and Alexis versus Franco and Andy. She scrutinized the teams for a second.

Probably as fair as you can get, she concluded.

Franco and Andy were playing defense, and they were both down in a three-point stance.

Tank was on his knees, bending down so that his head was even with Alexis's. They were talking intently, and Amber could tell, even from as far away as she stood, that Alexis wasn't happy with Tank's play. He looked chagrined. He'd been tracing something on his hand when Alexis held her own hand up in the universal sign for stop. Alexis began speaking. When she was done, Tank's shoulders were shaking with mirth. Then, he scooped her into his arms, dropped a quick kiss on her cheek, and held out his fist to her. Alexis bumped it, and when he set her down, Tank was in the position of center, and Amber's little sister was the quarterback.

"Amber, you're drooling on my door."

Amber snapped her head away from the glass it had been leaning on and turned guiltily to Molly. She tried to be subtle as she wiped her hand across her mouth.

"You actually moaned," Molly teased before she burst into laughter.

"Holy shit. That's so fucking hot," she gasped. "I think what's left of my reproductive system just sputtered and clenched."

Molly continued laughing, the fuel of Amber's comment adding to her giggling.

When Molly got ahold of herself, Amber finally felt the twinge of her blush fade. Molly offered her a beer, which she gratefully accepted. They settled in the kitchen, the camaraderie between them easy.

"Did I ever tell you when I knew I was in love with Franco?"

Amber coughed out a mouthful of beer. "Um, maybe not appropriate to be telling his daughter."

Molly laughed. "I promise, it's G-rated."

"It'd better be," Amber threatened.

"You'll remember, I'm sure, because it involved you."

"Me? That's weird."

Molly's lingering smile morphed into a dreamy seriousness, the force of the memory taking over. "It was that night."

Amber's stomach dropped. She didn't need any explanation for what night Molly was talking about. When Amber remembered it, in her mind, she always referred to it with the same moniker—That Night. She didn't like to think about it or recall it. Even the day before the night, when she'd realized she'd fallen in love with Tank, the magic of that day always got lost in the horror of That Night.

That Night when the agent had approached Tank and Tank had cheated on her and her life seemed to implode. Again.

"Actually," Molly clarified, "it was that day, in the tunnel."

Amber closed her eyes for a brief second, not really wanting to remember that. If she had to subtitle that day, it would be The Tunnel, The Blow Job, The Aftermath. Shaking it off, she gave Molly all of her attention.

"You almost ran up and hugged Franco. And you should have seen the look on his face when he realized you were going to hug him. It was like he imploded with sunshine."

Amber smiled at Molly's inadvertent use of Tank's nickname for her.

"He didn't look like he could be any happier."

"Until I ruined it, you mean?"

"Well, not really. It was the whole thing, from start to finish—your exuberance, then your reluctance, and even the horror on your face when you seemed to remember that you'd forgotten to hate him. All of it played out in the way he looked at you. Then, when Tank introduced you to Chantel and Franco stepped in? Holy shit is right. I would have followed him to the ends of the earth in that moment. There is just something so sexy and irresistible about a man who loves a child, and he obviously loves you. I was done for. I decided right then to start looking for a new job because there was no way I was going to be able to stay away from him."

Amber sighed. "Okay, that's pretty fucking cool."

"Yeah," Molly concurred dreamily.

And Amber couldn't help smiling at the dopey look on her friend's face. The love Molly had for Franco made Amber's heart feel gooey, hopeful, and sunshiny.

Fuck! This was not helping with her distant objectivity.

Amber took a sip of her beer.

And Molly switched gears. "How's work?"

Their respective careers in college athletics gave them a lot to talk about. But, this time, Amber frowned a little at the topic.

"It's good. But, for the first time since I've gotten there, I'm bored."

Molly's eyebrows shot up. She placed her beer on the counter and picked the knife back up. She arranged the vegetables she still needed to cut and began the rhythmic chopping. "I thought that might eventually be the case, but I'm surprised to hear that."

Amber cocked her head to the side. "Really?"

"Don't get me wrong. The Operations job is a good fit for you, but I know your passion lies elsewhere."

Amber shrugged. "Yeah, I guess. But this is really the first time that I've felt like I'm going through the motions. I've done everything, and I've perfected all my tasks—for me. The way we've implemented procedures is perfect for me. So, I'm restless."

Molly took a quick sip of her beer. She pulled her eyes away from her task and leveled her gaze on Amber. "Are you sure it's the job that's making you restless?"

"Yeah, of course. What else?"

"Tank?"

Amber scoffed. "No. He has nothing to do with my job."

Molly merely pursed her lips. "So, have you thought about looking for something else?"

"No!" Amber exclaimed, amazed with the direction of the conversation. "I couldn't leave Whitey."

"Sure you could. He expects you to at some point."

"I wouldn't go that far."

"Amber, do you think Whitey is surprised when coaches leave? His staff, those positions—they are merely stepping-stones for the best and the brightest. Whitey knows that."

"I haven't really thought about it like that."

Molly took a deep breath, like she was girding herself for what she was about to say. "I wasn't going to bring this up. Franco and I have talked about it, and we haven't heard any complaints, so I didn't think you'd even be interested."

"Interested? In what?"

"Our Director of Player Personnel position is about to open up. I bet Ken Swonson would be ecstatic to have you."

Amber didn't say anything for a minute. It would be a lateral move. In some football offices, it would be considered a step down, depending on how the head coach ran things. She wouldn't necessarily have a direct line to the head coach. But running the recruiting activities at a major Division I institution? She could get on board with that. She knew Molly was noting her reaction, watching every pro and con form in her head.

"I need to think about it."

Molly looked pleased. "You should absolutely think about it."

"But, Molly, don't mention it tonight, okay?"

Molly nodded. "Okay. But why?"

"If I make the decision, it has to be because of everything, except for Tank. And I need to do that without him knowing."

Molly wrinkled her brow. "Amber," she scolded, a tone of disapproval.

"I just..." Amber started, attempting to explain. "I just need to make this decision in isolation. I don't want to think I'm planning my life around him."

"Well, first, this is the perfect job for you, so I don't know how you can say that. You'd be moving closer to your family and most of your friends."

Amber waved her hand. "I know, I know, but please, I just have to do this my way."

Molly reached out and touched her hand. "When I took this job, I was running away from something, from Franco. Do you know how much better it would have been to know I was running toward something instead?"

Amber had an answer to the question, but the doors behind her swung open, and all the noise she'd been expecting when she walked in surrounded her. The As scrambled in the door, vying for her attention. Before she knew it, she had both of them in her arms, and each one was attempting to talk louder than the other as they explained the football game.

"'Ber, we tied," Andy said after Alexis conceded the floor.

"Yeah, I was corback."

"*Corback*, huh? Why didn't you let Tank play quarterback? You know, that's his job."

"But Papa said he chokes," Alexis told her.

Amber couldn't stop the snicker her baby sister had startled out of her.

For the first time, she glanced up and met Tank's eyes from across the kitchen. He was staring at her the way she'd been drooling over him earlier in the day. She recognized that heated gaze that was heavy with future possibilities. She couldn't tear her eyes away from him. She wanted him to look at her like that every day, to see her and know every dream could be found with her. He walked to her, trancelike, as if he were on some mission he had to fulfill. When he was a couple of inches away from her and the As, he dipped his head between the three of them and dropped a sweet kiss on her mouth. She almost combusted at the enchanted moment.

"Hi," he murmured.

"Hey," she managed to get out.

Tank stepped back from her but not before Alexis launched herself into his arms. Amber pushed her nose into Andy's neck, inhaling the sweet fragrance of little boy sweat mixed with grass. He giggled, and the sound grounded her. Pulling away, she looked around the room, and she saw that Franco and Molly wore identical expressions of wonder.

THIRTY-ONE

Tank leisurely ran his hand along the planes of Amber's back, loving the feel of her pliant, smooth skin under the ministrations of his touch. Tucked up under his chin, she sprawled along the length of his body, her left leg bent across his hip and her right aligned with his. They'd been a tangle of limbs throughout the night, reluctant to leave the cocoon they'd woven.

"I love being able to touch you." There was nothing overtly sexual in his delicate tracings, more just an appreciation for his ability to actually do it.

Amber snickered. "Skype wearing thin already?"

He pinched her on the hip. "Funny."

"What are we doing today?" she asked.

"Feel like working out with me?"

Amber pushed up onto her right arm, peering at him. The look on her face told him all he needed to know.

"Yes. Are we swimming?"

"No. I want to throw."

She wrinkled her brow, her displeasure as obvious as her interest only seconds before. "I'm a shitty target."

Tank feigned shock. "Sunshine, are you trying to tell me that you can't catch a ball?"

She scoffed at him and dropped heavily upon his chest. His hands found their places, little magnets drawn to the coves of her body.

"I can catch, just can't run very fast," she mumbled, like he didn't know her running ability was hampered by her the ankle she shattered in the accident.

His fingers trailed down, offering comfort with the easy touch.

He nuzzled the top of her head, peppering it with kisses. "You know I just like to get you on the football field." He rolled them over and trapped her body, gathering her hands in one of his and pulling them up above her head. His mouth latched on to the scarred tissue under her ear, and he gave an exaggerated suck, eliciting a giggle and wiggle from her body.

"Shit, that tickles," she gasped out as he continued to tease her.

"You, on a football field?" He nipped and sucked his way over to her mouth. "So damn hot." He lifted his head so that they were looking at each other.

"Oh," she said, understanding dawning, "this is to fulfill some fantasy you have."

"I've had to get creative over the last four weeks," he explained plaintively.

"I'm sure you have. Not used to waiting for what you want, huh?" she teased.

"I've been waiting years for you," he stated, the mood suddenly shifting from light and playful to intense and heavy.

They stared at each other. Tank knew she was trying to figure him out. It wasn't about if he was being honest. Him wanting her seemed to be a universal truth, like one plus one equals two. And she wasn't measuring his desire. Whatever she was seeking, he wanted her to find it. He wanted to be a playbook she could easily decipher.

She looked away from him, and he let her.

He dropped his scruff-covered chin to her collarbone, gently rubbing against it, making her squirm. Her head moved back and forth, attempting to dislodge him.

"Tank!" she exclaimed on a laugh. "Stop, please."

When he looked up at her, their eyes connected, the seriousness of his last statement evaporating in the silliness of the moment.

Tank dropped a quick kiss on her lips before springing his next bombshell on her. "After we work out, lunch with my mom?" he said like a question even though he had no intention of letting her get out of it. Then, he released her hands and rolled off of her. "I'm going to shower," he stated, escaping quickly.

He should have stayed, taken the brunt of her refusals. But, instead, he hightailed it into the bathroom, leaving Amber alone with her thoughts about his plans. He needed to play all of his cards, to add up all the deficits for her.

Chantel Jones would be a problem. As much as he loved and respected his mother, she did not approve of Amber Johnson. He didn't have to think hard to remember his mother's shock when he'd introduced her to Amber. Just closing his eyes, he could practically feel the bite of the tension in the air. In the aftermath of everything that had happened on that fateful day, he sometimes glossed over his mother's reaction to Amber. He didn't mean to keep pushing Amber's limits with little things. But he had to address this part because the two women in his life needed to get along.

He hadn't been exactly forthcoming with Chantel. There were things you shared and many you didn't. His guilt and remorse over his actions toward Amber stayed hidden away, buried deep under the persona he'd erected. Chantel knew things had gone bad. She also knew Tank had wallowed in the outcome of those events. She, like no one else but Tilly, could see the shadow of sadness underneath the veneer of greatness. Had she known the whole story, Chantel would have undoubtedly championed Amber. But, with just smatterings of truths and a host of evasions, she could only see her son's sorrow and hurt. Holding Amber accountable for a morose Tank seemed the only course of action. Chantel and Tank hadn't spoken of any of it, but Tank knew his reunion with Amber was not something his mother was likely to celebrate.

To make matters worse, Chantel loved Madison. On paper, Madison was perfect for him. She was brilliant, funny, connected, and African-American. No matter how many times he'd attempted to explain the relationship they shared, Chantel had been secretly—perhaps not so secretly—hoping for Tank to make his relationship with Madison official. Madison was Chantel's choice for Tank.

"Like follows like," she was fond of saying.

But how could he explain to his mother that there wouldn't, couldn't be anyone else for him?

Chantel had called him when the pictures of him and Amber in the park surfaced.

"Is it her?" she had asked, like she'd been waiting for it.

When he affirmed Amber's identity, Chantel didn't spout off and warn him away. She knew better than to try to sway him. She didn't tell him to be careful or to think about what had happened last time.

He heard something like a, "Harrumph," on the other end of the phone and just managed to hold back a smile.

That was why her parting words, "Don't hold out hope for something that's never going to happen," irritated him.

Turning on the shower, Tank stepped into the spray, wondering what today might look like. He scrubbed vigorously, washing away a layer of guilt. He knew Amber needed to trust him again. But, as he let the scalding water wash over him, he wondered if maybe he needed to absolve himself of the guilt he felt for his actions and for what had followed.

The door to the shower opened behind him, and he waited. Amber stepped to him, her arms wrapping around him as the front of her body molded to the back of his. Her hands rested on his abs. She didn't speak, and he didn't try to make her. He laced his fingers through hers and held on, enjoying her feel. Most often, be it the distance between them or the complete lust he experienced when he saw her, their touches led somewhere. A kiss to a deeper one, a caress to a flame, a lick to a taste. All morning in his bed, his touches had been explorations and chartings, familiarity and knowledge. Wrapped in her arms right now, he experienced an unfamiliar intimacy. Immobilized by the warmth spreading throughout him, he tried to hold on to the swirling emotions, to keep it all within his sights, a moment to savor. Without words, she communicated some point to him, and if he concentrated, he'd get it. Her fingers tightened around his, and he wondered if she was agreeing without a fight.

Did she sense, as he did, that they stood on the proverbial cliff, poised to step over the edge?

The last time he'd suggested she meet his mother they'd butted heads, both testing their respective boundaries. He conjured the look of horror on her face and bit back a smile at the memory. He'd always pushed her. Even when he'd deliberately pushed her away, he believed she'd come back to him. When she didn't, he was genuinely, shockingly hurt. *But, really, what right did he have to that?*

He couldn't spend their lives constantly thinking he needed to make it up to her. His thoughts drifted back to the night they'd been together in his kitchen when sex had been about distance, not intimacy. If he wanted a future with Amber, he needed to find a way for both of them to move beyond the past.

THIRTY-TWO

Playing with Tank on a football field made the idea of having lunch with Chantel Jones something Amber could live with. Tank the athlete should have been a persona she knew, someone she was familiar with. But, as they traversed the field, a cloak of focus descended between them. Amber became part of the background of his workout.

A little unnerved, she wondered if there was anything, any activity in the universe, that was so engaging she could cease to see, feel, or hear Tank Howard. If it existed, she'd love to explore it, so she could escape him, even for a moment—like during this weekend. Tank overwhelmed her, made her want so much more for them.

She thought about Molly's unexpected job information the day before. Any decision she made today would bring her closer to Tank, so she shrugged it off, putting it away to contemplate when she could achieve some physical distance.

Tank sauntered toward the bin holding the footballs. He picked one up, flipping it around. Even from where she stood on the other side of the field, she could see the ball dance on his fingers. She pictured those fingers moving along her skin, digging in, and heat flooded her face. Grateful for the space between them, she turned, hiding her embarrassed smile. For her, just the thought of him was enough to make her blush, enough to have her rethinking her life.

"Sunny," Tank called across the expanse of the field. She turned back to him when he yelled, "Catch," and sent a ball on a perfect trajectory.

She barely had time to put her hands up before it was upon her. The sting of the ball hitting her hands could have made her drop it, but she held on, mostly to maintain her dignity. She wouldn't have heard the end of it if she'd dropped it. She glanced down at the ball and looked up in triumph. But Tank was already on her, his hands gripping her at the waist, as he half-tackled her to the ground. He pillowed her head with his hands, cradling her skull, absorbing any impact. But he couldn't quite hold himself away from her. His leg slid between hers as he hugged her to him, rolling over so that she was above him.

"Nice catch," he commented, his smile radiant.

"Did you mean to throw it so hard?"

He grinned his answer before he leaned up and nipped at her bottom lip. "I knew you'd be ready."

"Like I'm ready to have lunch with your mom?" she quipped before she could think better of it.

"I had dinner with your dad last night," he reminded her.

Rolling her eyes, she moved off of him and dropped to her back on the turf. He turned to face her and pushed up onto his elbow, so all she could see was a backlit Tank, haloed by the sun. She almost scoffed at the image of an angelic Tank.

Tearing her eyes away, her gaze settled on his shoulder. It wasn't that she didn't want to spend time with Chantel. On the contrary, she wanted to get to know her, to pick her brain, to discern the secrets to Tank. But, much like the invitation he'd offered her all those years ago, it felt premature.

He traced the outline of her mouth before his callous hand cupped her jaw, the hardened patches somehow comforting her. His thumb swept her mouth. And she forgot what she'd been thinking about.

"Look at me," he said gently.

She met his gaze.

"Lunch is probably not going to be fun. She's either going to subtly ignore you, making you uncomfortable, or she's going to grill you, making you uncomfortable. I can never tell. But you're going to be a part of my life, and she is a part of my life. I want to start to connect the two."

"Yeah, yeah," she murmured. "I got it."

He gave her a half-smile. "I know you do." He leaned down, his mouth hovering. "I have total faith in you," he said.

And she knew he meant it.

His lips brushed against hers, more a touch than a kiss. "We gotta go," he whispered, the vibrations ghosting along her mouth.

She pushed up and kissed him, hard to his soft. He climbed to his feet and held out his hand to her. When she twined her fingers with his, he tugged, and she was suddenly on her feet. They walked off the field together, the footballs forgotten, the moment heavy.

They quickly reached the car, and the nerves Amber had held at bay came rushing back. All of her self-talk about taking this slow and concentrating on sex washed away like a wooden bridge in a roaring flood. She was thinking about leaving a job she loved for an unknown quantity. She was actually contemplating relocating. Casual had left the building a long time ago.

So, what was a little lunch with the mother of the man sitting next to her?

If she could think about moving, whether or not the job was potentially perfect for her, she could certainly handle lunch with Chantel Jones.

Lunch with Chantel Jones was a disaster from the moment Tank and Amber walked into the restaurant.

They'd left themselves enough time to clean up after Tank's workout. But showering together wasn't the best idea, and by the time they got out and dressed, they were late. Tank's tension filled the car, an unpleasant odor of suppressed nerves permeating the drive. It left Amber on edge. The restaurant was another eclectic café. The old, converted house had crown molding and a coffered ceiling. Amber studied the building as Tank pulled her through the restaurant to a four-top table off in a corner where Chantel waited with an aggravated look on her face.

"You're late," was the auspicious greeting.

Amber's hope for a pleasant meeting dimmed.

Tank merely smiled. He pulled a chair out for Amber before greeting his mother with a kiss to her cheek. "I was practicing," he said, a light tone that was in direct opposition to the heaviness of the mood in the car.

Amber appreciated his ability to defer but felt the color in her cheeks heighten as she thought about why they were truly late. He might have been practicing a different position in the shower because they'd left the field in plenty of time.

"You remember Amber," he introduced. His knowing smile in Amber's direction told her that he had picked up on her blush.

"Hi, Miss Jones." She stumbled over her greeting, deciding in a split second between Chantel, Miss Jones, or Mrs. Jones. Complicated salutation. Complicated past. Complicated present. Amber maintained eye contact, almost daring Chantel to rebuff her.

"Nice to see you again," Tank's mom said.

Somehow, Amber knew it was genuine.

They made small talk while they looked over the menu, while they waited for their food, while they ate. Amber settled in, belatedly feeling stupid for the angst she'd harbored for meeting Chantel. This was nothing like she'd imagined.

Tank leaned forward and pulled his phone from his pocket. Amber watched as Chantel grimaced, her displeasure apparent.

"Hawk," Tank offered as an explanation. "Be right back," he said before he stood and walked toward the door at the front of the restaurant.

Amber continued to study Chantel, whose gaze remained locked on Tank's retreating form. Here, she appeared more demure than Amber remembered. Maybe her memory was tainted, but the day they'd met in the tunnel, Chantel seemed like she was six feet tall. Now, Amber knew Chantel was actually a couple of inches shorter than she was. She had beautiful almond-shaped eyes that reminded Amber of Tank. Her black slacks and silk shell were classy. Amber wondered if she always dressed so formally, but then it dawned on her that it was Sunday, and Chantel had likely come from church.

"Come to any conclusions?" Chantel's voice snapped, catching Amber off guard.

Amber's eyes jumped up to meet Chantel's angry gaze. "No, I really haven't."

"About my son, too, if I've read the situation right."

Amber leaned back in her chair, relief coursing through her. This was what she'd expected, primed for on the ride over. Amber didn't want to play coy, but she was so tempted. "You're correct," she said instead.

"He has to get down on his knees for you to forgive him and move on?"

Amber wished she knew the answer to that question herself. She fought off the urge to shrug and roll her eyes. "I haven't quite figured that out," she answered more honestly than she'd intended, Chantel's stare like a truth serum.

"You probably need to get to figuring that out. Tank's too good of a man to have to prove himself over and over again." Chantel's gaze never deviated from Amber's, issuing a challenge.

Amber contemplated asking if Chantel knew what Tank had done, but she found that she couldn't conjure up any of the residual anger she'd clung to for so long. Finally, Amber glanced away, searching for Tank, hoping he would come through the door and save her from this conversation.

Chantel picked up her glass from the table, drawing Amber's attention back to her. "I don't have to know exactly what happened," she began. "I'm sure it was worthy of your anger." She took a sip, eyeing Amber over the top of her glass before setting it down. "But I'm pretty sure a three-year penance should about cover it."

Amber remained silent. There wasn't anything for her to say. She had no easy answers for Chantel, and if she had, she wouldn't have supplied them anyway. When she finally came to a conclusion, the first person she would tell was Tank.

But the manners her father and Nona had tried so hard to instill in her reared up.

"Sure," she said demurely. "I don't think either one of us has really determined anything yet. It's more like a wait and see." She smiled gently, softening the edges of her response.

Chantel sat back, and Amber knew she was being assessed and judged. She wanted not to care, but Tank's earlier words echoed in her mind. The woman across from her was Tank's only family. Amber wanted to get along with her, but Chantel seemed to have some problem that prevented her from accepting Amber.

"Wait and see," Chantel repeated. "I guess, if you feel like you have the time for that. If it were me, I'd be worried he might get tired of waiting and go back to the girl who seemed to accept him, no matter what," Chantel stated.

Amber blinked, disbelief spiraling through her, and her temper finally snapped. "You mean, Madison?"

Chantel smiled. "She's been there for him for the last couple of years. I'm just saying, you might want to make up your mind before the decision is taken away from you."

Amber had no words. She imagined she flopped around, like a fish with no water.

She stood. "If you'll excuse me, I need to use the restroom." She placed her napkin on her chair and turned, controlling every movement.

When she returned, she survived the rest of lunch—barely.

The things she needed to think about stacked up in her brain like a pile of newspapers waiting for the recycling bin. She couldn't figure anything out with Tank around.

Their trip back to his loft was much the same as the drive to lunch. Silent and heavy. They'd each retreated into their own space, which was weighed down with fear and expectation. She didn't explain what happened at lunch when they returned to his house. They exchanged empty words and loaded actions.

She packed.

He watched.

She feared.

He hoped.

She left.

THIRTY-THREE

JUNE

The next two weeks flew by.

Tank texted her the day she left Atlanta after lunch with his mom, asking her to let him know that she'd arrived home. She did. Then he tried to call a couple of times, but she let his calls go to voice mail, and when he didn't leave a message, she didn't call him back.

She never took the time to explain what had happened between her and Chantel. Explanations would have accompanied excuses and assurances. She decided against those now when distance was what she craved. The seed of change planted by Molly had sprouted and taken root. She longed for clarity, some innate knowledge of surety. In a Tank-dominated universe, could she independently change the course of her life without inadvertently diverting her orbit more firmly in his magnetic pull?

Amber embraced the separation for what it was—a vacuum where she could redirect the course of her life. Her first step though, much like three years ago, began with Coach Whitehurst.

Amber followed Whitey into his office and took a seat in front of his desk. She looked around because she hadn't spent much time in his domain.

They'd meet in the war room to drink coffee and review the day before everyone else showed up. She and Whitey worked what seemed to be full days prior to the regular office hubbub.

What's that Army slogan?

We do more before 9 a.m. than most people do all day.

That was the kind of rapport she'd had with Whitey for three years. When she walked through that door to join his staff, she was a kid. Sure, she was a kid who had survived a lot of craziness, but she was still a child. During her time on his staff, she grew up a lot. She was wiser than she had been—but not necessarily smarter.

So, she felt some serious trepidation about the conversation she was about to have with him.

"So," Whitey said as he leaned back in his chair and propped his feet on his desk, "what's so important that you had to make an appointment?"

Amber should have known Whitey wouldn't beat around the bush. She shifted to the side and crossed her right leg over her left. "I wanted to discuss something with you."

He laughed. "I gathered that."

When she didn't pick up the conversation gauntlet, he dropped his feet to the floor and shifted forward. Leaning his elbows on the desk, he skewered her with a look she'd seen on his face but never had it directed at her. "Actually, there's something I've been meaning to talk to you about."

She took the out he'd offered. "Oh, yeah? What's up?"

"I got a call from a friend of mine. He was asking some questions about you."

For a split second, Amber thought he was talking about Tank. But then she realized how stupid that thought was, and she pushed it aside. She'd been doing that a lot recently—pushing thoughts of Tank out of her mind.

"Me? Who was asking about me and for what?"

"Ken Swonson."

Amber grinned. She couldn't help it. Sometimes, she forgot how small the world of college athletics really was. She wasn't sure if Molly had dropped some subtle hints or if Coach Swonson had found out about her from someone else, but she took it as a sign that maybe this was the right move.

"Really?"

Whitey smirked. He knew that she knew where this conversation was going. "We gonna play it that way?"

Amber laughed then, too, and the tension ebbed. "Funny. It's just hard for me to go there." She started to get choked up, and her face flushed with embarrassment.

Whitey could handle a lot, but there was no way she was going to let him see her get teary-eyed. She composed herself while Whitey pretended to look at his phone, which they both knew was a prop because, as he'd said on numerous occasions, he hated the fucking thing.

"There's a job I'm interested in, and I wanted to get your opinion on it."

Whitey's face went soft, and for the first time since she'd started working for him, he looked at her with a fondness that bordered on parental approval. This time, she pretended to occupy herself while he composed himself.

"Whatcha got?" he finally barked, the familiar bite back.

"Swonson has a Director of Player Personnel position open." She took a deep breath, knowing that, once she opened this door, there was probably no going back. "What's your take on him, his organization, and the job?"

Whitey's face became intent. "He's a good man, honest. He does everything above board, which I know is important to you. He has to recruit against me, so he's at a disadvantage there."

She smiled when he winked at her.

"This is a competitive conference, as you know. He's a young coach. He came up through the ranks, definitely paid his dues. He has some organizational management issues. But he'll learn. And, of course, if he surrounds himself with a strong staff, he'll give me a run for my money." Whitey paused, but she knew he wasn't done, so she stayed silent. "He reminds me of another young coach I knew. Steadfast, honest, hardworking. He left me when the time was right. Makes me proud on most Sundays."

Amber didn't need to acknowledge that she knew he was talking about Franco. She got it, and it helped. Everything he was saying supported the research she'd already done. As of yet, she hadn't found a reason not to at least look into the job.

"As far as the position, I like you in Ops. You're organized and a hustler, so nothing falls through the cracks. But I also know about your secret activities in the film room."

For the second time, her mind flashed to Tank, and she thought about the secret little activity they had performed in the film room. She could feel the heat rising in her cheeks, but she tried to focus on what Whitey was saying.

"You got an eye for talent. We all know that, so I think you would be good at the job. With your ability to manage people and information, you'd be an asset to his program."

Whitey didn't compliment. You knew you were doing a good job because he trusted you with information and responsibility. So, his praise wrapped around her and warmed her, made her proud.

"Swonson wants you, sight unseen. Not sure who he's been talking to, but he's already impressed. If you throw your name in the hat, you'll have a job offer. You really just have to decide if you want it."

He stopped talking, rolled his chair back, and propped his feet back up onto his desk.

Amber leaned back in her chair and thought about what he'd said. She wanted to say more, mostly to thank him for everything he'd done for her, for taking a chance on her, and for letting her learn. She somehow knew, if she didn't take the opportunity to talk to him now, she wouldn't get another one. "I'm worried about leaving you high and dry."

"Camp's ready to go."

She nodded even though it was a statement.

"I'm sure every travel arrangement that can already be taken care of has been."

"Hotels are booked with the exception of postseason. Charters are lined up. When the budget closes at the end of June, I'll have all the requests for payments turned in. Game-day operation meetings are on everyone's calendars."

Whitey held up a hand. "I don't need a rundown. That shit bores the hell out of me."

"Right," she said.

"No offense, but I'll have the best and the brightest contacting me the moment word leaks that you might be leaving. I won't even have to work to fill the job."

She wanted him to say that he'd miss having her around and maybe beg her to stay because he knew no one could do the job like her.

Talk about ego.

But Whitey wouldn't do that, and she knew it. He'd let her go and wish her well, but he wouldn't beg anyone to stay with him.

"I..." She tried to come up with the words to express her gratitude. "Thanks for everything, for taking a chance on me."

But he waved her off. "Keep me posted," he said, dismissing her.

Amber stood and turned, walking to the door.

"You're gonna be great, kid," he said just as she stepped through the doorway.

At least, she thought that was what he'd said.

After she'd contacted Coach Swonson, things moved at warp speed. She applied and then drove over for a two-day interview. The time there convinced her she was making the right move. Ken Swonson was a force, and Whitey was right. She could see her father in the young coach, and that comforted her.

He'd handed her a list of the top one hundred prospects and asked her to evaluate them by ranking them according to whatever system she wanted. A small part of her felt disloyal, sharing her system with a man she didn't know when she'd never even shown it to Whitey, so she left out parts of it. She was still able to make her point, and she knew he was impressed. He played devil's advocate on a couple, and they had a pretty healthy debate on the importance of putting the right pieces in play.

Amber had stopped by Franco's on her way home and spent the night there. Neither Molly nor Franco asked about Tank, and Amber didn't offer any information.

But, on her way home, as she drove through Atlanta, her mind could no longer block out the thoughts.

Before she could even think about what she was doing, she ordered Siri to call Tank. As the Bluetooth in her car connected, every muscle in her body tensed. She couldn't decide what she was hoping would happen, and when he answered the phone, she relaxed into the seat, her reaction a true tell of her feelings.

"Hey," he answered. His voice floated through the car, cutting through the road noise and smoothing her out like a hot iron on wrinkled fabric.

She didn't respond as she tried to figure out what to say.

"Please tell me this isn't a butt-dial, Sunshine." His voice came through again, loud and clear and pleading.

"Hey," she managed, a wobbly version of her voice.

"Where are you? Sounds like you're driving."

"Seventy-five, eighty-five."

"You're in Atlanta?" His voice boomed, part-disbelieving, part-hoping.

"Driving through," she responded.

She was almost out of reach. If she hadn't wanted to see him, she would have called when she passed I-20. But she called as soon as she hit the connector. She could still exit on Freedom Parkway and backtrack to his house without really going out of her way.

"Stop. I'll come meet you. Where are you?" His words were rushed, like he knew she was going eighty miles an hour, and if she kept driving without some deliberation, she'd be out of reach.

"Name a place in the Highlands. I can be there in ten." She *almost* couldn't believe the words coming out of her mouth.

"Neighbor's."

She disconnected. She wasn't sure what she was doing, but as she pulled off the highway and drove toward Tank, everything about her lightened. So, she had gotten scared and hadn't talked to him in two weeks. It wasn't the end of the world or their budding relationship. She knew she had to figure things out, and it wasn't fair of her to shut him out like she had. As much as they were familiar, they were also new. So what if his mother didn't approve of her? She would eventually; Amber was sure of it.

But she owed Tank an apology…and maybe a blow job.

She turned onto North Highland Avenue and into the parking lot of the restaurant. By some miracle, she was able to pull right into a spot. She sat for a moment, collecting herself. Pulling down the visor, she did a quick makeup check. Somewhat satisfied, she grabbed her purse and opened the door. She got out of the car and turned.

"Shit," she jumped. "You scared the crap out of me."

Tank stood two feet in front of her, sheepish in his expression. "Sorry. I saw you pull in, and basically, I hurdled the railing to get to you." He grinned.

She smiled back. "Hi."

He stepped to her, his hands quickly finding their spots—left hand on her scar, right hand on her hip—and he pulled her forward. His mouth landed on hers with an inelegant thump, but his lips immediately gentled the intrusion, softly and unhurriedly kissing her. They both sighed into the kiss, the contact electric and soothing, exciting and familiar. She wasn't sure how long they stood there, kissing. But Tank began to relent, pulling away by dropping little kisses on her mouth.

"I missed you," he said, his lips skating along her scar.

"I'm sorry," she whispered. "I just wasn't ready to answer any questions yet."

He stayed pressed against her, his head bent low. "I'm not pushing," he replied just as softly.

"I know," she murmured. "But maybe you should."

THIRTY-FOUR

Tank released Amber from the confines of his arms, but he clasped her hand, interlocking their fingers and directing her across the parking lot onto the deck of the restaurant. He maneuvered her around the tables until he came upon the one he'd been sitting at, waiting so impatiently for her to arrive.

The patrons seated around them clapped loudly, teasing Tank about his hurdle over the railing.

"If I hadn't known you were an athlete, I would have figured it out."

"Dude, you sailed over the rail. I thought you were chasing a criminal."

Tank tried to play it off, not wanting to draw any more attention to himself and Amber than his stunt already had. He pulled out a chair for her and sat down, acknowledging the good-natured ribbings with a couple of waves around the deck. He was still flying high from Amber's phone call, so the teasing going on around him did nothing to penetrate the high he was enjoying. Even the people who approached for an autograph, pulling his attention from Amber, couldn't dampen the elation he was experiencing.

He'd been wallowing for the last two weeks. He didn't want to crowd her, so he kept his attempts at talking to her to one a day even though he had the desire to drive to Alabama every day. It was a long two weeks.

Reaching over, he laced his fingers through hers again and dropped his other elbow on the table. "It's good to see you, Sunshine," he said when the hubbub had finally receded.

She smiled at him, and he couldn't fight the wide grin on his face.

"You, too."

"Were you visiting Franco? How are the As?" Immediately, she shot him a guarded look, and he returned it with a questioning one. "Is something going on?"

Her eyes shifted away from his.

When she didn't answer him, he asked, "Is this a difficult question?"

She laughed uneasily. "No," she finally said, shaking her head. "I stayed with Franco last night. But I was here, interviewing with Coach Swonson."

Tank didn't know how to react. He wanted to hurdle another railing or maybe the building, Superman-like. "Oh?" he said, regulating his voice, disguising the glee he was feeling.

Working for Swonson meant she could live with him, or they could buy something in between. It smacked of opportunity and openness.

She held up her hand, reading something on his face he'd tried but failed to hide. "It's a great position for me. Director of Player Personnel."

"Nice," Tank said, infusing his voice with the enthusiasm he'd felt a second before. "How'd it go?"

Amber smiled. "Really good."

"What was good?"

Amber was rarely effusive, but when it was about football and scouting, he could get her to the point where she wouldn't shut up.

"The position is perfect for me and my skill set. He wants me to review film, to help the direction of their recruiting efforts. He gave me the top one hundred prospects from last year and asked me, based on how I typically evaluate, who I would have recommended for his program. I fudged my system a little bit in case I don't get the job, but it was a really good discussion. And he challenged me on a few of them, but I think he was just playing devil's advocate. I like him, too. He kind of reminds me of Franco, but I'm not sure if I would have come to that conclusion on my own or if Whitey planted the seed in my head." She shrugged with something that looked like indifference, but he could tell how excited she was about the possibilities. "I could see myself there."

"That's awesome. I'm really happy for you." He was really happy for her, but he was also stoked about having her in closer proximity to him. But he didn't say that, didn't give in to his urge to plan their lives now that she was going to be within his reach.

"Yeah," she said softly.

They sat there, staring at each other. He had no idea what she was thinking about. Those damn shutters she was so excellent at donning interfered with his probing gaze. A picture flashed in his mind of Amber holding Alexis and Andy, his imaginings replacing her siblings with children of their making. He wanted it all, and he wanted it with her.

"So, you think you're going to take the job?" He tried to hold back his crazy sense of elation at the thought of her living right down the street from him.

She hesitated before she answered. Her eyes slid away from him and then back. "I haven't gotten an offer yet, but I'll probably take it."

"Very cool," Tank said, nodding.

His phone vibrated in his pocket, breaking the spell. He reached back and pulled it out. At the same time, Amber dived into her purse to get her ringing phone.

He glanced down at the display and looked up at Amber. "Tilly," he said, holding the phone out to her.

"Keira," she returned, flashing her phone in his direction.

They each quirked a brow and then accepted their respective calls.

Tank followed Amber to Tilly's house. He pulled into the driveway behind her and scrambled out of the car. He opened the door and waited for her to alight from the car. They couldn't stop grinning at each other, and they walked to Tilly's door, hand in hand.

"Any guesses?" Tank asked as they waited for Tilly to answer the door.

Amber shrugged. "None."

She was about to say something more when Tilly ripped open the door.

"Damn! That was fast." He stepped aside to let them in.

"Looking good," Amber said, going up on her toes as Tilly bent down for her to plant a light kiss on his cheek.

Amber was right. Tilly was decked out in a three-piece suit, but Tank wasn't surprised because Tilly often dressed like that for work.

"Shouldn't you be working?" Tank asked as he walked through the door.

The three of them made their way through the long hallway and into the kitchen.

"I'll explain in a minute," Tilly responded.

Keira was standing rather stiffly in the middle of the room, looking like she didn't know what to do with herself.

Amber immediately went to her friend and pulled her into a quick hug. "Hi! You look amazing. I love the dress."

Amber moved back but kept her hands on Keira's shoulders, studying her. Amber cocked her head, and Tank could tell she was coming up with some conclusions.

"What's going on, Keira?" Amber asked softly.

"I'm so glad we caught you before you left town," Keira said.

Then, she leaned into Amber again—seeking comfort maybe, but Tank couldn't be sure. Keira looked beyond Amber, searching for Tilly. He walked over and circled behind, wrapping his arms around Keira and dropping a kiss on her head.

Keira's head tilted to the side, so she could meet Tilly's eyes. "You want to tell them, or should I?"

Tilly chuckled. "Uh, no. This is all you."

"Fair enough," Keira answered. She looked back at Amber and then met Tank's curious gaze. "We're getting married in"—she glanced at the clock on the wall over the sink—"two hours. And we were hoping you would be our witnesses, our bests, our people."

Tank couldn't help it. He lifted his stare to Tilly, trying to silently ask him if this was what he wanted. They'd talked about it a lot recently. Tilly had threatened to kidnap Keira and fly to Vegas just to get her away from all her family drama. He didn't know if Tilly had finally won or if this was truly Keira's idea. Tilly's gaze bore into Tank's. Then, Tilly's face broke into a wide smile, and

Tank had the answer he was seeking. Tilly was happy about this, so it was a good thing. Tank let himself feel Tilly's excitement.

Amber laughed, like she was in on some joke. Then, she tugged Keira out of Tilly's arms and hugged her. She softly said something in Keira's ear, and Tank watched as Keira's eyes filled with tears. Then, her eyes closed as she was absorbed into Amber's hug.

Tank moved forward then, hugging Tilly. "Congratulations, man," he said. As soon as Amber released her, Tank wrapped Keira up in a huge hug. "Proud of you," he murmured for her alone.

"Thanks," she whispered back.

When all the hugs had been swapped, Tank got to the questions of logistics. "I don't think I should show up at the courthouse like this, huh?" He waved his hand down in front of himself, indicating his workout shorts, flip-flops, and Dri-FIT shirt. Amber had caught him as he was walking out the door of the gym. "I've got to run home and change."

"I guess I can wear my interview clothes," Amber said.

"Nope," Keira said. She reached for Amber's hand. "I have something for you."

"Wait, isn't the best person supposed to have something for the bride?" Amber teased.

"You can make it up to me later," Keira said, pulling Amber along after her. "Tank, we'll see you in a bit."

Amber offered him a jaunty smile and a wave as she followed Keira out of the room and up the stairs. Tank watched her disappear from sight and then peered over at his friend.

"You're looking a little smug," Tank remarked.

Tilly chuckled. "In about two and a half hours, I'll be feeling really smug."

"How much cajoling did you have to do?"

Tilly's smile faded away. "None, man." He shook his head. "I thought it was over. She was a mess. Then, your girl kicked her ass. She came home from lunch with Amber a few weeks ago, and she proposed to me. Got on her knees and apologized. Said she knew we were already engaged, but she didn't want to wait to get married, and she didn't need her family's approval to love me." Tilly's big shoulders moved up and down in a shrug. "I knew that, ya know. She just needed to get there."

"All right," Tank said, clapping his hands together like he would before he left a huddle, "let's do this. You're with me, right? Can't see the bride before the wedding."

Tilly cackled. "Bro, I've been with her all day."

"Yeah, but it'll be better this way."

Tilly seemed to contemplate that. Then, he smiled. "A'ight."

Tank walked to the bottom of the stairs. "Sunshine," he called.

Amber appeared on the landing a moment later.

"Tilly's with me. I'll send a car to get you two. Toss me your keys, so Tilly can drive your car."

Amber wasn't a girl who enjoyed being told what to do. But she winked at him from her perch above him and dug into her pocket. She dropped the keys down to him.

"See you soon," she said, smiling wide.

Their eyes held, and all sorts of sentiments were exchanged without any need for words.

Tank turned away from her, giddy about their plans for the afternoon.

Tilly followed Tank to his house. Tank changed clothes, and he called in a favor to rent a limousine for the rest of the day. They arrived at the courthouse before Amber and Keira, even with a stop at a florist on their way.

The ceremony was simple but heartfelt with Tank and Amber acting as their witnesses. Then, the four of them were chauffeured to an exclusive restaurant in downtown Atlanta. After dinner, Tank and Amber left Tilly and Keira, so they could enjoy their wedding night. By the time they arrived back at Tank's, they were a little drunk, a lot sentimental, and slightly silly.

Tank grabbed a couple of beers and pulled Amber into the elevator. "Hang on the deck for a bit?" he asked as he dragged her against him and dropped a kiss on her head.

"Yeah," she murmured. The elevator ascended, and Amber leaned further into Tank, snuggling into his chest. "Today was a great day."

"It was," he agreed.

They came to a subtle halt, and the door slid open. Tank kept his arm around her, leading her to the couch. He sank down near the arm, situating her between his thighs. He handed her one of the beers and snaked an arm around her body, pulling her against his chest.

"You all set?" she teased when he finally stopped moving and took a sip of his beer.

"I managed that without losing a sip," he joked.

"We got interrupted earlier," Amber stated.

"We definitely did."

"If I get the job, I'm going to take it."

Tank beamed. He was thankful she couldn't see him.

"I didn't call you sooner because I wanted to be able to make an objective decision about the job without my feelings for you being a part of it."

Tank sat back, putting some distance between their bodies, pushing her gently forward. She turned her head, so she could see him, and Tank averted his gaze. When Tank didn't meet her eyes, she looked forward and tensed in his arms. He valiantly withheld his glee. He knew she wouldn't be fighting this so much if she could control her feelings, and that made him pretty freaking happy.

"Maybe it's the beer and champagne, or, shit, it's probably all the love we've been surrounded by for the last six hours. But I'll be closer, and I thought maybe we could give this a go."

"A go?" Tank asked. "Can you clarify what that means exactly?" He couldn't see her face, but he could practically feel the roll of her eyes.

"A go. A relationship," she said, exasperated.

Tank chuckled. "Isn't that what we've been doing?"

Her head dropped back onto his chest with a thud. "Yes, but seeing each other once a month is way different than having daily access to each other."

"Daily access." Tank let those words roll around in his head. "The only way we'd have 'daily access,'" he teased with hand quotes, "was if you were living here with me."

Amber solidified like a tree in the Petrified Forest. "That's not what I meant," she said stiffly.

He nuzzled up to her, his cheek resting lightly against hers. He turned slightly, so his mouth was level with her ear. "But it's what I meant."

Her chest rose as she pulled in a great gulp of air. "It's too soon. We just had a two-week fight."

"It was a standoff. We never even got to the make-up sex," he said, laughing. He kissed her below her ear and then let his mouth skim across the rigid skin of her scar. Her breath hitched, and he fought his grin. "Look, let's do a trial run. If it doesn't work for you, I'll help you find a house."

"Oh, a trial run? Pretty smooth, Howard."

"What do you have to lose?" he asked, his voice dripping with sincerity.

He wanted her here. He wanted to wake up with her every day. He wanted what Tilly had just gotten.

"I have to think about it."

"I can live with that."

He didn't want to push her, so he was content to let the subject drop.

For now.

THIRTY-FIVE

Amber rolled out of her bed and pulled on Tank's sweatpants, the first article she could locate among the sea of their discarded clothes. They hung from her narrow hips, no matter she rolled them. Reaching for a coffee mug, the pants slid again, and she huffed in frustration. Tank came up behind her, settled his hands on the waistband, and rolled them up before rubbing his whisker-roughened chin lightly up her scar. His big hand grabbed the mug from her, and he turned away, beating her to the coffee.

"Lots to do today," he stated as he handed her the full cup, before filling one for himself. "And I have a hard time staying focused when I'm around you," he finished with a smirk.

Moving her coffee mug to the side, she leaned into Tank, content to stand close to him. He placed his mug on the counter and settled his hands on her waist, pulling her to him and settling his chin on the top of her head. Her chest heaved with happiness.

"Good to see you, Sunshine," he said. Then, he dropped a kiss on her head and stepped back.

Amber glanced around the room, taking in the boxes and newspapers they'd left scattered around last night. They'd been too tired to clean up much of the remnants of their work but not too tired to make up for the time they'd spent away from each other over the last week.

The movers were scheduled to arrive in the morning. Things had been busy. Her resignation, her instructions for her successor, her trip to Athens to look for apartments. She was a hamster on a wheel, attempting to get everything organized for her move. After her exhaustive search for a place to live, she made a decision to rent a studio for six months, so she could learn the lay of the land. When she said as much to Tank, he was supportive while reluctant to actually agree with her.

Then one night Tank appeared at her door. She didn't even get an opportunity to speak. He picked her up, carried her to her room, and spent the night thoroughly seducing her. When her body was sated and her mind slightly atrophied, he snuck in the reason for his visit.

"Don't sign that lease," he pleaded. "I know you think it's too soon, and there are still a lot of things hanging out there between us. But we can make this work."

He didn't say anything else that night, but when he departed the following morning, he dropped a quick kiss on her forehead and said, "You could have a night like last night every night."

Still basking in the glow of the having Tank's full attention, she didn't volunteer a response. The idea got stuck like a loop in her head, making any other options wan in comparison.

When the lease agreement had arrived in her inbox, she stared at it, knowing she didn't want to sign it. If she let herself remove the shackles of her inhibitions and nerves, she knew exactly what she wanted to do. She wanted to live with Tank. She wanted to come home to him every night. She wanted to work her twelve-hour days and sleep, curled up next to him. She wanted to be there for him at the end of a Sunday when his body hurt, and he needed someone to rub him down or wait on him. She wanted him.

"Come on, Sunny. We still have to finish the kitchen. And I have to leave in"—he stopped to look at his watch—"two hours." He loaded up dishware she'd bubble-wrapped the night before. He finished that task and moved on to the next as Amber watched, paralyzed. "When do the movers come?"

"Tomorrow," she answered absently. She finished her coffee and picked up a box. "We're doing the right thing," she said softly.

Her statement stopped Tank mid-motion. She wasn't exactly sure which reserve that thought had come from—the one for self-preservation or perhaps the one left for wanting things that were too good to want. But here, as they stood on the threshold of this monumental change in their lives, she realized her fears and lack of trust existed in great quantities. She wondered what he'd do with all of her anxieties. He seemed to have a direct line on assuaging everything she threw at him. But that was easy with distance between them.

How would they fare day in and day out when the most amount of time they'd ever spent together was three days straight?

The plate Tank held suspended in midair was gently placed back on the counter. He leaned back, giving her physical space. Then, he shrugged his shoulders. "I figure this is fish or cut bait, right?"

Her eyes widened, the matter-of-fact delivery surprising her. "Yeah," she said more confidently than she felt.

He nodded. "Right. So, what do you have to lose?"

You! "Nothing."

Tank laughed. "You wreak havoc on my ego, Sunshine."

"What's that supposed to mean?"

"When I asked what you had to lose, you were supposed to say, 'You, Tank.'"

She snickered. "Oh, yeah?"

"I mean, I am Tank Howard," he said as he stalked to her. "The least you could have done was pretend."

"There's no pretending. I am scared of that," she declared.

Damn this man!

The blush that stained her cheeks did not go unnoticed by Tank, but he didn't comment on it. Instead, he merely said, "Well, that's not going to happen. End of story."

If she'd had her way, Amber would have left the hallowed halls of Ayers in the dead of night with her little box of personal items and a handwritten note for all the people who had touched her life in the last three years. Unfortunately, Nicky was not going to allow her to leave without any fanfare. Somehow, he'd managed to get Whitey to agree to host a going-away party for her at his house. As far as she knew, no one got invites to Whitey's house. So, she had no choice but to attend.

Her last night in town, she pulled on her favorite skinny jeans, a silky red tank top that flared out at the bottom, and a pair of platform sandals. Then, she headed out to Whitey's farm.

It wasn't a huge gathering—just the coaches, their significant others, and a couple of the people Amber had worked closely with over the years. As she pulled in, she allowed herself to acknowledge her fears about seeing Steele. They hadn't spoken since the awkward exchange in her office. She'd seen him but always with another person around, and all their conversations had been work-related. She hoped, tonight, it would remain status quo.

She mingled with the coaches, took a good ribbing for being a traitor, and spent some time with Whitey. The night was winding down when Nicky called for everyone's attention. She wished she'd thought to get out of there sooner, but she'd been enjoying the camaraderie. Her biggest concern about her new job was establishing the working relationships needed and earning the respect of the people around her. Now, as she was about to leave this group of men she'd worked with, she felt that fear more acutely. It took time to earn respect.

"As excited as we are for Amber's new journey, we are obviously sad to see her go," Nicky said.

"Hear, hear," was called out from around the room.

"Our resident videographer put together a book of memories, quotes, and pictures for you to take with you."

Amber stepped forward and took the book. She opened it to the first page and saw a letter from one of her favorite athletes. Tears threatened, so she shut the book.

"I'll look at this later," she said quickly.

There were some laughs from around the room.

"But we also wanted to give you something to remember us by—the real us."

"You mean, the *us* from the war room?" she quipped.

"Exactly," Nicky said. He handed her a box, unwrapped. "You know I can't wrap," he said.

She opened it up to find a three-foot mascot of her new school dressed in a State football jersey. She couldn't help the unabashed laughter. "You guys are crazy. Where am I going to put this?"

"On Tank's mantel," someone said.

The guffaws from around the room were contagious.

Amber enjoyed the teasing, knowing it would be a while for her to feel this comfortable in her new environment.

When she finally said good-bye, she was grateful to Nicky for making her participate. She left him with a big hug and a promise to see him during his vacation in July. He was incredibly stoked to be able to say he actually spent the night in Tank Howard's house.

It wasn't until she was at the door to leave that Steele approached her.

"I'll walk you out," he said, gently taking her arm.

She fought the desire to step on his foot. Letting him lead her out the door, she waited impatiently for him to say what he wanted to say.

"You're making a mistake," Steele started.

"Oh my God! We've been over this. Do you realize that all of your protesting is making you lose two of your closest friends?" she said. She picked up her pace, not wanting to be around Steele anymore.

"Who? You and Tank?" He laughed. "I think I'll survive."

Amber stopped walking and pulled away from him. "I'm sure you will," she said cuttingly. "It will just be a fucking lonely existence."

If she thought she'd get a rise out of him, she was sorely mistaken.

Steele merely shrugged. "If I were you, I'd watch your back. Being with Tank means you're suddenly interesting to a whole lot of people." With those ominous words, he turned and left.

Amber watched him walk away, her heart heavy. For two years, they'd been friends. She didn't understand who he was right now, and she was sorry that the man she'd been close to seemed to have left the building. If she was feeling that way, she could only imagine the hurt Tank was feeling.

For a brief second, she considered Steele's parting words. But, as she got into her car and began the drive to Tank, she forgot about Steele and her fears.

She hurried from the party, intent on getting to Tank's tonight. The movers had picked her stuff up the morning before and dropped it off. She didn't want Tank to have to handle all of it by himself.

The drive went by quickly, so when she pulled into their driveway and hit the preprogrammed button for the garage, she was struck by the fact that she was home. The word slid through her mind, feeling right in a surprising way. She parked and got out of the car to find Tank leaning against the doorframe, backlit by the kitchen light.

I could get used to this.

Then, he was moving forward and sweeping her up in his arms, spinning her around in a happy display. All the doubts she'd had eroded under the weight of his certainty.

"Good to have you home," he said.

Even though she knew he'd deliberately chosen the word, it did nothing to diminish the impact of it. And, when they made it upstairs to their bedroom, the sweetness of the moment stayed with her.

Later, she would think back on this night and remember only the homecoming she'd gotten from Tank. Maybe she should have remembered Steele and his warning.

THIRTY-SIX

JULY

Tank settled into the booth, surveying the restaurant. It was one he'd frequented with Madison over the last couple of years, so he didn't need to peruse the menu. Instead, with nothing to occupy him, he took out his phone and scanned the ESPN headlines, but nothing seemed to jump out at him.

His mind was on this impromptu meeting with Madison. He hadn't seen her since she left Tilly's house the night he was with Amber. They'd exchanged a couple of texts and talked a few times, but the consistent friendship they'd shared had dwindled to check-ins. It happened so naturally that he didn't really notice. His ability to let go of a friendship that had sustained him over the last few years surprised him. He never thought he and Madison were simply friends out of convenience, but he wondered now if that were the case.

He glanced up as Madison pulled open the heavy door of the restaurant and waltzed in. She nodded to the hostess while ambling directly to where Tank sat. The casual observer wouldn't notice the determination hidden underneath the blasé front, but Tank could tell that whatever had prompted this lunch was important.

He stood when she arrived at the booth, and they shared a brief friendly embrace—one you might lend to a distant cousin you were meeting for the first time, certainly not a friend and former lover. When Madison took a seat, Tank followed.

"Hey," she said.

Tank nodded his greeting.

She smiled at him. "It's been a while. It's good to see you."

Returning her smile with one of his own, he leaned back, studying her. "You, too."

The waitress arrived with waters. "The usual?" she inquired.

For the first time since she'd called him, Tank relaxed. The familiar greeting seemed to take the edge out of both of them.

Madison looked up at the server. "Yes, please. All the way around."

The girl nodded and left them alone.

"Thank God for the waitress," Madison exclaimed, her straightforward manner returning instantly. "Shit, for a couple of seconds there, I felt like I didn't even know you."

Tank grinned. "Sorry."

Madison waved him off. "It was me, too. I didn't think it would be so weird to see you." The tension drained away from her, and Tank could see her visibly relax. "I'm nervous about what I have to tell you, and I just locked up."

"Can't say I've ever heard you admit anything like that."

"I know. And you'd better keep it to yourself." She winked at him, and just like that, they were back to normal.

They chatted for a few minutes, catching up on the gaps of the last few months. Standard information was exchanged, stuff you could garner from a text message, information lacking tone and feeling. Madison was biding her time, and Tank was content to let her, knowing that whatever she had to say was going to change things.

The waitress deposited their food, and Tank watched as Madison tracked her movements away from the table. Then, Madison's gaze swung back to him. She leaned forward, like a conspirator, while Tank fought his desire to lean away from her.

"I just finished working on a story," she began.

Tank eyed her coolly as a bubble of unease began to percolate in his belly. She'd paused, and Tank realized she was waiting for him to acknowledge her statement. He nodded with trepidation, the green light she sought from him painful to concede.

"I decided to leave the sideline-reporting gig. There's a new sports news show called *The Shot Clock*. It's like *60 Minutes* for sports."

"That's great," Tank said, knowing she'd wanted her career to go in that direction. "I'm happy for you."

This wasn't grudgingly bestowed.

"Do you get to choose the stories, or are they given to you?"

This was something else she'd wanted—the ability to pick what she reported. She would have settled if the show was the right fit, but if she were writing her dream, she would have penned editorial discretion.

Madison shifted in her chair, and Tank noted the movement. She was nervous. She looked away from him for a split second. Tank's right hand nervously curled around the bottom of the seat, something to ground him.

"Both," she finally managed. "The first story started out as mine. I was chasing a lead. But, when the lead seemed pointless, I tried to bail."

"Tried?"

Madison didn't answer him.

"Why do I get the feeling this story has something to do with me?" he finally asked.

"Not you per se," she said.

Tank rubbed his hand over his face, his frustration apparent, his patience gone. "Madison, just say what you came here to say. This is getting old, fast."

"Are the rumors about you and Amber true?"

Tank leaned back in the booth, answering some need to put distance between them. "I didn't realize there were any rumors."

Madison rolled her eyes. Some time ago, that expression had made him laugh because it was so unlike her polished facade. Today, it made him want to sneer.

"Are you living together?" she asked.

Tank studied her. "Is this on the record?"

Never in their relationship had he asked her that. He probably should have protected himself. But Madison was on his side, not out for a story or an inside scoop on his life. He didn't feel like that right now. Some sliminess crept between them, making him long for a shower.

"Touché." It was a murmur before Madison glanced away from him again.

Done with the bullshit, Tank rose, pulled out his wallet, and threw three twenties on the table. "I'm out."

"Sit down, Tank," Madison quietly demanded.

The tone of her voice freaked him out.

He wanted to keep walking but found himself planting his ass back in the booth. He dropped his elbows on the table and leaned slightly forward, more menacing than intimate. He kept his voice controlled, but he was done with the games. "I have no idea what is going on, but my patience is at an end. So, lay it out for me, so I can get the fuck out of here."

The guileless expression he'd admired through the lens of a television screen suddenly seemed more threatening than anything he could imagine hearing.

"I've been investigating the death of Rowdy Daniels." Something must have shown on his face because her lips curved up into a merciless smile. "Yeah, I thought that name might mean something to you."

She toyed with the silverware on the table while keeping her eyes locked on him, and Tank's anxiety spiraled. Madison didn't normally fidget.

"I guess you already knew about the accident."

Tank continued to peer at her, hoping his face lacked expression. He'd never mentioned the accident. In fact, even after getting caught in the closet with Amber, he and Madison never broached the subject of his past relationship. Amber's disfiguring accident that left her ex-boyfriend dead was not up for discussion.

"After the police refused to press charges, the Daniels family looked into a civil suit. Wrongful death or something like that. They were convinced she was drunk, and that was what caused the accident. But the tox screens all came back negative."

Tank had known most of this. As she spoke, he found himself curious about what had sent Madison off to chase this particular story.

"The family subpoenaed her medical records. What they found there made them back off entirely. It was truly an accident. No malicious intent, no alcohol or drugs involved."

Tank tried very hard to maintain his disinterest, as if he had known all of this information already. But he couldn't hide the surprise or curiosity over what would make Rowdy's family stop their pursuit of blame. He knew Madison noted his surprise because her eyes flashed with triumph. She knew something Tank didn't, and that made her happy and smug.

"You don't know, huh?"

"Know what?" He tried to shrug it off, stem the wound so that the circling shark might lose interest and look elsewhere.

"What caused the crash."

He shrugged. "Nah. They're called accidents for a reason, right?"

Madison chuckled, an all-knowing sound, one he imagined a defensive end might release right before he pounded Tank into the ground.

Madison leaned back this time, relaxing against the plush cushion of the booth. "It was a medical emergency actually," she said, her seemingly innocuous attitude cloaking the obvious excitement and anticipation rushing through her.

Her eyes glittered, and Tank belatedly realized this was like foreplay to her. All of the cues were there, and the cauldron of bile threatened to spew up from his stomach.

"You've heard of an ectopic pregnancy?"

Tank swallowed audibly and nodded. He knew where this was going, and all he could think about was that Amber had been pregnant with someone else's child.

"Sometimes, there are no symptoms at all. I'm not sure if she had any issues prior, but apparently, that night her fallopian tube burst. They think she experienced extreme dizziness or fainted. That's how they ended up wrapped around the tree. The doctors had to perform emergency surgery to remove the tube in addition to operating on all of her other injuries." This time, it was Madison who shrugged.

Tank didn't even attempt to hold back the, "Fuck," that flew out of his mouth.

"I figured you didn't know," she said matter-of-factly, like she'd just told him the sky was blue. "Sad really. The chance of her ever getting pregnant again, pretty slim." She paused briefly, letting her conclusion hang in the air between them, before she said, "Anyway, that made it particularly difficult for his family to pursue any suit."

"So, end of story," Tank managed to say.

Madison smirked. "Absolutely not. It's a great story. I mean, obviously heartbreaking but sensational all the same. We are going to use it to announce the Ronald "Rowdy" Daniels IV Memorial Scholarship that his family is endowing."

"Right," Tank muttered.

He wanted to hit something. The asshole who'd messed with Amber's head was going to get immortalized with a scholarship.

Perfect.

And his ex-friend-with-benefits was reporting it.

Even better.

He studied her across the table, itching to leave but knowing he needed to stay seated, that there was more to come. Madison hadn't disguised her ambition, nor had she hidden her killer instinct. Nothing about this moment should have come as a surprise for him. Yet, leveled at him, her dreams of journalistic stardom looked harrowing.

"What else?" he finally asked.

"You're assuming there's more?"

"Isn't there?"

"Yes," she answered demurely, appearing nervous again.

Whatever came next was worse, he gathered. But he was confused by the change in her demeanor—shark to guppy in five seconds flat. About her story, Madison was fierce. He wasn't going to be allowed to interfere or sway her, and he didn't see a reason to try. While Amber might be uncomfortable with the retelling of her worst nightmare, she hadn't done anything wrong, and she would get through it. But whatever else Madison had left to share, it made her uncomfortable, and that made Tank constricted, the tentacles of worry and fear squeezing him.

"I'm sorry," Madison said, meeting his gaze.

"For what? The story?"

"No. I'm not sorry about that. That is going to be money." She sighed. "I'm sorry for what I'm about to tell you. I know this is shitty timing, and I'm willing to do whatever I have to in order to keep things good for you."

"Madison," he groaned.

"I'm pregnant," she said in a rush. "I'm almost one hundred percent certain it isn't yours, but that one night…"

She looked away, and Tank remembered that night of the engagement party in the foyer of his house. He sat still, a statue of himself, unable to move or talk.

"But, soon after that, I was with someone else, and the timing..." She shifted in her seat. "The timing works in his favor, not yours." She waved her hand. "That's probably the wrong word to use—*favor*—but you know what I mean."

"Madison," Tank said, trying to infuse his tone with patience, "why are you telling me this if you're so sure it isn't my child?"

"I don't want the other guy to know."

Tank couldn't help it; his tells showing—a heaving breath, rubbing his head. All the implications ran through his mind. Madison didn't want the other guy to know. Everyone would assume the baby was his. She wasn't going to tell anyone that the child didn't belong to Tank. Amber would think Tank was the father.

"Madison, please. You have to know, this will not go over well for me."

"I know. And I'm sorry, but I'm asking you to help me here."

"Help you? At the expense of my relationship with Amber? Are you high?"

She snorted. "I definitely won't be getting high anytime soon."

"Fuck!" Tank muttered.

"I know. I still can't believe I got myself into this situation."

Tank didn't know what to do with the frustration, anger, and disbelief coursing through him. That Madison was asking him to do this when she knew what Amber meant to him didn't make any sense.

"Madison, you owe me a better explanation. What the hell is going on?"

She looked away from him, trying to hide the fact that her eyes were welling with unshed tears. "At first, I thought it was genuine. He whisked me out of town, and we spent a couple of weeks away from everything and everybody. I believed him when he said he'd been biding his time, waiting for me to be free. It was nice—to be the person someone was waiting on instead of the filler."

"Shit."

She shook her head. "No offense. You and I went into our relationship with our eyes wide open. I have no regrets. I just didn't really get the difference."

"Okay," Tank said, reassuring her that he wasn't offended. "But I'm lost here. It sounds like this was not a bad thing."

"At first. Then, a couple of weeks after, he called me up, and he handed me the Rowdy Daniels's story on a silver platter. Wanted me to chase it. He thought there was more to it and that I could uncover something that would cause Amber and you trouble."

Tank thought he'd experienced every shitty feeling in the last hour, but somehow, he knew he hadn't reached the bottom of the despair pit quite yet.

He took a deep breath and plunged. "Who?"

"Lamarcus Steele."

Tank blinked against the harsh light of truth.

"He didn't care about me at all. It was all some twisted shit to get back at you for whatever reason. And I can't let him near this child."

"I'm sorry you're in this situation," he said. He laid his hand on top of hers and squeezed. "I really am. But I can't help you this way. I refuse to do that to Amber, fake or not." His tone was harsh, his anger obliterating any sense of sympathetic empathy.

He saw Madison stiffen right before her eyes narrowed, and he was once again that kid in the tunnel, having his life turned upside down.

"I'm not asking you," she replied calmly. "I'm sorry, but you don't have a choice. If you don't, I'll make sure Amber knows the truth about her father."

"Franco?"

"No. Her real father."

THIRTY-SEVEN

Tank walked to his car in an angry huff. He wanted to peel out of the parking lot, to leave skid marks on the street to match those that Madison had just left in his life. He flung himself into the driver's seat and turned on the car. It was as far as he got. He sat, paralyzed, unable to come up with the best way to play this.

Tank remembered the feeling of helplessness. An unreal sense of the series of events. A movie he was watching with twists and turns. A plot so masterfully written that the scene had left him breathless with disbelief. His father's agent waiting for him in the tunnel with his teammates twenty meters away from him. Leaving Amber in a New York hotel room. Being surrounded by his closest friends and his coaching staff when they discovered the truth about his encounter with his father's agent. It had taken him almost four years to finally right all the wrongs he'd committed. Then, Madison had pummeled him with the most explosive bits of information to once again push his future happiness just outside his reach.

He thought about how he could make it all go away, how he could spare Amber. He was seconds away from calling Hawk and engaging all the lawyers Hawk kept on speed dial. If he could think of a way to keep her in the dark, he would. It was like he hadn't learned his lesson. He would have given anything to push her away and keep her safe from the craziness of his life. Every time they were on the brink of happiness, something would come along to shatter the possibility.

He drummed his fingers on the steering wheel, weighing his options. Then, he grabbed his phone from the console and dialed.

The phone rang in his ear, reverberating like a ticking bomb, each ring a countdown to the inevitable.

On the fourth shrill sound, he finally answered, "Hey. What's up?"

"We need to talk. I'll be there in thirty minutes."

Tank didn't say good-bye. He shut down his phone and dropped it back in the cup holder. He didn't want to be tempted to call Amber or to answer if she called. He could not talk to her right now.

He carefully maneuvered his way out of downtown Atlanta. When he made it to the highway, he picked up speed, happy for the unspoken rule of the fast driving required in Atlanta. The monotony of the drive didn't settle him though. Instead, he felt caged, restless. He had no idea how to have the conversation required of him. He wasn't sure he could be sane.

It took him twenty-five minutes to arrive at his destination. He didn't pull into the driveway though. He stopped a couple of houses away and tried to come up with a plan. As he sat there, breathing deeply, his blood slowed, and the pounding of his pulse calmed.

The information could be wrong. Madison could have lied. Relief seeped through him.

He slid the car out of park and continued the rest of the drive.

He pulled into the driveway, shut off the car, and grabbed his phone in one continuous motion. He pushed open the door and alighted from the car. Stalking to the front of the house, he reached out and rang the bell. He shoved his hand into his pocket to hide the adrenaline shake.

When the door opened, Tank looked directly at him. "You alone?" he asked.

Franco tilted his head, his deep brown eyes studying him. Tank could feel the perusal, the scrutiny, and he knew Franco understood the seriousness of the moment. Then, Franco's whole demeanor changed, and he stepped back. His head dropped, and his hands reached up and scraped through his hair. He shrank right before Tank's eyes.

"You know," Franco said, his words directed toward the ground.

"Fuck," Tank muttered.

Any possibility of Madison's information being incorrect dissolved.

Franco's head came up, and Tank flinched at the look of despair on his coach's face.

"How?" Franco asked, his voice a timbre shy of its usual pitch.

"Madison," Tank answered.

Franco nodded and then pulled the door open wider, so Tank could follow him inside. They made their way down the hall and into the formal living room. Franco sank down into one of the two big leather club chairs, and Tank dropped into the love seat across from him. They sat in silence for a while, avoiding any eye contact, each lost in their own private hell.

Finally, Franco cleared his throat. "It was just never the right time to tell her, and then over the years, it became less and less important. She was mine, damn it!" His voice rose, and his fist pounded ineffectually on the plush leather of the chair. Desolation burned in his eyes.

Tank understood. But that didn't make any of this okay.

"You cannot tell me this without her here. I do not want to know any more than I do without her knowing." His voice was both adamant and pleading.

He could not absolve Franco, and Tank knew he would want to forgive Franco, for a thousand reasons. Amber would hate this. She would absolutely loathe knowing that Madison had known this secret about her, and she'd had no idea. Madison's involvement would burn almost as much as the truth was going to burn. And Tank wanted to be able to tell her truthfully that he didn't know this before her. He wanted to go through this with her. If he could give her this one thing, it would be that he was there for her, not for any other reason.

"Call her," Tank said. "Call her, and tell her to come here."

Franco nodded and stood, leaving the room, presumably for his cell phone.

Tank couldn't relax. Every muscle in his body was rigid with a toxic combination of regret, fear, and sorrow. If he'd stayed away from her, she wouldn't be here—in a place where the one truth in her life was about to be exposed as a lie. Madison wouldn't have bothered her. Steele would still be her friend. No one would have been interested in this story.

How was he going to explain to Amber that this was entirely his fault?

"They're just finishing at work." Franco's breath stuttered out of him. "Molly and Amber will be here soon," Franco said from the doorway.

"Okay," Tank answered, thankful for the slight reprieve.

For a little while longer, all was right in Amber's world.

Tank heard the door chime, like a final buzzer in a game when the two-minute drill had lasted two minutes and five seconds.

Time's up.

The chatter was loud as Molly and Amber entered.

"Mike?" Molly said, obviously looking for direction.

"In here," he responded.

He'd moderated his tone, Tank could tell, as he tried to disguise the trepidation permeating the room. They wouldn't know until they walked in.

Just one more small deception.

"Hey," Molly greeted as she walked into the room with Amber trailing.

"Hi," Amber said.

He heard the happiness in her voice when she saw him sitting there.

She walked directly to him, at the same time asking, "What are you doing here?"

He pulled her onto his lap when she reached him, and he kissed her hungrily, not caring at all that Molly and Franco were seven feet away from him.

Tank's hands engulfed Amber's chin, and he desperately shoved his tongue into her mouth. She held back for a split second, and then she gave into the kiss. Whether she sensed his anxiety or was truly happy to see him, he'd never know. For the moment, he let himself get lost in her. He relearned the caverns of her mouth and memorized the taste, fearing she'd never let him explore her plush mouth again. She finally pulled away. When their eyes met, he saw the confusion there.

"Happy to see me?" she quipped as she rested her forehead against his.

"You have no idea," he whispered. Then, because he needed her to know, because he was done with holding back from her, he said, "I love you."

She stiffened against him and pulled away, so she could study him. "Okay," she said quietly.

His hands found her hips, and he shifted her, so she was still on his lap, but she could see Franco and Molly, too. She turned her head, looking over at her father and his wife.

Then, she turned back to Tank. "What's going on?"

"Amber," Franco said, "I need to tell you something."

Her eyes searched Tank's, and his fingers dug into her side.

"I got you," he whispered.

Amber's nostrils flared. He sensed her uncertainty.

She inhaled deeply and then looked back to Franco. "Okay," she said.

Franco's hand reached involuntarily for Molly's, and she grabbed it. Molly's gaze snapped to Tank's, and he saw the moment Molly understood something was seriously wrong. Her eyes widened, and she visibly stiffened.

"You know I had another sister," Franco began.

Amber nodded. "Yeah, Angela. She died when you were seventeen."

Franco took a fortifying breath. "Right. Well, we were Irish twins. She was ten and a half months older than me. Growing up, we were inseparable. Each other's confidants, champions, whatevers. If either of us needed, the other responded. Until she went to high school, and I was still in eighth grade. Then, she met Tim. And they became inseparable. One of those puppy-love stories." Franco paused and looked away, like he was looking into the past. "He was a good guy. I loved him for my sister. Even when he got her pregnant when I was sixteen."

Amber's whole body stiffened, like she knew the punch line.

"Wait!" Amber held up her hand in the universal sign for stop. "You're not my father?" she asked, her voice raspy and halting, like shattered glass with sharp pieces.

"In every sense but biologically, I. Am. Your. Father!"

Tank could see Franco holding himself back from going to Amber. He could tell Franco wanted to snatch her up and hold on to her. But he didn't move. So, Tank held tight, holding all the pieces of her together, until she tried to stand. Then, as much as he wanted and needed to keep her with him, he sensed her need to get away. He pulled her in and held her close, trying to convey all the things he was feeling. Then, he let her go.

She stood abruptly. "You knew?" she said to Molly.

Molly shook her head, her expression as surprised as Amber's.

Then, Amber turned to Tank. "You knew?"

"Only that. And just today."

She began to shake her head from side to side, like she could dislodge the truth. "What the absolute fuck?" she muttered.

"Amber," Franco pleaded. He stood, too. He moved toward Amber, and she backed away. "I need for you to listen to me."

"No!"

Tank wanted to go to her, but she was a wounded animal, and her need for space overshadowed his need to hold her.

Franco stopped a couple of feet from her. "From the day you were born, I was there with them. Nona was supportive, too. You were probably the most loved baby ever born."

The last statement stopped everything. The whole room experienced a collective sign of tenderness. Even Amber's gaze softened.

"What happened to them?" Amber asked.

"Car accident," Franco said quietly.

"What happened?" Amber breathed as her eyes widened.

He cleared his throat, his agitation and discomfiture somehow greater. "Tim lost control of the car. They spun and came to rest in some trees. Died on impact." He stopped talking, but the pregnant pause meant more was coming. "You were in the backseat. Complete unscathed."

Amber's intake of air into her lungs reverberated around the room. Her hand came up to her mouth, smothering a scream, a moan, a question. Tank would never know.

"She had named me guardian. We lived with Nona while I was in college. And, when I graduated, I adopted you. You know all the rest. You know I took care of you. Everything else, you know is the truth."

"The truth?" she spit. "Whose fucking truth?"

Tank knew Franco wanted to respond, to reassure her, but he finally understood he needed to let her have a moment to get this all out.

"Why are you telling me this now? You've had years to tell me. All this time, this is why you've downplayed having a daughter. So, why the fuck is this coming up now?"

Franco's eyes darted to Tank, and Tank's heart dropped. Amber's wild eyes followed Franco's gaze and locked on Tank. It was like he was in the hotel room again, laying his heart on the line.

"What does this have to do with you?"

"Madison was—"

"Are you shitting me?" she said, cutting him off, her voice an octave higher than normal. "Madison Shepard knows about this? Fuck! What the fuck?"

He didn't want to tell her. He wanted to take it all away and protect her from all of it. But he knew he couldn't hold back even though he was going to completely shatter her world.

"Steele gave Madison some leads on Rowdy Daniels."

Amber flinched, and Tank hated himself even more.

"She was following the leads, and she figured it all out."

"So, this is a story for your fuck buddy?"

This time, Tank flinched. "Amber," he said tenderly, the word a caress, like the way he'd whisper her name before he buried himself inside her. He saw the thread of understanding, the way her body responded to his tone. She relaxed for a moment, and he took advantage. "She's not going to use this in her story. She's using it to keep me from saying that the child she's pregnant with isn't mine."

The dulled edges she'd shown seconds before hardened into razor-sharp borders. "She's pregnant?"

Tank nodded.

"Who's the father?"

He took a deep breath and rubbed his hand along the back of his neck. "Steele."

"How do you know it's not yours?" she asked.

"I don't." Everything drained out of her then. "But the timing isn't right. She doesn't think it's mine, and I don't either."

Amber scanned the room. She took in the three of them—searching for an ally, he thought. He saw the moment she decided she couldn't trust any of them.

"I gotta go. Don't..." She shook her head and started toward the door. "Don't you dare—any of you—don't you dare come after me."

Then, she ran.
And no one followed.

THIRTY-EIGHT

Amber had nowhere to go. For the first time since she'd moved in with Tank, she regretted it. The desire to curl up in Tank's plush bed overwhelmed her. The smooth weight of his cotton sheets, his cushioned comforter, Tank's hard body butted up against hers—it all beckoned her. She wanted the safety of his house. As she drove, it struck her that, in her head, she was suddenly referring to the house as *his* and not theirs. She traversed the roads from Franco's in a daze, wishing for an escape from all the truths they'd thrown at her.

Her fingers clenched and unclenched on the steering wheel. She tried to remember anything Franco had ever said to her about her mother. *Did he tell her that her mother had left her with him and split? Had she ever asked? Did she make it up in her head?* It was all so confusing because she couldn't recall ever having a conversation about her mother. She'd just accepted that Franco was her father. She'd never even missed having a woman to guide her.

Nothing exonerated him in her mind.

She couldn't think. She had to get somewhere to think. Grabbing her purse, she reached inside for her phone. Without considering anything else, Amber called Keira.

"Hey," came the happy newlywed voice through the line. "How are you?"

Amber didn't even bother with a greeting. "I need to talk to Madison. Text me her contact information," she demanded.

She heard Keira say something before she disconnected, and the phone's home screen reappeared. Then, she waited as she drove aimlessly on the back roads through the outskirts of Atlanta. She didn't have a destination in mind, but after an hour of wandering, she wasn't totally surprised when she found herself on the road in front of Tank's loft. Her choked laughter sounded in the car as she let herself acknowledge her desire to be there with him.

She didn't have any reason to be angry with him. He hadn't done anything wrong. Even if Madison were pregnant, it had happened before her. *And, if Steele had sent Madison down this path, how could she be angry with Tank?*

She pulled the wheel sharply left and skidded into the driveway. She pushed the button in her car, the one Tank had programmed, that let her into the garage. She parked, and relief seeped into her bones, calming her.

Home.

Amber had no idea how long she'd been sitting upstairs. She'd stripped out of her work clothes and tossed on a pair of sleep shorts and one of Tank's T-shirts. His scent clung to the material, wrapping her up in the illusion of him. She'd taken the elevator to the loft upstairs and pressed all the buttons to let the night air envelop her. The smells of summer and the city filled the space. One deep breath, and she could be somewhere else, a different memory wrapped in the colors of summer—a day on the lake with Keira when she was thirteen, an hour of rehab when she'd first awoken from the accident, a morning with Tank on the turf. Things that hadn't changed just because everything she thought was true was really a lie.

Around midnight, just when Amber didn't think she could keep her eyes open for another second, the elevator dinged behind her. Until that moment, she hadn't realized she was waiting for Tank to appear. She thought she conjured him from all of her musing, but with his approach imminent, her body stiffened. He might have seen it because he paused in his pursuit to reach her.

Sensing his indecision on what to do, she murmured, "I didn't realize I was waiting for you."

He was on her in a second, his arms wrapping her up, even as he held himself away from her. "Been calling you for a while."

She had forgotten her phone in her purse. "I left my phone downstairs."

His thumb lightly rubbed her back, just making sure she knew he was there. "I'm just glad you're here and that you're safe."

"At first, I didn't know where to go. I was homeless."

He stiffened. "This is your home. Our home."

She didn't reply. What she wanted to say would hurt him, and one of them bleeding today was enough.

"Franco's pretty frantic right now. Can I text him to let him know you are okay?" Tank asked.

She merely nodded. She understood Franco's worry, and although part of her wanted to make him sweat, it didn't seem fair. One of Tank's hands dropped from her waist. She saw the light from his phone glow in her peripheral vision. Whatever he texted, he did it one-handed. His other hand stayed her against him, like she might flee at any second.

Amber sensed Tank's desire to talk, to pick her brain, explore her heart, try and figure out just where her head was at. But weariness hit her hard.

He scooped her up. Foregoing the elevator, he cradled her close and walked deliberately down the steps. Pulling down the comforter, he slid her body between the sheets and tucked the blankets up under her chin.

"I'm going to close up the loft," he whispered near her ear before softly kissing her on her forehead, the caress of his lips a comfort.

"Come back," she responded.

"Count on it."

Then, he left her, and she burrowed deep into the covers she'd dreamed of when she left Franco's house. She drifted until Tank crawled in behind her. Then, she slept.

Amber woke before dawn, the weak light sliding through the plantation shutters. Tank remained wrapped around her, his arm slung around her waist, his knee shoved between her legs. She shimmied away and made her way to the bathroom. Taking a quick shower, she dressed haphazardly, only concerned with getting out of the house before Tank woke up.

Her purse sat on the counter where she'd flung it the night before. Searching it, she found her phone and tapped it, checking to see if the information she'd requested was waiting for her. Embedded in the overwhelming amount of text messages, she found the one she sought.

Disarming the alarm, she hurried to her car, knowing Tank would wake shortly. She plugged her phone in and mapped the address. She didn't think about what she wanted to say. She merely drove, her only thought her first stop—the coffee she knew she would need to survive the day.

Before she knew it, she was pulling up to Madison's secure building. Keira must have sensed her desperation because she'd included a code. It got her into the underground parking deck and up the elevator. Before she could second-guess herself, she was knocking on Madison's door. Her first attempt went unanswered.

So, she knocked harder and almost smiled when a frustrated, harried voice called out a greeting, "Who is it?"

"Amber," she responded.

The door quickly popped open, like Madison couldn't quite believe Amber would show up at her apartment. Even forced out of bed, Madison Shepard appeared unfazed. If Amber had hoped for an advantage by showing up unannounced at seven in the morning, it didn't appear she had one. Madison didn't even look shocked to see her. Holding out one of the two coffees she'd picked up, she pushed her way into Madison's condo.

Glancing around, she took in the designer decor with a mental shrug. After her quick perusal, she made her way to the right, the direction she imagined the kitchen would be. Following a short hallway, she turned into a black-and-white marble showcase kitchen. There were three barstools pulled up to a high bar, so she took a seat in one of them and finally took a sip of her coffee. Inhaling both the scent and the taste, she relaxed against the back of the stool. Madison had followed her, but rather than sitting, she leaned against the counter across from the bar, watching Amber with open curiosity.

Instead of speaking, they each sipped their coffee, appraising each other.

"Little early," Madison commented.

Amber leaned her head to the side. "Last night, it was too late," she offered as an explanation.

"I guess Tank told you about the baby," Madison said smugly.

"Among other things," was the only response Amber offered.

"Hmm. Well, maybe you should tell me why you're here."

"I guess I'm trying to figure out your angle. Are you hoping Tank will come back to you?"

Madison scoffed. "Why would I want that?"

"I'm not sure. Why would you want to pawn someone else's child off on him?"

Madison's eyes narrowed. "You don't know that it's not his child."

"You don't know that it is. But you know, I get why you would want it to be his over the alternative."

This time, Madison's eyes widened. "Thought he was your best friend."

"Yeah, that all changed the night we kissed," Amber said nonchalantly. "Some people just don't do well with rejection." She enjoyed the way Madison's back stiffened. "And, once Tank and I started to get back together, he just couldn't handle it for some reason. Although I'm confused about the timing. When did you guys hook up?"

"What is it you hoped to accomplish by coming here?" Madison said, her patience apparently at an end.

"My parentage doesn't matter. You can tell the whole world that Franco's not my father. It will only make him look like a better man than most people already think he is."

Madison looked astonished.

"You thought Tank wouldn't tell me, didn't you?"

Madison looked away from her, biding her time, sipping on her coffee. Then, she turned back to Amber, a malicious glint in her eye. "You know, this might be Tank's only shot at fathering a child, especially if he stays with you."

The comment hit exactly where it was intended. Amber had had no idea Madison knew about the circumstances surrounding her accident. She tried to don a disinterested mask, but Madison watched the cut bleed open. Amber hated that Tank had heard about it from Madison, but there wasn't anything she could do to change it.

"You know, the more I learn about you, the more I think you and Steele are perfect for each other. Bitter and wanting lives that clearly aren't yours. You do know he used you, right? I mean, he took complete advantage of you, using your jealousy for his own nefarious purpose." Amber smiled, a sliver of victory. "You basically deserve each other. Too bad that child of yours won't get as lucky as I did."

Madison clearly had taken all she was going to. "I think you should leave," she said.

Amber stood and walked toward the door. She didn't know what she had been hoping to accomplish. Perhaps Madison would think twice before she tried to blackmail Tank next time. Maybe she just wanted to show Madison that she and Tank were a united front. She wasn't sure, but she felt a little bit lighter as she walked toward the door.

"You can't stop any of this information from getting out. Especially since all of it is the truth."

Amber turned before she reached the door. "Do your damnedest. Just remember, that last time, Tank might have been with you, but he was wishing he were with me."

Amber wanted to pretend she was better than Madison. But her self-righteousness died the moment she got to her Audi. She flung herself into the seat as the expectation of relief shattered. There was no relief in sight. The gaping pit in her stomach was still there, growing with the knowledge of an imagined history. She'd hoped confronting the source would sew up some of the tears, but her excursion to Madison's hadn't made her feel much better.

Again, for the second time in mere hours, she didn't know where to go. Tank was waiting at home for her, but her need for him the night before had left her too exposed to be with him today. She didn't think she could open herself up as he tried to heal her. Her head dropped against the seat.

It took her a moment to name the feeling. At first, she thought it was despair. Then, she thought maybe it was just sadness seeping through her. It wasn't until she put the car in reverse, thinking of driving home, that she realized she felt unprepared. She hadn't been prepared for this tremendous need she had for Tank. All the ground they'd gained in the last months was slipping away, like a sinkhole swallowing ground. She needed a time out.

Tank would start training camp tomorrow. She could make it through the day. Then, she would have two weeks to figure out how to get her life back.

THIRTY-NINE

An entire week passed before Amber reached out to anyone. Tank had left days earlier with no fanfare. The big night out they'd planned before his report date never happened. Instead, he'd given Amber whatever she needed, which she appreciated.

When she'd first arrived home from Madison's, he allowed her the space she demanded. But, later that night, when she craved release and the escape that only Tank could give her, he handed that over as well.

The only hesitation he'd shown came as he went to kiss her good-bye. "I'm going to talk to you every day. Right?" he'd asked.

Even with all the battered spaces around her heart, his question hit her, one more bruise among the many. She nodded, not trusting her voice. Then, she watched him throw his bag into the Maserati and leave.

She'd worked insane hours in the days that followed, the new job providing enough of an excuse to escape. Molly tried a couple of times during the week to reach out. Amber managed to avoid every gesture with a legitimate work reason. She knew Molly was just waiting her out.

So, when Saturday arrived, Amber hesitated for only a brief moment before she texted Molly with a request to see the As. She wasn't ready to go to her father's house, so they decided to meet at a park near the house.

When she pulled up, she noticed Alexis and Andy waiting impatiently with Molly near the playground. Their little faces lit up with smiles Amber could see all the way across the expanse of green between them. Those expressions provided balm to all the nicks and cuts on her heart, and she found herself eager to hold them in her arms. She left her purse and locked the door. Then, she turned and ran to them, her ponytail hitting the back of her neck, her legs carrying her to the As as fast as they could. The moment she began her sprint, Molly unleashed them, and they came flying to her, a whirl of giggles and hair and wobbly legs. She slid, gently gathering them in her arms, as she tackled them to the ground, a mess of limbs. The three of them laughed and stayed on the grass, rolling and tickling.

But Alexis, ever impatient, began to whine about the slide. They made their way over to the playground, and for the next hour, Amber indulged their every request. She was sweaty and lighthearted by the time they made their way to lunch.

Molly ordered a beer, and Amber followed. They all ate, but the twins couldn't keep their eyes open, so Andy curled up in Amber's lap and Alexis, in Molly's. She ran her fingers through his sweat-dampened hair and then looked up. Molly was studying her across the table. Amber met her gaze for the first time since she'd arrived.

"Are you okay?" Molly ventured tentatively.

Amber took a deep breath and broke the eye contact. "Right now," she said softly, "I'm pretty perfect." She smiled sadly. "But other than that? I'm not really sure."

Molly remained quiet. She took a sip of her beer, adjusted Alexis, and took another sip. Amber wondered if she was trying to figure out what to say or how to say what she wanted to say.

"You have every right to be angry, pissed, hurt."

"I know," Amber replied simply.

"I'm angry, too."

In all her thoughts over the last week, Amber had forgotten that Franco had kept it from Molly. Now, she wasn't sure how she felt about that, but she could tell that Molly's thoughts were far from ambiguous.

"You have every right to be angry, pissed, hurt," Amber mimicked, not sure why she wanted to take her anger out on the woman in front of her.

Molly sat back, readjusted Alexis in her lap, and glared at Amber. "You're going to play it that way? Like I'm somehow the bad guy here?"

"No. Shit. I'm sorry," she said, immediately contrite. "I'm just a week out of practice with dealing with anyone I care about."

Molly smiled slightly. "Even Tank?"

Amber looked away and then back. "Training camp."

Molly pursed her lips and narrowed her eyes. "Convenient."

For some reason, her response made Amber laugh. "Yeah," she admitted. "Couldn't have come at a better time."

"Why do you want to avoid Tank? He didn't really do anything wrong."

Amber thought about what she wanted to say. She knew Tank was innocent in everything that had happened. His only connection was through Madison. But even that was flimsy because, without Lamarcus Steele, Madison might never have gone down this path. Yet, if she hadn't gotten involved with Tank again, her life would have gone on, and she could have discovered the truth the way it should have been discovered—when Franco told her.

"Have you asked him why he never told me?"

"Have you?" Molly retorted.

Then, with the hand not holding her daughter, Molly reached out and grabbed Amber's hand across the table. The whole motion was awkward with them both holding children and a wooden table between them. But something like comfort flowed through the touch, and Amber experienced her first real warmth in days.

"No," she said.

"Maybe you should."

Amber rolled her eyes. "Yeah, maybe."

Molly let it go, and Amber's respect for her increased. They talked about work and how she was fitting in at her new job. They kept it light, and before they knew it, they'd had a couple of beers, and the As had woken up with renewed energy.

"Walk," Molly suggested.

They ambled down the street, an ice cream shop as their destination, a twin in each hand.

"You've forgiven him?" Amber asked suddenly, curious about Molly's reaction.

Molly laughed. "Uh, *forgive* might be a little strong. I'm listening."

"How does that work?" Amber wondered aloud.

"Oh, that's a much bigger question," Molly teased. Then, her smile drifted away, and she said, "Let's get them some ice cream, and while they are occupied, we'll talk."

Once the twins were settled with their ice cream, Molly picked the conversation right back up. "He's devastated. You know that, right?" she began.

Amber swallowed audibly. "I imagine he's pretty frantic."

She could picture him perfectly. His hair was probably wild from running his fingers through it repeatedly, his eyes heavy with worry.

"Yeah," Molly said softly, pained, as if she were him.

The waves of empathy washed right up to her shore, but Amber tried to shake them off.

"Anyway, he feels bad for not telling me but not bad enough to apologize for withholding it since he never told you. That's a really hard line for me. I'm far more black and white than your father."

Amber flinched involuntarily, and she wanted to cry because she couldn't hear that word without questions bombarding her.

Molly ignored it. "He has a perfectly good explanation for not telling me. He never told you, and he didn't want to betray you by telling me first. And, as much as I want to flay him for not sharing with me, I get it. So, I'm not only mad at him for not telling me, but I'm also mad at him for making me see his point of view and, shit, for understanding it."

"Double whammy then?"

"Right. Twice as mad. And, to top it off, your father in a conciliatory mood? Well, let's just say…" Molly fanned her face.

Amber blushed. "Please don't take that line of thought any further. I might not forgive you."

Molly laughed. Then, her smile fell away. "He wants to be sorry for not telling me, but he's not because you're who you are to him."

Amber turned away, knowing she'd invited this but not really sure if she was ready to hear it.

Molly didn't demand her attention, but she continued, "I know you're not ready to hear this, but I'm going to say it anyway. You are his daughter. In his heart. In his soul. There is no difference in the way he looks at you and the way he looks at the As. I promise, I am not exonerating him in any way, but don't make this about him not being your biological father. He is your dad. He would never recover if you decide not to forgive him."

"I just don't understand what the big deal was. Why even try to hide it?"

"He's the only one who can answer that for you."

"Yep," she said.

"So, you want to tell me what's going on with Tank?"

"Not really," Amber answered on a snicker.

Molly joined in, chuckling.

"You know how you have to negate any declarations of love that come in the middle of or right after sex?" Amber asked suddenly.

"Uh, sure," Molly answered uncertainly. "Did Tank tell you he loved you in the middle of sex? Kinda cliché," she quipped.

"Ha! No," Amber said.

She stayed silent, watching Andy unsuccessfully navigate his ice cream. She reached over and grabbed the cone from him. Licking up the melting concoction from around the cone, she handed it back to him. He glanced up at her, pouting.

"I was cleaning it up, champ." Her explanation did nothing to appease him. Shrugging, she turned back to Molly. "He's told me he loves me only twice."

Molly's eyes widened, but Amber didn't try to explain. She didn't necessarily want to admit that she'd never even said those words to him.

"Both times, we were at a crisis point. The first was in the hotel room the night he won the Heisman. The other was right before Franco came clean." She didn't want it to bother her, but it did.

"I hope you aren't asking me if I think if that man loves you."

"I'm not sure what I'm asking. Every time we're close to that elusive almost happily ever after, something crazy happens. It's like there's some reason we shouldn't be together. I don't know."

"Three years ago, I'd have agreed with you. I think a lot of women would have accepted his apology and taken him back. I always admired you for walking away. It was the right thing for both of you."

Amber appreciated the vote of confidence. She still wondered sometimes, mostly when she was wrapped up in Tank's arms, sated physically, if she'd been out of her mind to walk away.

"He didn't hesitate this time. Franco said Tank had called him right after he left Madison. He didn't try to handle it alone. He didn't try to find some way around it. He knew you were strong enough to handle it."

Amber had thought about that. She dissected every part of the information. Taken it apart and turned it over, looking for chinks in the armor.

"Madison told him about the cause of the crash. And the lingering implications."

"What a bitch," Molly hissed.

Amber laughed. "That's not what you said a couple of months ago."

"I know, I know. Trust me!"

"I didn't get the chance to tell him myself. I think, of everything, that's what makes me the most mad."

"Would you have told him?"

"Of course. I just hadn't figured out a where and a when."

There was a pregnant pause between them.

"Did I just say that?" Amber whispered.

Molly reached out and squeezed her shoulder. "It's different. But, yeah, it's hard to tell someone you love something that you know will be hard to hear."

"Point taken."

"I wasn't making a point, Amber. There's no comparison here. And I want you to know, I don't expect you to just forgive your father. I just hope that you will."

Like in the restaurant, a rush of love and warmth stole through her. She reached out and grabbed Molly's hand. They stayed like that for a moment, an exchange of strength and understanding. Neither one of them remarked on the rarity of these moments between them; they merely held on.

FORTY

Camp had always filled Tank with anticipation and excitement. Two weeks on the field with his future team—what more could a guy ask for? But, this year, camp meant two weeks away from Amber at a time when she actually needed him. Or maybe that was a pipe dream because Amber was truly one of the most independent people he'd ever met.

The phone calls they'd shared during the last fourteen days were a bit stilted, short, and worrisome. He disconnected every night, swamped with thoughts of the ever-widening gap between them. He didn't try to broach the subject of her father because he knew that was the surest way to increase the space. So, he asked about work, spoke about his work. But her disinterest about what was happening on the field made his fears greater.

The day he'd left, Amber had come clean about her visit to Madison. He wasn't sure what reaction she'd been hoping for, but her parting words to Madison made him sputter with laughter. Only Amber could have pulled that off. He recoiled mentally as she admitted what she'd said about his last encounter with Madison. Truth that it was, he hated that Amber knew he'd slept with Madison the night he saw her again. When he thought about the possibility of Amber being with Steele that same night, it had driven him crazy.

On a circular loop, he thought about all of it. And, in the back of his mind, during the entirety of camp, he wondered if he would come home to an empty house.

The thought dominated his ride home. When he pulled into his garage and saw her Audi parked in its spot, he grew dizzy with relief. He put the Maserati in park, and his head dropped to the steering wheel as he stole a moment to gather his thoughts. He had no idea what the next couple of hours would bring, and he found he was afraid to walk through the door. If she said she was leaving him, he was certain he would bar the door and find some way to keep her there until he could convince her otherwise.

Great headline that would make.

Finally, the suspense a ball in his gut, he stepped out from the car. His mind tripped on images of her, a scroll through their recent history. Grabbing his bag from the trunk, he manned up and opened the door. The house was quiet but not empty. He could feel her presence without seeing her. On the kitchen counter sat a bouquet of flowers, much like the ones he'd tried and failed to surprise her with that first time. They were in a vase, which made him smile. He'd never actually decided how to give them to her.

He heard strains of music pumping through his audio system coming from the loft. As tired and beat up as his body was, he didn't bother waiting for the elevator. Instead, he took to the stairs, two at a time, up both flights, the fastest he'd ever run indoors. He reached the top and turned to take in the room before him.

Amber's elbow rested on the back of the couch, her chin perched on top of it. Her head was slightly tilted, her shoulders above the back of the couch. Her hair was piled high on her head. Her scar, the lovely stretch of skin that made her who she was, was on display. He smiled as he took in her attire. Just his jersey. He wanted to rush toward her, but he leaned casually against the wall, crossing his ankles and his arms.

"Good to see you, Sunshine," he said, modulating his voice as best as he could. Every muscle in his body was alert. This was a homecoming he had wanted but was afraid to hope for.

Amber smiled tenderly. "Hi," she said sweetly. "Welcome home!"

The panic of the last two weeks must have shown on his face because her expression changed.

"You knew I'd be here, right?" she inquired tentatively.

He shrugged, trying to downplay his irrational fear.

"Right," she whispered.

She unfolded from the couch and sauntered toward him. His jersey reached her mid thigh, and he was fairly confident that, underneath it, she was completely bare. His blood began to rage, pulsating through his body. He was certain that she could see the pulse point on his neck vibrating with his need.

She didn't stop until she was pancaked against him. Her hands clutched his and she pulled them away from his chest. She wrapped them around her and then draped hers around his neck. She got as close to him as humanly possible.

"I missed you," she said clearly. "And you don't ever need to doubt me being here." She leaned up and planted a kiss on his lips.

Like a matchstick touching a fuse, his control snapped. He wasn't sure what kind of kiss she'd envisioned, but he took control, delivering a bruising one. A tsunami of feelings whipped around them—his hopes, her fears, his worry, her disappointments. They were exchanged in a furious meeting of lips, tongues, and teeth. It was a claiming, a possession.

He picked her up without releasing her mouth and turned her pushing her up against the wall. Her legs wrapped around his waist and she pushed into him, rubbing her bare, wet heat against his raging erection. His need was a tangible presence and he thrust, moving his jean-clad length along her seam. His left hand snaked around her, so he could hold her in place as he freed his right hand to unbuckle and unzip his pants.

"Please," Amber gasped next to his mouth. "I need you." She bit gently on his bottom lip. "Hurry," she groaned.

There was nothing soft or gentle, nothing cautious or questioning when he released his dick and slid into the warmth of her body. The capitulation and acceptance he'd been craving for years overwhelmed him. He could feel it in every line of her body, in every word she whispered, every touch she ventured. He moved in and out of her in uncoordinated, frenzied motions. But even in his mindless need he knew the tells of her body—the exaggerated inhalation of air, the quickening of her muscles clamping down on him, the lust-filled look in her eyes. He wanted more than just her body in that moment. He reached for her hands with one of his and pinned them above her head.

"Look at me," he demanded as he held her body of the precipice of an orgasm.

Her languid brown eyes were an essay of emotions he could easily read.

"God, I love you," he whispered, the tide of his emotions too much for him. He slammed back into her, just where she needed him, the murmurings of her words lost as they both went over the edge.

Night had come at some point. A time between kisses and talking, during caresses and traded secrets. They'd relocated to their room, and they lay in bed, limbs entwined, draped with sweat-dampened sheets. Tank's hand flitted leisurely up and down the line of Amber's spine, and her thumb swept unthinkingly along his beard-shadowed jaw. They'd talked in bits and spurts, sharing things they'd kept hidden away over the last two weeks, unimportant tidbits that meant nothing and everything. It wasn't until the moon was high and every other topic had been exhausted that Tank thought to ask about Franco.

Amber's thumb stopped its stroking, but otherwise, she banked her reaction to his question. "I'm not sure I'm ready to talk to him," she explained. "I'm not sure when I'll be ready, but I think it will be like a lightning strike. Suddenly, one day, I'm going to wake up, and I'm going to need to talk to my dad. But, until then, until I feel that unmistakable draw, I'm going to wait."

She didn't say anything for a moment, and Tank let her have the time.

"I did talk to Nona. She didn't fill in any blanks or make anything different. She only told me what I already knew."

"What's that?" Tank inquired.

He absorbed her shrug.

"That he loves me, that I couldn't be any more his daughter than I am. That he would never intentionally hurt me. And, I mean, I already knew all that."

"True," Tank said.

He wanted to push her in Franco's direction, but he knew her too well to do that. She'd get there when she was ready and not a moment before.

"What's your superpower?" she asked suddenly.

"What?"

"Haven't you ever gotten that question in an interview? If you could have one superpower, what would it be?"

"Ah," he said, getting it. "Teleportation."

"Ooh, that's a good one." Her hand paused in its ministrations. "I'd always said speed. And then, for a while, after the accident, it was invisibility. For obvious reasons."

Tank couldn't help it when he hugged her close for support.

"I'd never once wanted to be able to survive fatal car accidents." This time, it was a whisper.

He didn't have any response to that, nor did he think he could come up with something if he'd had time to prepare for it.

She squirmed against him, and he wondered what she was working herself up to.

"We need to talk about Madison. And Steele."

"I don't want to talk about Steele," he said. "And I'm pretty sure I don't want to talk about Madison either."

Tank chuckled, and she pinched him in retaliation.

He yelped. "What was that for?"

"We do need to talk about her and the baby."

"No, we don't. Madison agreed to a paternity test." He rolled over, taking her with him so that he rested above her, his weight supported by his elbows. "Right before camp, I submitted a blood sample for a noninvasive prenatal paternity test. It's ninety-nine-point-nine percent accurate. I'm not the father."

"Oh," Amber responded.

He pushed up, so he could get a better read on her face. What he saw confused him. "I thought you'd be happy," he stated, perplexed.

She smiled tentatively. "I am."

"Then, what's going on in that head of yours?"

Her eyes locked on the ceiling—to gather her thoughts, he presumed. He gave her a moment, but when she didn't look at him again and didn't say anything, he pushed up onto his knees. He flipped over and leaned against the plush fabric headboard. Reaching for her, he scooped Amber up and set her on his lap, so she was straddling him. His fingers gently took her chin and tilted her head up, so she had no escape.

"Talk to me," he pleaded.

"You know everything Madison told you is true."

"Yeah," he said.

"The cause of the crash?" she said, questioning him.

He nodded.

"I mean…there's no guarantee I can get pregnant. I might not ever be able to have your children."

"I know."

"Since we met, I've been trying to tell you that I'm a bad bet."

Everything in him screamed at him to handle the situation correctly. But his heart began to beat rapidly, panic rising. He did not want to fuck this up. "I did some research," he began.

She smirked. "Oh, yeah?"

"Yeah," he said with a grin as his heart rate started to regulate. "There's no guarantee that you can't get pregnant either. Our odds, they're stacked against us a little more than the average couple. But there have been so many advances in helping women get pregnant."

"So, you're willing to risk it?"

He smiled softly. "I'd risk anything for you."

"Anything?" she said on a wobbly breath.

"My career, my money, anything. And you're taking a risk, too. How do you think I feel? I hate that, every time we figure things out, something happens. I always manage to mess up your life."

Amber pushed in closer to him, as if his corporal body could absorb hers, like there was a better way to merge their lives.

She took a deep breath. "Always with the ego," she said, her face buried against his neck so that he felt the words rather than heard them.

Tank stiffened against her. Then, he felt her shake, like her tears took over. Tank shifted, uncomfortable. He'd said the wrong thing again. Then, he noticed the difference. Her smile curved against the line of his Adam's apple. He gently pushed her away from him. Her mouth was indeed smiling, and her eyes twinkled with mischief. He smiled back, so happy to see that look on her face, to hear the laughter spewing from her mouth.

"Oh, you got jokes?" he said, teasing her with a nip against her mouth.

"Well, the world does revolve around the great Tank Howard."

"Really?" he asked as he flipped her onto her back. He shoved his mouth against her scar, nipping and kissing, rubbing his scruff-covered jaw against her, making her squeal and writhe. "That's what you think?"

"I mean," she said between giggles, "I'm in the presence—"

"You'd better watch it," he warned, digging his fingers into her most ticklish spot.

"Of greatness," she managed to eek out between her shrieks of laughter.

He laughed with her until this one second when she was stretched out underneath him, her hair a dark halo around her face, her body lined up with his. Tank watched, reveled in the feel of her, the joy she brought him. He stopped laughing and took it all in. It was a moment before she noticed.

She calmed and reached up, her hand flat against his cheek. "What?" she asked.

"I love you," he said simply.

She smiled. "I know," she answered. "I love you, too."

EPILOGUE

MONDAY-AFTER THE SUPER BOWL

The sun shone unabashedly through the windows of the suite because they'd forgotten to pull the blackout shade the night before. They might have considered it, but with the lights of the city reflecting off the bay, they'd opted for the view. The backdrop it provided for the Super Bowl victory celebration was too perfect.

"Sunshine," Tank whispered, nudging her on her side, "it's time to get up. Daylight in the swamps. Literally."

Amber rolled over, hair a mess, with the remnants of her makeup leaving telltale marks under her eyes. Even like that, she was the most beautiful woman he'd ever seen.

"Ugh, I'm not ready." Then, she turned and buried her head under the pillow.

Tank pulled it off of her and gently hit her with it. "Let's go. We've got a bet to settle."

Amber instantly perked up, her smile mischievous, as she sat up, cross-legged. His jersey hung precariously off of one of her shoulders. She looked sexy as hell, and he suppressed his desire to tackle her back onto the bed. They had things they had to do today. And he had people waiting for them.

"Shouldn't Super Bowl Champs and MVPs get to sleep in?" she complained.

"You're kind of cute when you're tired," he teased. He leaned forward and gave her a quick kiss because he couldn't resist. But he cut himself off. If he took too much, he'd have to satisfy his craving, like an addict. His fists dropped to the bed, so he was braced right in front of her. "Seems to me like someone is trying to weasel out of the settling up."

"I've been telling you for weeks that I've got this."

"Then, get in the shower."

Amber rolled her eyes but complied. Moving off the bed, she sauntered toward the bathroom, a little extra shake in the hip. He held back a laugh. When she got to the door, she looked back over her shoulder, no doubt making sure he was watching. Then, she whipped his jersey over her head and dropped it on the floor next to her feet. She stood, framed by the doorway, his living fantasy.

And that was way too much temptation to pass up.

They ended up being late.

Tank had planned carefully. He'd found a cute art deco café with a booth in the back for privacy. It seemed appropriate. He'd considered a couple of other locations, but none really stuck out in his head. They were more than a favorite location.

After they'd gotten out of the shower and dressed, they'd made their way down to South Beach. He had his postgame wrap-up with his mom. This time, getting Amber to come with him took zero effort. As soon as Amber had given herself over to the inevitability of being with him, Chantel embraced her wholeheartedly. She also secretly took credit for pushing Amber to admit to the depths of her feelings for Tank. Today, their brunch didn't last long, and finally, Tank was leading Amber to the bar to settle their bet. They ambled unhurriedly along Ocean Drive, checking out the sights.

"Breakfast was nice," Amber said randomly.

Tank smiled. "It was."

At one of their breakfast dates midway through the season, Tank had left Amber and Chantel to go to the restroom.

He was walking back through the restaurant, coming up on their booth, when he heard Chantel say to Amber, "All I had to do was dangle the Madison carrot in front of you, and you folded like a house of cards."

Of course, Amber argued her side.

She and Chantel didn't always agree, but they trusted each other enough to actually argue their points. Since he had to work to win any fight with either of them, he often enjoyed being a spectator to their bouts.

Amber and Chantel's relationship had been the easiest to navigate over the last couple of months. Amber still hadn't called a truce with Franco. But slowly, Tank could detect the easing of her anger and betrayal. Like last night, after their Super Bowl victory. When the families joined the team, Amber walked out with Molly, helping her manage the As. Tank watched as Amber took Alexis to Franco.

She deposited Alexis in Franco's arms before leaning in and kissing him on his cheek. Some whispered words in Franco's ear brought a glow to his eyes.

Tank had hoped Amber would have come to some peace with everything by now, but she just couldn't seem to put it behind her. Last night had been a step forward. It had taken her three years to forgive Tank, and he wasn't sure Franco could handle much more.

And Tank had plans. He needed Amber to move on, so the two of them could embrace the future.

But he understood the need to hold a grudge. He hadn't gotten around to talking to Steele yet either. Not that Steele was handing out apologies. But it still hurt. And not having Steele in his life anymore hurt, too. Especially for big things, like Super Bowl wins and for what he had planned for today.

"You okay over there?" Amber asked.

He squeezed her hand. "Yeah, just taking it all in."

She studied him. "There's a lot to take in, isn't there?" she commented, a glint in her eye that he recognized.

He smiled. He released her hand and slung his arm around her shoulder, pulling her close. He kissed her on the top of her head and towed her with him as he ducked into the bar. He made his way to the booth he'd reserved. When she sat, he took the seat across from her.

"You got it?" he asked.

"Of course." She smirked as she reached into the little purse slung across her chest. Grabbing her wallet, she rifled through until she pulled out the napkin they'd written on almost a year ago.

"Hand it over," he said.

She narrowed her eyes. "Why do you get to unveil?"

"MVP. I'm pulling rank."

She considered him.

"Fine!" she said as she pushed the napkin across the table.

He picked it up and sent her a wicked grin. Carefully unfolding it, he placed his side down.

He read what was written in her elegant handwriting.

> *Predictions*
> *AFC Champs: Atlanta*
> *NFC Champs: Arizona*
> *Super Bowl Champs: Atlanta*
> *MVP: Tank Howard* ♥

With all her smack-talk over the last few weeks, he shouldn't have been surprised that she'd predicted everything. But her belief in him was overwhelming. He kept his gaze fixed on the napkin in front of him, needing a moment to collect himself. She dazzled him on a regular basis, but this...

He cleared his throat. "What's with the heart?" he asked, his eyes still fixed on it.

Her fingers slid comfortingly along the length of his, and he looked up to find her gaze locked on him. She didn't answer him.

"The heart?" he asked again.

"I don't know," she said. "Maybe even then I knew I loved you," she said softly, like a caress.

He smiled before he pushed the napkin to her. "Flip it over."

Her eyes narrowed. "There's no way you predicted this. You would never have picked Arizona."

"Flip it over, Sunshine," he ordered again.

She rolled her eyes and flipped the napkin over. Then, she froze. Her other hand, the one not already held in Tank's, reached over and traced the letters, but she didn't look up.

Tank got a little impatient, and his nerves amped up. But he stayed silent and waited for some reaction.

A tear hit the table, and he couldn't wait any longer. He released her hand, stood up, and moved to the other side of the table. He sat down and pulled her onto his lap.

"Hey," he said tenderly as he tilted her chin up. "You're killing me here."

She buried her face in his neck. "That was almost a year ago," she muttered.

His nerves were stretched tight, but he managed a short laugh. "Yeah, well, if I'd had my choice, this would have already happened."

She giggled once, and the vise gripping his gut began to loosen.

"Seriously, Sunshine," he murmured against her hair.

She picked her head up, her brown eyes luminous with unshed tears. Her hands came up and cradled his jaw.

"I love you," she breathed before she pressed her lips against his for a brief kiss.

"Okay," he said, uncertainty clouding his voice.

"And, of course, I'll marry you."

His hands came up to mirror hers, and he dropped his forehead to hers. "I love you," he said.

Their mouths met then, a promise of forever sealed with a slow, deep kiss. When they surfaced, he moved her off of his lap. He stood up from the booth, digging in his pocket. When he retrieved the ring, he dropped to his knee on the outside of the booth.

Amber's smile dominated her face. She swung her legs to the side of the booth and reached out, so her hands were draped around his nape, her fingers meeting in the back of his neck.

"I talked to Franco a while back," he said. He hated the shadow that dimmed the light in her eyes, but she needed to know about the ring. "He gave me your mom's ring. It was a simple gold ring with a small diamond in the middle and two rubies on the sides. I thought about using pieces of it but figured you should be able to decide what to do with it. Instead, I just used the same design but bigger and platinum and onyx. It's more you."

He slid the ring onto her finger, and she dived into him. He stood, a little unsteady, both physically and emotionally, and held her.

"Is it a done deal yet, Sunny?" Iman said from a seat at the bar.

Tank smiled as she pulled back and looked at him. "I asked our friends to stay to help us celebrate," he said a little sheepishly.

Tilly, Keira, Iman, Hawk, and Nicky stood up from the bar. They all surrounded them, offering up their congratulations.

Keira hugged her close. "Hey, don't forget this," she said as she reached out for the napkin. "So damn cool," she said, studying it.

Predictions
Marry me?

"I'll take that," Amber said, picking it up and gently folding it. "Have to frame this as soon as we get home."

"Round of drinks," Iman said.

They all started in the direction of the bar.

Amber's hand stayed Tank. "I need to make a phone call," she said.

"Of course," he responded, a little confused.

"Do you think they have Wi-Fi here?" she asked.

His eyes narrowed. "Pretty sure. Why?"

"I want to FaceTime."

"Okay. Who're ya calling?" he asked finally since she didn't seem to want to offer anything up.

"I want to call Franco."

He pulled her close and dropped a kiss on her head. "Good. Want me to wait?"

"Yeah." She took a deep breath and reached for his hand. Placing it on her still flat belly, she said, "I want us to see his face when we tell him he's going to be a grandfather."

It took Tank a second. "A what?"

THE END

Thank you for reading the conclusion of Tank and Amber's story.

Please consider leaving a review on your favorite book site.

CONNECT WITH J. SANTIAGO

Sign up for J. Santiago's newsletter:

https://mailchi.mp/bf94c1c685b4/jsantiagosubscibe

AUTHOR'S NOTE

S tatistics on the rate of reporting sexual assault.[1]

RAINN, 2015, The Criminal Justice System: Statistics, RAINN, https://www.rainn.org/statistics/criminal-justice-system

---

[1] Department of Justice, Office of Justice Programs, Bureau of Justice Statistics, National Crime Victimization Survey, 2010-2014 (2015); ii. Federal Bureau of Investigation, National Incident-Based Reporting System, 2012-2014 (2015); iii. Federal Bureau of Investigation, National Incident-Based Reporting System, 2012-2014 (2015); iv. Department of Justice, Office of Justice Programs, Bureau of Justice Statistics, Felony Defendants in Large Urban Counties, 2009 (2013). (This statistic presents information together, which originated from separate studies. RAINN presents this data for educational purposes only, and strongly recommends using the citations to review any and all sources for more information and detail.)

During Tank's explanation to Amber, he mentions a group, TeamUP. Although TeamUP is fiction, it is based on the National Consortium for Academics and Sport's program Huddle Up. The outreach of this group is both groundbreaking and relevant.

THE POWER OF THE HUDDLE

Huddle Up leverages the transcendent power of sport to eradicate gender violence, in all of its forms, and the sexism underpinning this abuse. In sport, the huddle is a powerful symbol of togetherness, a place where many become one. In the huddle, teammates convene to reinforce their union, challenge & support one another, and communicate strategy. In the huddle, teammates forget past set-backs, galvanize conviction, and always have a unified front against the opponent. Huddle Up harnesses that power by challenging, educating, and empowering participants to be "all-in" to defeat our opponent—sexist abuse.

Huddle Up addresses the full continuum of abusive behaviors and empowers participants to understand how misogynistic language, sexual harassment, gendered bullying, sexual assault, rape and domestic violence are linked together. This understanding inspires participants to have the courage to challenge behaviors on all levels of the continuum.

ABOUT THE AUTHOR

J. Santiago is a graduate of Villanova University and the University of Pennsylvania. She gets her love of sports from her fifteen-year career in the field and a houseful of boys who love to play. A former English and history teacher, she understands and embraces the power of stories in our lives.

Connect with J. Santiago

Sign up for J. Santiago's newsletter:
https://mailchi.mp/bf94c1c685b4/jsantiagosubscibe

Like J. Santiago on Facebook:
@j.santiagonovels

Join J. Santiago's Reader Group:
http://www.facebook.com/groups/184363652197039/

Follow J. Santiago on Twitter:
@skywalkerxnl

Connect with J. Santiago on Instagram
@santiagonovels